Praise for the writi

Danger Zone

"*Danger* Zone is one fast-paced ménage novel *not* to be missed by the talented Sierra Cartwright."

— Victoria, *Two Lips Review*

"DANGER [Z]ONE is a brilliant first book in the HAWKEYE series..."

— *Romance Junkies*

Bend Me Over

"True to form, Sierra Cartwright has written a scorching story full of wickedly intense pleasure and kink."

— Bella, *Fallen Angel Reviews*

"Push your own boundaries and pick up this book. I promise you won't be disappointed."

— Roberta, *You Gotta Read Reviews*

Double Trouble

"...an intense, passionate exploration of domination and submission between these three dynamic characters."

— Laura Scott *Just Erotic Romance Reviews*

"...a sensually overwhelming and downright smoking hot story that blends excitement with a touch of romance..."

— Shannon, *The Romance Studio*

Loose Id®

ISBN 13: 978-1-61118-353-5
HAWKEYE: BEND ME OVER
Copyright © October 2010 by Sierra Cartwright
Cover Art by Marci Gass
Cover Layout and Design by April Martinez
Publisher acknowledges the author and copyright holder of the individual works, as follows:
BEND ME OVER
Copyright © November 2009 by Sierra Cartwright
MAKE ME
Copyright © October 2010 by Sierra Cartwright

Printed in the U.S.A. by
Lightning Source, Inc.
1246 Heil Quaker Blvd
La Vergne TN 37086
www.lightningsource.com

Contents

BEND ME OVER

Dedication

For MG—thanks for the wonderful help! For BAB and her wonderful husband, Don, I love ya and appreciate your patience. And for the crack editorial team at Loose Id, with special gratitude to Kym, Jill, and MT.

Chapter One

Oh crap.

The sight of the large if gorgeous man on her porch when she was heading out for her run scared the snot out of her, and Aimee leaned her whole body into the door and tried to slam it shut.

His booted foot stopped her efforts. Not just a booted foot, she noted a bit wildly, a massive booted foot, the leather showing nicks, bumps, and bruises from years of hard work.

Crap, crap, crap.

Her heart slammed into overdrive.

"Trace Romero," the man said, pushing back against the door.

A potential bad guy wouldn't introduce himself, would he? What the heck did she know, beyond a few spy movies? Her sister was the one with a gun; Aimee was the nerd with the iPod, ponytail, workout gear, and a scientific mind that rarely shut down.

"I'm with Hawkeye. Your sister sent me."

Her breath whooshed out.

If he was from Hawkeye and knew her sister, she should feel relieved. After all, she too worked for Hawkeye, Inc., one of the world's most exclusive security firms. As the world changed, became more global, more dangerous, there were more resources that needed protecting—celebs, corporate barons, and their family members. And there were areas in which the military wasn't authorized to operate.

Since its mission was to keep the planet and its inhabitants safe, Hawkeye added employees by the dozens every month, and its hiring rate showed no signs of slowing down. Aimee guessed this man was probably former military or a former cop, but that didn't matter to her.

She had no intention of letting any man, even one who looked like Trace Romero—*especially* one who looked like Trace Romero, tall, dark, and dangerous—inside her house.

She cursed herself for having called her sister in a panic. It was just like her protective older sibling to call out the cavalry. "You can tell her you were here and I sent you away. Mission accomplished."

"If I don't answer your phone when she calls, I might as well turn in my resignation and throw myself off Pikes Peak, save her the effort of hunting down my sorry carcass."

Aimee's running shoes slipped as he pushed on the door. For all the success her efforts were having at keeping him out, she might as well be trying to hold back a Colorado blizzard.

Maybe she couldn't beat him when it came to brute strength, but she could batter his ego and get under his defenses. "I can't believe a big, strong man is frightened of my sister!"

"Scared shitless," he admitted.

"Damn." She groaned. His ego was intact enough not to rise to her bait.

She heard him draw in a breath before he said, "We can do it my way, Aimee." He paused for a couple of beats, then added, "Or we can do it my way."

Through the small opening, she saw him move inexorably forward.

She hated having people in her space. It was bad enough sharing the fifteen hundred square feet with an obnoxious parrot that never shut up, but she refused to share with someone who would touch her stuff, eat her food, discover her secrets...

He'd been in her life less than thirty seconds, and he'd already interrupted her run, throwing off her routine. Unless she was so focused on her work that the rest of the world ceased to exist, she kept a rigid schedule.

The brute of a man budged her back another few inches. "You can stop the Big Bad Wolf act anytime," she said. But a panicky little part of her was afraid it wasn't an act at all.

"Step away from the door, and I will."

So maybe she didn't carry a gun and act all tough-ass, but she'd learned a few things from listening to her sister. If you can't go through, go around. "Okay. You win."

He stopped pushing. She counted to two. When he let down his guard, she grunted and then shoved forward with every scrap of irritation she could summon.

But her pissed-off best wasn't good enough.

His foot was still firmly lodged in the entrance.

Within seconds, he filled the space.

Good God, he was big. Bigger than big.

Instinctively she took a protective step back. No matter how mad she was, she would never be able to win against this man.

He dominated the space and sucked up the air she'd been intending to breathe. He stood well over six feet tall, and his shoulders almost filled the entire width of the opening. Faded blue jeans snuggled his hips, and a well-worn navy T-shirt hugged his torso.

She, who rarely got flustered, just stood there and blinked. He made her oh so aware of being a woman. In her shorts and sports bra, she felt small, vulnerable, while he was spectacular, from his angular cheekbones to his military-precision black haircut and rich, deep brown eyes. His skin was dark, emphasizing his Spanish heritage, and it might have been a shade or two richer for being in the sun. Damn, she was always a sucker for men who looked like him.

But before her mind could race off, she became hyperconscious of the set of his jaw. It brooked no argument, and intuitively she knew this man spelled danger to her.

She wondered if he would continue to stand in the entrance and argue with her, but he didn't. He grabbed her by the shoulders, unceremoniously moved her back a foot, then released her long enough to turn, slam the door, turn both locks, and slide the safety latch across...all before she could even draw a protesting breath.

"My way," he reminded her.

From the other room, Eureka squawked.

"What the hell is that racket?"

She should probably tell him about her attack parrot, but it would be a heck of a lot more fun for him to find out himself; well, fun for her, if not him. "It's a bird."

"Inside? A pet?"

"He owns me," she said, as if that said it all. When it came to Eureka, it did.

"Anything else I need to know about?"

That was a loaded question. "How much do you know?" Surely her sister had left her *some* secrets.

He raised his eyebrows. "How much is there to know?" he countered.

"I'm pretty boring."

"That's why someone broke in?"

"It was probably a random thing. Kids." She wished. Hoped. But she knew better. She'd dashed out for her morning coffee, extra-large vanilla soy latte, and come straight back. She hadn't been gone even half an hour.

When she returned, the back patio door was open, and the only place anything had been disturbed was her home office. Her electronics were still in place; none of her jewelry was missing. Even her emergency stash of twenty-dollar bills remained untouched in her dresser drawer.

"The local police said there have been no other reported break-ins."

Which brought her back to her original question. *How much did he know?* Surely her sister hadn't told him what, exactly, she was working on. And as for the other—her deep, dark secret—please God, don't let him find out about that.

"I understand nothing was taken?" he asked.

She shook her head.

"Which means it wasn't a random thing, and you and Ms. Inamorata know it. Want to show me around?"

"No. Not really," she said, not even trying to disarm her words with a smile.

"My way," he said again. "You can show me, or I can look myself."

"There's not much to see. My bedroom, which you're not going into, my office, which you're not going into, my kitchen, dining room, two bathrooms, and my living room...which you're standing in. That's it. You can go now."

He took another step toward her.

Damn if he didn't look as good as he smelled, like a cool Colorado breeze and the spice of night.

Reluctantly she ceded the ground; just as fast, she regretted her action. Instead of remaining where he was, Trace took another step in her direction. This time she forced herself to stand still. She crossed her arms across her bare midriff, fighting the natural instinct to get the hell away from him.

"I will be going into your bedroom and your office. I'll show myself around."

Arguing with him was like trying to turn back a tornado. "Fine," she said with false bravado. "In that case, I'll just go for my run while you have a look-see." She started to brush past him. He grabbed her wrist, not hard but firmly enough to say he meant business.

"You run, I run."

"Me Tarzan, you Jane," she snapped.

"That's the natural order of things," he said.

She rolled her eyes, but her heart was pounding, at least 80 percent of her target heart rate. She wouldn't need a cardio workout if he stayed under her roof another five minutes. His touch bothered her. His aggressive style bothered her. But what bothered her most was her own, way-too-feminine reaction to him. "You're interrupting my schedule, Mr. Romero...Agent Romero. Whatever your name is."

"Trace."

"You won't be here long enough for us to get that familiar."

"Don't count on it."

She snatched her hand back from his grip. "Look, I appreciate what you're trying to do—"

"What I've been *ordered* to do," he said.

"But my sister overreacted, probably because *I* overreacted."

"Why would someone break in?"

She frowned. There wasn't a good answer to that question.

"Your sister is the least likely person I know to overreact," he said, his voice more patient than she'd heard it so far. "If she thinks someone should be here to protect your body and your secrets"—his glance started at her head and slowly traveled downward, igniting too-long-dormant senses—"then I'm going to be here for as long as she says."

"The police said they'd be happy to drive by."

"Periodically," he agreed. "But they're not going to provide the kind of protection I can."

"I—"

"Show me around," he said.

She sighed. "Can I finish a sentence?"

"Depends whether you're going to agree with me or not." He grinned then, and strange things happened to her insides.

"Just for the record," he continued, "there are other ways to shut you up. Who knows?" He leaned in a bit closer. "You might enjoy them. I would."

Her heart increased its tempo to at least 85 percent of her target heart rate. She told herself he wouldn't kiss her, told herself she wouldn't let him if he tried.

Right?

The phone rang, thankfully shattering the moment.

"That'll be your sister, for me."

The phone shrilled a second time.

She sighed. "Through there," she said, pointing to the kitchen. It wasn't lost on her that he was winning every single battle.

He nodded and headed into the heart of her home.

She trailed him, fully intending to eavesdrop.

"Bombs away!"

"What the…?"

"Eureka! No." *God, no.* But she knew it was already too late.

The phone, the shrieking bird, her tension, all created sudden pandemonium.

From nowhere and everywhere at once, Eureka flew into

the room, a fury of green feathers and obnoxious noise.

"Duck!" she warned.

Too late.

Eureka swooped low over Trace's head.

Aimee pushed her palms against her eyes, unable to watch.

"Crap!"

Her word exactly.

"Return to base," the parrot shrieked. "Return to base! Mission accomplished."

The phone stopped ringing. Eureka landed on his perch and rang a bell that hung beneath a mirror. Then silence, sudden and oppressive, echoed.

"Sorry about that," she said, slowly pulling her hands away from her face. "I should have warned you about his...tendencies."

"Does he do that a lot?"

"Only when he's upset. Hopefully he got the intruders. Bastards for leaving a door open, anyway. If anything happened to him—"

"I think he's okay," Trace said.

She was glad for his interruption. That ridiculous, bad-mannered bird was her best friend.

"Did he get me?" Trace ran a hand across the top of his head, then looked at his palm.

"You'll need to change your shirt," she said. For the first time, she smiled at him. "Since you probably don't have another one, you can just go home."

"Stubborn woman."

"Stubborn man," she countered.

"It will wash." He dragged the hem from the waistband.

"Er..."

He exposed part of his stomach. *Oh. My. Talk about tanned and toned...*

He pulled the shirt a bit higher. "Don't!" she said. "Please." Having him this close was bad enough; half-naked would undo her.

The phone rang again. Eureka squawked.

"No," she warned, looking at the bird.

Eureka stretched his neck out and looked at her. He cocked his head to one side, as if contemplating her order.

"No," she said again.

The bird began to preen himself, but he kept an eye on Trace as the man crossed the room.

"I mean it."

Eureka lifted a foot from the perch, as if considering his options; then he put it back down again.

"Good boy," she said softly to her unruly pet. She too had her eye on Trace. His boots were loud on her tile floor, and as large as he was, he dwarfed the space.

"Romero," he said, answering her phone.

"Is it my sister?" she whispered.

He nodded.

He was a man of few words, until he looked directly at her and said, "No. She hasn't been the least bit hospitable. I have a bruised foot and parrot shit on my shirt."

Rat bastard.

"Yeah, no problem." He held out the phone toward her.

Reluctantly she crossed to him, not wanting to get any closer to him than she needed to. Her mind might not have wanted him in her space, but her body most definitely did. Aimee Inamorata was not used to men upsetting her equilibrium. They had their uses, no doubt, and sometimes they were even good for conversation.

She took the handset from him and, to her sister, said, "Hey."

For the next two minutes, the oldest Inamorata gave Aimee hell, finishing with, "I know you can take care of yourself, but you've got to think about the project."

"Exactly," Aimee said. "Now you see the issue. I can't work with someone breathing down my neck."

"Is that what he's doing?"

Actually he *was* close enough that she could feel the warmth of him. And it wasn't all terrible. But it sure as hell was a distraction.

"How soon will you be done with the project?"

"I don't know. A couple of days. Maybe more."

"So it's not like he'll be a pain in your ass for more than a few days. Live with it, otherwise we can talk about a safe house."

"Not fair," Aimee protested.

"The project is too important," her sister said. "*You* are too important."

Aimee was the scientist, calm and rational, or she had been until ten minutes ago when Tall, Dark, and Dangerous showed up on her porch. She sighed.

"Do it for me?"

"This is under duress," she said.

"So noted."

Aimee hung up.

"The formidable Ms. Inamorata wins another round?" he asked. His arms were folded across his chest, and he didn't gloat.

"Could you look smug or triumphant or something? It's easier to dislike you that way."

"Surprisingly, most people like me."

She couldn't afford to be one of them, as easy as that promised to be with him standing only inches away and smelling so damn good. "You're right. That is surprising."

"I already checked out the front of the house and the backyard. I wish you had a privacy fence rather than a chain-link one."

"The neighbors have a dog."

"Good to know. Show me the rest of the house," he asked again.

If he wanted to explore, he could do it on his own. No way was she watching as he uncovered her secrets. "You still need to wash your shirt," she countered.

"I have a duffel bag in the truck."

"Why am I not surprised?"

"Deductive reasoning? I'm told you are a scientist."

"There is that."

"And I fully intended to stay, regardless of your reception. I do have workout clothes as well."

"But if we both go for a run, no one will be protecting the house."

"Wrong again. Your sister has a couple of details assigned. There's at least one stationed down the block."

She tugged on her ponytail. "She thinks of everything."

He headed for the front door. "Be back in less than thirty seconds."

She thought about locking him out, but Trace Romero was every bit as stubborn, and maybe more determined, as he was.

The dark glance he shot her, combined with that set of his jaw, promised retribution if she crossed him again. *His way*, his attitude screamed.

She stood in the doorway, watching him jog across the road to his big, black, badass sports utility vehicle.

Under other circumstances, she would find him unbelievably attractive. Faded denim hugged his powerful thighs and showed the long length of his legs. But if she were honest, she'd admit she liked the way they showed off his butt. No flat butt for Mr. Romero. It appeared as nicely shaped and as honed as the rest of him. She wondered absently what he wore beneath those ancient jeans. Tighty whities? Boxers? Briefs? Commando? Lord help her, what if there was nothing but that zipper between her and him?

Aimee mentally gave herself a shake. She shouldn't be having random fantasies about her jailer. She needed to focus on her project. Hawkeye was counting on her.

He grabbed an army green duffel bag from the passenger seat; then he slammed the door shut and sprinted back toward her. She noticed him give a thumbs-up to a white Suburban parked down the street.

Her sister really had called out the cavalry.

Aimee had to take a step back to let him into the house.

"Should I change in your bedroom?"

"That's off-limits, I told you."

Right there, in her entry, he pulled off the navy cotton shirt.

She should have known better than to forbid him to do something.

Carefully he wadded the T-shirt. She stood there, mouth agape. As she'd already surmised, he was seriously one sexy man. She might not like his being in her house, but facts were facts, and he was totally smoking, sizzling hot.

He had no excess fat around the middle, and a smattering of dark hair arrowed down the center of his chest to disappear behind the brass button holding his pants together.

Her pulse easily reached 87, maybe 88, percent of her target heart rate. She didn't need a monitor to tell her that. "I'll throw that in the washer," she said.

He handed the T-shirt over and bent to unzip his bag.

"Is that a freaking gun tucked in your waistband?"

"GLOCK," he said.

"No. No guns in my house. No way, no how."

He sighed, but he didn't stop rifling through his bag. And heaven help her, she couldn't help but cast a surreptitious glance at the contents, looking to see if he had underwear there. He pulled out a gray shirt, but she didn't see any boxers, briefs, or tighty whities. That realization didn't do much to tame her libido.

"I mean it, Trace."

He stood. "I appreciate that you don't want me here. I realize having a gun in your house is uncomfortable. I know I'll be invading your privacy."

"And?"

"Tough."

"Tough?"

He took her by the shoulders. "Tough."

When he released her, she slumped.

How did everything get to be so out of control? She hated this, despised all of Hawkeye at the moment.

Needing to do something useful, something she could control, she headed down the hallway to the bathroom that also served as a laundry room. A man in her house. Protective detail. A damn pistol. Two hours ago, life had been totally normal, now nothing was.

She turned on the washer to the smallest load setting. She had some darks she could wash, but throwing their stuff in together seemed...intimate.

She had never in her life washed clothes belonging to a man. During her brief and only live-in relationship, she'd been with a nice guy. Jack. He'd cooked half the meals, paid half the bills, did the grocery shopping and his own laundry.

After barely eight weeks, she'd realized she was so bored that she'd rather have a root canal than endure another missionary, vanilla night in bed. With a root canal, at least she'd get meds to numb the pain.

She was aware of all Trace's movements as he went through her house, invading her privacy without compunction.

She saw him enter her office, and she followed, standing and watching him from the doorway. He was thorough. He opened drawers and the closet doors, looked behind the curtains, checked the window. He pulled the cord on the drapes and said, "Leave them closed, if you don't mind."

She did mind, not that it mattered.

He moved aside her Georgia O'Keeffe print, and she clenched her back teeth together. "Have you seen enough?"

"Just doing my job."

When he left the room, she didn't follow him. Instead she went into her home office, moved the O'Keeffe back into place, and powered up her computer.

If she couldn't run, she could work, or at least pretend to.

Madre de Dios.

Trace hadn't been sure what to expect when Ms. Inamorata summoned him to her office. Fierce, loyal, trusted, the woman had looked rattled. She was always composed, calm under pressure, which was why Hawkeye trusted her implicitly and added her to his inner circle. Whenever a situation got out of hand, she could always be counted on to deal with it and with the local and federal authorities, smoothing over all the details. Hawkeye himself said she batted cleanup better than any major leaguer.

So when Trace saw her, blonde hair mussed as if she'd dragged a hand through it, worrying a pen between her teeth, he'd closed the door, taken a seat, and never considered refusing the assignment.

And now he was glad he hadn't.

Although Inamorata the younger was a self-proclaimed nerd, nothing could be further from the truth.

She had the sculptured body of an athlete, and a fiery personality that was contrasted by her blonde hair and made his protective instincts flare.

He opened her closet and wasn't surprised at all. She had half a dozen pairs of running shoes, lots of outdoor and sports gear, including a racquetball racquet—she definitely was his kind of woman—a bunch of slim-fitting skirts and slacks, and several blouses. The slinky black dress tucked in the corner intrigued him, and he had to forcibly remind himself he was here for work. If he'd met her at the annual holiday party, things would have been different...way different.

Technically after checking beneath her bed and in the closet and making sure the windows were secure, he didn't need to look any deeper.

But he was still a red-blooded male intrigued by an appealing woman.

He crouched in front of her bookcase. *Well, well.* Judging by the books on the bottom shelf, she had carnal desires that rivaled his own.

BDSM.

He wondered how much experience she had, what her interest level was. He toyed with the idea that she might be an avid practitioner, but he quickly dismissed the thought. She'd have picked up the signals earlier, once her panic had subsided. And she would have been more responsive once she was in his arms.

The idea of introducing her to a scene turned him on. Having her bent over, ready for his touch, appealed on every level. She was a spitfire, and when she capitulated, her surrender would be all the sweeter.

Protecting the professor's body had suddenly gotten more interesting.

He plucked a well-worn book from the set and flipped it over to read the back cover. The novel was about a woman who wanted to be a submissive and lied to a Dom in order to be accepted for training. Hard stuff, not a simple "tie me up while we enjoy some slap and tickle." No, Aimee's taste was a bit more extreme, very much in line with his practices.

He thought about looking in her drawers to see if she had toys. He'd told her he didn't mind invading her privacy, but even he had limits. Keeping her safe was one thing; snooping was another. Besides, it would be more fun when she showed him herself.

After returning the book to the shelf, he stood and left the room, but not before noticing that the bed, with a slatted headboard and footboard, would be perfect for restraining her while she begged him to punish her.

He paused when he passed her office. She pretended not to hear him.

Grinning, he continued into the living room.

He killed an hour; then he headed for the back door, intending to take another trip around the exterior of the house. He was going to leave the door open, but the crazy *loro* jumped down from the top of his cage and began a ridiculous waddle walk toward the opening.

Knowing Aimee wouldn't appreciate it if he turned the bird loose, he said, "Stay." Then he realized he had no idea whether it understood him.

He closed the door and swept the backyard from left to right, looking for anything that was different from an hour ago. He hopped the chain-link fence, acknowledged the team stationed near the house, and then circled behind her evergreen trees.

Everything checked clear.

Since the front door was closed, he returned to the backyard, this time using the gate. It squeaked, which he appreciated. One more sound to be aware of.

He entered the house, and Aimee was in the kitchen, a glass of water in hand. "Find anything interesting?"

"Everything's secure from outside."

"Good."

She turned, her ponytail swishing as she headed out of the kitchen.

"Along with a few books in your bedroom," he said experimentally.

She stopped walking. "You were right that you were going to invade my privacy."

He pushed a bit more. "You have an extensive collection of erotic fiction."

"I read a lot. I have a shelf full of murder mysteries as well." She slowly turned back to face him.

"BDSM?" he asked. She hadn't run. She hadn't shut him down, either politely or with scorching rudeness. She was a woman more than capable of cutting a guy off at the knees and stuffing his balls down his throat. But she hadn't. "You have at least half a dozen titles. You even have a couple of manuals on erotic restraints and a complete how-to on being a proper submissive."

Her mouth and body said one thing, but the heightened flush said another.

"Let's be clear, Mr. Romero—"

"Trace." Fuck, throwing her off her stride was fun.

She tilted her chin back, but he noticed that her breathing had changed just a little, becoming more shallow. "Just because there's a shelf full of murder mysteries doesn't mean I've killed anyone." She paused a long beat, then added, "Yet."

He raised a brow, considering her. She was a study in leashed intensity. Her legs, very shapely legs, were spread about shoulder-width apart, and her hands were propped on her hips. She glared at him. Her eyes were deep, dark blue. He'd seen the same color in the depths of a Rocky Mountain alpine lake at twelve thousand feet. He was sure she thought she looked formidable. To him, she was a challenge wrapped in an intriguing package.

Her bare midriff would fuel fantasies for weeks, maybe months. He'd be in some nameless South American jungle, and he'd get this very picture in his head, her bare skin and sexy little body. "But the fantasy…?"

"The fantasy of killing someone and burying his body in the backyard is very compelling at the moment," she said with a vicious little smile.

Oh yeah. He was hooked. "I have more than a passing interest in BDSM," he said. He kept his distance, moving to the far counter and leaning against it. He crossed his arms across his chest.

"Maybe I'll interview you for a scholarly book I'm planning to write on the topic."

"Ah. So your interest is strictly scholarly?"

"Certainly."

She couldn't tell a lie if her well-being depended on it. "Have you had any experience of your own to write about?"

"I don't have to face all the ethical dilemmas that I write about."

"True enough." Her blonde hair had been yanked back into a severe ponytail. Instead of being loosely held, barely swept back from her face, her hair was corralled into a confined knot. He wondered if the way she wore her hair was a metaphor for the way she ran her life. Trace relished the thought of her capitulation as he made her whimper in his arms. "There's a particular book about a woman tricking a Dom into training her."

"We are so not having this conversation," she said.

Anyone else looking at her might believe what she was saying. They might miss the clues her body was telegraphing, the way she folded her arms across her chest but ruined the effect by rubbing her hands up and down her bare skin, the way her gaze kept straying to the waistband of his jeans, the way she'd moistened her lower lip. Now that he knew what to look for, he saw she wanted this discussion every bit as much as he did.

"Think of it purely in scientific terms," he said. "Research for your book. Like you suggested, you can interview me. I'll be a resource. Have you thought about being trained yourself, actually going through the experience?"

"It's not about me," she repeated, but she was fidgeting.

"I find it interesting that none of the BDSM ones are about a female being the Domme." He took a step toward her. "None are strictly about bondage or fetish play. They all have a common theme. If they were all research, wouldn't you have a more diverse collection?" He pushed away from the counter and took a step toward her.

"I'm, er, just starting the research."

"I see. So I take it you've never been tied up before you were spanked, Aimee? And you have no desire to find out for yourself what you're missing?"

"No. None." She stood her ground.

He nodded curtly. "In that case, I won't keep you from your work."

She blinked, evidently unaccustomed to being dismissed. "Right." She left her water, forgotten, on the counter.

Aimee sat in her office chair, and her hands shook.

This was a nightmare. A living, breathing, ripped-from-the-headlines nightmare. And it was exactly what she wanted.

She wanted a big, strong man to sweep her off her feet. Wasn't that her fantasy? She'd dreamed of meeting a man as strong as she was, not some milquetoast who split the bills and the laundry.

Her perfect man would see through her carefully constructed facade to the needy woman beneath.

But now that he was here, in living flesh, offering her what she craved, she was scared right down to her size 6 running shoes.

It bothered her that her panties had gotten damp when he'd asked if she'd wanted to get trained. Her body was much more honest than she was. Yes, she wanted to get trained, and yes, she wanted to do it at his hands.

But couldn't take a risk, wouldn't take the risk. She was far too sensible for that. Wasn't she?

For the next hour, she tried to concentrate on work. Nothing happened, and she ended up zoning out, playing a few hands of solitaire.

She couldn't get thoughts of Trace out of her mind. His questions tumbled over and over. He hadn't bought, even for a minute, that she was doing research. He'd clearly noticed everything about her, like a good Dom would. He was paying attention to her reactions, probably more than the words that came out of her mouth.

She heard the back door open, heard it close again. He was definitely focused, and when he had something in mind, he followed through. She exhaled shakily. All that probably meant he wasn't through with her yet.

She was pretty sure she wouldn't be able to withstand it.

Keeping up the pretense, she stayed in her office when he reentered the house. He'd been gone three minutes and thirty-seven seconds, not that she'd noticed.

She heard his booted steps in the living room, then down the hallway. She flipped from solitaire to a spreadsheet and leaned forward as if studying a formula on the screen. He was in and out of every room, rechecking the windows.

She turned in her chair as he passed her office. "Does my sister know what you're into?"

"Yes," he said without stopping.

Curse him. Curse him, curse him, curse him.

He was out to drive her batshit crazy.

She swung back to the computer and dropped her head onto her desk.

Her sister knew his secrets, and she'd sent him here regardless.

She heard a muffled sound from the television in the living room. Cozy. Just *cozy*.

After another half hour of games, both on the computer and in her head, she went into the living room and stood in front of him.

"Aimee! Aimee!" Eureka called from the kitchen.

Trace hit the Mute button on the remote. That scored big points with her. Of course, how interesting was a Colorado Rockies baseball game, when they had no hope of even a wild-card slot in the playoffs?

He looked at her and waited. Couldn't he help her out, at

least a little?

"If you… If I…"

He waited, his brows raised patiently. Her mouth dried. This man was so appealing, his masculinity making her instinctively feel more feminine. "Have you ever trained a novice sub?"

"Trained? In what way?"

She closed her eyes for a minute. He was definitely not going to make this easy. "Introduced a woman to being a submissive." Her heart missed a beat. "Your submissive?"

"I'm not into lifestyle BDSM. I've had subs, and I'm happy to tell you about the experience. I don't require my subs to be full-time slaves, if that's what you're asking. But I often do require they wear collars."

She tried to keep her hands from going to her neck, and she settled for clasping them in front of her. "Where would you start? I mean, theoretically."

"Theoretically?"

"Research…for my book."

"The first place I start is with honesty. Then we go to trust."

Her mouth felt dry suddenly.

"I have no tolerance for bullshit. If you're curious, we can explore; there will be nothing theoretical about it. It will be raw, and it will be real. Your sister trusts me with your life. If you can do the same, be real, be honest, learn to trust, then say so, straight up."

Her mind reeled. "If I said I was interested, where would we start?"

Chapter Two

Trace's cock was rock hard.

Her innocence thrilled him. He wanted to be the one to introduce her, to explore the dark side with her. She licked her lower lip. Damn, if he'd ever seen a more appealing woman, he didn't remember when. "We'd start with you honestly answering a few questions. And you'd do that from that chair, right there."

It was his first test, and they both knew it.

With her energy level, he knew she would prefer to stand, maybe even pace. But it wasn't about what she preferred.

Slowly she crossed the room. Men moved toward a hangman's noose with more enthusiasm.

She sat, legs pressed together, across from him.

"How much experience do you have?"

"None."

"By none, you mean…what, exactly?"

She tugged on her ponytail, but not a single strand of hair became dislodged. "I have no experience. Nada. Zero. Zilch."

"You've never been tied up?"

"No," she whispered.

"Never been spanked?"

"Oh God."

He took that as a no. "Nipple clamps?"

"I own a set."

"But a man, a Dom, a master, hasn't put them on you?"

"Trace…"

"I asked you a question." Part of him was tempted to just draw her close and kiss her senseless. *Caramba.* She was so damn perfect.

"No."

"I'll watch you put them on." The color on her cheeks darkened to scarlet. Dios, he hoped she never lost this intriguing innocence. "Butt plug?"

"I have a stainless steel one. And no, no one has ever put one in me."

"Or fucked you with it?"

Her eyes opened wide and stayed that way for a long second before she blinked. "Certainly not."

His cock chafed against the inside of his jeans. "How much experience do you want to have?" He pictured her bare bottom over his lap, her body wiggling as he pressed one hand to the small of her back and then used the other to teach her a thing or two. He wondered if she'd fight to be quiet while he pleasured her, while he punished her. Or would she give into it completely, abandoning all reserve while she was perfectly responsive?

Instead of answering him, she asked one of her own. "How much experience do you have?"

It was a fair question. He opted for the honesty he would soon demand from her. "I've had several subs, two of them long-term. I ended my last relationship about six months ago, with no animosity. She just couldn't handle how long I was gone from her. I don't blame her, and if I saw her at a club, I'd happily play with her. I love exploring a woman's boundaries, your boundaries," he clarified, "and pushing them."

He saw her take that information and feed it through her extensive brain.

"You're interested in it too. The psychological implications along with the sexual ones. My guess is you want a man you can't steamroll."

"Not fair."

"But true?"

She frowned.

"It takes a strong man," he said, "to tame a strong woman."

"I don't need taming."

"Or spanking?"

"Or spanking," she said, but the words were unsteady.

They were still separated by several feet, but he saw how hard she struggled to breathe. He continued to push. "You have no desire to be so outside yourself that you experience orgasm after orgasm?"

She blinked.

Into the sudden silence, he asked, "How long, Aimee, since you've been with a man who's been so focused on you that your pleasure was the only thing that mattered?"

"That's not what BDSM is about."

"Oh? Enlighten me. What is BDSM all about?"

"Not having this conversation," she said again.

He was relentless. "Tell me, Aimee. What is it about?"

"It's about your…" She stopped; then she scowled, a deep furrow appearing between her finely sculptured eyebrows.

Her innocence appealed to him on so many levels. It had been years since he'd been with a woman who wasn't jaded.

Such depths were hidden inside Aimee. He could see it in her eyes, and he wanted to be the one who showed her everything she craved.

His cock began to throb, and not just from the anticipation of eventually fucking her, but from the knowledge he'd be the first to dominate her.

She started again. "It's about the Dom's pleasure. About the sub being so focused on her Dom's pleasure that she, or he, takes pleasure from that."

He hadn't missed her Freudian slip. "Maybe to some people," he said. "And if you've got a great relationship, that definitely is part of it. While I have certain expectations from a woman who submits to me, I also make certain she receives pleasure from me. Take out your ponytail."

Her mouth opened before she snapped it shut again.

"Tell me you're not curious." He waited. "Tell me you're not wondering what the first thing is that I might do to you. Tell me you're not anticipating obeying my commands."

"I…"

"Honesty," he reminded her.

"Yes," she whispered.

He stood and closed the distance between them. He put his hands on her shoulders and pulled her up. Every motion deliberate, wanting to communicate with her on a level that words never could, showing he was controlled, that he could be trusted with the gift of her submission, he tipped back her head with the pad of his thumb.

She was so small in his hands. The top of her head barely reached his chin. He meant what he said. He wanted to explore her boundaries, shatter them, but she would be a willing participant each step of the way.

Her mouth slowly parted.

"I'm going to kiss you," he said. "And you're going to kiss me back." He waited for a response.

She nodded.

"But first, you're going to take down your ponytail."

His second test.

Aimee knew exactly what he was doing. Or at least she thought she did. In her fantasies, none of this head-game stuff existed. A Dom issued an order, his sub complied. There was no hesitation.

But the reality was so much different.

She was questioning everything, including her own sanity.

The feel of his thumb pressing inexorably beneath her chin was breathtaking. His right hand gripped her left shoulder with undeniable force. Yet she knew, totally, she could get away if she wanted. She could have dodged him earlier, could have turned around and left the room. But she didn't want to.

Despite her wildest dreams, all the books she read, the chat rooms she studied with academic interest, it went against her nature to willingly submit to anyone. After their parents died, it had been her and her big sis against the world. They'd both struggled for scholarships, had worked full-time jobs while attending school. At times she'd had three roommates just to make ends meet. Aimee had learned self-sufficiency early, and she liked living her life that way now.

Trace captured her gaze. With the force of his own, he compelled her not to look away. Truthfully she didn't want to look away. She wanted to get lost in the depths of his brown eyes. His scent, his presence, overwhelmed her.

"Scared?"

"Not at all."

"Liar."

He said the word without malice, but quickly enough for her to realize he was watching her intently. He'd told her he wanted her honesty, and regardless, she wouldn't be able to hide from him. Suddenly that terrified her more than anything ever had.

He continued to wait.

"Yes," she admitted. "I'm scared." That wasn't an easy confession. Life had taught her not to show weakness, and standing here emotionally exposed revealed her every vulnerability.

"Take out your ponytail," he repeated.

They both knew this was about more than her hair. It was about him exerting his will and whether she'd comply. It was her first step. If she pulled the band from her hair, she was submitting to him, and she had no idea where it would end. "I've never done anything like this before. I'm not sure exactly what to do."

"But you're intrigued? When you masturbate, it's what you think about."

"Yes," she whispered, feeling heat chasing into her face once again. She tried to look away, but he held her chin more firmly. She had never admitted to anyone that she masturbated, maybe because of some deep belief that it was wrong. And here he was, assuming she did, not questioning.

"Take one step."

"What if it's the one that sends me off the edge of the cliff?"

"It will be," he promised.

Her nerves shot, she laughed, the sound nervous, bordering on brittle. "That's reassuring."

"The option is not to take the step," he told her. "That's certainly your choice. I won't force you into anything, ever. But let me ask you this, Professor. What's more risky, taking the chance or never knowing the outcome? Never knowing if it's right for you? Never experimenting? Never knowing if fantasy is better than reality?"

She mulled that over thoughtfully. Even though it wasn't really in her nature to turn herself over to anyone, she thought about her relationship with boring Jack. The lack of excitement hadn't worked for her either. Jack had never told her what to do. He politely asked, then thanked her when he turned off the light. For what, she'd wanted to ask, for being as unimaginative as he was?

"But after you take down your hair, you're going to take off your sports bra."

She was?

"Then you'll cup your breasts and offer them to me."

She shivered, from fear, from excitement.

"And then…"

There was more?

"If you choose to take that first step, you'll beg me to suck your nipples until they're hard."

Oh. Uh.

He leaned in and drew her lower lip between his teeth, gently at first, then with a bit more force.

Resistance eased away.

Almost instantly she gave herself over to the slight pain, buried beneath intense pleasure. She wanted to let her inhibitions slide, wanted to be with a man strong enough to urge her to dig deeper.

And this man did.

Intuitively she knew he was the one she'd been waiting for.

While he held her captive, her thoughts continued to tumble. Resist? Submit? Take a leap? Retreat in fear?

He continued the pressure on her lower lip. Rational thought was all but impossible.

Subtly he changed what he was doing, demanding entrance

to her mouth.

Willingly she surrendered.

She liked to be kissed, and this man knew how to kiss. He tasted of temptation and determination. There was no hiding from him or his demands.

Her arms went around him. She flattened one palm on his back, and with the other hand, she dug her fingers into his black hair. She raised on tiptoes to meet him more completely.

Within seconds, she knew he'd been right.

He was kissing her, and she was kissing him back.

Their tongues met in thrust and parry. She had a taste of what sex with him would be like, and she wanted more. She liked his insistence, and she especially liked the way he drew her tight against him and held her there. She felt safe in his arms. And like her sister had intended, Aimee felt protected.

Finally, like she did with most decisions in her life, she stopped the internal debate. She'd looked at the pros and cons unemotionally, and she made up her mind. Better to take the risk and find out...

She pulled back from him slightly, letting go with the hand she'd feathered into his hair. She reached up and pulled out the band that cinched her hair.

Expert that he was, he'd continued to kiss her, hold her. But she noticed his eyes had darkened almost imperceptibly.

He released her shoulder and then ran his fingers through her hair, fluffing it, playing with it.

She was no less a prisoner now, though, since he cradled the back of her head.

He slowly drew back, ending the kiss, then finally, after one last nip, let go of her lip. "Good girl," he said.

The approval in his husky voice sent a tiny jolt of excitement through her. She'd taken that first step. Instead of terrifying, it was liberating.

"More?" he asked.

They both knew what he meant. Was she ready to go deeper? Would she follow all his orders? Slowly, her lower lip throbbing, she nodded.

Then he let her go entirely and took a step back.

Eureka flew into the room in his usual graceless, noisy manner. She realized he'd called her name a couple of times, and she hadn't answered. "Everything's okay," she told him.

He cocked his head in Trace's direction.

"Nap time," she told the bird.

"Nap time," he repeated.

"Return to base," she said. "I'll be right back," she added to Trace. She exhaled, grateful for the reprieve. Covering Eureka's cage would take a few minutes, giving her enough time to drag her breathing back under control and to think about whether she was truly prepared to take action on Trace's request.

Sitting where he instructed and taking out her ponytail had been minor compared to his next request. If she took the third and fourth steps, she knew he'd demand a fifth, then more, until she was truly submitting to him.

"Return to base," Eureka said. "Nap time." He hopped onto his perch; then she put her hand in front of him. He climbed onto her forefinger and said, "Wheee!" as she placed him in his cage.

She grinned at him, not at all upset. She covered the cage, and the thought that she could have lost him earlier this morning sent a cold chill up her spine.

This wasn't fun and games, not that she would ever allow herself to lose sight of reality long enough to think it was.

Her pulse rate had returned to near-normal when she went back into living room. Trace was still there, in much the same place she'd left him, but he'd turned off the television. Another point in his favor.

He said nothing. He folded his arms across his chest, waiting, watching.

He looked sexy but unapproachable, which in a weird way only made him seem even sexier. It was as if this man had opened up her brain to take a look at what made her tick.

Her older sister always told her to live with no regrets. Aimee realized that if she were to look back on this moment ten years from now, she would regret being timid more than she would regret taking a chance.

She boldly went to stand only a foot or so away from him. Her heart rate had surged to the level it would have if she'd actually gone for her run.

Trace said nothing, and she might have thought he was uninterested in her decision, except for the barely perceptible way his eyelids momentarily shuttered his eyes.

She hooked her thumbs underneath the elastic of her sports bra and then pulled the material up and off. She closed her eyes as she dropped it to the tiled floor.

"*Muy bonita*," he said. "Very pretty."

That raw huskiness in his voice thrilled her. She'd be a lemming, if only his voice urged her on.

She opened her eyes to see him looking at her intently. "Touch me?" she asked, the words more a plea than she'd intended them to be. She had wanted to sound forceful, perhaps a bit demanding, and certainly competent and in control, like she always was. But standing in front of Trace, she was none of those things. She was a woman who wanted this man's hands on her half-naked body. "Touch me, Trace."

"Offer yourself to me," he reminded her. "Beg me."

She noticed the bulge at his crotch. He was as turned on as she was. That knowledge was heady and all she needed. Rather than succumbing to embarrassment like she ordinarily would, she kept her gaze focused below his belt as she cupped her breasts in her palms. Quietly she said, "I want you to suck on my nipples."

"Look at me."

The words, in the silence, were a whiplash.

She looked up and kept her gaze focused on his face. Drawing a steadying breath, she softly said, "Please, Trace, suck on my nipples. I need…"

He waited in that patient, maddening way of his.

"I need your touch. I want to feel your hands on me. I want your mouth on my breasts, your tongue on my nipples." She lifted her breasts a bit. "Please, Trace." And she did want it, need it, need him.

His motions deliberate, he unfolded his arms. Her body felt weak as nerve suddenly deserted her. Then he was there, his arms around her, supporting her, one palm pressed against the small of her back, the other cradling her nape.

He lowered his head to capture a nipple between his tongue and top teeth. Then he sucked, hard.

Her knees buckled.

He caught her, sweeping her from the ground and carrying her down the hallway to her bedroom.

"Please," she whispered.

"I haven't even started with you yet," he promised, setting her on the floor.

He put his pistol on the nightstand. She was so caught up with what he was doing that she didn't even protest the gun being in her bedroom. Her arms fell to her sides as she surrendered to him. He sucked her right nipple while he pinched the other between his thumb and forefinger. She arched her back, asking for more.

"Keep still," he told her.

"Keep still?" Had he lost his mind? Because she was definitely losing hers. She'd never experienced anything like this, exquisite and painful, creating a demand from the inside out.

"Part of your lessons," he said, returning to her nipple and torturing it relentlessly.

She'd taken the first steps, she realized, and he was exerting his will more powerfully. He'd force her to be an active participant. Already she was learning there was nothing passive about being involved with him.

She began to squirm. Heat flooded her body. She wanted more. More pressure. More intensity. She wanted to orgasm.

"Distract yourself," he said. "Think about something else, anything else other than how your body is responding to what I'm doing. Think about the fact I want you to keep still. Think about pleasing me."

"I…"

"Can," he told her. "You can. You're a runner. Breathe. Use the same techniques you use there."

"But—"

"Breathe." He suckled, gently at first, then with unyielding force.

She squirmed. She was coming undone. He couldn't possibly have any idea what he was asking of her, demanding of her. He'd assigned her a task, and she was doomed to failure. Staying still was nearly impossible with the way he tormented her. She'd never realized how sensitive her nipples were, never knew she could get so totally turned on from breast play.

She tried to follow his instructions.

When the only thing she could think of was how much she wanted to come, she forced her thoughts to her project and looming deadline. She met his gaze, saw the slight smile that toyed with his lips before he moved that skillful mouth to the tip of her other breast.

She wanted to do what he said, she realized, wanted to please him, wanted to see him smile at her.

He moved one of his hands between her legs. Helplessly, shamelessly, she ground her crotch against him, wishing she'd taken off her shorts, and he responded, unerringly finding her swollen clit and pushing his thumb against it. When she could no longer breathe in a controlled way, she settled for panting. Hearing his instructions echoing in her mind, she tried to fight the orgasm. She tried to hold it back, tried to keep still.

He moved to her other nipple and bit. She cried out.

The orgasm caught her. In a powerful wave, it crashed into her, over her.

She moved faster and faster against him, riding the wave of the climax, her pussy clenching.

He kept doing what he was doing as she ground it out, damn near achieving a second orgasm.

She was shattered. Complete. Overwhelmed. He continued to hold her in his strong arms, offering support and whispering soft, reassuring sounds.

Seconds later, when her breathing had returned to normal and her brain regained its functionality, she realized she was lying on the bed and he was beside her. She placed her head on his chest and said, "That never happens quite so fast."

"You're as responsive as I hoped." He kissed her forehead.

She'd always believed there was something wrong with her. When she'd been at MIT, her roommates had talked about their experiences, and she didn't have much to share in return. She slept with few men, achieved the big O with even fewer. It seemed her friends enjoyed sex a whole lot more than she did. But now she was wondering if she'd just been with the wrong men.

"How are you feeling?"

"Satisfied." She wanted to wrap her arms around herself. "I'd love to curl up and drift off to sleep for a few minutes." Even better, she wanted him to hold her as she dozed. And when she awoke, maybe they could do it all over again.

After only a minute, maybe two, she lifted her head off his chest, not entirely sure she was comfortable with the intimacy. She wasn't the kind of woman who relied on men, who turned to them for comfort. Self-sufficient, and independent, she needed no one. She ignored the little whisper inside that said it might be nice to allow someone to get close, might be nice to share the load, might be nice to have someone to hold on to, at least sometimes.

She met his gaze. Was it possible to get lost in the depths of his eyes?

A small smile played at the corners of his mouth, until he said, "You were disobedient."

That got her attention.

"You didn't have permission to come, sub."

"But…" She needed permission to orgasm?

"I told you to distract yourself, to think about anything but the way I was pleasuring you. I told you to keep still, to concentrate on pleasing me." He paused, maybe to let his words sink in. "This time, I'm feeling generous. I'll let you choose your own punishment."

Sleepiness was banished. Nerves dried her mouth. "You want me to choose my own punishment? For orgasming without permission?"

His gaze returned to the collection of books on the bottom shelf. "I think you know exactly what I'm asking of you."

Erotic fear churned inside her.

This man would never let her off the hook. Secretly she didn't want him to.

She had already started to trust him. Her sister had handpicked him, and the older Inamorata would kick his ass from Colorado to Colombia if he hurt her, and the long arm of Hawkeye would hunt him down wherever he tried to hide. Despite those realizations, terror made her freeze in place.

"But I will tell you this. No matter what punishment you choose, it will start with your being totally naked," he said.

While he was still dressed. Suddenly she knew that was part of it. He was stripping her defenses, one by one, starting with her ponytail, continuing with her sports bra, and now with the rest of her clothing. She saw the power in it. Nowhere to run. Nowhere to hide.

"Now."

Chapter Three

Even as she questioned if she'd actually go through with it, she climbed off the bed and took a couple of steps backward. She toed off her shoes, holding on to the dresser top for balance.

She bent to take off her ankle socks.

He stood there, saying nothing.

Her nipples were still hardened into little pebbles, the cool whisper of air from the overhead fan keeping them taut.

She hooked her fingers beneath the band of her shorts and wiggled until they slid down her legs. She stepped from them, leaving them in a pile on the floor with her other discarded pieces. They both knew she could have simultaneously removed her underwear, but she didn't have the guts for that.

"A thong?"

She nodded.

"Leaves your ass bare. Are you always hoping for a spanking, Aimee?"

"No!"

He laughed.

But…maybe. There was a reason she chose her underwear, she knew, even if she didn't admit those things to herself.

He patiently waited while she discarded the scrap of material. The crotch was damp from her earlier climax and from the continual wetness his words caused.

Finally she stood there in front of him, naked. She tipped back her head, then folded and unfolded her arms a couple of times, not quite sure what to do with them.

"Lovely," he said. "I had no idea whether or not I'd find you shaven."

She was. But she wasn't sure he approved.

"I like you bare," he said, eliminating her worry. "I would have shaved you myself."

That idea sent a tiny shiver down her spine. To have him so close, so intimate, while she was totally vulnerable.

"When in doubt, keep your arms behind your back."

"Do you miss anything?"

"With you? I plan not to."

There was a little frisson of excitement that passed through her body at his words. That his attention was so focused on her... It was heady indeed.

She moved her hands behind her back, and she realized that thrust out her breasts a little more.

"Keep your legs spread, whether you're kneeling or standing. Farther," he said. "Shoulder width, at least. I always want access to your pussy."

Her insides felt molten.

"Face away from me."

She turned.

"Now bend over and grab your ankles."

Bent over, with her legs spread, she would present an obscene image. Humiliation threatened to pull her into an undertow. She almost protested, but she stopped herself. He knew exactly what he was asking her to do. She had been honest about her level of experience, and he'd been honest that he'd had submissives before. Aimee was willing to bet he was as skillful with his first woman as he was with her. He had the instincts that made him an operative her sister trusted. And he had a way of looking at her, of reading her that made him adept at knowing which buttons to push.

This time, he didn't repeat his command. He just waited.

She could refuse, or she could embrace her fantasy.

She bent and grabbed her ankles. The sight of the world upside down was too much, and she closed her eyes.

As she waited, schooling herself to be patient, she focused on the sound of the overhead fan and felt the air on her exposed parts, and she wondered what he was doing.

Looking at her, that was for sure. Thinking? Planning? Enjoying the sight? Please God, she was vain enough to hope he liked what he saw.

All her senses seemed supercharged.

She inhaled the scent of him, that intoxicating blend of man and spice. She hungered, she realized, for the sound of his voice. That strong, unyielding tone was a lifeline. Suddenly she felt adrift.

"Spread your legs a few more inches." He got off the bed and moved in behind her. He used his right foot to exert pressure against the inside of her right ankle, forcing her into the position he wanted. "Your ass needs to be stretched by that plug."

She told herself she couldn't actually die from feelings of mortification.

"You've never been fucked with a plug, but have you had anal sex?"

"I tried it once, in grad school."

"Tell me about the experience."

When this was over, she'd have no secrets left. "It was awful. I'd had too much to drink, and so had he. It hurt. He never actually…" She swallowed, not something that was easy when she was hanging upside down. "There was very little penetration. He ended up... Ah... He didn't last long enough... I mean... He came all over the sheets."

He stroked her between the legs, long, sweeping motions with his large fingers.

"You're wet," he said.

She was.

"Your body is so responsive, so honest." He parted her labia and glided a fingertip across her clit.

Involuntarily her body jerked.

"Nice," he said. "But keep still."

This time, she struggled to obey. He feathered her clit again, and she gasped. But instead of moving, she squeezed her eyes shut just a little more and drew a deep breath.

"Quick learner," he said. He pressed a finger firmly on her clit. She moved forward a scant inch, trying to get away from the maddening, delicious intensity of the feeling.

He put a palm against the middle of her back, keeping her bent and preventing her from moving away. Then he increased the pressure on her tiny, already swollen nub.

"Trace," she said. Unbelievably she was feeling a tiny orgasm already building inside. She told herself she could come from just this tiny amount of sensation, but she knew she was wrong. It wasn't just about his touch; it was about his mastery of her. It was the combination of the words he used and the force he exerted.

Even she could smell her arousal.

He began to move his finger in a tiny circle, and at the same time, with his palm, he held her firmly, making sure she couldn't escape his touch. "Distract yourself," he reminded her.

She whimpered. Her hips began to sway, even though she fought against it. "Actinium," she said. "Aluminum.

Americium."

"The periodic table?"

She didn't answer him; instead, she focused. "Antimony..." She trailed off as he continued his relentless assault on her body. "Argon... Please! Please stop. Otherwise I'm going to come."

"Not yet."

"Trace!"

"Hang in there."

"I—"

"Breathe!"

Her knees were threatening to give out. She could barely hold on to her ankles. Thinking about anything except what he was doing was impossible. She needed to let him know that, but she couldn't find the words. "I..."

"I want you fighting it out, Aimee."

She did. Her eyes still scrunched closed, still panting, she said, "Arsenic, astatine, barium..."

"Now," he said, sliding a finger inside her. "Come now."

The orgasm swamped her. She lost her footing as her knees finally buckled, but he was there, holding her, supporting her, never letting her crash headlong into the ground.

He scooped her up and carried her to the bed. He lay down with her, careful to keep his boots off the mattress. He held her close, cradled her tenderly, her head on the soft material of his T-shirt. "Thank you," she whispered. Until now she'd never understood why the female subs in the stories she read would be so appreciative after a climax. She figured they were because that's what their Doms demanded. Now she knew differently.

She would have never survived his actually entering her. She would have splintered from the inside out.

Her gratitude wasn't just for the earthmoving orgasm. It

wasn't just because he'd relented and given his permission. It was so much deeper. Her gratitude was for all that and the way he read her so perfectly, recognizing what she needed, when she needed it, and for having her hang on longer than she might have so that the experience was even deeper. Most of all, it was for catching her, caring for her when she wasn't sure she was able to.

"Have you decided?" he asked, his breath warm against her hair.

"Decided?"

"What your punishment will be."

She swallowed. She'd totally forgotten, and she told him that, adding, "I hoped you'd forgotten too. Or that I'd gotten a reprieve. You know, kind of like time off for good behavior."

He laughed. "No chance. You're always expected to obey me. Good behavior will not mitigate disobedience. So what's it to be?"

"Can I get back to you on that?" She wasn't sure she could take anything more. Aimee was convinced she was at the edge of her endurance.

"Within the next thirty seconds. Sure."

"Trace!"

"Tell me, in your reading, in your most private fantasies, when you've imagined yourself being punished, what that experience was like."

Again, he didn't ask if she had those kinds of thoughts. He assumed she did, and he would probe until she revealed the details. She was already learning that he wouldn't allow her to hide behind embarrassment. He wanted her secrets exposed, and he'd keep at her until they were. "There's always an awareness," she said, "about what I've done wrong, how I could have behaved differently." That naughty arousal was starting to unfurl again, despite how tired she was.

"You've read enough to know the difference between punishment and discipline?"

Was it possible for her face to get any hotter? "I think so."

"Tell me."

She wiggled around, trying to face him. The scratch of his denim jeans felt rough against her bare leg.

She thought of the way he'd masturbated her earlier, the way she'd ground her crotch against his hand. Her imagination took flight as she wondered what it might feel like to have his leg between hers as she rubbed against the strength of his thigh.

"The difference between punishment and discipline," he repeated.

"Punishment is correction. Physical..." Despite herself, she was picturing herself across his lap, her bottom exposed to his hand, maybe his belt. She shivered, and he drew her closer against him.

"I guess punishment could also be mental. It's meant to reinforce behavior that a Dom expects."

"Good enough. Discipline?"

"That trips me up a bit. Discipline can also reinforce behavior, but I guess there's a punitive side that's missing."

"Fair distinction. Discipline, with my subs, is also about training. It can be as painful as punishment. It can also be very enjoyable. For both of us."

"I think I'd rather be disciplined than punished."

"I'm sure you would. You mentioned the mental part of punishment. It can be very effective, so I use it sparingly. You don't follow an order, you'll be punished, generally very quickly."

"In that case, can we get this over with?"

"Nervous?"

"In college, I'd volunteer to take tests early."

"Masochist," he said. "It will make you a good sub."

"I want to be across your lap," she said. She couldn't believe she was admitting this, something she'd never told another human being. She'd always kept her secrets locked away, never hinting at them, never mentioning them to anyone. "And..."

He waited, as she should have guessed he would.

"Your hand. I want you to use your hand to punish me."

"Anything else?"

"And..."

"And?"

"I want you to take it easy. Virgin spankee, and all that."

He laughed. "When I said you got to choose your own punishment, I didn't say you got to choose all the details."

"It was worth a try," she said.

"Not really. Now you'll just get punished for trying to get out of your punishment."

Her stomach took a nosedive and landed somewhere around her knees. Good thing she was still lying down.

"How many spanks do you deserve?"

She squirmed. She had no idea what to suggest. Too few, and she'd be in trouble for that, no doubt. Too many, and she might come up with a number higher than one he'd choose.

"And how many extra for trying to get out of a hard spanking?"

She hadn't finished in the top of her class for nothing. "I think the ones for trying to get out of my punishment should be harder than the others."

He stroked her hair. It would be almost possible to believe they were lovers, just enjoying a few minutes of intimacy, rather than a Dom and a wannabe sub discussing her induction into BDSM.

"Do you agree?"

"In this case, that sounds reasonable. Still waiting for numbers."

"Ten," she said. "Ten for the first infraction. Three for the second. That's an additional thirty percent."

"If we started at a more reasonable twelve, what's the percentage, then?"

"More like twenty-five percent."

"And?"

"Four is reasonable," she said before he came up with something even more outrageous. She'd hoped to only take a handful of strokes for her first official spanking, and now she was at sixteen. "Do I get a safe word?"

"You have been reading. Do you want one?"

She wondered what it would be like to fly without one. None of the subs in the books she read went without a word to either slow down or stop a scene. "Krypton."

"*Preciosa*, I think you're going to be my kryptonite. Nothing else on the periodic table you'd rather choose?"

"I like krypton."

"Krypton it is. But I want you to know something, Aimee. It's my intention that you never need to use your safe word. I don't want you using it just because you're a little scared. I want you to discuss those things with me. This experience will be about taking you to the edge." Trace climbed from the bed and offered her a hand.

"Here? Now?" She took his hand and let him guide her up.

He pulled her against him and took hold of one of her wrists lightly, but with enough force that if she chickened out, she wouldn't make it far.

She'd always wondered what it would be like to actually be in this situation. But it was nothing like she imagined. In her own fantasies, she was always in control of her own reaction; she was never afraid: she welcomed anything her Dom threw at her. She was always the perfect sub. Well, unless she'd decided she wanted to be punished, in which case, she was very bad, just to get what she really wanted.

The reality was so different.

She'd always figured her imaginations would have to stay exactly that, flights of fantasy she indulged in on those rare occasions she pulled out her toys and books. She'd never dreamed she'd find a man who would take her, as he promised, to the edge.

She hadn't counted on her deepest, darkest secrets coming to light.

Now that they had, she realized she'd been completely unprepared for any of it. How could she have known that her heart would race like it was right now? She'd definitely had no idea her brain would feel as if it had been scrambled. She had not suspected that she could feel this sense of overwhelming arousal or that her Dom's voice—Trace's voice—would be something she would cling to. And she hadn't realized she'd turn to him for comfort, even as he was the one who caused her the pain.

He sat on the edge of the mattress, tested its firmness, then said, "Count each spank. Aloud."

She nodded, since her vocal chords no longer wanted to work.

"Oh, and Aimee?"

Since he was sitting and she was standing, they were eye to eye. His gaze was all-seeing. "Yes?" she whispered.

"You may not come."

She almost laughed. "You're forbidding me from orgasming from a *spanking?* You are kidding me, right?"

He grinned, and for a moment, she almost forgot to be

nervous. "If you orgasm, we'll have to start the spanking over."

No chance.

He exerted a small amount of force on her wrist, enough to let her know they were done talking.

She moved in closer, glad that he kept hold of her. If he'd lessened the pressure, she would have made a mad dash out of there… Well, after she found her clothes.

Blood was pounding in her ears. If he said anything, she didn't hear it.

He tipped her over his lap. She noticed how powerful his thighs were, how unyielding the strength of his muscles was beneath her belly. She was terribly aware of how much smaller she was than him. Of his strength and power. Of his masculinity.

She realized in only seconds that there was nothing for her to grip.

"Spread your legs," he reminded her.

She did, knowing how exposed she was. He could see everything, touch every part of her. She was upside down, across his lap, helpless.

A tendril of panic crawled through her, and the word *krypton* pinged around in her mind. Krypton, krypton, krypton. If her brain could have completed a circuit and gotten the word from her subconscious and out of her mouth, she might have used it.

As it was, in this position, even gravity worked against her, and her hair fell forward, framing her face, a few strands getting in her eyes.

"You okay?"

She thought she nodded, but he prompted, "Aimee? I need you to answer me."

Was she okay? She was terrified. Excited. Anxious. "Okay,"

she whispered. "I'm okay."

He rubbed her rear, and she liked the feel of his skin on hers. When he dipped a couple of fingers between her legs, she was stunned to feel moisture there.

"Nice," he said.

She forgot to be self-conscious. She just wanted him, wanted to be satisfied. He'd already given her a couple of orgasms today, and now she was craving another. If he'd just touch her *there...*

"Now point your feet inward."

That would expose her even more.

She fought against her natural inclination to refuse, to protect herself as much as possible.

"Point your feet inward," he repeated quietly, patiently. "Good girl," he said when she complied.

She hadn't been completely aware of following his order, but there was something hypnotic about him that compelled her response.

Before she was fully prepared, the first spank landed hard on her buttocks. Good God, *it hurt.* She started to squirm. Some people actually liked this? Were they out of their minds? And she was supposed to get sixteen of these?

But he was there, soothing the hurt with his palm.

"Count," he reminded her.

"One," she whispered. Then, a second spank landed. "Damn!"

"Damn is not a number," he said, and she was sure she heard amusement in his voice, which meant at least one of them was enjoying this torture.

"Two," she said. She wiggled. He placed a hand on the small of her back, effectively imprisoning her. He was so much bigger, so much stronger than her. She was aware of her vulnerability.

He spanked her again.

"Three!"

He rubbed over the sore spots, and she was surprised to find herself relaxing. It shouldn't be possible.

"Good. Relax into it."

"Relax into it?"

"If you fight it, your muscles will be tense. And you'll enjoy it less."

"Enjoy it. Right." Since she was still imprisoned, hanging upside down, she couldn't draw a full breath, and her words sounded muffled.

"I hope you do," he said. "I want you to."

He stroked between her legs, unerringly finding her clit. She moaned and shifted, trying to encourage him to put more pressure there.

"Naughty girl," he said.

He took away his hand, and she whimpered in protest.

He placed the fourth spank at that tender spot on her right side, on her thigh, right below her buttock.

She gasped but somehow managed the word "four."

He delivered the next one to her left thigh.

"Five." She whimpered. Tears swam in her eyes. The punishment wasn't even halfway over, and the four hardest ones were still to come. She wasn't sure she could do this. In fact, she was sure she couldn't.

"You're fighting," he told her, rubbing the tender areas. "Breathe into it." He slid a hand between her legs again.

No way could this be arousing her.

"You look so beautiful," he told her. "You were made to be across my lap with your cute ass begging for my punishment."

His words did something to her, just like what happened when she read. She had never had a man's words so turn her on before. But the appreciative tone in his voice almost made it all worthwhile.

He spanked her three times in quick succession. The pain was so fast, so stinging, she couldn't even count.

"Six, seven, and eight," he said.

Somehow, though, the pain receded quickly, leaving her warm. The overhead fan turned slowly, cooling the droplets of sweat that dotted her back.

Silently he masturbated her. She was wetter than she ever remembered being. Her hips began to jerk, from the combination of his touch and the heat in her buttocks and thighs. Her toes dug into the floor as she struggled for control.

"I wish you could see what you look like," he said. "How perfect. How desirable. Feel how hard my cock is from looking at your red ass."

"Trace!" Despite his earlier warning, the beginnings of an orgasm began to unfold. It didn't matter how much she told herself it was impossible: it was real. "Stop," she begged. "Please. Spank me. Spank me!"

"You'd rather I spank you than stroke your swollen clit?"

"Yes!" The word was somewhere between a demand and a plea.

He drew some of her moisture over the nub. His finger slipped effortlessly, and she was going to go out of her mind.

"You would prefer I didn't do this?"

Her body became rigid as she forced away thoughts of her impending orgasm. Silently she started through the elements of the periodic table again. *Actinium. Aluminum. Americium. Antimony. Argon...*

But it wasn't working.

The man was diabolical. Diabolical and good. He knew exactly what he was doing, just how to touch her to make her shatter. He could keep her on the edge as long as he wanted. But just as frightening, maybe more frightening, she knew he could force her past it at any moment.

Arsenic.

Now there was a good one.

Arsenic, arsenic, *arsenic.*

"Please…" She realized absently that the only word she wasn't thinking of was *krypton.*

"You're not going to come, are you?"

He slid a finger into her vagina, and she bucked against him.

She was no longer certain what she was begging for. For him to keep it up until she climaxed, or for him to stop so she wouldn't earn a second punishment.

"Tell me what you want."

"Spank…spank me!"

He did, finishing up the last four.

"Twelve," she said, barely able to breathe.

"How many more?"

"Twenty-five percent," she said, anything to distract herself. He still had one hand pressed against the small of her back. The other, he rested across the fleshiest part of her butt cheeks. Even though he wasn't touching her intimately, her pussy was throbbing. She was still moist.

"The last four are for what?"

"For trying to get out of my punishment." There was a change inside her. She felt more compliant, softer. She took a shallow breath. At the beginning, she didn't think she could survive the first six. Now she was mentally ready for the last four.

She tried to remember everything he told her. *Breathe. Relax. Don't fight it.* She focused on the last one and braced herself with her fingertips and toes. She spread her legs again, without being told.

"Could you be any more perfect?" he asked.

Patiently she waited, even though she wanted it to be over.

He spanked her right cheek so hard, her breath whooshed out of her lungs. She had no time to recover before he added another to her left cheek.

The third, a scorcher, landed between them.

Even without him touching her between the legs, she was damp. The idea of him looking at her, seeing her so exposed, made her want his touch in ways she'd never craved a man before. Not just any man, she realized, lying there, gently shifting. She wanted him. She wanted Trace, inside her, dominating her, seeing things about her that even she didn't recognize.

"One more," he said.

She closed her eyes, opened her legs wider, shamelessly.

He spanked her there, on her exposed vulva.

She screamed, her body going rigid as the pain ripped at her.

Instantly she was in his arms, but instead of holding her as she expected, he laid her on the edge of the bed. He knelt on the floor and placed her legs over his shoulders.

No.

He wouldn't.

She couldn't let him.

She'd never… "Trace…"

With his strong hands, ones that had just relentlessly punished her, delivering unimaginable pain, he kept her thighs spread wide apart. He kissed her tortured pussy, then licked her with long strokes of his tongue.

She tried to escape, but she was helpless.

He took away the pain and simultaneously made it worse. "I—"

"Come for me," he said. He entered her with two fingers, stretching her, seeking and finding her G-spot.

An orgasm, all the more intense from the physical assault on her private parts and mental assault on her thought process, swamped her.

She was dragged under, gasping and panting.

And when she recovered, he was there. He was lying next to her, trying to tame her messy hair. She blinked, unsure what to think, how to feel.

"How was your first spanking?"

It wasn't just the spanking, though; it was her first submissive experience, and it was the first time a guy had ever gone down on her. Any of the three would have been enough, but to combine them into a single encounter altered her.

She sought the right words to let him know what she was feeling. She couldn't find anything. It was difficult to believe she'd won a spelling bee in elementary school, when right now she wasn't sure she could spell her own name, her first one, not her surname. She settled for "unimaginable."

"Ready for your run?"

"Run?"

"Like outside, one foot in front of the other."

She turned to face him. "Are you serious?"

"Wouldn't want to get in the way of your schedule." He left the bed, and she wasn't sure she liked it.

He bent to take off his boots, and he tossed them in the general direction of her closet. The action made it clear he wouldn't be spending the night on her sleeper couch.

Then he unbuckled his belt, pulled it free of its loops, and dropped it on her dresser.

She lifted her head off the pillow. "You are serious." She dropped her head back down again.

Insatiably curious, she propped her elbows behind her and watched him unfasten the snap on his jeans and lower the zipper.

Oh. God. Oh God. Oh. God.

Commando.

And his cock was enormous. The color was beautiful, darker at the bottom of the shaft, a bit lighter near the head. His cock was hard, and it pointed straight at her. Her mouth dried.

She wanted him like she'd never wanted anyone before.

Chapter Four

"Uh, looks as if you need something more urgently than you need a run," Aimee said.

He did. He needed her desperately. He didn't remember the last time his cock had been so hard for so long. Since she'd stood in her living room, hands on hips, trying to stare him down with the ferociousness of her scientific personality, he'd been done for.

Trace Romero adored women, all women. Tall. Short. Slender. Voluptuous. Dark-haired, blonde. Most particularly, he had a thing for strong, independent women. When they surrendered, there was nothing headier.

But he knew a couple of things about a woman's first exposure to submission—and Aimee's needs specifically—and he tried to put being a good Dom higher on the priority list than his own needs. She needed to think about the experience, process it, maybe talk about it. He was determined to give her what she needed before he satisfied himself deep inside her body.

She licked her lower lip as she looked at him. Well, not him but his dick.

Sometimes it took all his discipline not to put the incessant demands of his body first. There was nothing he wanted more at this moment than to be buried to the hilt inside her pussy. He'd move, and his balls would slap against her. The knowledge that she was still sore from his spanking would just make it better for both of them.

Before he could give in, he unzipped his duffel and pulled out a pair of shorts. On second thought, he reached for a pair of briefs buried at the bottom of the canvas bag.

He bent and grabbed her thong and shorts from where they'd been discarded on the floor, and he tossed them at her. "Get dressed."

"I can't move."

He adjusted himself inside the restrictive briefs. "Maybe another spanking will convince you?"

"You wouldn't!

"Try me."

Clutching her clothes against her chest, she scrambled into a sitting position. "Anyone tell you you're diabolical?"

"The list is long and distinguished. Need help?"

"No," she snapped.

He put on his socks and stuffed his feet into his shoes. He already had them tied when she pulled on her thong.

"Bend over."

"Uh…"

"Bend over. I want to see how red your ass is."

She did.

He questioned his sanity, not for the first time. Her skin was still pink, with one tiny welt. He couldn't resist kissing it. He squeezed her butt cheeks, then pulled her back against his cock. *It wouldn't take much to push aside that scrap of fabric…*

"Yes," she whispered. "I want you, Trace. Take me. Please?"

She couldn't possibly want hard, raunchy sex as much as he did. And it would be so easy. He'd just need to push that tiny scrap of fabric out of the way and penetrate her while she was still bent over. She'd be wet for him; he knew it. He could smell her arousal. It ignited his male instincts, his baser urges. He'd slide in with a single dominant thrust and... Gritting his teeth, he asked, "Eight-minute miles?"

"I want you," she repeated. "I want you to hold me."

He heard a trace of vulnerability in her voice that nearly undid him. "I will," he promised. "After our run."

"In that case, seven-minute miles," she said. "As a warm-up."

"You are tough."

She swayed from side to side. A lesser man would have been done for. He grabbed her around the hips, holding her steady. "Get dressed." He swatted the upper part of her right thigh.

Disobeying him, she stayed in place.

He forced himself to move away. Christ. He needed to be made of steel to resist the temptation of the very desirable scientist. He tucked his gun in place, trying to ignore her.

She took a long time getting dressed, grabbing a fresh sports bra from her bottom drawer and strapping her slick little heart-rate monitor in place, and he was sure she was stalling. He met her gaze in the mirror that hung over her dresser. That tiny line between her brows was back. She was confused. Maybe feeling rejected. It took her several minutes, and she bent rather than crouched to tie her shoes. Finally she snagged a new hair tie and put her ponytail back in place.

"Ready?"

"I think I'll stretch first."

And she did, with her back to him, so that her ass was presented beautifully. If he'd been instructing her, he couldn't have given her more precise directions on how to make herself look beautiful, or turn him on.

She spread her legs even farther apart, and then she turned her torso slightly, dropping her head down so it rested on her right knee. She wrapped her hands around her ankle.

Helpless, a red-blooded male programmed to think of sex every eight seconds or more, he appreciated the long length of her muscles. He couldn't focus past his own vivid images, that of having her tied up with silk restraints, keeping her spread wide for him as he took her from behind. Blood surged in his cock. Had he been particularly bad in a past life? There had to be a reason he was standing here, being tortured.

She might have thought he had the upper hand as Dom, but the reality was, he was putty in her hands. He wanted to please her, wanted to give her experiences she'd never forget. He was absurdly delighted to provide her introduction to submission.

He ignored the flash of irritation that told him he wanted to be her first, last, and only. Life didn't work that way. You had interactions with people, and reality took you in different directions. She had her work, liked her insulated, scientific life. He lived for new adventures, blowing stuff up, covertly entering places where even the military wouldn't venture. The divorce rate among his friends made the national average look optimistic. His own track record wasn't much better. He'd had subs, but even women accustomed to pleasing their men and waiting patiently couldn't tolerate his lifestyle for long.

Still, the sight of her ass did unholy things to his libido.

Distraction being the better part of valor, he went into the living room. There was only so much a man could take.

He heard her in the bedroom; then she was obviously in her office, judging by the tapping sound he heard. He assumed it was her computer keyboard. He admired that she was a bit like him. Even though she was physically and mentally aroused, there was still time for work.

A few minutes later, she joined him. She pulled the cover

off the blasted loro's cage, and the bird blinked sleepily. Did they actually sleep during the day? "Good morning, Aimee," the parrot said.

"You can't keep it covered and quiet all the time?" He'd never been around anything except cats. That this thing seemed to have intelligence was a bit unnerving. "Does he need coffee now? Maybe the newspaper? Maybe a fried egg?"

Eureka lifted a leg and looked at him.

"Feeling's mutual," he told the fluffed-up feather ball.

"They can be very territorial, aggressive, ah, hormonal, for lack of a better word, at certain times of the year."

"And I suppose this is his time of year?"

"Be nice," she told him.

He wanted to point out that the bird started it.

"Going for a run," she told Eureka, offering him a piece of fruit from a bowl near his cage.

"Run! Run! Run!"

"Does he give you a curfew?"

"Seven-minute miles," she said with an evil smile. "And a lot of them."

He hated to run. He'd never admit that to her, but when he got cardio, he liked to be killing a ball. He didn't care what kind of ball—handball, racquetball, soccer, football—but he liked exercise with a purpose, particularly if contact was involved. *Especially* if contact was involved.

The sun was vanishing behind the Front Range, taking the day's heat with it. No matter where he traveled in the world, he liked to come home to the Rockies. They were tall, rugged, and badly behaved, much like him. Aimee locked the front door and tucked the key into a small pocket in her shorts. They started out, and he waved to the Hawkeye team in the sports utility vehicle. At the end of the street, he acknowledged a second team. He was aware of Team One getting out of the car. One of the agents would head toward her home, check the perimeter. The other would tail them.

"How many people have been assigned to watch my house?"

"Assigned to watch you," he corrected. "Four teams. Two teams, assigned to twelve-hour shifts."

"Plus you."

"Turns out I have a personal interest in keeping you safe."

She'd strapped on a heart-rate monitor. She checked it from time to time, and damn if she wasn't setting better than a seven-minute-mile pace. If he told her it was pushing his max, he suspected he'd never live it down.

She headed for the local high school's track.

He was supposed to keep up this pace, be aware of danger, and have a discussion about BDSM? Right now he'd rather have a cold beer. "No ill effects?"

"None at all." She had the nerve to smile at him. "But since you brought it up, why didn't you fuck me when you had the chance?"

He blinked at her words. He'd heard the F-bomb before, but not from erudite, scientific Aimee Inamorata. "Not because I didn't want to."

More quietly, she said, "I asked you to take me. You refused. What do you want me to think?" Without waiting for his response, she checked her monitor and stepped up the pace. "Six-and-a-half-minute miles?"

At that rate, she'd leave him in the dust and lap him in no time. He wasn't sure his ego could take that.

He could run. Or they could talk. He snagged her wrist while he was still physically able to keep up with her. He pulled on her, slowing her down. "I wanted to talk first."

"Talk?" She laughed. "You'd rather talk than have sex? Too much estrogen in your veins, Agent Romero?"

"Look, Aimee. You saw my cock. You know damn well I wanted you. Want you."

She yanked her wrist free from his grip and continued her relentless pace.

Not for the first time with a woman, he wondered how the hell he'd gotten so far off track. He wanted her to feel respected, not used, and all he'd done was piss her off. He could live to be a hundred and five and not handle women any better.

He struggled to keep up with her. "It would have been wrong of me to, in your terms, fuck you, right after a scene. Especially your first scene."

"And better to leave me confused?"

"That's why we're here." Why the fuck couldn't she see that? She had an analytical mind, was more given to science than emotion. So why didn't she get it?

"Now I'm really confused." She turned up the dial on her running.

Christ, and she thought he had no compassion? He'd been away from elevation for several months, but even if he'd never left the Mile High City, she'd still be smoking him.

Part of him—the one ruled by intelligence and the demand to preserve his own life—was tempted to let her pull ahead, work off some of her energy and frustration. She would eventually lap him, and then he could rejoin her. But he could never forget that his real purpose in being here was to protect her delectable body. No matter what intuition said, he couldn't afford to let her get more than a few feet away from him. Of course, the bad guys would have to be in better shape than he was if they intended to catch her.

He kept up for a half mile, then three-quarters of a mile. By the time they'd logged a mile, his shirt was plastered to his back, and he was mopping his brow.

She was barely sweating.

She checked her monitor, never breaking her stride.

He wondered if the agent trailing them was enjoying the sight of him having his clock cleaned by a woman who weighed a hundred pounds less than him and stood barely five feet five.

Enough was enough.

He snagged her wrist, more forcefully this time. He pulled her to a stop. He knew the language she spoke, and if that's what she wanted, that's what she'd get.

He grabbed her shoulders, fingers biting into her soft flesh. "Goddamn it, Aimee, we're going to talk. And if you even attempt an estrogen crack, I'll turn your ass over my knee right here. Want to try me?"

"You're messing with my goal."

"I'll mess with a whole lot more than just that, woman." He yanked her against him. Tugging on her ponytail, he held her prisoner. "We will talk about your experience," he said. "You'll tell me what you liked, what you want more of. You'll tell me what you didn't like. You'll tell me what frightened you and if you were tempted to use your safe word. You'll tell me what you want me to do to you when we get back to your house. And then, Ms. Inamorata, you'll be fucked thoroughly. Any questions?" Before she could do anything except gulp a drink of Denver's oxygen-starved air, he kissed her.

There was nothing sweet or seductive about his kiss. He wanted her to know of his own frustration, wanted her to understand how hot he was for her, how much he'd been holding back. She might not understand it was for her own good, but fucking A, she needed to get that it wasn't easy for him.

She held herself rigid, and her eyes were unblinking.

Goaded, he dragged her onto her tiptoes; then he moved

one hand to the small of her back, pressing her against him.

Aimee Inamorata gave as well as she received. She didn't retreat from his dominance. Instead she leaned into him, kissing him back, meeting his tongue, accepting it.

At her surrender, his kiss changed.

This woman was perfect for him. Strong enough to stand up to him, feminine enough to respond to his demands, strong enough not to be frightened of him, feminine enough to fire all his protective instincts.

She'd be the death of him.

Despite the physical exertion, his cock began to respond.

Slowly he ended the kiss. It was either that or find a secluded place where he could strip her naked and thrust into her, satisfying them both.

Her soft lips were red and swollen. Her cheeks had flushed to a soft apple red. And a few wisps of hair escaped the confines of her ponytail. Even though he was no longer holding her as tightly, she leaned into him of her own volition. "That worked for me," she said breathlessly.

The run might not have exerted her, but his kiss had. His ego took that piece of information and etched it in memory. "In case you were wondering, it worked for me too. You're a perfect sub, Aimee."

She looked up at him. Her eyes, no longer shooting fire at him, darkened the way they had earlier. There was a look about her when she capitulated. He wanted to keep her close, protected.

"If I promise to talk, can we run?" she asked.

"Eight-minute miles," he countered.

"Do you always have to have your way?"

"Pretty well," he said.

"Is that a male thing or a Dom thing?"

"It's the—"

"Natural order of things," she said.

"You're learning. I like a woman who's a quick study."

She rolled her eyes.

He released his grip on her.

She set the pace, and he fell in next to her. Talking wasn't comfortable, but at least it was achievable. "I want to know about your first experience," he said.

"Confusing is a good word."

He waited. After thirty seconds or so, he glanced over at her. That tiny line had appeared between her brows again. Forcing himself to be patient, a trait that had served him well in the military and as a Hawkeye operative, he remained silent. He didn't remember self-discipline ever being quite this difficult before her.

"I liked it, but I didn't think I should like it."

"Go on." He lengthened his stride slightly, matching hers.

"I'll be honest," she said. "Part of me, the strong, independent woman, thinks it's wrong to enjoy giving her pleasure over to a man."

"It's the—"

"If you say 'natural order' one more time, Agent Romero, I'll go for an Olympic speed record."

Her ponytail swished as she looked at him. At this point, if he took her, it'd be over in less than a minute. "I'll behave," he promised.

"It felt as if I was abdicating control."

She was. She had. But that part didn't matter. She was such a natural, he could just take it.

"When you had me over your knee…"

She checked her monitor, and this time he recognized it for

the stall tactic it was.

"I was totally exposed. At first I thought it was obscene. Well, actually, I still think that."

"But?"

"When you held me so tight, and I knew you were watching me, it was… At first it was disconcerting. As if I can't hide and I can't keep secrets from you. And now, with you demanding to know what I was thinking, for me to describe my experience. It's a little unnerving to realize how much you know about me."

"When BDSM is part of a relationship, honesty is even more important."

"The unexpected thing for me was how liberating I found the whole thing."

"Liberating?"

"I was able to give myself over to the experience totally. I let go. I stopped being self-conscious. And since you demand honesty, I'm not sure how I feel knowing that I got off from pain, but there it is."

"Erotic pain," he corrected. "Deliberately inflicted, deliberately placed, deliberately timed. I watched you every step of the way. I saw the way you responded, and I played on that. If something hadn't been working for you, I would have changed it up. I doubt you'd get off from random pain. What we did was very different."

She nodded. "As far as what didn't work for me? Your having clothes on. I want you naked next time."

"Deliberate as well. I wanted your introduction to be all about the act of your submission, not as a prelude to sex."

"You better not be telling me that sex has nothing to do with this."

He laughed. "No chance. I want my cock in your mouth."

She pulled her lower lip between her teeth.

"In your sweet cunt."

She momentarily closed her eyes. He couldn't have described how much he liked having the upper hand again. "And in your tight ass."

"I told you that I've never successfully... I mean..."

"Tell me."

"It was such a disaster. I am not sure I want to try it again."

"But you use the plug you have."

"Every once in a while."

"I'm going to ask you to trust me. It will be uncomfortable at first. But I won't hurt you. I'll start with a finger, then two, prepare you."

"I have to imagine having you doing that will feel differently than a plug."

He loved pushing her boundaries. "Having me do what?" He wanted to hear her say it. "No secrets between us, Aimee."

"I'm sure you fucking my ass will feel different than having a plug or a finger up there."

From spitfire to submissive in five seconds. Man, he wanted this woman.

"Yeah," he said. "It will. Especially since I'll have a finger on your clit, and you'll be fighting an orgasm all the way."

"Like I said. Different." Her words were brave, but her eyes were slightly shuttered.

"Were you tempted to use your safe word?"

"I was, the very first moment I was over your lap. For a few seconds, I thought I might be panicking when I realized how vulnerable I was. If my mouth would have worked—well, for anything other than gasping—I might have used it. But then you kept talking to me."

"I've never seen anything quite as spectacular as the sight of you across my lap. When you turned your toes inward, spreading your cheeks, parting your labia to expose all of your pussy, believe me, spanking you was about the last thing on my mind. I've never been with anyone like you, Aimee, and I want you to know that."

"Yeah yeah yeah." This time she stopped, dropping her hands to her knees.

When he stopped next to her, she looked up. Keeping himself from devouring her the way he wanted was one of the more difficult things he'd ever done.

"Now that we've got all that out of the way, now that you've opened up my brain and had a look inside and spanked my butt raw, *now* will you fucking fuck me?"

Through the years, Aimee had had a lot of guys try to get in her pants, especially when a party and alcohol were involved. But she'd never, ever asked a man to take her.

She'd literally begged Trace to have sex with her, several times, and he still refused. Agent Romero was annoying as hell, as frustrating as a failed hypothesis, and all the more sexy for keeping himself aloof. Wasn't that supposed to be a female trick? But here she was, wet, horny, and frustrated.

Now, back at home, he still hadn't taken her to bed. Instead he said they needed to eat. Food was the last thing on her mind.

Totally at home in her house, he'd gone outside to light the grill before coming back in to snag a few vegetables from the refrigerator to make a *pico de gallo* to go with a bag of corn chips he found in a cupboard. "Cilantro?" he asked.

"Men don't know what cilantro is," she said, opening a crisper drawer.

"Some men," he corrected. "As well as some women."

Even though she'd rather be in her bedroom with him, she didn't mind abdicating control of her kitchen. In fact, she didn't mind abdicating control of other things to him either. She tried not to think too much about the implication of that realization. She was strong and independent, resourceful and self-reliant. She told herself the situation with Trace was temporary, but she ignored the pit in her stomach that the thought caused.

He chopped and diced, then tasted and folded his arms across his chest.

"Something wrong?"

He scowled, then took another scoopful of the pico de gallo. "More salt."

He gave the salt mill a couple of more twists, then stirred it in.

She could get used to this, sitting back and watching while someone made food for her. "Better?"

"Nah. It's not just better, it's perfect."

"Humility is your middle name?"

"Honesty is my middle name. When I know it's good, why should I pretend otherwise?"

She rolled her eyes but dipped in a chip of her own. She took a bite, then closed her eyes as the flavors exploded.

"Well?"

"Okay, okay. So when you're right, you're right."

He grinned. He grabbed the barbecue tools from a drawer, kissed her quickly on the forehead, something she could really get used to, then headed outside. "My talents are needed."

She shook her head.

He tended to the steaks while she made a salad and uncorked a bottle of merlot, allowing it to breathe.

She had no interest in food, but he definitely did. As she was rapidly learning, what Trace wanted, Trace got.

She peeled a couple of mandarin oranges, and Eureka walked across the floor with his adorable waddle to collect his share of their dinner. "Hungry," he said. "Eat, eat, eat."

When Trace returned to the kitchen, the bird didn't get out of his way. Trace was forced to stay on the far side or the room, and she didn't even try to hide her smirk.

"Tell me why you think your house was broken into." He folded his arms across his chest and leaned against the counter closest to the door. He'd changed from his drenched shirt into another T-shirt, this time black. The top button of his fly was open, and he hadn't bothered with shoes or socks. The intimacy of the scene struck her. He was comfortable here; she was comfortable having him here. And in her contradictory mind, that very comfort made her uncomfortable.

"I've got your sister's ideas," he said. "I want to hear yours."

She didn't need a reminder as to why he was really here or that he'd soon be gone. Now that she'd had a taste of him, of BDSM, she wanted more. For crying out loud, she wanted sex. Sex, sex, sex, sex, sex. But she knew from experience that he wouldn't be dissuaded. When he wanted an answer, he got it. "How much do you know about what I'm working on?"

"It involves communications. Other than that, not much."

"We're working on a microchip that's so small, it can hardly be detected. Essentially, I'm working on a new application. We attach the chip to a bug, literally something that resembles a mosquito. The mosquito is controlled remotely."

"Like the drones being used by the military?"

"Precisely. In this case, though, the mosquito can inject a chip into a person, or an animal for that matter. For example, take me. I'm a bit reluctant to be a client of Hawkeye. Many Hawkeye clients are like me, at least according to my sister. Most people don't want to have a protection detail, because it reminds them they're in an unsafe situation. Some will even try to shed their detail. But say that person has a pet."

He glanced at the bird.

"We could, hypothetically, send a mosquito into a room and insert a chip into the pet."

"That'd maybe make Eureka good for something other than roasting."

The bird flicked a piece of mandarin orange in Trace's direction.

"Knock it off," she said.

"Me or the bird?"

"You. There's nothing wrong with Eureka's behavior."

"I was just pointing out that pets should be good for something. Take your neighbor's dog for example. It barks to warn you of impending danger. A good dog earns his food and an occasional chew toy."

She rolled her eyes. "Do you want to hear about the project, or would you rather point out Eureka's failings?"

"We don't have that much time."

He grinned, and she was like a giddy schoolgirl with a first crush. In fact, when Billy Johnson offered to carry her books in the fifth grade, she hadn't been this smitten.

"Really. I do want to know. This is a huge deal, and I'm curious."

"So once we've inserted the chip, either into a pet or a person, we could listen in to conversations. We could track a person's actions." She dumped the washed spinach from the colander into a bowl. "Obviously there are a lot of concerns about the chip and its technology."

"Privacy."

She nodded, glad to have the opportunity to really talk about this. She loved her work, but she rarely had the chance talk to someone who could be trusted. Her social circle was somewhat limited, and she spent most of her time communicating through e-mail or on chat with other teammates. If she didn't go out for her daily latte, her voice would probably dry up from disuse. "Let's say we're hired to protect the daughter of a company president, but she doesn't want a detail. Should we be allowed to chip her without her knowledge? Or her pet, or what about her pillow? And if we're trying to infiltrate an organization, say we're trying to rescue a kidnapped businessman in Colombia, we need intel, and this is a way to get it. Most people would say that's a good use of the technology."

"Agreed."

"But what if a man suspects his wife is cheating on him? Should it be okay for him to chip her, or the Chihuahua she puts in her purse before she goes out? Do the ends justify the means? And worse, what if it gets into the wrong hands? I'm working on the programming, but even I'm not sure how I feel about it."

"When you work on something with the potential for good and evil in the same package, it has to keep you awake at night."

"I think that's mainly why I run. To try and sort it out. If something I work on saves a life, especially that of a child, isn't that worth it?" Just as easily, someone else could end up dead. Both results could potentially be a result of her code.

Aimee wasn't a black-and-white person. She saw shades of gray. She liked to think it made her a better scientist; the truth was, it probably got in her way more than anything.

"You have the chip here?"

She shook her head. "I'm not a hardware person. So there's nothing here that anyone would be interested in. Well, except my computer. I am working with several others across the world on the programming code to operate the bugs and get the chip injected. But how could anyone have found out about the project, and if they did, what would have led them to me? That's the only thing puzzling me. All my neighbors, almost everyone I know, thinks I'm working on a new book about ethical implications of technology. People who know me either think I'm a writer or they know me to be an adjunct professor for the University of Colorado. That's why I think it's potentially a random break-in. I'm not as convinced that it's related to the project as..." She trailed off. "That's why I'm not as concerned as my sister seems to be," she said instead.

"You almost said her name."

"Did not." Not under penalty of death.

"Donna?"

She shook her head.

"Ruth?"

She laughed.

"Julie?"

Her sister's first and middle names were top secret at Hawkeye. Aimee had been sworn to secrecy, and it generally wasn't difficult to avoid mentioning them since she worked remotely and few people knew they were related. "You should check on the steaks."

"Do you know how much money is in the office pool?"

"Last I heard, there was a comma in it."

"Now there are two figures before the comma. I could take a trip to the Bahamas if I found out your sister's name." He leaned toward her. "And I could take you with me."

Eureka squawked in protest.

"Steaks," she reminded him.

"You're a cruel woman, Professor."

"Smart," she countered.

He went outside, and she added the tiny orange segments

to the salad, then liberally sprinkled some pine nuts on top. She used tongs to move a small portion into a bowl for Eureka before tossing in feta cheese and drowning the salad with homemade dressing.

"How far along is the project?" he asked, putting the platter of sizzling steaks on the dining-room table. "Wineglasses?"

"In the cupboard above Eureka's cage."

He looked at the bird. Eureka glared back.

"Water's good," Trace said. "We can skip the wine. Really."

She laughed. "Get the wineglasses, you big chicken. He's just a bird. You outweigh him by about two hundred or more pounds."

He moved, and Eureka hopped up on top of the microwave. He walked across it so that he was only inches from Trace.

Her parrot had never behaved so badly before. It had to be the hormonal thing, didn't it? She'd had male guests before, and she occasionally had parties. He was usually entertaining and charming, amusing people with his tricks. He seemed to be antagonizing Trace on purpose.

"Does he bite?"

"Not often."

"That beak looks wicked."

"Bill. Birds have bills, not beaks. And it can be. Wicked, that is. He could take a chunk out of your earlobe. Not that he will."

He reached over the parrot, and Eureka started coughing, or rather, playacting a cough. "Return to base," she told him.

If birds could scowl, he scowled at her.

She stood there resolutely. "Return to base," she said again, more sternly.

"Return to base," he finally mimicked, but he still didn't

look happy about it as he resumed his perch.

It wasn't bad enough that she'd had a break-in or that Trace Romero was taking up her life, but it was all compounded by the hostilities between her protector and her feathered friend.

Trace got out the wineglasses, all the while keeping a close watch on the bird. She might have laughed, if she were certain Eureka would actually listen to her, but since Trace's arrival in her life, she hadn't been sure of much.

He poured the wine, giving her more than she would normally have while working. If she finished the glass, she'd have no resistance at all toward him, not that she seemed to have any to begin with, and heaven knew what she'd tell him about her and what she hoped he'd do to her. Wine tended to loosen her mouth more than any other drink.

Feeling bad for the bird, she added a couple of more nuts to his salad before putting the dish in his cage.

"He gets to have part of our dinner?"

"He doesn't eat much."

"We could still roast him."

The bird squawked as if he understood Trace perfectly.

"He was kidding," she said.

"Not really. He probably tastes like chicken," Trace said under his breath. Before she could scold him, he repeated his earlier question. "How much longer will you be working on the project?"

"Hard to say. We have so many people working on it, in so many countries, that we're making advances twenty-four hours a day. We have occasional conference calls, sometimes via video."

"You can be naked on your next chat."

She blinked.

"At least from the waist down."

He offered her the glass. Without a thanks, she took it.

"Maybe with a plug in your ass," he added.

She took a drink, not surprised when the rich red liquid nearly sloshed over the edge.

"How would you like me to fuck you?" he asked, pulling out a chair for her.

Her mind swam, again, at his contradictions. He was asking outrageous questions, while at the same time exhibiting old-world manners.

She put down her glass while he slid her chair in.

"I could have you up against a wall," he said against her ear. "With your arms over your head, keeping you helpless."

Aimee was coming unraveled from the inside out. His breath was warm on her ear, and she smelled the wine he had sipped, soft spice layered beneath a bite of tannin, and him, all male and musk after their run.

"Or bent over, with you grabbing your ankles so that I can admire your cunt while I put a finger in your ass."

Had she known what she was asking for, demanding, when she kept asking him to fuck her?

"Maybe on your back, spread-eagle, tied to the bed while I flog your pussy until your clit is swollen?" With reserved restraint, he sank his teeth into that tender spot where her neck and shoulder merged.

If she hadn't been sitting, her knees would have buckled and her legs would have never supported her.

"Maybe on your stomach, spread-eagle, with a pillow underneath you, so your ass is begging for the spanking I'll give it?"

Were they really discussing her project only five minutes ago?

"Are your nipples hard?"

Her entire body was on fire.

He bit her again, then laved away the hurt with his tongue. "Are they, Aimee?"

"Yes," she whispered.

"And your pussy. Is it wet?"

"Very."

He took a seat across from her, then offered his glass in a toast. She clinked her glass against his, then took a big drink, meeting his gaze above the rim of the crystal. They made it all the way through dinner, albeit with her having too much wine and not enough food, before he made her stomach take a dive.

"Did you decide?"

"Decide?"

"Which is it going to be? Tied to the bed? Up against a wall? Or bent over? And if the decision is being tied to the bed, face up or facedown?"

Chapter Five

He watched the play of emotion across her face. A frown, that sexy scowl, the parted lips, as she thought through the implications. She would have liked all his choices, he knew, but not necessarily the twist he put on them. He knew what she wanted to say. None of the above. She wanted his cock. She'd made that more than clear. And this time, she could bet her sweet, sweet ass that she'd get it. But it would be on his terms, always on his terms.

"I need a shower first," she said.

"I'll clear the dinner dishes," he told her. "You go get in the shower. But cover up that damn bird first."

"His name is Eureka."

Flying fucktard was more like it.

She petted the bird before putting him in his cage.

"Night, night," he said.

Was it possible for birds to be psychotic, split personalities, maybe? The bird opened his beak—bill—and looked at Trace, then cocked his head to the side for her to stroke his back. The bird was enraptured by her. Well, at least that was one thing they had in common.

"I'll hurry," she said after covering the bird's cage.

"Take your time. I plan to wash your back." Trace topped off her wineglass. He liked this somewhat mellow side to her. She definitely wasn't tipsy, but there was something less self-conscious about her motions, more feminine, less reserved. "Oh, and Aimee…"

She stopped at the entryway and turned back to face him.

"You didn't answer my question. And I'm not letting you off the hook."

Her hand trembled, just slightly, and he grinned.

Five minutes later, he shut the dishwasher, refilled his own glass before corking the meager contents left in the bottle, then turned off the overhead light. A growling sound came from the direction of the birdcage. "You'll taste like chicken," Trace said aloud as he passed the cage.

After putting his wineglass on the nightstand near hers, he put his gun in the drawer and then joined her in the bathroom. The room was steamy and smelled of lavender, or what he thought might be lavender. Could have been any flower, he supposed, even rose or lilac. Regardless, it smelled fresh, feminine, and appealing, just the way a sub of his should smell.

His cock was hard, and he hadn't even looked at her yet. He stripped and dropped his clothes in the hamper with hers. He didn't think too long or too hard about what that meant; it just seemed more respectful than dumping them on the floor. Or that's what he told himself.

He slid back the shower door, and she looked up at him. Water dripped from her hair, and several drops clung to her long eyelashes. She held on to a round nylon-looking thing that was oozing lather.

"I can't say that a man has ever been in the shower with me before."

"I like being your first." He entered the shower and then reached to cup her breasts. He loved the dark, dusky pink of her small nipples and how quickly they hardened when he gently pinched them. She moaned, her knees going forward a bit. "Tell me how much pressure you like. How much feels like too much? How much pushes you past that point and makes your pussy throb?"

"Even your words do that to me," she admitted.

He tightened his grip a little.

Her mouth opened.

"You like that?"

"Oh. Yes. Yes."

He applied a bit more pressure, and her eyes closed. Even more and she gasped, panting. "That?"

"Hurts," she whispered.

"And this?"

She cried out.

"You didn't just come, did you?"

She blinked. Then she laughed nervously. "I guess that's the point where my pussy throbs."

"Did you come without permission, *querida*?"

"I guess I need to be punished."

Dios. Save him.

"Will you punish me, Trace?"

This time, she took an assertive role, and he was about done for.

She raised onto her tiptoes, dropped the poufy thing, then wrapped her arms around his neck. She leaned into him, pulling his head downward so she could kiss him.

Where he was demanding, she was a bit more tentative, but when he opened his mouth for her, she took a bit more of an aggressive role, finding his tongue, then retreating.

He liked the way she tasted. It was more than just the unique taste of her, more than the lingering sweet tartness of the wine. It was about her willingness to please him, her desire to make him want her in return. He'd kissed women before.

There was either a connection, combustion, or there wasn't. Being a scientist, she probably knew a name for it. All he knew was it worked or it didn't.

His cock throbbed against the softness of her belly.

She pulled away a little, long enough to look him in the eyes, and against his mouth, quietly said, "I love the sight of your cock."

Where the hell was his sweet, innocent submissive?

She folded a soapy hand around his cock and began to stroke him. As hard as he was for her, it would take her less than a dozen strokes to jerk him off. Half a dozen if... "Aimee!" He grabbed her hand.

She increased her pressure and made the strokes faster and shorter. The vixen. He tightened his grip, forcing her to stop.

"Do you like that, Trace? *Master?*"

Dios! How did he go from being in charge to being bewitched? "I didn't give you permission to touch me."

"I didn't ask for it." She bit his lower lip. Hard. "I wanted to touch you. And I want to suck you as well."

Had she used one of her mosquitoes when he was outside, planting something inside him that told her exactly what he wanted and how he wanted it? Something had definitely gotten under his skin. "I made the decision for you," he said.

"Decision?"

"But we'll practice in here first. Face the wall, Aimee." He liked her shower. It was big enough for both of them, with room to maneuver. She'd obviously spared no expense here. The showerhead was oversize, and it was adjustable, heightwise. The interior was tiled, with a built-in bench, something he was certain they would take advantage of when he got around to letting her suck him, something that, if he thought about it too long, would make him come at the first skin-to-skin contact.

She turned while he picked up the bottle of body soap from a shelf. "Hands on the wall," he instructed. "Above your head." Her sweetheart of an ass was temptation manifested. If he weren't careful, he'd forget he was supposed to be the Dom here.

He squirted some of the soap into his palm as he looked at the bottle. Lilac, not lavender. He'd been close. At least they were both purple flowers. He lathered both hands and smoothed them over her shoulders, then down her back. She gave a small moan that made his cock stretch and strain even harder.

Then he bent behind her. "Feet at shoulder width, Aimee."

She slowly moved into position.

Water ran over both of them, and this close to her, he inhaled the smell of her. It was all he could do not to bury himself there, all he could do not to lick her until she came all over his mouth.

He soaped her legs one at a time and adjusted the showerhead to rinse her completely. He cleaned the soap from his hands before stroking between her legs. Her pussy was slick from her own juices, and she needed no lubrication.

He moved his forefinger back and forth across her clit; then he brought in his other hand to spread her labia and pull back the hood of her clit. It amazed him how much he liked to touch her. The sound of her pleasure spiked his own. He wasn't generally into self-denial, but this woman made him want her pleasure more than he wanted his own.

She jerked and gave that tiny moan that he recognized as a precursor to her orgasm. She was so responsive, so easy to please. He gave her clit a tiny pinch. She gasped, her forehead falling forward to hit the tile.

The tiny pinch had interrupted her orgasm, and he easily slid a finger inside her.

Her breaths were shortened, little bursts of air, and he slipped in a second finger beside the first. "More?" he asked.

He saw her fingers splay above her head. "Yes," she whispered.

"Tell me."

"I want another finger inside me."

He finger fucked her until she rocked back and forth. It was hard not to get caught up in her reactions. In his less experienced years, he would have taken her while she was in a heated frenzy. But he wanted her over and over again, wanted her satisfaction, wanted her to enjoy all the experiences he could give her. More than ever, this was about her, testing her limits, taking her places she hadn't known existed. That he got to go there with her was just pleasure on top of pleasure.

"Trace," she whispered. "Trace. I want... I'm going to come."

He had guessed that a fraction of a second before she said anything. He stopped his motions, gently pulling out of her. She gave a halfhearted cry of protest but didn't say anything else. Trace adjusted the water, making sure it fell warmly on her body. He waited until her body quit shaking from the second denied orgasm. "I'm proud of you," he said.

"I didn't want you to stop."

"Yeah. I gathered that."

"You really are a sadist."

"A happy one, since I found an avowed masochist to play with."

"Beast," she said, stamping her right foot.

"Just think how spectacular your first anal orgasm will be."

She froze.

"Relax." He drew some of the moisture from her pussy back toward her anal whorl.

"Nervous," she said with a little laugh.

"I want you to trust me. I won't do anything you're uncomfortable with. We'll start with one finger, like we just did. And only when you're ready for a second will I attempt it."

"No sex?"

"Not until you're ready." He leaned in very close as he touched a finger to her most private area.

She nodded.

"When I push in, bear down, push your anal muscles back against me."

"You're serious?"

He took her earlobe in his mouth and gently bit. Then he trailed kisses down the column of her throat to distract her.

He felt her relax slightly, and he stroked her pussy with featherlight motions even as he put a small amount of pressure on her anus. "You're doing great," he said.

"You haven't done anything yet."

He brought his left hand up to cup her breast, and then he pinched a nipple. She yelped and arched her back as she tried to evade him. He took the opportunity to effortlessly enter her rear.

"Damn!"

He kissed the top of her head. "You're there," he told her.

"I've been making all that fuss about *that?*"

"'Fraid so."

She sighed exaggeratedly. "Much ado about nothing."

He moved his finger, stretching her slightly.

"I... Er..." She wiggled her hips experimentally. "I think I like that."

He couldn't wait to take her this way, filling her ass with his cock, driving it home, making her scream as she came. "I figured any woman who liked a butt plug really wouldn't object."

"Can you…? Will you try a second?"

"I'd prefer to use lube for that."

"There's some in the cabinet under the sink."

"Was that a please?"

"I want a second finger up my ass. Please."

He laughed. Quick study. She exceeded all his hopes, and he had had very high hopes. "Greedy little sub."

"I said please."

He left her for a moment, dripping water all over the tile floor. The lube was conveniently at the front of the extra toiletries and her lotion. He grabbed the bottle, flipping open the lid and squirting a dollop onto his fingertips before he even returned to the shower.

She was in the same position where he'd left her, even with her legs spread, waiting. At this point, she could lead him around by his cock and he'd follow her anywhere.

He backed up a bit instead of starting from where they'd left off. Even without his telling her, she arched her back for him. He wrapped one arm around her.

"Stroke my pussy," she told him.

"Happy to." He did. Simultaneously he pressed a finger against her rear entrance.

She pushed back against him.

"Old pro," he said. He kissed the side of her neck. He couldn't help himself, not because he thought it would please her, but because he wanted to. He wanted her to be his, and he wanted to mark her. He wouldn't actually do it, but damn it, he wanted to.

This surge of possessiveness was odd. In the past, he'd sometimes shared his subs, but the idea of sharing her pissed him off.

He moved his finger in and out; then, when he thought she was ready, he brought a second finger up beside the first and eased both inside her.

She gasped. "That's a little more challenging," she said. "You've got big fingers."

Her breaths were a little close together, as if she might be close to freaking out. He stroked her clit just a little faster.

"That... Yes. Right. There..."

"You like it?"

"Feeling overwhelmed," she admitted. "Feeling... It hurts... But I..." Then she screamed.

Her orgasm surprised him, and if he didn't guess wrong, it surprised her as well. He caught her as she collapsed backward into him.

"Sorry about that," she said.

"That one's a freebie. I think you earned it."

"No punishment?"

He wiped the water from her eyes as she tipped back her head.

"That's fair," she said when he didn't respond. "It was your fault, anyway."

"My fault?"

"Well, if you weren't such a skillful lover, I could have held on longer."

"Do we need to have a discussion about personal responsibility?" he asked teasingly. How long, if ever, since he'd teased a woman?

"I'd rather you finally fuck me."

"Can't you think of anything else?"

"Not really. No."

"I created a monster."

"There you go. A textbook example of personal responsibility. We both recognize it's all your fault."

"Where's your butt plug?" Keeping her supported, he pulled first one, then the other finger from her rear.

She wiggled around until she faced him. She pushed runaway strands of hair back from her face. "It's in the top drawer of my nightstand."

He turned off the faucet and reached for one of the towels she'd thrown over the shower door. After drying her hair and her face and trailing the towel down her neck and across her chest, he said, "Turn around."

Obediently, she did.

He ran the soft material across her shoulders, then down her back, before rubbing the towel across her buttocks. He crouched to dry her legs, before finally moving to her intimate parts. Her labia were swollen and reddened. If he'd ever seen anything more appealing, he didn't remember the sight. "Now the front." His voice was husky. If he didn't get her into the bedroom immediately, he'd take her right here in the shower.

After she was dry, he tossed the damp towel back on top of the door and snagged the other for himself. "Grab your plug."

She went to brush past him but stopped. She reached up and stroked his chin with the back of her hand. "You turn me on."

"Yeah?"

"Just in case you missed it." She squeezed his cock.

He bit out a curse. "Your plug," he told her.

"Aye, aye, sir."

That earned her a swat as she exited the shower stall.

He gave his body a cursory pass with the cotton towel, then grabbed the bottle of lube and followed his delightful sub into the bedroom. She was lying on top of the bed on her side, her head propped on her upturned arm. The stainless steel plug with its blue crystals at the hilt was on top of the dresser. "On your stomach, with a pillow beneath it."

He saw her breath catch and her eyes widen. "You're going to put it in?"

"Another time I'll watch you do it. But yes, I plan to put it in you."

She followed his instructions, her knees digging into the mattress. He put one knee on the mattress, near her, and then he liberally covered the stainless steel with lube. "Keep your legs apart." He placed the narrow, teardrop-shaped tip against her opening. She was lovely in her submission, and the sight of her completely exposed made his cock throb. "This won't hurt a bit."

She laughed, enough to loosen the tension, and he seized the moment. With a swift, sure motion, he sank it all the way in.

She gasped, and her hips jerked, but she settled almost instantly. "It's cold," she said.

"Dios. That looks beautiful. I may just always keep your ass full."

She squirmed.

"And maybe we'll get you a bigger plug, one that stretches you even wider."

She turned her head to look at him. "You're serious?"

"Maybe a glass one."

"You're scaring me," she said. "Again."

Her voice was breathless. He loved that about her. There was a quality to her voice when fear and trepidation melded into trust. It did strange things to him, appealed to his masculinity, made him want to protect her. He smoothed blonde strands of hair back from her face. "Haven't you learned I don't do anything until you beg for it?"

"A glass plug?" she asked skeptically. "I'm going to beg for that?"

"You will," he promised. He wiggled the stainless plug he'd just inserted, tugging on it, then sinking it back in. "Do you like that?"

"I do. A lot. I'm enjoying playing with you that way a lot more than I thought I would."

"I told you the choice was yours," he said. "Up against the wall, bent over, or restrained. But I changed my mind. When I fuck you for the first time, I want to look at you. I want to see your expression. And I won't restrain you because I want your legs around my waist as you draw me in deeper."

"Yes," she said, turning over and tossing aside the pillow. "Fuck me?"

"I thought you'd never ask."

"Rat fink."

He laughed. He left her long enough to grab a condom from his duffel. It seemed to take longer than ever to rip open the packet and roll the latex down the length of his shaft.

"I like to look at your cock," she said.

"I like to have you look at it." He moved between her legs, poised at the entrance to her pussy. "And touch it."

"Do you enjoy this?" She showed him what she meant, closing her hand around him tightly.

"Yeah."

She stroked him, slowly at first, then more vigorously.

His head fell forward. Control threatened to splinter. "I thought you wanted me to fuck you. If you keep that up, I'll tell you right now, lady, it ain't going to happen."

She actually stuck out her lower lip in a pout, but she

didn't stop the back-and-forth motion on him.

Propping his weight on one arm, he curled his other hand around hers, stopping her motions. "I want you to jerk me off," he said. "Later. Now I want to be inside you while your ass is full of that plug."

"Take me."

He needed no second invitation.

She was already wet, and he slid in the first inch effortlessly.

"I can feel the plug," she said. "It…"

"You okay?"

She inhaled sharply. "Yes." Then again, she said, "Yes."

He entered her slowly, feeling the plug himself. She was tight to begin with, and the size of the plug made the fit feel even more snug. He forced himself to grit his teeth and pace his strokes, not giving in to her whimpered urgings or his own body's demands.

He grabbed her wrists and imprisoned them above her head. He loved the way they looked together, his darker skin contrasting with her much lighter tone, his strength complementing her toned, long muscles, his dominance made more complete by her sweet submission.

About to go over the edge way too fast, he withdrew for a moment to pace himself and to drive her mad, just a bit more. He pulled one of her nipples into his mouth, biting it with more pressure than he'd used before.

"Trace! That's…"

"Too much?"

"Fantastic."

He moved to her other nipple, giving it the same intense attention.

Her head thrashed back and forth, and the sight of her

capitulation drove him to the edge. He sank into her, thrusting, riding her hard, wanting her to experience the madness that consumed him.

"I want to come."

"Beg," he told her. "Beg."

She whimpered. "Please? Please, Trace. I can't...I can't take any more."

He felt her body convulse beneath him. "A few more seconds."

"You're making me crazy."

She started to pant.

"Now," he told her, sinking his teeth into her shoulder.

She screamed. Her body bucked and trembled. Not for the first time, he thought of how perfect she was for him, strong enough to offer everything he demanded, soft enough to delight him.

After she came, he rode out his own orgasm. He bit out a curse in Spanish. The wait had seemed interminable, but it had been worthwhile. He hadn't had an orgasm this wrenching in months. Dios. There was something about this woman...

When she finally opened her eyes, she was looking up at him. She grinned and said cheekily, "Okay, so maybe you did want me."

"That'll earn you a spanking."

She stuck out her tongue. "You'll have to find the stamina first, Agent Romero."

"Woman, I always have the energy to spank your sassy ass." He released his grip on her wrists, and after disposing of the condom, he maneuvered them both around so that he held her against his chest. She wiggled her rear against him. He gave her a gentle swat. Then she turned to face him. The color of her eyes was lighter than he had ever seen before. Her mouth was open slightly. Her blonde hair was mussed all over her face. And he was ensnared, as surely as if she'd slapped a pair of unyielding metal handcuffs on him.

She drifted off to sleep, and he held her.

He didn't question the rightness of having her body pressed against his so trustingly. Nor did he question his own determination to keep her safe. It wasn't just about his job or the fact Ms. Inamorata herself would skin him alive if anything happened to her little sister. This was about what Aimee's innocence and responsiveness did to him. He'd keep her safe, no matter what.

When he was sure she was asleep deeply, he climbed from the bed and dug out a pair of shorts and a fresh T-shirt from his duffel. He had a hard time concentrating on what he was doing. It hadn't been thirty minutes since he'd drained his balls, but he was already getting hard again. Even in sleep, she was alluring, her hair in disarray, the dim light reflecting off the crystals in her plug when she moved. His body suddenly thought it was ten years younger.

He skipped socks and stuffed his feet into his running shoes.

After grabbing his gun, he walked through the house, then went into the kitchen. That damn bird growled again. "Tastes like chicken," Trace said.

After grabbing a flashlight from the countertop, he headed outside. The neighbor's dog growled softly, but it didn't bark like crazy. Certain everything was fine, he double-checked all the window locks, then went outside to talk to the crew. They'd be on until seven a.m.

"All's quiet, Romero," Daniel Riley said, rolling down the window.

The team, one man and a woman, were sipping coffee. Sara Stein and Daniel Riley. He knew them both. Hawkeye had so many operatives, everywhere on the face of the planet, but he knew these two, and he was glad to see them assigned to the job. Stein was steady, good with women, great with kids. Riley was young and ambitious. He volunteered for a lot of high-risk assignments, and he'd already received a big promotion.

"I hear it could have been a random thing," Riley added.

"I don't believe it," Trace said.

"Regardless, none of us are going to let anything happen to Inamorata's kid sister," Stein added. "No way in hell."

"You got an inside track?" Riley asked.

"Inside track?" Trace leaned forward. "On?"

"Her name. Ms. Inamorata's," Riley said.

"We've been talking about it, and we've decided we'd be willing to split the money with you," she said.

"The woman is closemouthed. But we can safely cross off Ruth, Donna, and Julie."

"I'll check them against the list," Stein promised. "She seems more like a Prudence or Catherine or Christine. Something more formal, uptight, you know?"

"But her sister is Aimee. Informal," her partner said. "So maybe it's a top-ten name, like Jennifer or Jessica. Maybe Emily."

"But look how Aimee is spelled."

"Yeah, I keep forgetting you're the genius."

Trace started to move away, then turned and came back. "Don't let anything happen to her."

"No chance," Stein said, leaning over Riley. "I'm more frightened of Inamorata than I am of Hawkeye himself."

"See, you keep proving that Mensa IQ," Riley said. "Hey, Romero. There's a nasty rumor going around that she kicked your ass when you went for a run."

"You keep proving your non-Mensa IQ," Stein said,

smacking her partner on the arm. "Keep your mouth shut."

"What? Why did you hit me? I was just repeating what I heard."

"Rumor's true," Trace said. "If she hadn't slowed down, she'd have lapped me a second time."

Sara Stein whistled sympathetically. "She lapped you once?"

He didn't answer that. Technically she hadn't, but she would have. "You can go running with her tomorrow afternoon. We'll take turns."

"Sorry, dude. I get off at seven," Riley said. "Happy to help, otherwise, you know? Anything for the team."

Trace rapped his knuckles on the vehicle's roof.

"Sweet dreams," Riley said, smothering a yawn.

Trace grinned, checking out the area as he jogged back across the street. There wouldn't be much time for sleep. He had more than a few things he planned to do with her, to her, and very few of them could be considered *sweet.*

* * *

Aimee sat up in bed and wrapped her arms around her upturned knees, very much aware of the plug still deep inside her.

Dozens of emotions crashed over her.

She hated waking up and finding the bed empty.

She was used to sleeping alone, and she liked her sleep, eight hours at a minimum, preferably nine, and on rare occasions, a full ten. This was the first time she ever remembered waking up and feeling lonely.

She told herself he wouldn't have gone far. But she listened intently and didn't hear him moving about the house. The bedside lamp was still on from earlier, but there were no other lights turned on.

As silence became more familiar, she became aware of the sound of voices outside. Not just his but others, likely one of the security teams. It reminded her why he was really here, of the danger he and her sister believed she might be in.

He wasn't here because he was a man who found her sexy and attractive. He was here on assignment, and when the assignment was over, he'd be gone.

They could play and have fun, he could push her to the edge of her sexual submission and fulfill all her fantasies—and a few she didn't know she had—but he'd move on soon. He'd be in a jungle somewhere, perhaps supported by the technology she was working on. He'd be rescuing some businessman, maybe a kidnapped child, or he'd be protecting civilians in a Middle East war zone, and she'd still be in Denver, Colorado, continuing on with her research, teaching classes downtown, running every afternoon...stagnant in her boring, rigid life, thinking about him, wondering what he was doing, who he was doing... "Damn. Damn, damn, damn. Damn."

She was not the kind of woman who felt sorry for herself. Her older sister made sure of that. Life threw events at you, but it was how you responded that helped you grow and change. Events didn't define who you were. You defined who you were.

Still, sex with him was incredible. Powerful. She reached for her wine. Who was she fooling? It was the best sex she'd ever had, and the reactions he'd wrung from her left her feeling emotionally vulnerable.

She liked falling asleep in his arms, enjoyed his strength, swooned over the way he touched her.

So now what?

Exhaling shakily, she took a fortifying sip from her wine.

She was scared. If she fell for him, she wasn't sure she'd

survive it. So that meant there was only one practical solution. She couldn't fall for him.

She could enjoy the sex and the interchange, but that was it. Swooning was okay. Fretting was not.

Aimee heard the front door close. He returned to the bedroom smelling of the cool Colorado evening.

"Didn't mean to wake you," he said.

"You didn't. Not really. I wasn't aware of your leaving the bed, but when I turned and you weren't there..."

"How does the plug feel?"

She slid her wineglass onto the nightstand. "Full."

"Uncomfortable?"

"Surprisingly not."

He crossed the room and toed off his shoes. He smoothed her still-damp hair back from her face. It amazed her how tender he could be. The contrast with his dominant personality thrilled her. She never knew what to expect, and that heightened the experience with him.

"Since you're awake, I'll give you two choices of what we can do to fill the time."

Her heart picked up a few extra beats. She looked up at him. A small, devilish smile played at the corners of his mouth. Whatever he came up with, he was going to enjoy it.

"I can take you bent over. Of course, with that plug in your ass, I won't be able to put my finger up there. But I can play with it." He paused a beat. "Or I can introduce you to bondage and tie your hot body to the bed, keeping you helpless while I fuck you."

He held her head between his hands and leaned forward to kiss her. She surrendered instantly. She loved the taste of him, the way the wine mingled with the bite of the pico de gallo he'd made for dinner. And she loved the way he started by drawing her lower lip between his teeth, then using his tongue to coax her into opening her mouth. This time his kiss was gentle as he silently asked for her invitation. She rocked forward, giving it.

Then he deepened the kiss, demanding more from her, forcing her to open her mouth wider as he simulated their earlier sex act. He probed. He sought. She could have no secrets from this man. Her pussy moistened, and her nipples hardened. Her whole body seemed to open in response to him.

When he ended the kiss, her mouth felt bruised, and she ridiculously had never been happier. She was nearly giddy with it.

"Well?"

"I want to be bent over." She could hardly believe her words had sounded so calm. But her earlier decision had liberated her. She wanted to enjoy sex with him. Why not wring every drop of excitement from their time together as she could? She'd already decided she wasn't going to allow herself to get hurt emotionally. So why not have fun?

"Nice." He released her and pulled off his shirt.

She loved the sight of his chest, the way the dark hair arrowed downward, the way she could see his muscles ripple as he stretched, and the sight of his brown masculine nipples… Her mouth watered, and she wanted to play with him the way he played with her.

He put the gun away, then shucked his shorts. As usual he was commando, and as usual his cock was already engorged.

"I can't get enough of you," he said.

"The feeling's mutual. I like the feel of your cock inside me. You should share more often."

He laughed, then offered her his hand. "Stand there," he told her as he helped her from the bed.

"Facing you?"

"For now. Spread your legs…as wide as you can."

She did, and he knelt in front of her. She shuddered. Big, strong, powerful Trace Romero was on his knees, with his mouth at her crotch level.

"Just making sure you're ready."

"I'm ready!"

He looked up at her, capturing her gaze. Then he leaned in and licked her pussy.

"I'm ready," she whispered.

"Gotta be sure you're really, really ready for me to fuck you as hard as I want to."

Within seconds, she'd be over the edge. That was probably his master plan. Push her over the edge and then punish her for it.

She placed her hands on his shoulders, trying to keep her balance. When he did…*that*…she could hardly hold herself up.

He spread her labia with one hand. With the other, he toyed with her plug.

"Ready," she said again, this time through gritted teeth. "Really, really wet," she said.

He kept at it, licking her pussy, changing the amount of pressure on her clit. His tongue was magic. He slipped his tongue inside her while he gave a particularly firm tug on her plug. Her whole body felt like it was on fire.

She moved her hands, digging her fingers into his hair.

"You were up to 'barium,' I believe."

"Thanks." She might have laughed if she weren't fighting so hard to hang on. "Berkelium, beryllium, bismuth…" Then thought became almost impossible, despite the fact she could recite the table backward. "Boron."

"You've got the most delicious cunt," he said. "I could eat you all day."

The graphicness of what he said just made her hotter.

He pulled out the plug even farther, then shoved it in. She was done for.

She screamed as she shattered.

He kept up his maddening motions, dragging a second orgasm from her.

"Now," he said, looking up at her and grinning, "you're ready."

Chapter Six

"I'm glad you're so fit," he said. "It'll make it easier for you to stay in position."

She turned her back to him, and he trailed his fingers down her spine, then into the crack of her rear. Every nerve ending felt as if it were being singed. This man knew how to touch her, where to touch her, and for how long to touch her. "How long are you planning to keep me bent over?"

"Until sometime tomorrow. Retribution for that run."

"You've got a mean streak."

"A mile wide," he agreed. "And a memory that doesn't quit either."

He exerted some pressure against the small of her back, and she spread her legs apart as she bent over.

He grabbed a condom, then moved in behind her. She wiggled her butt.

"You're a vixen."

She felt his cockhead against her pussy. Her breaths came closer and closer together, even though he'd barely started to touch her.

"So tight," he murmured. "Hot." He put his hands on her hips and held her tight as he pushed inexorably forward.

"It feels…different than anything else has." It had to be the combination of the position and the fact she was a little out of control. The blood rush to her head only enhanced the intensity.

She heard him grunt, and she took silent pleasure from the fact he was turned on. She loved that she had the same power over him that he had over her. Intoxicating stuff.

"Play with your pussy," he told her.

She nodded, or the best she could manage hanging upside down, and tried to do as he asked. It wasn't easy, being bent over with him impaling her, filling her, stretching her, making her feel even fuller since the plug was still in place.

She touched herself, and her clit felt sensitive. "It's swollen," she said.

"Good."

"Beast."

He dragged her backward and managed to snake his arm around her middle so he could hold her completely imprisoned while he fucked her. Having him so totally in charge gave her that now-familiar feeling of being able to let go, and she relished it.

She felt his orgasm building before she heard his deep groan of appreciation.

He held her, and he pounded into her.

His cock was hard, pulsing.

She wanted his orgasm as much as he demanded hers.

She remained in place as he shuddered.

"I'm not finished with you yet," he said.

"But…"

He jostled their positions a bit. "Your orgasms need to be a three-to-one ratio."

"I think I'm past that."

"You will be." He reached around and fingered her while he still had her pussy filled. The intensity of the angle combined with his unyielding and relentless pressure on her clit made her tremble.

"Don't fight it," he said.

He still held her, and he made his movements shorter and more intense. She called out his name, and the climax overtook her. "I think I'll sleep well this time."

He slowly withdrew. She couldn't quite manage to stand.

"A little help from your friends?"

"Please."

She wasn't sure how he managed to have so much strength and energy left as he drew her up. Her muscles were spent, and she'd forced him to keep up with her during the run, so she knew he had to be as tired as she was. He pulled back the bedcovers before lifting her onto the mattress.

"Stay there," he said.

She wasn't going anywhere for a very long time, even if he were to order it. But luckily he was giving her an order she could effortlessly follow.

She rolled onto her side, and a few minutes later, she felt him there with something warm and wet. Her eyes opened.

"Washcloth," he said. "Relax."

She followed his instructions, taking a breath and luxuriating in the way he cared for her. After soothing her clit and gently wiping her pussy, he used the small cotton towel to remove the plug. She exhaled. "Thank you."

He crawled in behind her and pulled her close, settling his cock between her ass cheeks before pulling blankets over them both.

"I think I might like this submissive stuff."

"You think?"

"Maybe," she said teasingly. "I may need a little more experience to know for sure."

He reached around and tweaked one of her nipples.

She yelped.

"Then tomorrow, I'll give you another lesson, and we'll see how that goes. You can let me know then how it's working for you."

"Three-to-one, huh?"

"At least," he said.

"Cumulative or daily?"

"Does your brain ever shut off, Professor?"

"Just asking. I like daily better. Easier to track that way. I won't be as tempted to start a spreadsheet."

"You don't want me to catch up. Admit it."

"You set the rules, Agent Romero. I'm just trying to understand them properly, well, so I don't have to be punished or anything. I wouldn't like that."

"Uh-huh."

Effortlessly he flipped her over and pinned her beneath him. "Hey!"

"I want you to shut up. I only know three ways to do that. One involves a gag."

"Uh…"

"The other two involve my anatomy."

He lowered his head toward her.

He captured her mouth in a kiss, and she tasted herself on him. Kinky, sensational stuff. And another experience to save for later, when they were no longer together.

"This working for you?" he asked, drawing away momentarily.

He didn't wait for an answer.

* * *

Coffee. Coffee would be good. Her usual fix of an extra-large vanilla soy latte would be even better.

Aimee dragged a pillow over her head to block out the bright Rocky Mountain sunshine.

Slowly reality returned.

She became aware of the tenderness between her legs and the fact her nipples were slightly sore.

She rolled over and pushed up onto one elbow. She saw the indentation on the pillow Trace had used. Even without that, she would know it hadn't been a dream. The scent of him lingered in the room. His duffel was on top of the dresser. His stainless steel watch took center stage on the nightstand. A discarded T-shirt hung from one of the bedposts. His presence dominated the space, even though he wasn't in it.

She heard him banging around in the kitchen.

Then Eureka chimed in. "Get up. Get up!"

"Tastes like chicken," Trace said, his voice carrying back to the bedroom.

She laughed. But she'd definitely have some damage control to do there. Trace had obviously left the bird covered up, and that would just annoy Eureka all over again.

"Get up! Get up!"

Aimee slowly realized that coffee wasn't just a dream or a need. The richness of its brewing scent had awakened her. She could get used to someone more ambitious than she was getting out of bed and turning on the coffee.

She'd always considered the idea of having someone around to be more than a bit obtrusive, and her ex had certainly proven that. He was useless; well, useless and annoying. Factor in that he hadn't turned her on in bed, and that was the trifecta of relationship doom.

Unlike her, she hadn't ever put together an official pros-and-cons list on the idea of living with someone. Until last night, there had been no point. Being put to bed and awakened by the scent of coffee could potentially outrank ten negatives, like doing someone else's laundry. She'd do two lifetimes' worth of laundry, without complaint, to have coffee waiting in the morning.

She debated what to wear into the kitchen. Obviously Trace had preferred her naked last night, but what were his expectations during the day? And how was she supposed to act?

This was more complicated than she had imagined.

With a groan, she collapsed back onto the mattress and pulled the blankets over her shoulders.

"Morning."

Trace stood at the doorway, his shoulder propped against the jamb. He held a steaming cup of coffee in hand. Her mouth watered, and not just from anticipation of her own cup of coffee, but from the sight of him.

He smelled fresh, of spicy soap, citrusy shampoo, and first-of-the-morning air.

Black T-shirts were made for him, and he could have walked out of a magazine ad for those blue jeans. Just open the top button and...

"I was hoping you'd join me in the shower," he said.

"I would have..." *Might have*, she silently amended. She was known to be cool, calm, and logical, but in this situation, she had no idea how to act.

"If you were awake."

"I seem to have burned up a lot of energy yesterday. From the run. From the break-in."

"Uh-huh."

Did he see through everything?

She sat up, dragging the sheet with her. She felt unaccountably shy with him standing there, looking at her as if he knew all her secrets, which at this point, he practically did. She smoothed her hair back from her face, but with the smile on Trace's face, he didn't seem to mind her dishabille.

"Since I'm such a smart man," he said. "I brought you coffee."

"You brought me coffee? That's for me?"

"I was afraid to come near without bringing a gift."

She scowled at it, but now she couldn't take her gaze off the steaming mug. "I don't suppose it has cream in it?"

"It does. Organic half-and-half."

"How...?"

"I figured there wouldn't be half-and-half in your refrigerator for any other reason than coffee. How'd I do?"

"I think I'll call you Sherlock."

He entered the room and sat on the edge of the bed. She accepted the mug with a grateful smile. Yeah, doing laundry for this man would be no biggie, as long as he got up before her every day and brought coffee in bed. That was an indulgence she'd never even considered before. "Perfect," she said, taking a long drink. "Thank you."

"Drop the sheet."

Instead of waiting for her to comply, he captured the high-thread-count cotton and pulled it away from her body. Her nipples hardened instantly, in response to the room's chill and the heat of his gaze.

"I'd keep you naked all day if it were up to me."

He cupped her left breast gently, and dampness flooded between her legs.

"Careful with the coffee."

He was a master. He had her exactly where he wanted her,

as usual.

She noticed, with a thrill, the differences in their skin tones, the white creaminess of her breast and the pink of her nipple, contrasted with his richer, darker color. Everything about this man gave her chills.

He tightened his grip slightly. She gasped. Watching her intently, he pinched her nipple between his thumb and forefinger. "You like that?"

"Yes," she said, gasping for breath.

"And this?" He tightened his grip.

She'd experimented with nipple clamps and never experienced anything so intense. Aimee could no longer speak. Her eyes closed.

"You are so amazing to play with," he said. He tweaked her nipple one final time. "Get dressed. Breakfast awaits."

She blinked the world back into focus. "Breakfast?"

"The meal between dinner and lunch."

If her brain weren't foggy from sexual arousal, and if he hadn't been smart enough to hand her a cup of coffee, she would have brained him with a pillow.

He laughed. With only a glance over his shoulder, he left the bedroom.

She took a few appreciative sips of coffee before getting out of bed. It was kind of strange to wake up naked. She had a few favorite nightshirts, several with pictures of Einstein along with some of his more-famous quotes, and even one with a picture of Richard Feynman. That, she realized, should have told her a lot about her life.

She hit the shower, and she stayed in there longer than she should have. It was totally decadent to have half a cup of coffee still waiting when she wrapped a towel around her. As long as she didn't focus on why he was here and how short the duration would be, life was good.

Since she had a lot of work to do today, and she was bound and determined not to let him interfere with it, she dressed in jeans and a soft T-shirt. And since she wasn't above being somewhat of a tease, she skipped wearing a bra.

She powered up her computer and checked e-mail. There was one from a twentysomething colleague from the East Coast. He was a mad-scientist hardware guy who wore in-your-face T-shirts and knew more stuff than 90 percent of the planet's population.

He'd been experimenting with a mosquito last night, and one of his neighbors had sprayed it with insect repellent. The spray had worked; evidently the stickiness clogged up the mechanics of the bug. That was something they hadn't spent a lot of time considering. The wonder kid had been up all night trying new things.

Shaking her head, Aimee opened up her integrated development environment to work on debugging her piece of the software. Ideally the IDE would find the flaw in her programming that sometimes made the mosquito's injector jam.

She'd spent days looking at it, to no avail, and time was ticking.

While the software chewed on her work, she headed back down the hallway.

The scene in the kitchen shocked her. Trace stood in front of the stove, his back to her as he sang in Spanish. She could get used to that, she decided. Any man who could operate a paring knife, a frying pan, a toaster, and a coffeemaker, all in the same morning, was her hero.

But it wasn't only that.

Eureka's cage was uncovered, and her feathered friend was on top of his cage, his foot wrapped around a slice of apple. Eureka still glared suspiciously at the human, but Trace had gotten her bird up and fed him—now that was above and beyond.

Giving in to impulse, not something she generally did, she crossed the room and slid her arms around his waist and held him tight for a few seconds. "Thank you."

"All this over coffee?"

"Mainly the bird," she said.

"I figured I should plump him up, put some meat on his bones, before we roast him for dinner."

"Bombs away!"

She looked over her shoulder and pointed at the bird. "Eureka, no."

He picked up the piece of apple that he'd discarded.

"You really should stop antagonizing him," she said to Trace, pinching him.

"I should stop antagonizing *him?* Hello, he's the one who dropped a bomb on me. On the food chain, humans rank slightly higher than birds, and if he were smarter, he'd figure that out."

"Tastes like chicken," Eureka repeated. "Tastes like chicken. Bombs away!"

She glared at the bird again, but he was eating, obviously having made his point. "He's smarter than you give him credit for. What's for breakfast?"

This time he looked over his shoulder at the bird. "Eggs," he said. "Lots of them."

She pinched his rear.

"Omelets," he said, reaching for a spatula. "With avocados and cream cheese."

"Can I hire you out after all this is over?"

"For sexual favors?"

"That too. Mostly, though, for your culinary skills."

"And here I thought you only wanted me for my body," he said.

"It's great that you've actually turned out to be somewhat useful. Up until now, I've always thought having a man around would be as helpful as having an extra toe."

"I think I'm insulted."

"You shouldn't be. I'm revising my opinion."

"Ah. You have evidence to support a new hypothesis."

"Precisely." She could stay like this for a very long time, with her cheek pressed against his back, inhaling his unique scent. And Trace didn't seem to be objecting either. "How can I help?"

"Set the table, and grab the pico we made last night."

Saying *we* was generous, since all she'd done was watch and eat.

He turned toward her then, seizing control like he always did. Before she could react, he had dropped the spatula and had her against the counter. His right leg was between hers, her crotch against his thigh. He dug his hand into her hair, holding her captive for his kiss.

She wrapped her arms around his neck and responded completely; she had no resistance where this man was concerned. As he'd obviously intended, she moved her pussy against his leg while he devoured her mouth in a demanding kiss.

Even though she'd had half a dozen orgasms last night, another was right there, gnawing at her.

He moved his free hand to her lower back, and the pressure he exerted changed her position a bit, bringing her in more firm contact with his leg. He had to know what he was doing, had to know its effect on her...

She came, hard, and with a whimper that was muffled against his mouth.

"Now," he said, "it's a good morning."

When her head stopped spinning, she grinned up at him. "I'm up one to nothing. And it's not even seven o'clock."

"I'll even the score later."

While she put colorful place mats on the table, her gaze kept straying to him. He was more than competent in the kitchen; he was at home. It frightened her, more than just a little bit, to realize how comfortable she was with him here. "More coffee?" She offered the drink as if having a man in her kitchen at this time of the morning were the most natural thing in the world.

"Black," he said. "Although after tasting the cream on your kiss, I'm tempted to have you put some in mine."

She refilled his mug, then grabbed herself a new one from the cupboard, adding a huge dollop of half-and-half.

He brought two plates to the table, and after she took the first bite, she sighed. The flavors melded on her tongue, complemented by the bite from the jalapeños in the pico de gallo.

"It'll do?" he asked.

"I may be up two to one after this."

"Guess you like my cooking." He grinned.

"Maybe you should be the scientist with those kinds of deductive-reasoning skills."

After breakfast, he said, "Go to work; I'll take care of this."

"Really? You don't want help cleaning the kitchen? What kind of male chauvinist are you?"

"Not a good one. But the idea of having you always ready for sex has a certain appeal."

She laughed and tossed her napkin at him.

"Work," he reminded her. "Unless you don't want to get anything done today. In that case, I'll have you tied to the bed in less than five minutes."

The image he evoked made her tremble. What they'd already done pushed at her boundaries, but it hadn't been frightening. In fact, it had been liberating. But could she trust enough to be completely vulnerable?

"You'd be the perfect man if you agreed to let me go get my soy latte in about an hour."

"Happy to take you anywhere you want," he said. "But you're not going alone."

No matter what, yesterday's break-in loomed insidiously in her mind.

Her landline rang, and she went to answer it while Trace cleared the dishes. When she heard her sister's voice, she said, "I've been offered half the money in the pot if I just cough up your name. I hear there's enough for a nice trip to the Bahamas."

"Won't matter if I kill you. You have to be alive to enjoy the trip."

"That's what I was afraid of." Aimee laughed, but her sister didn't. Her body chilled. "Something's wrong."

"Agent Romero is still there?"

"Of course he is. I don't want to be moved to a safe house," she said.

"Let me talk to him."

"I'm a big girl."

"Get me Romero, Aimee."

He was already walking over to take the phone from her. With a shrug, she gave him the handset and headed for her office and shut the door. Work could always be counted on to restore her equilibrium.

Aware of the deep rumble of his voice down the hall, she opened a spreadsheet and then logged into the program the Hawkeye team had been using and scanned the notes various teammates had made since her last log-in.

There'd been no breakthroughs, but one programmer in Buenos Aires had found another sequence that made the mosquito crash, literally, into a tree. He had attached a video clip, and she laughed and replayed it.

She sent a message that learning what didn't work moved them one step closer to knowing what did. That comment was met by a very quick "yeah, right," from someone in Baton Rouge.

Since her part of the puzzle involved injecting a nanochip into an unsuspecting person, she focused on her piece. She'd learned early on that if she focused on other peoples' work, she never get her own finished.

A message flashed across the bottom of her screen just as she became aware of being surrounded by silence.

Her sister knew. Trace knew. And now she did.

Jason Knoll, a Hawkeye programmer who lived near the small Colorado mountain town of Conifer, had been found dead in his office, and he could have been dead for as long as thirty-six hours. His computer was missing, and he had code written on his hand. She remembered her sister talking about Jason. As a fourteen-year-old, he'd written a game that had been purchased by one of the world's largest producers of video games.

She sat back, stunned.

Trace knocked on her door. Without waiting for an answer, he strode in.

"The break-in wasn't random," she said, still staring at the message.

"No."

He came up behind her; then he gently spun her chair so that she faced him. He caught her by the shoulders and pulled her to her feet.

He wrapped his arms around her, holding her tight, letting her lean on him. He didn't say anything, nothing meaningless or trite. He simply offered his strength. Gratefully, for the first time in her life, she accepted a man's support.

"He was a kid," she said. She tried to swallow the lump in her throat, and she valiantly blinked back the tears swimming in her eyes.

"I'm sorry," he said simply.

Emotions crashed into her, swamping her. "He was funny. Would have never harmed anyone."

Trace stroked her hair, cradling her as if she were precious.

For long moments, he said nothing. Memories of the team teasing and brainstorming with Jason flashed through her mind in a random, senseless order. She continued to lean on Trace, to inhale his scent and draw from his strength. How had he become so important to her, so fast? "Did they get any of his work?"

"Yeah."

She looked up at him, appreciating that he didn't try to lie to her or soften the news. "Then the rest of us will have to work doubly hard to get the project finished."

"Is your work backed up?"

"I back up remotely every night at midnight."

"Good. So you can access your work from anywhere?"

"Theoretically." Grief collided with reality.

"We're moving you."

She pushed away from him, out of his arms. "Moving me?"

"Wolf Stone, Hawkeye's right-hand man, has a remote place, a ranch really, fully state-of-the-art, in the mountains. Or we can go to my place."

Annoyance warred with the fact she should have seen this coming. "You're moving every person who works for Hawkeye? There are dozens of us working on this project. You can't keep everyone safe. Think about it."

"No one but you matters to me."

She didn't want to leave her home.

"We can do this—"

"Your way," she interrupted. "Your way or your way, right?"

He folded his arms in that implacable way she recognized and hated. Her lover was gone; the man who'd prepared breakfast and offered to wash the dishes had vanished as if he'd never existed. In his place was the hardened operative, a man who would give her no choice about anything once he'd made a decision.

"You've got ten minutes," he said. "I'd prefer you get ready in five."

"What about Eureka?"

"Can one of your neighbors—"

"Don't even go there, Agent. If I go, so does he."

"It's not practical to haul a parrot—"

"Were you not listening?"

He sighed. "You've got nine minutes." Without another word, he left the room.

She sank into her office chair. She resisted her immediate impulse to drop her head onto the desk. Aimee rarely allowed herself to feel self-pity. She learned early that crying didn't solve her problems; she just ended up with a headache on top of everything else.

With a resigned sigh, she pulled back her shoulders and forced herself to focus. He'd already had his gun in place, his watch strapped to his wrist. He was all business. If Trace said she had nine minutes, he meant it.

The front door slammed, and she checked her watch. Eight minutes.

She ignored the messages from her colleagues who were speculating about Jason's death. Instead she powered down her computer and gathered her notes, before hurrying into the master bathroom to throw toiletries into a travel bag.

The clothes Trace had worn yesterday were in the hamper alongside hers. It hadn't taken long for him to dominate almost every area of her life. As much as it chafed, she also realized she appreciated it. Dealing with Jason's death would be more difficult if she were alone.

She heard the sound of a truck being started, and she grabbed a suitcase from the closet. *Focus.*

She scooped a handful of lingerie from her bottom drawer, then tossed in socks. Packing workout clothes was probably ridiculous, but she needed the feeling of some control, and she decided she wasn't going anywhere without them. After tossing in jeans, T-shirts, and a couple of sweatshirts, she shoved down on the contents so that she could zip the piece of luggage.

She heard the front door close again, and the truck still sounded like it was running.

Trace joined her a few seconds later, grabbing his duffel from the floor and tossing it on the bed. "Close?"

"Yeah. Not sure I thought of everything."

He looked at her pointedly. "Toys?"

She blinked. "You're serious?" When he didn't answer, she realized he was totally serious. She opened her nightstand drawer. She felt the heat of embarrassment crawl into her face, even though she knew that was ridiculous. Surely she didn't have any secrets left from him. "There's no room in my suitcase."

He unzipped his bag again, and he had a wicked, toe-curling smile on his face. "I'd prefer to have them in my possession, anyway."

She tossed clamps and a plug, along with some lube, into his waiting duffel.

"Good girl."

His approval didn't matter. It shouldn't matter. She looked up, and he was studying her intently.

They were separated by only inches. She'd always been able to keep work and play separated, but with Trace, she was constantly aware and always hungry. The power of his presence intoxicated her, even as it frustrated her.

"I'll get your computer. You grab the bird. If the house isn't stocked with food, we can always eat him."

"Not funny."

"Who was joking?"

As she headed into the kitchen, she realized he'd done it again, kept her off balance, made her forget she was scared, made her forget she was angry with him.

"Want to go for a ride?" she asked Eureka.

"Ride."

She hadn't had him in a vehicle since the day she'd brought him home, and she really wasn't sure how well he'd do. "Say good night, Eureka," she said before covering his cage. She tossed some fresh fruit into a bag and then carried both into the living room. Trace had already put their luggage near the door.

She was reaching for the doorknob when he entered the room with her computer and said, "Wait for me."

"Aren't you being overly cautious?"

"This is your ass we're talking about," he said. "And I've become partial to it."

She noticed his GLOCK was in a shoulder holster. He put

down her computer, then opened the door.

A woman wearing black jeans and a black T-shirt, what Aimee now thought of as the Hawkeye uniform, stood on her porch.

"Bree Mallory," he said by way of introduction. "Aimee Inamorata."

"A pleasure, ma'am," Mallory said. "I've met your sister."

"You can cross off Donna, Ruth, and Julie," Trace said.

"Oh, and I'll give you Jennifer, Susan, and let's see, Elizabeth," Aimee added.

"Thanks for that." Mallory grinned, and Aimee liked the chink in the formal armor. The operative then grabbed the luggage and headed to the vehicle with it.

Aimee noticed that the back door of the SUV was already standing open, and so was the passenger door. "Always thinking ahead,"

"Always." Trace reached for the birdcage. Eureka growled like a dog. "On second thought, you take the loro," Trace said to her. "Flying feathered…"

With Mallory standing guard, Aimee loaded Eureka into the vehicle, putting the cage on the floor behind the passenger seat. Mallory kept her body positioned so that Aimee was never left exposed. That anyone felt that step was necessary sent a cold chill down her spine.

In less than sixty seconds, everything had been loaded into the SUV, Mallory had slammed the doors shut and they were on the road, a truck in front of them, a massive white Suburban behind them.

"I'm freaking out a little," she admitted as he rolled through a four-way stop without slowing down.

He looked over at her. "A little I can deal with. A little will keep you sharp. Just don't make it a lot, *si?*"

She laughed. "Are you always calm?"

"Not when I've got you bent over."

"How can you think of sex at a time like this?"

"*Pericita*, with you, I rarely think of anything else."

And besides, she was now thinking of something other than the danger. She was getting moist, just from his words and the way he glanced at her.

"Where are we going?"

"I promised you a soy latte, I believe."

Her mouth fell open. Could he be any more complicated? "You're going to get me a latte?"

"Not at your usual shop, but yes. I always keep my promises, Aimee. I want you to know that."

Chapter Seven

Trace Romero, trusted army guy, loyal Hawkeye operative, mission commander, had lost his mind. First he allowed Aimee to bring the loco bird with them; now he was stopping at a coffee shop. Others might accuse him of thinking with his little head rather than the big one. And they'd be right.

No one went deep with a parrot in tow, and they sure as sunshine on a stick didn't stop at a coffee shop on the way underground.

When he'd told Mallory, Daniel Riley, and the rest of the team that they were making a stop en route, they'd looked at him like he was the one who'd suddenly gone crazy.

Mallory had opened her mouth to argue, but when he'd turned his gaze directly on her, she'd shut up and nodded. She'd turned to the rest of the guys, three other men, and said, "We'll make it work."

They'd formulated a plan, and the smile of thanks Aimee had given him made everything worthwhile.

The very fact she had stayed calm when she might have panicked after learning of Jason Knoll's death, the fact she hadn't resorted to tears to manipulate him to stay at her house made him want to give her the world. He'd said she had ten minutes to get her life packed up, and she'd done it.

This woman, with her responsive ways, her sexy submission, and her crackling intelligence, had gotten under his defenses. For the first time in his life, he didn't object. Last night, she had boldly asked for what she wanted sexually, and she shot every bit as straight as the world's most finely crafted weapon. She might be a bit shy, but that she pushed past her inhibitions was intoxicating, every bit as much as his favorite bottle of mescal.

He intended to keep her safe and by his side for a very long time. He didn't wonder when he'd made his decision. He didn't wonder about the personality change deep inside. He wanted Aimee in his life, and he sure as fuck intended to be the only man she had sex with from now on. The rest, he'd figure out.

He parallel parked directly in front of the coffeehouse door, even though head-in parking was specified.

Mallory jumped out of the vehicle that parked behind him, and she was at Aimee's door in seconds.

"You want anything?" Aimee asked.

"Your ass back in that seat in under four minutes."

"Do you always have to be so bossy?" She sighed. "Wait, never mind. Don't answer that. Turns out it was a rhetorical question."

He grinned at her. The moment the door closed, Eureka growled. "I'll take care of her," he told the bird. "You, I'm not so sure about."

He took the break to adjust his cock in his pants. Having her so close kept him hard. He could fuck her three times a day and have energy to spare.

For a few seconds, he thought about the idea of having her all to himself, somewhere remote, somewhere out of danger, so he could focus purely on her and pushing her to the edge of her endurance.

The longer he thought about it, the more he liked it.

Danger had always been an aphrodisiac, but suddenly the thought of teaching her, disciplining her, at his leisure, held more appeal.

As he'd ordered, she was back in under four minutes. "Three minutes, fifty-seven seconds. You're getting better at this submissive gig," he said.

"You'll need some sustenance to keep up your dictatorial ways. Here."

"Nah. I can do that in my sleep. Using manners, that's what takes energy."

She offered him the small bag. "Lemon pound cake. Mallory said you have a weakness for it. She doesn't miss a trick."

"Just the icing," he said, sliding into traffic but nevertheless reaching into the bag to break off a piece of the pastry. "Thanks."

"Wouldn't have figured you for a sweet-tooth kind of guy."

"I'll take a bite out of anything that appeals to me."

"I'm wondering something."

He accelerated, nosing the speedometer just past the speed limit as he headed for the interstate.

"What would you do if I took a bite out of you? Here. Now."

"Want to find out?"

"I think I'm more of a scaredy-cat than I want to admit." She sat back and took an appreciative sip from her coffee. "Thank you for stopping."

"Thank you for not being a pain in the ass."

"You are such a romantic, and you have such a way with words. I bet you make all the women swoon." She stretched out her legs and crossed them at the ankle. "But I can forgive a lot with a cup of coffee in my hand."

Despite what he said, when he was working, he took his job seriously. Sex came second to everything else. Nothing mattered more than keeping Aimee Inamorata safe. It had nothing to do with her sister at this point, and everything to do with Aimee herself. But with her legs stretched out like that, he couldn't help the carnal thoughts. He wanted to see them spread as she was bent over, wanted them over his shoulders as he buried his face in her sweet cunt, wanted them wrapped around his waist, her heels in his back as she urged him to penetrate her deeper and deeper.

She made him want to be nasty.

"How does your ass feel this morning?"

She looked at him over the top of her cup. "My ass? Like my butt cheeks from that vicious spanking?"

"Vicious, was it?"

"Horrible."

"And you're hoping I do it again soon?"

"There is that."

"But I was asking if you're ready to have my cock up your ass."

"Oh." She choked on her coffee. "Yes."

He'd tried to prepare her to accommodate him, but not in a way that left her too uncomfortable to enjoy what he was planning for later. "Not too sore?"

"Honestly?"

"I never want less than complete honesty from you, *novia*."

"This whole thing with Jason's death is bothering me."

There was something different in her voice, a combination of wistfulness, and forcefulness that blended together in a way that gave her tone a sexy, husky quality. He waited for her to sift through her thoughts. He had plenty of practice waiting. He dealt with all kinds of reactions to traumatic situations, and he'd been in more than his share. Some people went into shock. Others lost their nerve, walking away or asking for reassignment. Some men went gunning for revenge. Plenty cried, raging at injustice. But everyone dealt in their own way.

He admired the way she held herself together, but he wouldn't have blamed her if she hadn't.

"My work, the work we're all doing at Hawkeye, is important. That someone is willing to kill to get it stuns me, sickens me, pisses me off. But it shouldn't really be surprising." She paused, and drew in a shaky breath. More than anything, that betrayed what she was really feeling. "I'm sure there's a team trying to figure out how someone learned about the project, and I'm sure my sister isn't sleeping more than a few hours a night, if at all." Her fingers curled tightly into the paper cup; it was a wonder it didn't crumple. "I have no doubt everyone is being protected so we can get the work finished."

She stared straight out the windshield, apparently not seeming to notice they'd left the city behind and that the breathtaking vista of the Continental Divide loomed in front of them with its snow-dusted top.

While keeping a vigilant eye on his beautiful passenger, his submissive, the woman he intended to care for, he shifted to the left lane to pass a slow-moving semi. Mallory and her driver followed.

"I'm glad you're here," she said. Then, still in that unblinking trance, she kept gazing into the distance. "I've made a lot of choices in my life. I've never regretted them, never questioned them...until now."

"And now?"

"I want to explore more."

He waited.

She looked over at him. Her mouth was set in a line. There were daggers of determination etched into her blue eyes. When she spoke, there was no room for argument in her tone. "So yes, I'm ready to have you tie me up, tie me down, and fuck me hard—including my ass." She put her drink in the cup holder.

Then she unfastened her seat belt and climbed onto the passenger seat backward. "And I want to know the answer to my question."

He glanced over at her before forcing his gaze back to the road. This stretch of I-70 wasn't as dicey as some, but it always demanded respect.

"What will you do if I take a big bite out of you, here, now?"

Bracing herself, one hand curved around the headrest, she shocked him by leaning across the distance.

She licked his earlobe.

He bit off a curse. Then Eureka added his own sounds effects.

Then she nibbled his earlobe.

"Woman."

"Just curious," she said, "about this…"

She sank her teeth into his shoulder. The pain rocketed through him, almost immediately replaced by white-hot heat. He kept both hands firmly on the steering wheel and fought for focus.

She then gave him a quick kiss on the side of the neck before getting herself situated and her safety belt refastened.

"You might not want to live quite so dangerously," he warned.

"And if I do? What if I want to live dangerously?"

When had she gotten so bold? Dios. He needed strength.

"What if I want you to punish me?" she asked.

He shot her a glance. She was looking at him. Her mouth was slightly parted, and her eyes were a shade lighter than normal, dancing with devilment. But there was something else layered with the devilment, a desperation, a hunger to be taken. He knew what she wanted. She wanted to feel alive. She might feel like she'd cheated the reaper, and she wanted to throw it in death's face. Surely she knew she was pushing him. Did she want to know it was safe to test him? Did she need to know she was safe with him? Did she need to explore the boundaries of how far she could go? "You will get what you are asking for, Aimee."

"And if I beg for it?"

Oh she knew all right; no doubt. She was pushing him harder, testing his limits. Once they got out of this situation, there'd be nothing he didn't show her. "Aimee..." His nostrils were flared from lack of air, and that wasn't because of the lack of oxygen at altitude. It was because his body had diverted blood from his brain to other parts.

"And if I beg for it, while I'm in front of you, on my knees...?"

"Woman..."

"If I do all that, will you take me over your knee and spank me? Will you make me scream your name?"

He lifted his hips to adjust his jeans.

She grinned. "I'll take that as a yes."

He'd give her everything she was asking for, everything she wanted, craved, hungered for. And then he'd give her more. "Take it as a yes."

* * *

She meant what she said to Trace, and she meant every word.

Jason's death had galvanized her. It hit her in a completely different way than her parents' deaths had. That loss had taught her how to be self-sufficient and how to look out for herself.

Now this...

She'd never been much of a risk taker. A hard worker, someone who was willing to push herself to achieve more and more, definitely, but she never ventured too far from safety. Even the men she'd been with had been safe. Boring and safe. And what had it gotten her? Being alone, not fulfilling her deepest fantasies.

The lesson she'd learned today was, carpe diem.

And she wanted to carpe the hell out of Trace Romero's diem.

He kept asking her to trust him. So what if she did? If she didn't, she knew the end result. He'd walk away in a few days, as soon as this situation was resolved, and she'd never see him again. But if she seized the opportunity, at least she'd have memories to keep her warm during the long Colorado winter nights. And who knew? One risk might lead to another.

"You're quiet," he said.

"Thinking about having your cock up my ass." She grinned when she saw his fingers tighten on the steering wheel. "I bet it will hurt at first."

"I'm sure it will."

He wasn't unaffected. She knew that from the way a small muscle ticked in his temple. "But I bet I'll get used to it."

"I'm sure you will," he agreed again.

"In that case, I bet I'll beg you to fuck me even harder."

"Count on it."

"And then—"

"Hello? Sub? Dom?"

"I know you're the Dom," she said, reaching for her coffee again. "Wouldn't forget it, even for a minute. By the way, thanks again for stopping for the latte."

She could look at him all day long. He kept his hair military short and brushed back from his forehead. His nose was a bit off center, as if he'd had it broken once or twice. It didn't detract from his looks at all. In fact, it made him look stronger, more compelling. He was a man accustomed to being in the thick of things. If something bad happened, she knew she could count on him. "Did I mention that I didn't put on panties when I got dressed this morning?"

His curse was uniquely him, a mix of English and Spanish, rich with the accent of his native tongue, clipped by his frustration. "I'll pull off at the next exit," he said, "and spank your ass, with God and half of Hawkeye watching."

She blinked.

"Want to try me?"

Part of her did. That small, naughty part of her was shocking. Who was she?

"Aimee?"

"Honestly? I don't know." But her heart was beating a little faster than it had been.

"You're an exhibitionist?"

"No! Well, not that I know of."

"You'd want to try it?"

"I'm…"

"You're open to it?" he asked.

"I'm not sure."

"We'll keep that on the maybe list," he said. "The maybe list had an opening since anal sex and spanking moved to the definitely list."

This time, she squirmed.

"Maybe Mallory would like to watch you get a bare-bottomed spanking?"

She tried to speak and couldn't form anything that didn't sound like a strangled cry. Despite her newfound "carpe diemness," there were things he would mention that might still make her nervous. Then again, her first spanking had been terrifying but thrilling too. She'd masturbated after reading spanking stories, but the reality of having her naked body across his jean-clad lap had made her fantasies seem like an old, black-and-white, reel-to-reel movie. Having his callused hand on her bare, exposed body seemed like 3-D in contrast.

He turned off the highway, and in the wing mirror, she noticed two other vehicles follow them. "Where are we going?"

"You never answered when I asked if you preferred my place or a Hawkeye property, so I made the decision for you."

"Shocking that you'd make a decision for me." But she said it without hostility. He had asked for her input, and at the time she'd been incapable of processing information, never mind making a decision.

"I decided on my place."

"Your place?"

"Not mine, technically. My family's," he corrected. "It's small, more of a cabin than a house. We use it for hunting, fishing, cross-country skiing, getting away. It's not grand, no television, but it's remote and private, I know the area, and it has electricity along with running water. It has two small bedrooms, one bathroom, and the kitchen, dining area, and living room are one open space. You should be able to work since we have cell service out there. If not, I imagine we'll find something to do so that you won't get bored."

"I do need to work on the project. And as long as you have cell service, my wireless card will get me into the network. I think all of Hawkeye plans ahead."

"We rented another cabin in the area, so the operatives can be close, and so that we can limit the number of people legitimately in the area. There's already food in the refrigerator, brought up from Denver so the locals in the nearby town won't be aware that we're there."

She shook her head.

"Along with an espresso maker."

"You're making me happy."

"And soy milk."

He really *was* the perfect man.

He turned off the pavement onto a dirt road. Eureka squawked.

"Sorry, guy," she told him. "Has to be a rough trip in a cage."

"We could always let him go. Lots of trees and friends around for him... I'm sure he'd be happy here."

"You really hold a grudge."

"Hey! That was my favorite T-shirt."

"I washed it," she said. "Good as new." Well, almost. With everything going on, she'd forgotten it in the washing machine.

"He can apologize anytime."

She shook her head. About twenty minutes later, the sun was blazing down in typical Colorado fashion. There were only a few high clouds in the sky, nothing to break up the shimmering heat. The highest of the distant mountain peaks were still dusted with snow, and if it weren't for the danger, she would be captivated by the scenery. He pulled off the bumpy road and slowed even more as he turned into what appeared to be a barely maintained driveway.

"Aimee! Aimee!"

"Almost there," she told the bird.

She was gritting her teeth by the time the small cabin came into view. It was rustic, as he'd warned, and it appeared to have been constructed from hand-hewn logs. What he hadn't said was how charming it was. Trees surrounded the small home, and a bright red hummingbird feeder hung from a pole. She noticed the numbers next to the front door were painted on colorful Mexican tiles. A small grotto accented with wildflowers, including columbines, stood to the right of the home. A statue of the Virgin Mary was on the rock, her hands spread as if in welcome.

He turned off the vehicle's engine but left the keys in the ignition. "Stay in the truck," he told her, "until one of us comes for you."

She nodded and released the latch to the safety belt. He reached into the back, and Eureka growled again.

"Who the hell taught him to do that?"

"His previous owners had a poodle that thought he owned the world. He terrorized their Rottweiler."

"No one could have taught it to say thanks? Maybe to purr? Or being wild here, to act like a bird?"

"Trace?" Turning to face him in the fading daylight, she ran a finger down his jawline. "Since you're the Dom, and I'm just a sub…"

"Why do I feel like I'm being set up?"

"Can you give me suggestions on how to shut you up? You know, respectfully…? I'm just asking because you can just shove your cock in my mouth to make me be quiet. And since you're the Dom, you can do it anytime you want." Boldly she grabbed his cock and gave it a squeeze, mindless of the other people around, maybe partially because the other people *were* around.

"For future reference, that'll work." He closed his hand over hers. "Stay here," he repeated before getting out of the car.

She would definitely do that again, she decided. She liked how responsive he was. The thought that she might have some power over him intoxicated her.

"Get up. Get up," Eureka said.

"Five minutes," she told him.

The three male Hawkeye agents went around the back of the cabin in opposite directions before heading into the woods. Trace went inside while Mallory stayed on the porch. That five people were charged with keeping her and her piece of the project safe was sobering.

Within thirty seconds, Aimee saw Mallory flash a thumbs-up. Thank goodness. Eureka wasn't the only one tired of the trip. She needed to stretch her legs, and food would be good too. The operative jogged over to the vehicle. Aimee opened her door while Mallory opened the back. "I'd like to get you inside as quickly as possible."

Mallory stayed close as Aimee grabbed the birdcage.

"I'll get everything else," the other woman said, staying behind Aimee, making sure she wasn't exposed.

She carried Eureka inside, aware of Mallory behind her every step. "Where do you want me to put him?" she asked Trace. "And don't even dare consider saying the first thing that came to mind."

Mallory laughed, then turned her laugh into a polite cough and headed back outside.

He grinned.

For a few brief seconds, he appeared younger, more carefree. She wondered how things might have turned out if they'd met under different circumstances. Would they have even been attracted to one another? Or would it have been just as incendiary? Would it have been as intense without the element of threat? Or would it have been even better because they had time to explore each other?

"The bookcase," he said, coming over to clear games and magazines from the top. "I'll be back in less than fifteen minutes, twenty, tops," he said.

Mallory brought in the rest of the luggage. "All of it in one bedroom?" she asked Trace.

He and Aimee exchanged a glance.

"One bedroom," he said.

So he didn't care who knew they were sleeping together. Absently she wondered if Hawkeye headquarters had posted a side bet about how long it would be before they were sleeping together.

"Please stay inside," he said.

She nodded.

Trace set up her notebook computer on the kitchen table and grabbed an extension cord from a drawer.

She uncovered the cage, and Eureka said, "Good morning, Aimee."

"I'm afraid your schedule is really off."

"His schedule isn't the only thing about him that's off," Trace said on his way out the door.

She refilled Eureka's water and cut up some fruit, but she left him in the cage, giving him time to adapt to the surroundings. As she powered up her computer, she was very much aware of the murmur of voices outside, with Trace's being the dominant one.

He was right about his family's cabin not being grand, but he hadn't mentioned that it was cozy. Even though there was a deer head mounted on one wall, and some sort of fur on the floor in front of the wood-burning fireplace, there were plenty of female touches, from the dried flowers in a brass water pitcher to the bright serape thrown over the arm of the couch. A colorful bowl sat on the kitchen counter, and a few family photos hung on one wall, between the door and a picture window. Some of the shots looked as if they'd hung from their places of honor for years, and the frames were mainly wooden, in bright primary colors, although a couple were constructed from hammered tin.

She wandered over for a closer look.

One appeared somewhat recent and had been taken outside the cabin. Trace stood next to an older couple. Maybe his parents? The man's arm was across the woman's shoulder, and they were both smiling. Trace had his arm around the shoulder of another woman, who was trying to juggle a small child on her hip.

"Three generations," Trace said, coming in. "My parents, my sister, and her oldest, Ricardo."

"Oldest?"

"She has another on the way, thanks be to God. Keeps Madre busy so she doesn't focus on my failure to provide her with a grandchild."

"You spend a lot of time with your parents?"

"As much as I can. Mi madre, I think she'd like you. She likes independent women."

She grinned. But before she could continue the conversation, he grabbed her. He slammed the front door shut, locked it, and had her arms above her head, his body pinning hers, before she could draw a breath.

He kept her imprisoned with one hand and with the power of his gaze. "You played with fire, baby girl, telling me you weren't wearing any panties…"

Now she couldn't breathe, didn't want to.

The man was masterful, and she wanted to be taken by him.

Keeping her gaze captive, he unfastened her jeans, working the zipper with impatience until its teeth surrendered the same way she did.

He dragged the material down past her thighs, and she wiggled until they fell to the floor. She did a little dance to toe her shoes off; then she kicked her pants aside.

He grabbed a condom from his pocket. "Hold this with

your teeth," he told her.

She dutifully opened her mouth and held the package with her teeth.

As he lowered his jeans, she realized how turned on he was, how hard his cock was. His breathing was as shallow as hers. "You asked how to shut me up," he said. "Fucking you ragged always short-circuits my brain."

She continued to hold the condom steady with her teeth, and he used that as leverage to rip open the package.

"Do you feel how hard I am for your sweet cunt?"

Her knees weakened.

"I want my cock in your pussy."

Since she couldn't speak, she nodded.

Somehow he managed to unroll the condom on his shaft, and then he took the packet from her teeth and dropped the empty wrapper on the floor. "Are you wet?" But he didn't wait for an answer; instead he reached his free hand between her legs. "You are," he said approvingly. "Very wet."

He gently pinched her clit, and she could have exploded right there.

"Very wet," he repeated.

She was grateful that he was strong enough to support her entire weight.

He nudged her pussy with his cockhead.

"Where do you want me?"

"Inside me," she managed, drowning in his eyes.

"Where? Where do you want me?"

"My pussy," she said. "I want you in my pussy."

He entered her about an inch, and then he pulled back again.

"Please," she said.

"Where do you want me?" he asked a final time.

Softly she said, "My cunt."

He smiled. "Open your mouth."

She felt dizzy.

"I always want your mouth open," he said.

She parted her lips slightly, and he slid his tongue inside her mouth at the same moment he bent his knees so he could thrust upward, entering her pussy with a single, powerful stroke.

Thoroughly dominated by him, she came instantly.

He continued to move his hips and simultaneously ravage her mouth.

This was so base. Both of them were still mostly dressed. Daylight radiated through the windows as they had raw sex spiced by danger with no promise of tomorrow.

She came a second time, her cry swallowed by his relentless kiss. She was still riding her own orgasm when she felt his cock harden even more.

He took two more long, powerful strokes, driving deep into her, burying himself before finally climaxing.

Her body shook and trembled. "Yes," she whispered when he ended the kiss. "I liked that," she confessed.

"Good." He dug his hand into her hair, keeping her head imprisoned as they looked at each other.

She could get lost in the rich depths of his eyes. God help her, she had it for him, bad. She might be seizing the moment, but she didn't want the moment to end.

"Later," he said, "I'm going to do it to your ass."

Chapter Eight

With other women, other subs, he'd had some restraint. With her...none. He wanted her. He wanted her again and again, from the front, from behind. He wanted to be in her mouth, wanted his tongue on her pussy. He wanted her bent over, tied up, outside, pinned to a tree. He couldn't get enough.

He had a job to do, and he wasn't besotted enough to ignore it or the danger. He'd keep her safe, no matter what.

But damn, thoughts of her were never far from his mind. And where his thoughts went, his libido followed.

He turned a knife on its side to smash a clove of garlic; then he glanced over his shoulder at her.

She hadn't left the kitchen table in a couple of hours. Daylight had faded, and he'd turned on a lamp; she hadn't acknowledged him or the fact it had been getting dark.

She sipped on a glass of water, and occasionally she shifted positions. Once he saw her with her bare feet pulled up onto the chair as she leaned forward. She was flexible, but he'd already found that out, and he definitely appreciated how limber she was.

Several times she'd muttered, and at first, he thought she might be talking to him, but she actually seemed to have no idea he was within a hundred miles. He caught her nibbling her lower lip, and a few times he'd seen her with a pencil behind her ear. She was focused on what she did, and even her damn loro was being quiet for a change.

He'd spent the majority of the afternoon outside with the other Hawkeye operatives, checking out the rented cabin, establishing a perimeter, assigning duties and responsibilities, making sure Riley got some rest. He'd been on duty all night. In typical Riley fashion, he'd volunteered for the extra duty, but Trace wanted the man fresh.

Chances were good nothing would happen. No one had harmed her when they had the opportunity yesterday. But Hawkeye, Inc. wasn't the best in the world by leaving anything to chance. Until the person who'd killed Jason was in custody—or dead, Trace's personal choice—Aimee Inamorata was his responsibility. He'd never lost a client, and he'd see someone in hell before losing her.

When he'd returned to the cabin, she hadn't even seemed to notice. He'd slipped his radio onto the counter and hung up his jacket before she even noticed he was there.

He growled protectively. The woman needed someone to watch over her, as oblivious as she was to the world.

He'd started cooking, and she'd only glanced over her shoulder once. She'd smiled, and the slight intimacy had caught him off guard. The fact she didn't comment on his gun was a step in the right direction as well.

Trace threw himself into slicing and dicing, needing to do something to burn off some energy. He sautéed onions and artichokes in some olive oil. As a finishing touch, he added in some garlic. Ingredients had to be tossed in the pan in the correct order, well, in his mind anyway. The truth was, it probably didn't matter. By the time he added enough cream and cheese, anything tasted pretty good. He turned on a burner beneath a pan of water and uncorked a bottle of Chianti. Getting closer.

"Bingo," she said.

"Bingo?"

She blew out a breath and tipped back her head. That exposed her neck, and if he didn't have one hand wrapped around a skillet, he might have been tempted to cross the room and lick the column of her throat.

"That might have done it. Only one way to find out."

"How's that?" He gently shook the pan, not only so the garlic didn't burn, but he needed the distraction. It had been what, two, maybe three hours since he'd had her against the door.

"I'm going to upload my code to the project coordinator so they can run it in the field."

"What have you been working on?"

"Debugging... Remember I told you about the mosquito and the chip? My piece of the puzzle is the code that makes the actual stinger penetrate the skin, so the chip can be injected. Sometimes the stinger was jamming, and there didn't seem to be a reason for it."

"But you might have solved the problem?"

"They'll probably run it all night to see if it fails. It's always possible, more than possible, that I solved one problem, but more may exist."

"The scope of it seems unbelievable."

"It is. Even I can't believe it. I really didn't think I had the skill set to work on this, and without other people to bounce ideas off, I probably wouldn't have. Jason, he was one of the best."

He heard her voice choke up, but she continued. "He was a prodigy, hacking into computers before he was ten, and not always for altruistic purposes. By fourteen, he was writing games. He had one of those unique minds. He's a big loss to the world, not just to Hawkeye." She pushed her chair back from the table, and her bird squawked.

"There are dozens of us working on various pieces of the

project; not everyone works at the same time. Most of us have other things we're also developing. Like I mentioned last night, some are hardware people, since we had to fabricate the individual parts and make them all work together."

She gave Eureka another piece of fruit. He ate more often than they did. "Something smells good"—she crossed the room, came up behind him, and slid her arms around his waist—"and I'm not talking about dinner." She slipped her hand down the back of his pants and squeezed his butt cheek. "I'm a little sore, but I want you again."

He could get used to this. She was good company, a quick study, and she matched his voracious sexual appetite.

"How hungry are you?" she asked.

"Wanted to make sure you kept up your energy."

"Will dinner be ruined if you finish cooking it later?"

In way of answer, he switched off the burners. He turned the tables on her, capturing her by the waist and swinging her onto the countertop. She squealed and ended up laughing; the bird freaked out, calling, "Bombs away!"

Half-panicked, he glanced over, but the bird was still confined to his cage. Not a bad place for him to be all the time, in Trace's opinion. "Put your legs around my waist."

She did, and he jostled her from the counter and completely into his arms.

"You can't carry me!"

"Yeah?"

She grabbed his shoulders, still laughing as he walked toward the bedroom. He tipped her unceremoniously onto the mattress, and she scrambled to her knees, facing him. She crawled toward him, reaching for his fly. "Dom? Sub? New concept for you, I know."

His implied threat did nothing to frighten her or put her in her submissive place. She even had the nerve to look up at him as she unbuttoned him and slid down the zipper.

"Just doing what you want, Master," she said saucily, "anticipating your orders, your needs. Just trying to be a very good sub."

Any better, she'd be the death of him. "Get off the bed."

She froze. She'd heard the change in his tone, and she respected it. Impossibly, his cock got even harder.

She dropped her hands and moved about until she stood on the floor near him.

"Strip."

She glanced up at him before quickly looking away again. He noticed that her hands shook as she pulled her shirt over her head.

Next came her jeans. She hadn't put shoes after they'd had sex earlier. Saved him some time. "On your knees," he told her as he finished undressing. "Now suck my cock." Cum already leaked from the slit, and she licked it off.

She cupped his balls with one hand, and she closed the other around his shaft, squeezing firmly. Yeah, definitely a quick study. It'd take her about twenty seconds to send him from where he was into an orgasm. Shouldn't be possible, he told himself, not after all the ejaculations he'd had in the last two days. He put a hand in her hair and drew her back. "Bend over the bed."

He helped her up and moved her into the position he wanted her, with her body wide open, exposed to him, for him. He left her long enough to find the lube. He'd taken her toys at her house, and he grabbed the nipple clamps in his bag. He held them up in front of her.

"Uhm…"

He recognized her tone, and it excited him. Her voice betrayed anticipation wrapped in nerves. She might want to panic, but she was resolved to trust him instead. Intoxicating stuff, trust. Better than the abandoned Chianti. "Play with your nipples," he said. "Make them hard."

"I'm feeling a little embarrassed," she admitted.

And more than a little aroused, he wanted to say in return. He could smell her from here. Every time he pushed her boundaries and she obeyed, he fell a little deeper for her.

He opened one of the clover clamps and tested its bite on his pinkie. Nasty little thing. He smiled.

He took his time getting the bottle of lube. He liked watching her squirm and writhe on the bed as she followed his orders. Her hips swayed enticingly. She might be embarrassed, but she put that aside to give him the show he wanted. "Keep it up," he told her.

Her torso was pressed into the bedcovers, and he moved in beside her. He maneuvered his hand beneath her to squeeze her right breast.

She made a gentle mewing sound, but she didn't protest. In fact, she moved just a bit so he could have better access to her body. He pinched her nipple and kept tightening the grip until she gasped. Her breaths were ragged little bursts, and he imagined the pain ricocheted through her.

He released her pebble-hard nipple; then, when she inhaled sharply, he affixed the first clamp.

"Crap!"

"Does that hurt?"

"It's awful!"

He reached between her legs and found her wetter than before. "Uh-huh."

"Trace, please…"

He slid a finger through her slick folds. She pushed back against him. "Please, what?"

"I'm turned on!"

"That was the idea," he said. He reached beneath her to plump her other breast and torment her nipple mercilessly. She squirmed, but she never tried to escape. "You're a perfect submissive, Aimee." He clamped the other nipple, and she yelped.

"I've never been so turned on," she said, dragging in air.

He tugged gently on the chain that connected the clamps.

"Damn it!"

"You may not come," he told her.

"Trace! I... Please..."

He pulled on the chain again. "I want you to keep still."

She inhaled sharply several times, obviously fighting for self-control. Educating her in his evil ways was its own reward.

She was completely hot for him, and she fought each of her own impulses in order to give him what he wanted. He could keep her like this forever.

He drew some of her moisture backward and pushed a finger against her rear entrance. She swayed, but she didn't try to break out of position. In fact, she moaned in encouragement. "More?" he asked.

"More. Please."

He inserted his finger the rest of the way, and she exhaled softly. He gently finger fucked her ass, stretching her with each small thrust.

"More," she whispered again.

He withdrew his finger, then flipped open the top to the lubricant. He squirted a huge dollop into his left palm before discarding the bottle. "I want you to talk to me," he said. "Tell me what you're feeling, if it's too much. I won't stop, not unless you use your safe word. But like I told you, it's my intention that you never have the need for it."

"Trace...? Master...? Shut up and fuck me already."

He slapped her ass, halfheartedly, but the action obviously caused her clamped tits to rub against the mattress, and she squirmed.

He sheathed his cock in a condom and lubed his finger. He wiped his hands on some nearby tissues. "I love seeing your entire cunt and ass exposed like this," he said. "I love the fact your pussy is already dripping." He played with her clit before inserting his finger in her ass again.

When he drew it out, he added a second and slipped them in together. She pushed back against him the way he'd instructed her.

"It is harder," she said.

He bent so he could lick her pussy. She moaned and shifted, opening herself more. "So beautiful," he told her.

He stroked, licked, and finger fucked until she was on her tiptoes, with her fingers digging into the bedsheets. She was panting his name, or some blend of Trace and Master that made it one word.

He placed his cock against the entrance of her ass. "Keep breathing," he told her. "Bear down like you're trying to push me out."

"Ow!"

He kept moving forward slowly, but when she said, "Hurts!" he pulled back and then thrust forward slowly.

Eureka shrieked.

He wondered if they made miniature bird gags.

Trace worked it, and her, using all his restraint. He wanted to be buried deep, wanted to fuck her with all the intensity that clawed at him.

"Bromine," she whispered. He recognized her technique to distract herself. That she was trying so hard to please him made his pulse pound.

She could use her safe word at any time, but she hadn't.

"Almost there," he promised her, burying himself a bit deeper with each motion.

"Where? Hell? Have I been really, really bad?"

"Oh yeah," he told her, leaning over to whisper in her ear. "Really, really, really bad. So bad you're good." He reached beneath her and gave the chain a brutal tug, and at the same time she arched and cried out, he sank his cock home.

She clawed at the bedding. "Damn it! Damn you!"

"*Bueno*," he muttered. He gritted his teeth momentarily. He could come in less than three seconds if he weren't careful. "Muy bueno."

"For one of us!"

"So tight. So hot." He released the chain he'd tugged on, and instead he stroked her clit, fingered her cunt.

"Trace..."

"*Mi amor?*"

"Please tell me your cock is all the way in." Her words were shaky. "Please."

"You're all the way there." There was a sheen of sweat on her back that showed her struggle. Her pussy wasn't as wet as it had been, and he wanted this to be good for her, really, really good.

He moved inside her, a little at a time, but as he did, rocking back and forth, he kept up the pressure on her pussy, increasing it, decreasing it.

After a few seconds, she began to respond, no longer fighting, and not just cooperating but participating.

"Uhm..."

"Yeah...?"

Since she was facedown, her words were muffled, but he understood her perfectly. "I might like this."

"You might?"

"I might."

"How will you know for sure?" He stroked her clit with short, frantic motions. Her hips bucked beneath him; he rode her hard. He tucked an arm beneath her belly, giving her support, tilting her pelvis so he could go even deeper.

"I…"

She shuddered in a way that signaled that her orgasm was gathering. Trace knew he shouldn't feel pride, he should just be happy she was going to get off. But for fuck's sake, he was proud of her, of the way they fit together, of her trust in him. Maybe pride came before the fall, but so be it. He liked being the one to introduce her to BDSM, liked being the one to turn her over his knee for her first spanking, and he sure as hell liked having his dick up her ass. And he'd better be the last.

"Can I come?" she asked.

She wouldn't be able to stop it if he kept up what he was doing…

"Trace! *I need…* Please!"

Without his permission, she climaxed. He felt the clench of her muscles, smelled her heat. This woman was hot…and *she was his.* He came deep inside her, showing her just how much she belonged to him.

* * *

"Duty calls," he said.

Aimee yawned and stretched beside him. "Can't we just stay in bed for the next ten days or so?"

"Much as I'd like to…" He kissed her on the forehead and

then climbed from the bed. Aimee gathered the sheet around her. After he'd sexed her up, he'd removed her clamps and held her tight against him while she dozed. But she'd already learned there was no such thing as Trace just drifting off to sleep. No matter how intense the session, he'd still leave her in bed to check things out.

"Besides, dinner awaits."

On cue, her stomach growled.

He laughed. "No, I'm not bringing you dinner in bed."

"Spoilsport."

He went into the bathroom and returned with a damp washcloth to clean her up. She rolled over onto her back and shamelessly spread her legs. He took his time, probably more time than he needed to. "You spoil me."

"Get used to it."

She'd like to, but they both knew this was fleeting. She had her work, he had his. Hawkeye kept him on the move. She was a job. Sexually, even though they connected well, she knew she was just another woman in the line of his subs. Still, she was glad for the experience. She looked at him and dug her hands into his hair, holding him close. This time she kissed him deeply and demandingly, moving her tongue until he took charge. Then she opened for him, trying to communicate everything she couldn't say with words.

She watched him pull on his jeans and shirt and put socks and shoes back on. That damned gun was never far from sight either. "Do you ever go barefoot?"

"Never when I'm on duty, rarely when I'm off."

Things he took as matter-of-fact never even crossed her mind.

"Twenty minutes," he told her.

She didn't hurry, enjoying the sounds of him moving

around the kitchen. Muted light spilled into the room, and the evening held the barest hint of an upcoming fall chill. If she closed her eyes and pretended, as long as he was with her, everything was right with the world.

Savory scents finally roused her. She pulled on her discarded clothes. "Good morning, Aimee!" Eureka said when she came out of the bedroom.

"Poor thing will never get it straight," she said, gathering her computer and books and moving them into the living room.

Trace might have repeated, "Poor thing," mockingly, but since she couldn't be sure, she ignored him.

"Point me in the direction of wineglasses and silverware."

"Wineglasses and plates are in that cupboard." He pointed the tip of a wicked-looking knife toward the corner.

"Do you have a license to use that thing?" she asked.

"What, this?" He tossed the knife in the air, then caught it.

"As much sex as you've had, you'd think your testosterone level wouldn't be quite so high."

"It's all about balance."

Men. She poured them each a glass of wine; he left his untouched beside him as he dumped pasta into the boiling water and added a pinch of salt.

She finished setting the table, and he brought over the food He even generously put a fresh slice of orange in Eureka's cage.

"Tastes like chicken," the bird said, walking across his perch, away from the fruit.

She laughed, even though she tried hard not to. "You really are a talented man," she said as the tastes of the artichokes and garlic combined with cheese and cream melded on her tongue. "This is the second best thing I've had in my mouth today."

"Aimee," he warned, his hand pausing midway to his mouth.

"Just sayin'," she said. Trying to appear innocent, she took another bite of the pasta. "And just wondering when you're going to tie me up."

"Insatiable."

"You're kind of like Frankenstein's creator. You thought you knew what you were doing."

"I know exactly what I'm doing...keeping you wet and horny works well for me."

No matter what she said, he always had the ability to take it one step further and make her even more turned on.

After dinner, she saw him glance repeatedly at the door. "I'll do the dishes while you go play secret agent man."

"That's generous."

"Not really. I want you in bed with me. If we work together, that'll happen faster."

He put on his holster and slid his GLOCK into it. It was hard to imagine any danger out here in the remoteness of the Rockies. But she knew that's the kind of man he was, a protector, from a long line of protectors.

She let Eureka out of his cage to explore his new surroundings while she did the dishes. Since she'd had him, he'd never been out of her house, so she wasn't sure exactly how he'd behave. He perched on top of the cage, not venturing far.

Trace was gone a long time, and she kept glancing at the door. She was contemplating a second glass of wine when he returned. "All quiet on the western front?"

"Everything checks out."

"But...?"

He shrugged. "I don't know. Something..."

"Intuition?"

"Gut," he said. "Something doesn't add up. But I don't

know what."

She leaned her backside against the sink. She hadn't seen him like this before. A frown furrowed his brow, and he crossed through the cabin, straight for the phone. He didn't glance her way. "Trace?"

"Log on to your computer. See if there's anything new."

She grabbed the notebook from the coffee table in the living room and powered it up. Her heart was pounding, and she figured it was somewhere around 70 percent of her target heart rate, definitely aerobic. She kept glancing over at Trace. He was a study in restraint, from the economy of his motions to the way he held his body, the phone tucked between his ear and shoulder so his right hand was free. "You're making me nervous," she said.

"Romero," he said.

She eavesdropped, not making a pretense of ignoring his conversation, since it was presumably with her sister.

"Nothing," he said, just as cryptically as he had been with her when she asked him a question. He listened for a moment, then said, "Any leads?" He listened for a few more moments, then said good-bye.

"Talk to me, Trace," she said, crossing to him. "There's nothing online, except tributes to Jason and wild speculation— it was burglars, it was a random thing, it was suicide, it was one of his friends who wanted to get his hands on the technology, terrorists, everything except aliens from Area 51."

He leaned against the counter where she'd been only minutes before. He steepled his hands and drummed his forefingers together. "Do you mind making coffee? A full pot?"

"We going to be up all night?"

He looked at her. "*You're* not. I'm going to gather the team for a strategy session."

"Here?"

"Yeah. I'd rather keep you here than drag you with me to the other cabin, and I'm not leaving you alone."

Even after the break-in at her house, she hadn't been terribly concerned, but now, her heart rate wouldn't slow, even though she practiced some yoga breathing. She made the coffee while he headed back outside.

Five minutes later, he was back, smelling of the cool evening air and with a determined set to his jaw. Thirty seconds or so later, the rest of the team showed up.

"Where's Riley?"

"Finishing a perimeter sweep," said Mallory. "Top of the hour."

Trace nodded. "I'll perform the introductions. Aimee Inamorata," he said. She smiled, and she wondered if it looked as stiff as it felt to her. "Agents Laurents and Barstow. You know Bree Mallory."

Both of the men nodded, but she'd never keep them straight. They were dressed alike, much like Trace. They both had on long-sleeved black shirts, black pants, and boots, and they wore no personal items. They were both within an inch heightwise, with dark hair, brown eyes, and athletic builds.

"Is there an assignment sheet for overnight duty?" Trace asked, dragging a chair back across the scarred floor and taking a seat.

Everyone else relaxed at that, and everyone else sat. Aimee, though, carried the coffee carafe and stout mugs to the table. She'd seen him interact with her, but to watch him in command of a crew was an entirely different thing. She understood him better. There was no way he couldn't not lead, dominate, in a relationship. It was who he was. Command came effortlessly; giving it up would be what took work.

"We drew straws, three-hour shifts."

"I'm first," Mallory said. "Nine p.m. to midnight."

"Midnight to three," one of the other men said.

"I come on at six. But everyone will be getting up around that time."

"Leaves Riley with three to six."

"Short straw," Mallory said.

"Give me the drill," Trace said, pouring the first cup of coffee for himself.

"We all have radios," Mallory said, "and beginning at nine, we're doing half-hour perimeter sweeps. We'll report anything suspicious."

"No matter the time," he clarified.

"Yes, sir."

Feeling more than a little useless, Aimee carried creamer and sugar, along with a couple of spoons, to the table.

There was a knock on the front door, and all the agents exchanged glances. Trace nodded in Mallory's direction; the woman headed across the cabin. Trace and the other agents stood, and Trace moved closer to her. She wanted to scream with frustration. This was not happening. She was a nerd, a college professor, single woman who wrote books about ethics, not someone who needed the country's best and brightest protecting her.

She suddenly understood the application of her mosquito even better. She now had sympathy for the people who might have a chip shot under their skin. Being in protective custody sucked. She wanted to insist she didn't need a handful of operatives around. She just needed to be alone, at her own house. For the first time in her life, she wanted to crawl out of her own skin.

Trace held up three fingers, and he ticked them down one at a time. When all his fingers formed a fist, Mallory pulled the door wide.

The group exhaled in unison when the man at the door entered the room.

"Riley," one of the men said.

Mallory closed the door behind him. Eureka chose that moment to freak out. He squawked like a banshee, all feathers and fury as he flew at Riley. He issued no warning before unloading on the man's head.

She stood there for a moment, horrified. "I'm sorry," she said. "Eureka! Return to base!"

Trace looked at her. *I'm sorry*, she mouthed again. "I think the trip disturbed him."

"You think?" Mallory asked, laughing.

Riley glared at Mallory and at the bird.

Aimee headed across the room, trying to capture the frantic bird, but he had no interest in being subdued. Finally, in desperation, she asked Trace to toss her a dish towel. He did, and she threw the towel on top of Eureka, trapping him.

"Good thing you have time for a shower," Trace told Riley.

"Yes, sir."

Everyone seemed fixated on looking at his hair, staring, while at the same time pretending not to notice, until Mallory finally said something. "That's what you'll look like with gray hair, huh?"

"Comedy Channel is having open mic night," he told her.

"Report?" Trace finally said.

"Nothing unusual. Perimeter checks clear."

The meeting continued while she wrestled Eureka back into his cage and covered him up.

The group finished their coffee, then headed outside. Trace joined them on the porch while she cleaned the coffee cups.

A few minutes later, he came back inside. "I'm not sure what came over Eureka. He only acts that way when he feels threatened or if I'm being threatened. Not sure what that was about. He wasn't bothered by any of the other operatives. Maybe it was just too many people."

"And maybe he just has no manners."

"He is only a bird. Not real high on the IQ scale."

"You keep trying to tell me how smart he is." He headed for the phone again. After only ten seconds, he said, "I want full background checks on every member of the detail. And I want to speak with Sara Stein. Find her." Then he hung up and looked at her. "Your loro could have bad manners. He could have a birdbrained IQ."

Chapter Nine

She was as stubborn as the mountains were high. She frustrated him on every level, and he wanted her more and more with every passing minute.

"You can make it an order," she said, "and I'm still not going to bed."

"I want to make it look like we are." He admired her, even though she frustrated him. He saw the fear in her eyes, the uncertainty. He knew she hated this whole thing. Nerds didn't get into trouble, she'd told him. Maybe not, but it had found her. Still, she didn't complain.

Without any more arguments, she went into the bathroom and brushed her teeth. "I'm changing into running clothes," she said.

Since he was not planning to sleep at all, he couldn't argue.

He grabbed his flashlight and radio and then turned off all the overhead lights. He placed everything in the bedroom where he could reach it, waited a few minutes, then turned off the light.

On the bed, he held her tight against him.

"I hate this," she said.

"Don't blame you."

"I like that about you."

"What?"

"What's the saying? You don't try to blow sunshine up my

ass."

"Thank you. I think." He kissed the top of head and waited for the change in his senses. His eyes would adjust to the night; he'd become more attuned to the outdoor sounds.

He was aware of her body against him, holding him but not clinging. And that was a perfect description for her personality; it made her a marvelous sub. She counted on him, depended on him, trusted him, but she didn't need him to define who she was. He'd had a relationship or two fail because of that, but she was solid. Steady.

"You really think I could be in danger."

He thought about lying. But he only thought about it for a moment. If he demanded honesty from her, he owed it in return. "Yeah, I do. Not likely. Possibly. But I won't leave anything to chance where your safety is concerned."

"Riley."

"He shouldn't be here. He was supposed to get off at seven a.m. His partner wasn't there when we rolled...but he was. Doesn't necessarily mean anything." It gnawed at him that Aimee's computer hadn't been taken. Jason's had. Why break in and leave her computer behind? Unless having the woman herself was the goal?

"Eureka might have bad manners," she said.

"Like you said, he didn't attack anyone else. I want you to stay here."

"I'd prefer to go with you."

"I can move through the woods better alone."

"I don't like this," she said.

"You've got your cell phone?"

She nodded against him.

"You've made sure it works?"

She softly said, "Yes."

"Call your sister and update her. All goes well, I'll be back in twenty minutes, after having a chat with our young man."

* * *

Aimee hoped his instincts were just on hyperalert, seeing trouble where none existed. As he went to slide from the bed, she grabbed him. "One kiss?"

"Oh yeah."

He kissed her. Hungrily. Demandingly. Insistently. He bruised her mouth, leaving no doubt how intense his feelings were for her. She drank it as sustenance, needing his reassurance.

She hardly heard him cross the living room, and she doubted she would have known he was gone except for the soft *snick* of the lock being slid home.

Obeying his last order, she called her sister. Following his lead, or maybe his paranoia, she dialed the phone from beneath the blankets so the glow wouldn't be seen.

* * *

Part of him thought he was all kinds of loco. Hawkeye subjected their operatives to the most stringent background checks. They ferreted information every bit as thoroughly as the bureau did. Not surprising, with as many former Feds as they had working for them.

Riley had several commendations. And it wouldn't be at all unusual for the man to volunteer for overtime; in fact, it would be expected. He was an ambitious young man, and Trace had worked with him before, finding his conduct exemplary.

So he was headed for the agents' cabin wearing night-vision goggles, moving counterclockwise, *all because of a feathered freak he considered a fucktard?*

* * *

"Nothing?" Aimee repeated.

"Nothing at all," her sister affirmed.

"That's good news, isn't it?"

"Most likely. You're telling me he went out into the woods because Eureka dropped a bomb on Agent Riley? Seriously?"

"Seriously," Aimee said, laughing a little.

"Keep me posted. And when Trace comes back, tell him we have a call in to Sara Stein. We're sending someone to her house as well. Tell him we're also checking why the relief guy didn't show up this morning."

* * *

He'd spent too many years as a hunter not to recognize that faintly metallic smell on the night air. He froze, backed up, got his bearings, and moved cautiously.

The scent got stronger and stronger as he moved farther away from the cabin.

Then he saw her. Bree Mallory was lying on the fucking ground in a pool of blood; it was a miracle she hadn't already bled out.

Shit.

He fell to his knees.

The bastard had slit her throat.

"Tried," she whispered. "Tried… Stop him."

"Riley?"

She whispered, "Yes."

He calculated his options. He didn't want to leave her,

didn't want to leave Aimee alone. If he keyed his radio, he would alert Riley. If he didn't, no one else would know, and there'd be no backup.

"Go," she whispered.

He would never, as long as he lived, forget the gurgling sound when she tried to speak. "Fucking hang in there, Mallory." He grabbed a kerchief from his back pocket to help stanch the blood flow, and he propped her up. He keyed the radio once. If the other guys were paying attention, it would be enough. Regardless, it was a good guess Riley knew the jig was up.

Goddamn bastard was going to pay.

* * *

She heard a faint sound outside. It could be anything, she knew. From the wind, to an animal, to Trace returning. But when Eureka growled, she knew it was none of those. She moved into the kitchen, keeping her back to the counter. Silently she moved toward the dish drain and grabbed the vicious-looking knife she'd seen Trace use earlier. Then, as silently as she could, she moved to the closet in the back bedroom.

It took half a dozen tries, but the front door finally gave way in a barrage of splinters.

Frantically she pushed redial on her phone, trying to connect with her sister.

"I don't want you dead," Riley said.

Good thing, because she had no intention of ending up dead.

"Let's do this peaceably. No one will get hurt."

"*Aimee?*"

She prayed her sister was smart enough to figure out what

was going on when she didn't say anything. It was her big sister's job to be smart, thinking things through where others didn't.

The landline rang, and Aimee stayed where she was. *Keep thinking, Sis.*

Her hands felt slick and inept curved around the hilt of the knife. She glanced at the phone on the floor. The line was still open, which meant her sister hadn't hung up.

The unmistakable sound of boots on the wooden floor made her mouth dry.

The phone rang a second, then third time.

Her breath was strangling her. Way past aerobic zone and into anaerobic. She tried to suck in a breath and steady her nerves.

She hoped he saw her computer on the coffee table. Since she'd downloaded her work, Hawkeye, Inc., already had her revisions. Her computer wouldn't be much use to him now.

"Come out, come out, wherever you are."

Was he certifiable?

Eureka growled.

"You shut the fuck up!"

She clamped a hand over her mouth. If he hurt her stupid bird...

The phone rang a fourth time, then settled into interminable silence.

Why didn't he just take the computer and go?

"I want you, Aimee. Only you. You're more valuable than anything, don't you get it? Just come out, and no one else will get hurt. You can save them all. I promise I won't slit your throat like I did that other little bitch's. But it's up to you. If you don't want to come out and play, I'll just wait here for big, bad Romero. I'll shoot his ass while you watch. It'll be on your head. You want to save him, don't you?"

Trace had only ever asked for one thing from her: trust. At the time, she'd had no idea what that would entail. But he was assigned to cover her ass, and she knew he'd do it, and she had to believe that—oh yeah, and keep herself alive long enough for that to happen. If she gave herself up, he'd be beyond pissed. She almost laughed. Who'd have thought she'd be more concerned with Trace being pissed than facing a madman with a gun.

The longer this dragged on, the better. Between her sister and Trace, the cavalry was on its way. She had to believe that.

Light flooded the master bedroom.

She squeezed her eyes shut. She'd had no idea that panic could so completely consume her brain, shutting down the circuits. She wasn't operating from her higher brain any longer, but from the animalistic part that demanded she survive.

She heard his every move, the scrape of his shoes on the floor, crashes as he upended things and threw them.

Then there was silence, followed by the chill of his laughter as he ripped down what had to be the shower curtain and rod.

"You're running out of places, Aimee, and I'm getting a little mad at you. You don't want me to be mad, do you?"

Cadmium, she told herself. Surely, somewhere in her brain, she remembered something she could focus on. *Cesium*. Something to keep the blinding panic from consuming her. *Californium…*

There was a squawk of his radio, and he said, "Oops. They're on to us. We don't have much time. Let's go see your sister."

Then she understood. It wasn't about her. She was a means to an end. If he could get that far, he could get to Hawkeye himself.

He was telling the truth when he said he wanted her alive. He wanted her as a hostage.

Her breaths were shallow, hollow, when he flipped the switch for the back bedroom. Every instinct urged her to run.

"Are you under the bed, Aimee?"

She hated the way he used her name, implying there was an intimacy between them. Her skin suddenly felt like spiders crawled over her.

He was moving closer, she heard him, the sound dragging down her spine. She saw him; as hidden as she was, he couldn't see her, yet...

She swallowed convulsively when the barrel of his gun entered the closet; then, with the gun pointing in, he ripped back the door.

Scared senseless by the suddenness of the motion, she screamed and lashed out, stabbing him, focusing on his arm. She stabbed him, over and over, slashing and gouging, not caring about anything except getting that gun out of his hand.

"Bitch!" he screamed, reaching in, grabbing her hair, and slamming her head into the wall.

* * *

A scream tore across the night.

Not just a scream. A scream from *his woman.*

Consumed with fury, Trace shoved the door of the cabin.

He bit off a curse. All bets were off. Daniel Riley was a dead man.

Then he smelled it. Sulfur. The goddamn son of a bitch was going to try to burn them all to hell.

Gun drawn, he moved quickly through the cabin to the back bedroom.

The sight astounded him.

Riley was on his knees, trying to light the oil from a smashed kerosene lamp. Aimee had her body wrapped around his ankle, pulling on him for all she was worth. Blood pulsed from his arm, and blood streamed from her temple.

"Freeze," Trace said.

Riley looked up and smiled, and he dropped the lit match.

Trace reacted. He grabbed Aimee from the floor. Instinctively she turned herself into his body. It was then that he realized the fucking traitor had doused her with the oil as well.

Fighting his fury, Trace headed for the living room and grabbed the stupid bird's cage on the way out the door.

Laurents and Barstow were thrashing through the woods, ripping off their night–vision goggles when they got closer.

"What the fuck?" Laurents asked.

"Riley's in there."

"Goddamn. It's your cabin, sir."

"I've got the only two things that matter. He cut up Mallory, left her in the woods. Counterclockwise on the perimeter." He nodded at Barstow. "Go."

Laurents moved the vehicles, and after he popped open the back of the Suburban, Trace said, "Go after Mallory." Trace placed Aimee in the back of the Suburban, and he grabbed a blanket to wrap her in. Her eyes were wide, and she stared at him, her eyes unfocused. "Got your damn bird," he told her, struggling to suppress his own emotion.

"Aimee! Aimee!"

He pulled the cover off the birdcage so the loro could see her. For once he sympathized with the flying freak.

"I'm good," she told them both. "Really. I just keep seeing his blood. I…I stabbed him."

He had no words. She'd done the only thing she could, and he was proud of her. But she needed to sort this out in her own mind, make sense of it any way she could. It could take time, he knew, and lots of it.

He smoothed back her hair, and his hand came away covered in her blood.

No matter how long it took her to recover emotionally, it would probably take him longer.

Within minutes, the sound of sirens pierced the night.

"You know," she said, attempting a smile, "this time, I'm glad the cavalry is here."

* * *

Trace had no idea how Ms. Inamorata arrived so quickly, but even from the company jet, she'd been solving problems. Mallory was still alive, and she might make it, thanks to the helicopter Inamorata procured.

Inamorata crossed over to him first, and she looked as perfect as ever, not a single hair out of place, makeup perfectly blended, and she was in her own uniform, a pencil-slim skirt, feminine blouse, and heels. She carried a briefcase, and there was a smaller bag slung over her shoulder. Rue the man who didn't think she kicked ass and took names.

As she moved closer, he saw the betrayal of emotion in her eyes, so like her sister's. Unshakable Inamorata, Hawkeye's right-hand woman, was walking in her own nightmare. She had to know Aimee would have never been dragged into this if it hadn't been for her. Despite that horror, she'd been making things happen, arranging the cleanup, making sure everyone was taken care of.

"Concussion, most likely, according to the doctor you pulled out of bed," he said without being asked. "Nothing more."

She nodded. "Thank you." She looked over her shoulder at the still-smoldering structure, or what remained of it. "You'll get a new cabin."

"My parents will appreciate it. Anything on Sara Stein?"

"We found her."

"And?"

"She's in the hospital. He was a bastard."

"Not mourning the loss," Trace said. He'd been keeping an eye on the cabin to make sure the pissant didn't crawl from the flames. It gave him satisfaction to know Riley would continue to burn in hell.

"Where is my sister?"

"Back of the Suburban...talking to a shrink."

"I'll get you back by her side in less than ten minutes."

"Five, or I make a scene."

"You really care."

"Five minutes, Inamorata."

"Romero..."

"Five minutes."

* * *

"How bad's the headache?"

Aimee grabbed hold of her sister's voice like the lifeline it had always been. She looked up and smiled.

"Family," Inamorata told the counselor, one of their own. "You can have her back tomorrow; tonight, she's ours."

The counselor nodded and left.

"You'll need to be debriefed, all sorts of formalities."

"I kind of figured."

"You'll have as many people to talk to for as long as you want. There's going to be no pressure to return to Hawkeye, I promise you that. And I'm afraid Trace has only given me five minutes with you...something about a scene otherwise."

"He would too."

"This is about you, Little Sis. If you don't want him, he'll be gone."

"I think I like him."

"He's a pervert."

"Turns out, so am I."

The sisters exchanged smiles; then tears swam in Inamorata's eyes. "Jesus, Aimee... I'm sorry."

"You couldn't have known." This was the first time in their lives that she'd been the one to soothe her big sister. They held hands, and Aimee repeated, "You couldn't have known."

"I'm supposed to keep you safe."

"I'm glad I got to be part of stopping him."

Still, she accepted the comfort when her sibling wrapped an arm around her shoulder. They were still like that when Trace rejoined them.

"Scram," he told Inamorata.

"Silver-tongued devil," she said.

"I want the nicest hotel room in Winter Park."

"It's yours. You'll have cell phone service when you hit the town limits. You'll have a text message with directions."

Aimee was stunned, and not just from the blow to the head. Her sister was taking orders from Trace, and she seemed happy to be doing it.

The dynamic astounded her. Her sister had always looked out for her, now she was not so voluntarily abdicating the position.

"Here's a bag of stuff you might need, extra clothes, toiletries. They're my clothes, so they're probably too big, but Trace will take you shopping tomorrow."

"And Hawkeye will pay the bill," he added.

"Of course." She started to walk away; then she stopped and looked back. "Take care of her."

By the time she'd finished the sentence, he'd scooped Aimee into his arms. Aimee laid her head on his shoulder. "I could stay here all night."

"I have other ideas for you, if you're interested in them."

"Do they include us being skin to skin?"

"In the shower, then in the bed. I'm supposed to wake you up a number of times through the night to check on you. Any ideas how I should do that?"

"Maybe one or two."

Epilogue

"Tie me up?"

"Aimee…" The woman had him exactly where she wanted him. When she was naked on her knees in front of him, he could deny her nothing. When she did *that* with her tongue to the tip of his bare cock…

She'd been asking for it for weeks, and he'd been heroic enough to resist her. Until now. That scar on the side of her head still bothered him, and she'd told him, more than once, to get over himself.

"I've been thinking—"

"I hate when you do that." She gave his balls a squeeze that made him catch his breath.

"I want you to bend me over the bed and tie me that way."

The image alone was enough to nearly make him come.

"I want you to fuck me hard."

The rest of her sentence went unfinished. *Like you used to.* They'd argued every day for the first two weeks. She accused him of treating her like porcelain. He hadn't argued back. She was right. And so what of it? He was going to keep her safe and protected, even from him.

She gave his shaft a long, loving lick. "Bend me over, Trace."

"Aimee, I'm warning you."

She looked up at him earnestly. "This isn't working for

me."

His heart stopped. Those were the words he lived in dread of hearing. They'd spent the last three weeks on the Southern California coast in a beach house provided by their employer. Trace had wanted to take her out of the country, but she wouldn't leave Eureka behind.

Except for having the bird with them, the first two weeks had been perfect, with long walks on the beach, hitting all the tourist traps, feeding her at all the restaurants. But the last one had been more volatile. As her strength returned and the nightmares stopped, she wanted their sex life to return to what she called normal.

"I've tried it your way." She sat back on her heels, dropping her hands to her thighs. "I want it to be like it was."

"I nearly fucking lost you." He reached for her, willing her to understand his pain.

"Do it! Do it," she shouted. "Grab my hair."

He sighed and dropped his hand.

"Except for that, everything's perfect."

"So leave it alone, damn it."

"No! Because without that, it's not real. We're not real. You kept asking me to trust you enough to tie me up. Trust yourself. Trust me. Trust me to set the limits, trust me to let you know if I can't do it, trust me to let you know if it hurts. And it won't."

"You were at the hands of a madman."

"And I kicked his ass."

He laughed.

"Well, that's my story, and I'm sticking to it. And I'll kick yours too, if you treat me badly. Don't you get it? That freak wins if he steals what we had."

"You've been seeing a shrink."

"It's not just psychobabble. It's the truth. He had delusions of grandeur. It was only a fluke that I was related to the very important Inamorata and he was assigned to that particular project. But if he steals our relationship…"

"I'm afraid of hurting you."

"If you do, I'll tell you."

"We'll do this my way."

She sighed. "This feels familiar."

"When we return to Denver, it will be with my ring on your finger."

"Wait—"

"My way, Aimee."

"My sister's right. You are a silver-tongued devil. Was that a proposal?"

"No. It was a statement of fact."

"I'm marrying you?"

"Within six months."

"What if I don't want to get married?"

"My way. And to be sure you don't forget it, you'll wear my collar as well."

She was so wet for him, because of him. He'd made her life complete. She couldn't imagine a future without him in it. "Can I, er, pick and choose this dominance stuff?"

"Take it or leave it." He dug his fingers into her hair gently.

She surrendered instantly, turning her head into the cradle of his palm.

"You're the one who doesn't get it, querida. I'm never letting you go. I'm applying for a job at headquarters. I should be home more than I'm gone."

"I want us to live at my house."

"Or something bigger, eventually. For now that's fine."

"And I want to keep Bella."

"I thought we discussed that. I'm the Dom."

"Bella! Bella!"

He glanced over at the two annoying-as-hell parrots. They'd been at the beach a couple of days ago, and there'd been an animal-adoption booth set up as part of a city festival. She'd fallen in love with a parrot that needed a home. The rescue people weren't sure how Bella would do with another parrot, but Aimee had begged all of them to let her give it a try, and what Aimee wanted, she got. He was putty in her hands, and he was afraid she knew it.

They were closing in on the end of the trial period. Now it seemed he'd end up with two of the flying idiots. It confounded him how two parrots could make five times the noise of one.

"Uhm, theoretically Eureka won't be as possessive of me if he has a mate."

"Everything with that loco is theoretical. Idiot that he is, he'll probably think he's in a ménage."

"Isn't the Spanish word for parrot *loro*, not *loco*?"

"Whatever."

"Your cock is hard."

"You're on your knees in front of me." Nothing like pointing out the obvious. All he needed was her within a one-mile radius to get hard.

"Tie me. Fuck me."

He tightened his grip in her hair, and she closed her eyes on a soft sigh.

"Take me…" She looked up at him and licked her lower lips seductively. "Bend me over, *Master*."

"Over that chair, sub. Legs spread, your cunt exposed, your hands gripping the chair legs."

He'd thrown her off balance, he saw. She'd pictured what she wanted, but how badly did she really want what they'd had?

"Yes, Trace," she whispered.

"You may crawl."

She blinked. "Yes, Trace."

His cock hardened even more. She draped herself over the chair as he'd instructed. And now, for both of them, there was one last test. "Point your toes in." She was experienced enough to realize that would just make her presentation that much more erotic. He left her there for long minutes, enjoying the view. She moved her position slightly a couple of times, but she didn't protest or try to stand. He gave her every opportunity to call a halt to this, and all she did was sway her hips seductively.

He moved around her deliberately, using Velcro cuffs to secure her in place.

He dipped a hand between her legs and found her wet for him, wetter than she'd ever been for him.

In the distance, he was aware of the surf; in here, he was aware of the roar of the blood in his ears.

He sheathed his cock with a condom and took her. Hard. Fast. Digging one hand into her hair, supporting her with another, he pounded, pistoning, penetrating deeper and deeper.

"Yes! I want you. Fuck me. Fuck me *harder*. Now."

She was a demanding little sub, and she was all his.

She came without permission, something he'd definitely have to correct, and it was with a scream.

For once, the parrot didn't seem to care.

Within seconds, way ahead of his planned schedule, he groaned loudly as he ejaculated. Satisfied, he slapped her rear as he pulled out. "You made me come too quickly."

"The sub is sorry, Master."

She'd be the death of him.

"Perhaps the Dom would like the sub over his lap for a

spanking later?"

He spanked her flank again, and she stunned him by whispering, "Thank you."

He released the cuffs and carried her to the bed. "Your punishment, mi amor."

She curled up next to him, in the protection of his arms. Together, they looked out at the ocean. "Yes?"

She turned back to him; he focused on the tiny scar, but this time, he saw it was healing, maybe like they were. "You'll get me hard, by whatever means you can think of..."

"Yes, Master."

"So I can fuck you again, up the rear."

"I thought Master would never ask..."

MAKE ME

Chapter One

"Inamorata. Stay."

Wes Lowell snagged her wrist and held her firmly, preventing her from getting out of bed. She looked over her shoulder at him. His dark hair, rumpled from their vigorous sex, fell temptingly across his forehead. His gray eyes were more smoky than usual, which meant he was good for at least one more orgasm.

Her body responded with a flood of pheromones. She wanted him. He was sin and naughtiness rolled into one sexy package.

She straightened her spine and called on all her mental reserves so that she didn't yield to the seductive pressure of his grip on her wrist and crawl back into his arms. "I can't."

"Just tonight."

It was tempting—*he* was tempting. A white sheet covered his lower body, but that meant his oh-so-appealing chest was bare, and she always loved the way that thin strand of dark hair arrowed down, disappearing into his groin.

She stopped herself from touching him. Temptation, she knew, started with a single step. Before long, you were committed, distracted from your work, answering to someone else, and you had to consider their opinions before making big decisions. No. *Definitely not for her.*

And definitely not with Wes Lowell, her friend and lover, sometimes coworker, an alpha male who was her equal professionally, intellectually, sexually.

And that was the real problem. She wanted him every bit as much as she wanted not to want him.

With any other man, she might have relented and given her driver the night off. With anyone else, staying would have meant nothing, and she'd have been able to keep an emotional distance. She'd get up in the morning, have breakfast and coffee, then smile and wave good-bye without looking back or even sparing a second thought for the man she'd slept with.

But Lowell was different. Every time she left his bed, it took hours for her to regain focus. She thought about him, mentally replaying their lovemaking. She'd be reading a report, crunching data, making risk assessments, when a thought of him with his tongue *right there* on her clit would blindside her. Desire would swamp her.

Once, a few months ago, she'd had a moment of weakness. Late at night, restless and alone in her king-size bed, she'd reached for the phone to hear the gorgeously modulated tones of his voice as he whispered her name and told her what he wanted to do to her.

She'd resisted the impulse, but the fact she'd even had the weakness bothered her.

Despite her resolve to be strong, the bed had seemed larger than it ever had. A feeling of loneliness had crept over her, and she'd been aware of every noise in her ridiculously large downtown loft.

For all those reasons and a dozen more, Inamorata had to leave. "I've got a car waiting." She pulled her wrist. "Duty calls."

"Duty? Or are you running away again?"

Because the argument was familiar and way too freaking close to the truth, she gritted her teeth. "It's late."

"Two a.m.," he said. "I'll make sure you're up in time to make it to work."

"Let me go, Wes."

He clenched his jaw and slowly released his grip.

She slipped from the bed and put several feet of safety between them before scooping her lacy black shelf bra from the hardwood floor. Half her clothes had ended up in an untidy pile on the floor, and the other half were strewn across the footboard.

She stood facing him as she did a reverse striptease. She took her time, wanting him to want her.

He propped a pillow behind his back and sat up. He watched her unblinkingly. There wasn't anything about Wes Lowell that wasn't intense, and she'd long ago gotten over the embarrassment of having him study her while she dressed, or undressed for that matter.

She pulled on her matching scrap of a thong and grinned when he gave an appreciative wolf whistle.

"No one would suspect the reserved and conservative Ms. Inamorata would wear that kind of underwear."

"I've never heard you complain."

"You never will."

His voice reminded her of midnight and moonlight. It was dark and rich, and it sent a shiver through her body.

She started rolling a stocking up her leg, aware of the fact he hadn't looked away.

She smoothed the silk into place and was reaching for the second stocking when a loud barking shattered the silence.

Lowell's medium-sized mechanical dog raced into the room and skidded across the newly refinished floor in a cacophony of yelps and nips before crashing into a nightstand.

"Bentley!" Lowell warned. "Behave."

The yipping contraption shook off the mishap and all but danced toward her. The mutt was as lovable as he was accident-prone, and far too many of his characteristics were reminiscent of his builder.

Bentley turned circles, snatched one of her stockings in his mechanical mouth, and then raced for the door.

"Did you pay him to do that?" she asked, stunned by the dog's speed and daring.

"What can I say?" He shrugged. "Bentley doesn't want you to leave either. He gets an extra-long battery charge tonight."

She sighed. Even if she retrieved the stocking, it would be ruined. Thank goodness the bad-mannered mutt hadn't stolen her shoes. Those nasty metal teeth would make the finest designer leather into a chew toy.

She removed the single stocking and rolled it into a ball.

"Sorry," Lowell said.

"Really?" She raised her eyebrows. "I doubt it."

He shrugged.

She stuffed the lone stocking into her purse.

"A little cold tonight to have your legs bare," he said.

"I'll survive." She wriggled into her skirt, then stepped into her high heels. She shrugged into her silk blouse and began buttoning from the bottom.

His gaze never left her.

Finally, reluctantly, she grabbed her leather bomber jacket from the bedpost.

"Let me." He climbed from the bed in all his naked glory. A pillow fell to the floor beside them.

The sight of his body always amazed her, the rugged lines, the masculine sinews. Even though he was a self-proclaimed geek, his body was that of an athlete. He might have a scientific calculator in the nightstand, but he had push-up bars beneath the bed.

His cock was more than halfway hard, jutting toward her, despite the fact he'd come less than five minutes before.

She wished he'd stayed in bed. Right now, leaving was about self-preservation.

He helped her into the jacket and adjusted the lapels.

"Thank you," she whispered, aware of his scent and the way he dominated her space. Breath strangled in her throat.

He secured both of her wrists behind her back with a single hand.

"Lowell…" Her heart raced. She needed to get away.

He exerted pressure, forcing her onto her tiptoes. "Open your mouth."

"Lowell—"

"*Open your mouth.*"

Confused, and more than a bit excited by his tone, she opened her mouth. His kiss wasn't soft or sweet. It was brutal in its intensity as he staked a claim. He didn't try to coax a response; he commanded it.

His kisses always left her breathless, yet the depth of this one was different.

He tasted of demand, spiced by power. If he'd been dangerous for her before, he was doubly so now.

She ached to wrap her hands around his neck, and she tried to pull away, but he held her wrists prisoner.

He'd always been a kind and considerate lover, but this… Wow.

His tongue went deeper in her mouth, and she was lost. *Oh yes.* Yes. She wanted him. Yes, she desired him. Yes, she wanted to be in his bed and never leave.

His cock was fully hard, and it pressed against her stomach. She was turned on, and so was he. Her breaths came in struggled bursts, and all rational thought stopped.

Before she could figure out what he was doing, he ended the kiss and turned her around. Within seconds, he had her bent over the mattress. "Wes!"

He kept her wrists secured against her spine, and he dragged up her skirt, bunching it around her waist before stripping off her thong.

The cool Colorado night air crept across her exposed flesh.

"Lift your right foot."

She hesitated.

"*Do it.*"

She surprised herself by obeying. There was something about his tone that took away her will.

He pulled the underwear away, then said, "Now lift your left foot."

This time, she knew she couldn't win. Instead of fighting it, she gave in.

He tossed aside the thong. "Lovely."

She struggled futilely, knowing he was looking at her, seeing her vulnerability. She was smart enough to be scared.

"Spread your legs farther apart."

Oh God.

She couldn't believe this was happening. Outside of a club setting, she liked having the upper hand sexually, enjoyed setting the pace, being in charge. Until tonight, he'd seemed mostly content with that.

"Do I need to repeat myself?"

Barely able to breathe, trapped, subdued by his strength, she spread her legs a few inches farther apart.

He was there, his right foot against the inside of her ankle, forcing her even wider. For the first time in her life, she felt somewhat helpless, and it was frightening. "Wes…"

"Don't fight it," he said against her ear.

The sound of his voice reassured her.

"Don't fight me."

She held on to the lifeline of his voice. She'd known him professionally for two years, and he had a solid reputation at Hawkeye, Inc., for being resourceful, creative, and damn smart. He stayed with cases and people long past the time others would have given up in frustration. Which might be part of the reason they'd been intimate for the last six months. He'd worn her down.

Over the years, she'd refused his multiple offers for coffee or drinks or a hike up the Apex Trail. But in her one moment of vulnerability half a year ago, he'd been there. He'd helped her forget, and he'd never mentioned the event that she saw as a weakness.

He'd made love to her, held her, and let her go as soon as she wanted to leave. There'd been no awkward need to snuggle or have breakfast together. He'd been everything she craved.

A small part of her, though, wanted more. She enjoyed making love, but like a lot of agents, she was an adrenaline junkie.

Making love was…nice.

In the past he'd been a perfect gentleman, even in the most lustful moments. He made sure she was okay, and he made certain she was satisfied. Hawkeye trusted Lowell. She trusted Lowell.

She wasn't sure whether she to be nervous or thrilled beyond words.

She knew it felt out of control, and part of her liked that.

"There are rumors about you, Inamorata."

Her heart thundered. "Rumors?"

"You've tried BDSM."

She squeezed her eyes shut. "I can't believe you'd listen to rumors, Mr. Lowell, let alone believe them."

"Usually there's some truth behind them," he said, leaning in closer. "You were seen at a club in San Francisco with your pretty little ass exposed for some dom to spank. Maybe you want more than a spanking. Maybe you want a beating. Is that what turns you on? Having your ass so red you can't sit down? Is that what makes your pussy weep?"

His strong thighs pressed against her.

She might deny she was turned on, but if his cock got even just a bit closer to her heated pussy, he'd know the truth.

"I've been waiting for you to give me a hint, to ask for what you really want."

"I'm satisfied by the sex we have." *That*, at least, was the truth.

"But when you're alone, when you masturbate, what do you fantasize about?"

"I'm too busy to masturbate."

"Liar." He laughed; the sound was seductive. "A woman as responsive as you, a woman who loves sex as much as you do? You masturbate, Inamorata." He gently sank his teeth into soft flesh of her neck.

She yelped and arched, trying to escape.

"Don't ever lie to me, to yourself. Understand?"

She couldn't think, couldn't answer.

"Inamorata?"

"Yes," she said, finally, afraid she might drown in mortification. But as she spoke, she gained confidence. Either that, or it was bravado, she wasn't sure which. "I masturbate." A lot. He was right about her sex drive and energy. A good orgasm relaxed her faster than a glass of wine. But two could play his game. He wanted details; she'd give them to him. "I fantasize about being tied up, about forced orgasms, about being across a man's lap for a blistering spanking."

"Why haven't you told me?"

"It's never seemed important. I know people I can go to for that."

Wes sucked in a sharp breath.

She didn't know if he was angry or if the idea of someone else doing her aroused him. Regardless, this conversation was starting to get too deep into her personal life, and she wasn't sure she wanted him there. She gave him her famous aloof smile that was designed to keep others at a distance. "I have scenes with people who want the same things I do—release, pleasure, a mindless fuck," she said. "So sue me."

"Why haven't you asked me to beat you?"

The same reason she didn't stay the night or have coffee the next morning. Because she needed to protect herself emotionally. "I always go to a club. It's anonymous. It's fun. It's over in an hour, an hour and a half. No strings, nothing awkward that needs explaining or discussing. I never see the man—the dom—again. It's never been part of a..."

"Say it."

She couldn't. Wouldn't. She had no intention of acknowledging something to him she wouldn't admit to herself.

"A relationship?" he guessed "Is that the word? You've never had BDSM be a part of a relationship."

"We don't have a relationship," she said. Or more truthfully, she didn't want to have a relationship, didn't want to consider this anything more than a series of one-night stands with a man who satisfied her. Mostly.

"Inamorata, I'm not going to beat you. You've pissed me off way too much for that. But I sure as hell am going to fuck the lies right out of you. And when I'm not furious at you, then I'll punish you."

Desire, raw and carnal, shot through her.

He stroked her pussy. "*You like this.*"

"Yes," she whispered.

"Tell me what you want."

With his fingers, he pulled back on the skin shielding her clit, exposing that tiny nub. Every nerve ending screamed. She felt as if she were suffocating. Her jacket seemed too tight, his grip on her too secure.

"Tell me what you want," he repeated.

"More…"

"More of what?" He stroked her clit. "This?"

She moaned.

"Or this?" He slipped a finger inside her and then pulled it out.

Before she could do anything other than whimper, he began fucking her with his finger.

She tossed her head from side to side. She was so close to coming she could crawl out of her skin.

"Maybe this?" He pressed his thumb on her clit, hard. And he inserted a second finger along with the first.

"Damn it!" An orgasm loomed only seconds away.

"Tell me," he said.

"I like *that.*"

"Be specific, Inamorata."

She'd never been shy about requesting what she wanted sexually, but this seemed obscene.

He lessened the pressure, the bastard. "I like it when you put a lot of pressure on my clit."

"Like this?" He pressed his thumb lightly against her.

"More. Harder." He did, but not quite enough. Almost. Almost, but not quite. She pushed her body back a bit, taking what she wanted. "I need more. *Please.*"

"This?"

He pressed harder on that tiny nub. "Yes." She started to see stars.

"What else?"

"Fuck me. Fuck me with two fingers." She couldn't believe she was saying this, admitting this. When she played with doms, she took a somewhat passive role. If they wanted her to be a schoolgirl, she became a schoolgirl. If they wanted her to be a naughty maid, she was a naughty maid. But this…? Voicing what she wanted, the pressure that pleased her…?

"Like this, Inamorata?"

Oh. *Yes.* He kept a steady pressure as he rhythmically pushed in and withdrew his fingers. She tried to wriggle backward so he could go deeper, but he kept her immobilized. "Damn you, Wesley Lowell. Don't stop. I want to come."

"I want you to tell me what you want. Exactly what you want and how you want it," he said. "I'll make sure you get it. But make no mistake, from here on out, we'll do this my way." He took a breath and then quietly, very quietly, asked, "Understand?"

She understood.

Until this moment, she had decided when they saw each other; she had decided how long she stayed in his bed and at his house. She'd never joined him for dinner or stayed for breakfast, and she'd never invited him back to her downtown Denver loft.

"Say it, Inamorata. *Say it.*"

"I understand." A part of her had wondered how long he'd allow her the upper hand. A few times, before she'd fallen asleep, she'd considered what she might do if he got tired of her dictating the terms of their relationship. He was a strong, powerful man, patient and tolerant as well. But even he had to have limits. She had hoped his willpower wouldn't exert itself for a few more months. In her mind, the relationship would be over the moment he pushed for more. But now that he was… Damn him. "I want you inside me," she said as he kept up the relentless torment.

He turned his fingers slightly and unerringly found her G-spot. She drew in a shuddering breath as the climax began to build.

He knew it too, if the way he pulled out of her was any indication.

This was torture. "Wes," she protested.

"Please…?" he prompted.

She couldn't, wouldn't beg. Ms. Inamorata, Hawkeye's right-hand woman, had never begged for anything in her entire life. At work, she politely requested things get done. People who didn't comply right away had a good reason or they were replaced. As sure as the sun set over the Rockies, Inamorata would not be begging for an orgasm.

He plumped her clit, pushed on it, and simultaneously reinserted a finger inside her and pressed against her G-spot. Only a few more seconds… She moaned.

Again he pulled his hand away.

"Please…?" he prompted a second time.

"Lowell…"

"Please let me come, Sir," he said, coaching her.

No. She struggled to get away, but his strength effortlessly subdued her. She knew, though, that if she really insisted, he'd let her go.

"Beg for me. Let yourself go. Surrender."

This was no longer about sex. It was a battle of wills. It was also an internal battle. She didn't want a man who would be this demanding. She didn't want anything serious with any man. Why couldn't he leave it alone and simply enjoy casual sex like other men? "I…I want…"

"Say it," he whispered.

"I want to come."

He said nothing as he continued the relentless onslaught.

"Wes!"

"Beg, Inamorata."

She was lost. Suddenly she wanted the orgasm more than she wanted to be in charge. "Please," she said softly. "Please, I want to come. Damn it, Wes, I'm on the edge."

"Baby, when I let you come, I promise it will have been worth the wait."

Let her? Let her? "You're not going to let me come?"

"Not yet. I want you thinking of me. I want you calling me Sir."

Think of him? She wouldn't think of anyone else. She'd been doing the reverse striptease to make sure he thought of her, and he'd totally turned the tables.

In that moment, he terrified her. He had control physically. Worse, he had her emotionally. She felt shattered. She should wrest herself away from him, put on a fresh coat of lipstick, then call out a good-bye over her shoulder as she headed out the door. But she did none of those things. She was needy, helpless beneath him, and she made no attempt to get away.

He kept both her hands imprisoned, and she felt him shift positions, kneeling behind her. "Oh no," she said. She wasn't sure how she could survive him.

"Stay still."

He licked her, front to back, and she cried out.

When she felt his tongue against her rear entrance, she shuddered. While she wasn't shy, she'd never experimented anally, and the firm press of his tongue against her tightest hole stunned her.

"Relax, Inamorata."

He gently bit her right butt cheek.

She cried out.

Bentley raced into the room, yipping at his master.

"Out!" he commanded.

Ignoring him, the dog turned excited circles around them, all but bouncing up and down.

"Sit!"

The mechanical contraption did, right next to her foot.

"Not there. In the corner," Wes said. With a long-suffering sigh, he added, "I'm going to build him a kennel."

The dog gave a high-pitched whine, as if he had understood every word.

Wes grinned at the dog. He'd been working to perfect a pet for his niece, an animal lover whose allergies made dog ownership impossible. Obviously, there were still some issues. "Corner," Wes said.

With a whimper, Bentley sulked off.

"Now, where were we? Oh. Right. I was licking your cunt and tonguing your ass."

This time she whimpered.

Methodically he ate her.

She rose on her tiptoes and pushed back against him, silently asking for more.

He kept her torso pressed against the mattress. And damn him, he continued his maddening pace, not speeding up, but slowing down when she was ready to come.

He sucked her clit into his mouth and slowly entered her vagina with two fingers. Then, pulling away, he said, "You're slick."

"Yes."

"And you're going to beg to come."

"I already did."

He laughed. "Again."

She was shameless. "Please." This time there was no fight. He'd proven his point. He'd won. This time, in the bedroom, he was in charge. "Please let me come, Sir; make me."

He moved in a bit closer, licking, sucking her clit, sliding his fingers in and out of her vagina. He stopped for a moment and found her G-spot.

Still balanced on her high heels, she pushed her hips backward, all but pleading for release. "I'm going to come, Wes."

"Do it."

He still held her captive.

He pressed his thumb against her anal opening, and she screamed as the climax swamped her.

Her body convulsed. He continued to touch her, taste her as she came.

"Wes…"

"Ride it," he told her.

She did. Not able to fight it, or him, she relaxed into it. But before the wave receded, a second one followed.

She shuddered, trying to arch her back, trying to wriggle away. But he was as determined as he was strong. He kept her imprisoned, relentlessly driving her on.

Her pussy clenched. Her entire body seemed to tingle.

He pressed a finger firmly against her clit, and she screamed out her orgasm.

She lay there for a few moments, stunned, shattered, aware of the cool, crisp cotton sheets, and more, the strength of his body. She felt the contrast of their bodies, his steel muscles against the softness of her skin. The contrast reassured her.

He released the pressure on her clit and eased his fingers from her pussy. For a moment, she felt adrift, wanting him to hold her. That had been demanding and powerful and, if she had to be honest, one of the most fulfilling sexual experiences she'd ever had.

If she weren't careful, she could get addicted to this, to him.

And Inamorata was determined not to need anything from any man.

She forced air into her lungs, trying to steady her pulse as well as her emotions. "You can let me up now." Her voice didn't sound half as strong as she'd hoped. Frustrated at the way her body was betraying her, Inamorata shoved her body weight backward and jerked apart her wrists.

The fact she managed to get away said more about his lack of resistance than her strength.

She shrugged and then rotated her shoulders several times as she straightened. She smoothed her skirt back into place and then turned to face him. She forced a casual smile. "Thanks for the orgasms."

"Don't."

She put her palms flat on his bare chest and pushed him back a step. She forced herself to ignore his erect cock and clenched jaw.

Bentley jumped up, dashed across the room, skidding and barking, grabbed her thong from the floor, then galloped out the door.

"Guess you'll be buying me a closet full of new lingerie," she said, feigning a lightness she was nowhere close to feeling. She grabbed her purse from the nightstand and slung it over her shoulder.

"Inamorata…"

"I'll find my own way out."

"The hell you will, woman."

Instead of waiting for him to pull on a pair of jeans, she left the bedroom. She didn't have a lot of experience finding her way to the front door in the darkened house. He always walked her out, commanding Aston, his whole-house computer, to turn on the lights as they walked through the rooms.

Each time she was at his house, the routine was the same. Outside, he'd kiss her one last time while the driver waited, his gaze averted. Only then would Wes hand her into the car. He'd stand on the sidewalk, Bentley next to him, arms folded across his chest until she was out of sight.

She suddenly realized how badly she'd learned to count on that routine.

She hurried through the great room, wishing there were more ambient light. But he used blackout window treatments for privacy.

Bentley danced around her feet, and Wes's curses echoed off the walls.

She forced herself to take a deep breath to gather her composure.

Wes had thrown her completely off her game. She was known at Hawkeye, Inc., for being emotionally rock solid. But he'd left her reeling. She'd been enjoying their occasional hook-ups, but now that he'd uncovered one of her secrets, and oh so decadently, he was even more dangerous. She didn't want him knowing how badly his touch, his taste affected her.

"Damn it, Inamorata! Wait!"

"Good evening. Cindy?"

She jumped at the sound of the disembodied voice. She thought she'd gotten accustomed to having a computer, with a way-too-human, far-too-sexy English accent talk to her.

"Nice try," she said. "But my name's not Cindy. Please let me out, Aston."

"You're leaving for the evening, Annabelle?"

"Yes on the leaving. No on the name. Please let me out."

The lock turned.

"Bridget?"

"No." Usually Aston's attempts to guess her first name amused her, and in the months she'd been sleeping with Wes, they'd been through the alphabet more than once. Tonight, though, she wanted out.

"Until next time, Ms. Inamorata."

She pulled open the door, aware of sounds from the bedroom. Wes would only be a few paces behind her. She used her foot to keep the determined Bentley from following her outside. "Go get Wes," she said quietly.

The dog's tiny mechanical ears moved forward.

"Wes. Where is he?"

The dog looked over his shoulder. His little tail wagged madly.

"Go get him, Bentley!"

Bentley seemed to compute her order. His ears moved back into position. He turned and jumped up once before trundling toward the back of the house.

Her driver had her inside the vehicle by the time Wes, wearing unbuttoned jeans and nothing else, appeared on the porch.

She collapsed against the leather seat. She tried to feel guilt for leaving—okay, running—but she couldn't. At the moment, her need to escape overrode everything else.

Her cell phone rang. A handful of people in her life had custom ringtones—Hawkeye, her sister, and Wes. She always knew which calls to answer—and which she could ignore.

When she recognized Wes's ringtone, she considered answering, for maybe two seconds. But she'd left in the middle of the night because she needed time and space. He overwhelmed her, made her think, made her feel, made her want. Her pussy tingled. Her breasts ached.

Fantasies of him tying her up, making her beg, of his hand spanking her, of him forcing her onto her knees crawled through her mind. The force of her desire for him terrified her. Sex was one thing. BDSM was another. And heaven help her, that's exactly what she was considering asking for. The tiny serving of his dominance had made her want more. More desperately, she needed to be independent.

With a sigh, her finger trembling, she pushed the button to send him to voice mail.

Within thirty seconds, the phone rang again.

The man was persistent.

She knew she should be flattered. Half the women who worked stateside for Hawkeye, Inc., had a secret crush on him. Most women would shove her out of the way for the opportunity to be fucked by the handsome, intense, well-built—oh yeah, definitely well-built—Wesley Lowell.

For the second time, she sent him to voice mail.

When she felt stronger, more capable, less needy, she'd return his call. Probably within the next few days.

Maybe.

* * *

In frustration, Wesley pushed the End button and slammed down the phone.

The confounding woman had driven off without even looking over her shoulder, without giving him a second thought.

He sure as hell knew it had nothing to do with her not being sexually satisfied. There had been nothing fake about her cries of frustration, her moans of satisfaction. More likely the brave, tough Inamorata was scared shitless. At least he hoped so. That way he'd have company.

Still, everything he knew about her pointed to the fact she wasn't a coward. Her running away had been chickenshit, and he'd had no intention of letting her off the hook.

He'd gone back inside and grabbed his cell phone from his office desk and punched in her number.

After two rings, she'd sent him to voice mail. Inamorata rarely, if ever, turned off her phone. In the six months they'd been doing this, she'd never turned it off, not while she dozed, not while they were having sex. He'd even known her to answer a call from Hawkeye while she was in the bathroom.

Jaw clenched, he'd picked up the phone and pushed Redial. After one ring, he'd gotten her crisp, professional voice-mail message.

He'd ended the call a second time.

Goddamn her and her independence.

He'd never met a more frustrating, irritating, intriguing, irresistible woman. He wanted her. Wanted her bad.

He ran his hands through his already messy hair.

Wesley Lowell had rarely been at a loss with a woman. He adored women, enjoyed everything about them, from their soft curves to their sometimes mercurial moods, to the way they fit so perfectly in his arms. He loved taking care of them, bringing them breakfast in bed, enjoyed being out with them in public, having a nice dinner or a pizza and a beer.

Most especially he liked being in bed with them; he liked sex hot and dirty, down and rough, sweet and slow. He liked making love. He liked fucking. He liked bending a woman over a bed. He liked tying her hands to the posts. He liked reddening her sweetheart ass and hearing her plead for more.

Unfortunately he had a short attention span.

The allure of each new woman wore off quickly. He was restless, easily bored, wanted change. But his infatuation with Inamorata hadn't lessened over the months; it had intensified.

He didn't like wanting her as much as he did. It made him uncomfortable. But there it was.

If his attraction had been based solely on the thrill of the chase, he would have lost interest a few weeks ago when they'd left their clothes on his great-room floor and he'd taken her across the back of his couch.

Instead, fucking her in the great room had stoked his hunger. Fulfilling each fantasy only fueled the next one.

Inamorata was multifaceted, uninhibited in bed, committed to her work, loyal to those who worked for her, and uninterested in having anything resembling a relationship with him. He wouldn't say he was obsessed with her. But damn close to it.

He had seen tonight coming.

He wanted more from her. He wanted to take what they had to the next level. Clearly she didn't. Tonight's collision, in what he wanted and what she wanted, had been inevitable. He'd spent the last month debating every one of his actions. He'd been as deliberate with the way he handled her as he'd been with examining blueprints.

And tonight, he'd lost patience.

He was tired of her throwing back the covers and walking out. He was tired of not knowing when—if—she'd be back. He was tired of giving in and letting her have her way.

He debated his next action. Wait? Or go after her? Do the caveman act, throw her over his shoulder, and keep her prisoner until she admitted she was his? Invite her for a candlelit dinner?

He discarded that idea immediately. There was far too much testosterone in his system to play the besotted knight.

Dragging her by her ponytail was much more what he was in the mood for.

Bentley came over. He sat and wagged his metal tail, his head cocked to one side. One of Inamorata's stockings hung from his mouth.

* * *

"I'll pick you up at eight, Ms. Inamorata?"

"Perfect, Ricardo," she said to her driver, stepping out of the car. The Colorado fall air felt cool on her bare legs. Darn that Bentley for stealing one of her stockings. And damn Wes for encouraging the lovable mutt's bad behavior. "Thanks," she said as Ricardo closed her door.

He walked her to the front door of her building.

Even though the ride down the mountain and back to her loft had taken almost half an hour, her insides still buzzed from a mixture of nerves and excitement.

Not that anyone would know, but her hands shook slightly as she swiped her key card for access to the building. Wes hadn't gripped her hard enough to bruise, but the memory of his touch lingered.

She punched the elevator button to take her to the third floor. Ricardo tipped his nonexistent cap and headed back to the car.

Her phone rang again. With a sigh, Inamorata ignored yet another telephone call from Wes, sending him to voice mail. She knew and accepted that she was taking the coward's way out. She almost always answered phone calls, even when she knew a difficult conversation would follow. She believed in dealing with things straight up.

Sexy, overwhelming Wesley Lowell took everything she believed in and stood it on its head. Tonight had proved he was more man than she wanted. But that didn't stop her pussy from moistening every time a thought of him danced through her mind.

Since she didn't know what to do about him, she decided she'd think about it later in the day, when the thought of him wasn't so prevalent, when the memory of his touch didn't sear her skin, when the scent of him didn't linger on her clothes.

She exited the elevator and walked down the hallway toward her loft. She opened her front door and then froze. She'd turned off all the lights before she left, and yet the kitchen was ablaze with hundreds of watts. Then she heard a groan. Feminine. Soft. Agonized.

She pulled her pistol from her purse, reached for her phone, speed-dialed Hawkeye, and then dropped her bag in the hallway. He answered on the first ring, despite the fact it was nearly three in the morning. He sounded every bit as awake as he did at noon. "Someone's in my place," she said. "At least one female. Groaning."

"Want the police? Backup?" Hawkeye asked.

She appreciated that he didn't ask for any details. He'd know she'd give them if she had them. And no one inside the Hawkeye organization liked to involve the authorities unless absolutely necessary. "I'll let you know."

She clipped the phone to her skirt's waistband so she would have both hands free. Slowly she moved into the wide-open space.

Near the master bedroom, she saw Martha, her housekeeper, on the floor, arms bound behind her. Whoever had done this to Martha had crossed her ankles and secured them with duct tape. The woman's body was curled into a fetal position. For added measure, the assholes had slapped a piece of the tape across her mouth. Since the vacuum cleaner and the hardwood-floor polish were still out, the perpetrators had obviously attacked soon after Martha had arrived, meaning she'd been trussed on the floor for hours.

Inamorata fought back her emotional response and focused on her training.

Secure the area.

She crouched and touched Martha's shoulder reassuringly. "Be right back," she promised.

Despite her resolve to stay calm, no one—no one—fucked with hers. Martha had been with her for a dozen years, and Martha was the mother Inamorata wished she still had. She'd kick the ass of whoever had done this. "Is anyone else here?" Inamorata asked.

Martha groaned in response and tried to shake her head. But tears leaked from her eyes.

Steeling herself, Inamorata searched the rest of her home before closing the front door and dialing the phone. "My housekeeper," she told Hawkeye. "Bound on the floor. No blood. All else is secure. I'll keep you apprised."

After putting away the cell phone, she went into the kitchen. Her morning coffee cup was still in the sink, reinforcing that Martha had been attacked soon after she'd arrived. Forcing back her shoulders, Inamorata grabbed a knife from the top drawer. Then she changed her mind. It would probably be easier to cut through the tape using scissors. Unwrapping the tape would probably be best, but she didn't have the patience for that.

Inamorata spoke quietly and soothingly to Martha the entire time. "We'll get that tape off you," she promised, crouching next to Martha. She placed her gun on the floor, within easy reach. "This may hurt."

Martha nodded.

There was no easy way to get the tape off the woman's mouth, and Inamorata grimaced as she pulled it off. "Sorry," she whispered.

Martha babbled incoherently for a few moments.

"I'll get you some water in a second," Inamorata promised. "But first, let's get the rest of it off. I need you to keep really still." Truthfully, Martha's muscles were probably so stiff and cramped it was doubtful she could move at all.

The woman quietly sobbed.

"Are you hurt?" Inamorata asked. *Other than the obvious.*

"Head."

Inamorata nodded.

"No police," Martha said, the words choked, hoarse.

Inamorata cut through the tape at Martha's wrists. Bastards had done a hell of a job. She forced her jaw to unclench. "Easy," she said. "Slow and easy."

Martha cried out, likely as circulation returned.

"The pain will diminish," Inamorata said. "Breathe." She caught Martha's gaze and exaggerated her own breaths. Martha's eyes were wide, unblinking. More than pain lurked in the depths. Martha was scared.

"Sam," she said.

"Sam?" Inamorata had met Martha's son a number of times over the years. He'd been in and out of trouble as a teen, but last she knew, he had a steady job.

"They have Sam."

"Who? Who has Sam?" She cut through the bonds securing Martha's ankles.

"Men."

Martha moved her legs slightly and groaned again.

"Take your time," Inamorata said.

She patiently remained at the woman's side, gently massaging her extremities. A few minutes later, Inamorata offered assistance when she saw Martha struggling to sit up.

"They hurt him yesterday. Today, they came here, and they gave me a warning."

"What do they want?"

"Your help."

"Mine?" She sat back on her heels.

"It's all my fault," Martha insisted, tears rolling down her face.

"Stop. The behavior of bad people is not your fault."

"It is," Martha said. "I talk about you all the time. I'm so proud of you."

Inamorata smiled, but it was automatic, not sincere as she raced to put together what Martha was saying.

Silently she unwrapped the remaining tape, noticing how chafed the woman's skin was. She'd skin those bastards alive.

"Sam—he talked about you, bragged about you too."

"It's okay," she said.

"They said they would kill him if you call the police."

"Okay. No police." Worked for her, at least for now. No law enforcement meant fewer questions, fewer explanations needed when she kicked ass and left bodies strewn about.

Just then, the front door banged open. She leaped up and grabbed for her gun. Martha screamed.

Inamorata positioned herself in front of Martha.

"What the fuck is going on here, Inamorata?"

Chapter Two

"Wes." She lowered her gun. After a shaky exhalation, she concentrated on forcing her heartbeat into a regular rhythm. "You're lucky I didn't shoot your ass."

"You might wish you'd taken the opportunity." He closed the door behind him.

He didn't walk across the room, he stalked, devouring the distance, dwarfing the space. With him looming over her, she suddenly felt small.

"Start talking, woman."

A dozen questions crowded her mind. How the hell had he known there was an issue? How had he found out where she lived? "Put a lid on it, Wesley Lowell. Show some manners or leave. In fact, just leave. We're busy here."

She looked up at him. There was no doubt, with the way his arms were crossed over his chest and his legs were spread, feet planted firmly, that he was here to stay.

Despite her attempts to be cool and in charge, a very female part of her was glad to see him. A very tiny part was happy he cared enough to be mad. A larger part wanted to preserve her sanity, her privacy, her ability to function competently. His being there made her aware of being a woman.

"Talk," he said.

She sighed. Even Hawkeye himself didn't dare intrude on

her life like this. But Wesley Lowell could outstubborn Hawkeye. He might even be able to outstubborn her. "You're frightening Martha."

"No, he isn't," Martha said, although her voice sounded a bit shaky. "About time you met a man who stands his ground with you."

He grinned.

Inamorata groaned.

"Three men have my son, my Sammy," Martha told him. "And they came here looking for Ms. Inamorata. I'm worried about her."

"I am too," Wes said, quietly.

"I can take care of myself," Inamorata said.

"Of course you can," Martha agreed. "But I do feel better with a big strong man being with us right now."

"Let me help you to the couch," Inamorata said, changing the subject. "And I'll get you a glass of water."

"I'll help her. You get the water," Wes said.

"She's been traumatized by men," Inamorata snapped. Was he dense? And why the hell did he think he could barge in here and issue orders?

"And she said she feels better having a big strong man here. That would be me."

"The other ones are bad," Martha said. Her lips moved a little, but it was more of a ghost than a true smile. "This one isn't so bad."

Outnumbered and knowing when she was beat, Inamorata picked up her pistol and headed for the kitchen.

After placing her gun on the table, she took a glass from the cupboard and then ran the tap until the water chilled.

When she entered the great room, Wes was helping Martha to the couch, cradling the older woman's arm and walking a bit behind her, encouraging her to move only as fast as was comfortable for her.

This was the same man who'd stormed in here in a blaze of anger? The man who had imprisoned her wrists, bent her over the bed, and used his hands and mouth to make her beg for an orgasm?

His gaze met hers, and she shivered.

His eyes narrowed, and even from that distance, she saw his eyes were a steel gray color. This wasn't the sexy charcoal color of their lovemaking, a color that told her he was weak with desire for her. Nope. This was unadulterated fury.

His tenderness was for Martha and Martha alone.

He arched his brows, sending a message she received loud and clear. He wasn't done with her yet.

After helping Martha onto the couch, Wes crossed to the fireplace and rested his elbow on the mantel. He was here to stay. If it were up to Inamorata, she'd kick his overbearing, pompous, demanding rear right out the door, no matter how he tempted her and no matter how hot and tight that rear was.

Oddly, though, his presence reassured Martha. As much as he made Inamorata seethe with resentment, she couldn't deny his patience with Martha. Which left Inamorata stuck.

Inamorata sat on the couch next to Martha. The woman's shoulders were hunched, and her hands were in her lap. She absently rubbed her right wrist with her left thumb.

"Water?" Inamorata offered.

Seemingly jolted out of her thoughts, Martha accepted the glass and took a hesitant sip. Water sloshed over the rim, spilling onto the floor. Her eyes widened. "I'm sorry," she said. "I'll clean it up."

"Nonsense."

"I've got it," Wes said.

The woman's hands continued to tremble, and Inamorata took the glass and placed it on the coffee table.

"Guess I'm more upset than I thought."

"You have every right to be upset," Wes said, returning with a handful of paper towels. After blotting the mess, he continued, "Start at the beginning."

"Sam"—she looked at Wes—"that's my son."

He nodded as if he didn't already know the information.

Inamorata noticed he didn't make any attempt to move back to the other side of the room.

"He's a good boy. Really."

Inamorata's gaze connected with Wes's. If he were such a good boy, none of them would be here right now. Neither of them said anything.

"Go on," Wes said.

"He was telling some of his new friends that I worked for you."

"Did he mention Hawkeye?" Inamorata asked.

Martha returned to rubbing her wrist. "Yes."

Wes folded his arms, then, seeming to realize how intimidating that could look, dropped them.

"Tell us more about his friends," Inamorata said.

"He met them at work."

So he still had a job.

"He's working downtown, in one of the skyscrapers," Martha said, with more than a hint of pride. "He's in computers. Anyway, they were all over at the house the other night. It was Sunday; I'd made a pot roast and vegetables. I'd baked some bread too. One of the boys was asking about you, if it was true you worked for Hawkeye, Inc., if it was true you're pretty high up in the organization, if it was true you actually know Hawkeye himself." She lowered her gaze to her hands and remained silent for at least a minute.

Inamorata patiently waited.

Martha sighed. "Anyway, I didn't hear from Sam on Monday or Tuesday."

"Is that unusual?" Inamorata asked.

"No. Not since he got himself an apartment on Capitol Hill. But he always comes for Sunday dinner. He has to take the bus. On Wednesday—"

"Yesterday?" Wes asked.

Martha blinked, as if trying to sort out the days. "Yesterday. Yesterday, yes."

Inamorata offered the water to Martha again.

The woman's motions were exaggerated, and she used two hands to hold the glass steady and take a small sip.

Wes paced, but when Inamorata glared, he sat on the ottoman of her favorite leather chair. She wasn't sure she liked having him in her space, making himself at home; she'd been right to keep all their hook-ups at his place. He propped his elbows on his knees and leaned forward, resting his chin on his linked hands.

Inamorata took the glass and placed it on the table.

"On Wednesday, yesterday, Sam called to tell me that he loved me and that he was sorry."

"Sorry?" Wes asked.

"I thought he meant for all the years he'd been in trouble. You know, when he was a teenager, after his father died." She swallowed and looked at her hands again. "Then while I was here working, I got a call from one of the boys who'd come over last Sunday. He said they had Sam and a message...message for you."

When they involved Martha, they'd involved Inamorata. Inamorata had gotten that message loud and clear.

"He told me not to call the police, or I'd never see Sam again." Her words caught on a sob.

Inamorata took Martha's hands and then breathed deeply, deliberately, until Martha followed suit.

"He...he hung up. I was going to call you..." She trailed off and frowned. "My phone—I don't know where it is."

"We'll find it," Inamorata promised.

"They came here before I could make the call. There were two of them. They must have followed me, I think. They didn't say anything, not a word. The big one—I think his name is David—hit me on the head. When I woke up, they were gone and I was on the floor." She shuddered.

"Security cameras," Inamorata said to Wes.

"On it," he responded. "I'll also need your phone number..."

"Ms. Montano," Inamorata supplied.

Martha gave her phone number, then shook her head. "No. Wait. That's one I used to have."

Inamorata grabbed her phone and checked her address book for Martha's number. She read it off.

"Got it." He nodded and then repeated it.

No dim wattage coming from his brain.

"You calling Hawkeye with an update?" he asked her.

She nodded.

"I'll be back in ten."

For once, she wasn't upset Wes was around. His techy, geeky skills could come in handy.

He walked toward the door. "I'll lock it," he said.

Martha's gaze followed him. She continued to stare at the closed door.

"Let's get you to the hospital," Inamorata gently said to

Martha.

The woman shook her head. "I'm fine."

"You were hit on the head," Inamorata countered.

"The doctors will ask questions."

"I'll get you a doctor from Hawkeye."

"No." Martha's eyes widened. "I'm okay. I'll be fine. No doctors. They'll ask questions. Then they'll notify the police."

"A Hawkeye medic won't involve the police," Inamorata said.

"You promise?" Martha's brown eyes were unblinking, as if she wanted to trust but couldn't. The stakes were life-and-death for Martha—her only child. The woman loved her son as much as Inamorata loved Martha.

Inamorata took her responsibilities seriously. Squeezing the woman's hand reassuringly, she said, "You and Sam are my first priorities. I'll take care of you. I'd prefer if you let me move you to a safe location."

"I want to go home."

She understood that sentiment. If she assigned a protective detail from Hawkeye, they could keep Martha safe. "If I have any reason to believe that's a bad idea, you will be moved."

"But—"

"I'll let you go home for now."

When Wes knocked on the door a few minutes later, Inamorata let him in and then excused herself. She walked toward the bedroom, dialing the phone as she went. She closed the door behind her, then, when Hawkeye picked up on the first ring, succinctly outlined the situation.

"I'll organize resources," he told her.

"Wait! That's my job."

"I'm not so out of touch I don't know how to use a Rolodex."

"Database," she corrected. "We don't use a Rolodex anymore. We use a database."

"I'd better call my assistant."

"Martha will need a medic. Send an agent—no, make that two, for protective detail. And I'll take a geek to trace cell-phone calls, coordinate GPS positions, look into Sam's supposed friends for motivation."

"I've made Lowell available to you."

"Thanks, but no." The man was already insufferable.

"Want to tell me what's going on there?"

If she understood it, she would.

"He's already on-site," Hawkeye said. "Engaged in the situation."

Inamorata didn't respond.

Silence pulsed over the line.

"Lowell's the best," Hawkeye said. He paused for a few more seconds, then asked, "Do you want the best?"

She sighed. "Lowell it is."

"The building manager already uploaded the video he requested. We've got a couple of names at least. Lance, David. Martha's son, Sam. We've got pictures."

That was fast. But then, what else had she expected? She'd been attracted to Wes—the confounding man—partially because of the rumors about him and his mental prowess. About a year ago, because of his involvement with a FBI case, he'd been written up in a national magazine, despite Hawkeye's attempts to keep a low profile in the press.

"Get us whatever information you have on Sam. We'll get a link uploaded to Lowell with what we've got. Have Martha identify who's who."

"She got knocked around."

"Do the best you can. Let Lowell work his magic."

She opened her mouth to speak, and Hawkeye cut her off. "Don't let your personal feelings interfere with what's best for a case."

"Have I ever?"

"Once."

"Below the belt, Hawkeye." They were both silent for a moment. She did remember the time in the heat of the Arizona desert, seemingly half a lifetime ago, not long after her rookie year. She'd made mistakes, and the nightmares still haunted her.

"Yeah. That was unfair," he agreed. "But you asked. No one is perfect, Inamorata."

Her mistakes had sharpened her senses, made her a better operative, and honed her skills. But Hawkeye was right. She would be a fool to refuse Wes's talents. She tried not to let Hawkeye hear her sigh. "I'll use him."

Without another word, Hawkeye ended the call.

She pushed the End button and slowly returned the phone to the holster. Her shoulders sagged, and she let out a long, slow breath.

Without warning, her bedroom door opened. "Do you have any respect for my privacy?" she asked.

"You didn't call."

She frowned. "When?"

"When you got home. When you realized there was something wrong."

Her frown deepened. "Why would I call you? I notified Hawkeye."

He clenched his jaw so hard she saw a pulse tic there.

"You're pissing me off," he said.

"I'm not trying to piss you off, I promise. It never occurred to me to call you," she admitted.

"I ought to turn you over my lap right now. We've been in a relationship for six months, goddamn it."

"We don't have a relationship. We don't have a commitment, a promise, anything. I don't owe you an explanation about where I am, who I'm with. When I have a work case, I don't talk to you about it. In fact—"

"Enough, Inamorata."

"We've hooked up every once in a while," she said, tipping her head back to meet his glare. "That's hardly a relationship."

"What do you call it?"

"I don't know." She fought her irritation. He was way out of line, and it was clear he disagreed. Men. "Friends with benefits."

"Friends *is* a relationship."

"Fine. Okay. Consider us something else. I don't know. Fuck buddies."

"Now I'm seriously pissed." He took a step toward her.

She stood her ground, despite the self-preservation instinct—hell, despite common sense—that urged her to take a step back. "I have work to do. This discussion—argument—can wait for another time."

"No. It can't. I'm tired of you running, Inamorata. I'm more than tired of you denying what we have."

"Can this wait? Martha is—"

"Martha is in the bathroom cleaning up. I walked with her, but she didn't seem to need any assistance. As for you, woman, you can quit running away, emotionally as well as physically."

"Screw you, Lowell. I'm not—"

"No, you're not. Not anymore. Not running, not hiding."

"Let me finish a sentence."

"I would if what you were going to say next wouldn't get you in more trouble."

She sighed. He knew her better than she knew herself. She wanted him, every bit as much as she wanted *not* to want him.

His speech pattern, the way he walked, with purposeful and determined intent, the way he looked at her, as if there was no one else on the planet for him except for her—all of it combined in a magical way that made him irresistible, that made her libido slam into overdrive.

Heaven help her.

He closed the distance in a few easy steps. "King-size bed," he observed. "With four posts." He curved his hands around her shoulders.

While his grip wasn't tight, didn't hurt, it was unyielding and left her with no doubt he was a man who was intent on dominating her.

"Who's tied you to them, Inamorata?"

"I lost count. Ten different men. Maybe a dozen?" What was it about him that goaded her? "Jealous?"

"No."

That pulse ticking near his jaw became more and more pronounced. His "no" had been quick, and it had been an obvious lie. She would be stupid to push him further.

"It doesn't matter if a hundred men have tied you to them, Inamorata. I'll be the last."

She shuddered. With that clipped tone of voice, she believed every word he said. "That's a big assumption, Mr. Lowell. A bold one."

"It's a promise, Ms. Inamorata. And I'll make your ass so red you'll forget about any man other than me."

He dug his hands into her hair and made a mess of the locks she'd tried to tame. No one in the last six months had seen her hair mussed, except for him.

"You'll beg me to spank you. And you'll scream when I

give you permission to come."

"More bold words?" Dear God, did her voice sound as shaky to him as it did to her? *Bravado*—that was the sound.

"More promises," he countered.

Using his grip on her hair, he pulled her head back. He kept one hand fisted in her hair, and with the other, he cradled her head.

This kiss was unlike any other.

Wes Lowell was the gentlest lover she'd ever been with. Until tonight. Now, he demanded capitulation.

She resisted at first, but his onslaught was relentless. And truthfully, this man did something to her that made her respond, whether she wanted to or not. Her body betrayed her mind's resolve.

He tasted of determination, spiced with anger. He wasn't only punishing her with the kiss; he was marking her as his. Instinctively she knew if she stopped him now, there would be no going back. She wouldn't be invited to his house again. He'd walk away. She wasn't ready to admit they had something more than hot sex. It definitely, in her book, wasn't a relationship. She didn't share enough of her life, enough of her mind or emotions to honestly say they had a relationship. She didn't trust him enough for that. She'd never trusted a man that much.

Pulling back, he said, "Open your mouth wider, Inamorata."

After licking her upper lip, she did.

"Wider."

He kept her gaze imprisoned. She couldn't look away now if she tried.

"Better," he said approvingly.

He thrust his tongue deeply inside her mouth. He wasn't simulating any sex act they'd enjoyed. This was far more intense. She shuddered, knowing when they were intimate again, it wouldn't be lovemaking or sex; it would be raw fucking.

Her insides were a puddle of desire.

The harder he pushed her, the more she wanted him, and he seemed to recognize that.

She knew about Dominance and submission. She'd played BDSM games since she'd dated an older man while she was still in high school. Because she'd lost her parents early, Inamorata had grown up fast. Boys her age, with their groping and uncertainty, had never interested her. Because she acted mature, no one had raised an eyebrow when she lied about her age. So she'd been with twenty-five-year-olds when she was barely eighteen. She liked self-assured men, or she had, until right now. Right now, he was unsettling her, and that infuriated her.

He eased back a little. She responded by leaning into him more. Suddenly she didn't want the kiss to end, didn't want this—*whatever it was* going on between them—to end.

She met the next gentle thrust of his tongue with a parry of her own. He groaned. She reached up to wrap her arms around his neck. Submission, she knew, wasn't about something being taken from her. It was about willing surrender.

She heard water running in the sink.

Slowly he ended the kiss.

"I'm not finished with you," he said.

"Is that a warning?"

"Take it how you want," he said. "I meant it as a promise."

His words, his tone, the set of his mouth didn't scare her—they turned her on. A frisson of electricity danced up her spine.

"I'll look for Martha's phone while you compose yourself." For a moment, he imprisoned her chin between his thumb and forefinger.

He held her gaze for a few seconds longer than she was comfortable with, and she read determination in the set of his jaw. Without another word, he left.

She released a breath she hadn't realized she was holding.

Just how well did she know Wesley Lowell? Despite the fact they'd been involved, she didn't really know him. Until tonight, she hadn't suspected the depth of his temper. She'd had no idea he was interested in tying her up and spanking her. She'd had no idea he was frustrated with their involvement and wanted more.

And now this… He'd remembered Martha was bothered about losing her phone. He was as kind and compassionate to an older woman as he was edgy and overbearing with her.

Inamorata sank onto the edge of the bed.

Her shirt had come untucked from her waistband. Her skirt had gotten twisted around her thighs. And her hair—the unruly thick strands settled on her shoulders and curled around her face. Professional, she was not.

Another reason to avoid him.

Inamorata didn't *do* rumpled.

She wrestled her hair back into place, then smoothed her black pencil skirt, and tucked in her blouse.

More in control, she rolled back her shoulders and headed for the great room.

If she'd been any less self-possessed, she'd have missed a step when she rejoined Wes and Martha.

Wes was on his hands and knees, peering beneath the couch. Martha stood nearby, wringing her hands.

Inamorata cleared her throat.

"Still looking for Martha's phone," he said, glancing over at her. "She's worried her son is trying to get hold of her."

Damn him for being so likable.

Hawkeye was already working behind the scenes to access Martha's cell records. Likely they knew whether Sam had been trying to call. She knew that. Wes knew that, so he was just trying to soothe a frantic mother.

"Found it," Wes said.

"Thank you, thank you, thank you," Martha said.

"Looks as if it's turned off." He was powering it on as he walked toward Martha.

"I need to check the voice mail." She took the phone and frowned at it. "I don't know how. No one ever leaves me messages."

"I've been told I'm pretty handy at that kind of thing," Wes said. "Let me help."

His phone and Inamorata's both signaled incoming messages. She opened hers to find pictures of the men from the building's security cameras. She guided Martha to the couch and sat next to her. "Do you recognize any of these men?"

"That one." She pointed. "David."

"Any last names?"

Martha frowned. She began rubbing her left temple in tiny circles.

"It's okay," Inamorata said, touching Martha's shoulder reassuringly. "If anything comes to you, let me know." Truthfully she was surprised Martha had done as well as she had. The emotional and physical trauma had to have taken a toll.

The intercom buzzed, and Inamorata excused herself to walk over and answer the summons. She pushed a button and a strong, no-nonsense female from outside the building said, "Sara Stein here, as requested."

Inamorata raised a brow in surprise, surprised to hear

Stein's disembodied voice. The other woman hadn't been back on active duty long, and to have shown up here, she would have volunteered for the assignment.

Stein was young and until recently had been one of Hawkeye Inc.'s most promising protective agents. Even though it had been her sister's life on the line, Inamorata thought Stein's actions had been exemplary. Stein hadn't agreed, insisting she should have seen her partner's treachery ahead of time.

Inamorata hadn't wanted to approve Stein's leave, preferring to assign the woman to another case, have her work through the angst and doubt and learn to trust her judgment again.

But in a rare moment of disagreement, Hawkeye had overridden his right-hand woman's decision and signed Stein's request, granting her as much unpaid time off as she wanted.

When Stein walked through the door, she met Inamorata's gaze squarely. Inamorata realized Hawkeye had been right. Stein looked rested, fit, and ready for duty. She'd found her way back. "Good to see you."

"I won't let you down, ma'am."

"You never have."

Laurents and Barstow, two good-looking specimens of men if she'd ever seen them, showed up next. And they weren't just tall, dark, and classically handsome, they were talented and tough.

The cavalry had arrived.

In minutes, and despite the fact it was sometime before four a.m., her home had become command central. Hawkeye hadn't lost his touch or, evidently, his Rolodex.

A medic arrived next, a man whose skills had been tested in a trauma center and honed on Middle Eastern battlefields.

"No doctors," Martha said.

With the arrival of each new person, her agitation level had visibly increased. And now the frantic movements of her hands never stopped. "They said no cops."

Sara took charge, kneeling in front of Martha. "You're following their directions perfectly. This man is from Hawkeye, and he's not a real doctor."

Inamorata shot him a look of apology.

He shrugged as if to say no offense taken.

"You're doing great. Your son would be proud of you. And you're going to take care of yourself, so that when we get him back, you can fuss over him. Does he have a favorite food?"

"Chocolate chip cookies."

"Mine too. Will you bake some?"

Inamorata folded her arms, impressed. Who knew Sara could soothe as well as kick ass?

Now that the woman was relaxed, the medic put Martha through a series of tests that meant little to Inamorata. "If we weren't going to have agents with her all night, I'd want her in the hospital," he said.

He scribbled down a few things for Stein. "Call me if her headache gets worse. Watch for confusion, imbalance, vomiting, changes in her pupils. And of course, loss of consciousness or convulsions."

Stein nodded. Inamorata trusted her efficiency.

Sara helped Martha stand and assisted her into her lightweight jacket. "He didn't call," Martha said, her eyes wide and unblinking as she stared at her phone.

Inamorata knew Martha was likely numb, and that wasn't all bad. The body needed to process horrific events in small pieces.

"He didn't call," she repeated.

Inamorata hugged the woman, held her close while the

tears finally fell.

Wes met her gaze over Martha's shoulder. This time, the resolve in his posture reassured her. He might have just met Martha, but he'd go above and beyond for her. Inamorata appreciated that, even if she didn't appreciate his interference.

Laurents headed for the door, presumably to get the vehicle in position. Hawkeye's protective agents were the best. They dealt with people in the most emotionally debilitating moments of their lives. They had a unique blend of compassion and detachment that kept them sharp and kept their clients alive.

After a minute, Sara moved in, telling Martha very slowly and clearly that they were going to get her home. Barstow led the way while Martha leaned on Sara.

Martha looked over her shoulder.

"I'll be in touch," Inamorata promised. "And if you hear anything, I want you to contact me anytime."

"You'll look out for my Sam?"

Inamorata smiled reassuringly and made an X on top of her heart.

When the door closed behind them, she exhaled.

"I'll stop by in the morning to check on her," the medic said, closing his mysterious bag. "I'll send you an immediate update."

The man found his way out. Suddenly there was deafening silence, and she was alone with Wes.

"You need some rest," he said.

As much as she wanted to argue, and might have another time, just on principle, she nodded. She'd like to be able to work round the clock, and still could if the situation demanded it, but she knew resting gave her an edge. "I'll catch a few hours before heading to the office." Infuriating man just stood there, either intentionally or obtusely not taking her hint that he should leave. "You should get some sleep too," she said.

"I'm planning to." He took a step toward her. "With you."

It must be lack of sleep, her brain slowing from exhaustion, but she knew she couldn't have heard him right. "With me?"

"The bad guys were in your loft, Inamorata."

"And?"

"You would have liked for Martha to go to a safe house. I'd like you to be somewhere safe also."

"I'm a trained professional. There's a difference."

"Not so much in Hawkeye's eyes."

"What are you saying?" Her heart slowed by several beats per minute. She knew, feared, his next words.

"I'd hoped you'd see reason. I'd hoped you'd see the bigger picture and what's best for the case. But I'll bottom-line it for you. You're not staying here. You have only two other choices. Your car is waiting outside."

"You're annoying the crap out of me, Lowell."

"Deal with it. You can go to my place or a safe house."

She opened her mouth to speak, but he waved a hand, silencing her.

"Hawkeye assigned me as your protective detail. His decision isn't open for negotiation, nor is mine."

Chapter Three

"I don't need a protective detail."

He'd already gone through a litany of her arguments in his head. "Probably true."

"I don't want protection."

"Too bad; you're getting it."

"You're the wrong choice."

He raised his brows and reined in his temper.

"You're not…" She folded her arms across her chest. Her chin was set at a stubborn angle.

"Not…" he prompted.

"Objective enough. We're involved."

"Now we're involved? When it's convenient for you, we're involved?" Anger gnawed at his gut. He'd thought he'd been prepared for any argument, but he hadn't been prepared for that one.

"You know what I mean."

"No, Inamorata. I don't." He stepped toward her and took her by the shoulders gently, much more gently than he felt like being.

"We're not allowed to protect family members, close friends."

"Will you go to a safe house?"

"No chance." She raised her chin a notch. "I'll lead this

investigation. I'll find Sam. And I'll find the bastards who hurt Martha. She's one of mine."

More than ever, he admired her. She loved fiercely and protectively. He wondered what it would be like to be someone she cared about. "I'm Hawkeye's compromise," he told her. "If you're unwilling to go with me, he'll have Wolf Stone take over your responsibilities until this is resolved."

Her mouth opened slightly before she obviously realized she'd betrayed her emotions. "It's my case. My responsibility."

"You know Stone is the best."

"After me."

He smiled. He did love her spunk. "After you."

She looked at him, tipping back her head a little more so their gazes connected. Her breaths were shortened. Her green eyes flashed fire. Outside the bedroom, Inamorata clearly didn't like taking orders, didn't like being backed into a corner.

She shrugged out of his grip. "I'm calling Hawkeye." She turned her back to him and walked toward the bedroom as she dialed the phone.

She closed her door firmly behind her.

He heard the soft tones of her voice but couldn't make out any words. While he waited, he cleaned up the area, throwing away the scraps of duct tape that had been used to secure Martha. He didn't know where to put away the scissors, and it made his blood hot that this was the first time he'd been to her place. And if Hawkeye hadn't called, Wes would still be waiting on an invitation that might never have come.

He pulled open a drawer and found a well-organized place for silverware. He opened a second drawer and found an assortment of knives and a space big enough for the scissors.

Everything about Inamorata's loft was as meticulous as the woman herself. Nothing was out of place, and she didn't have any of the piles of paper and miscellaneous electronic parts that were the hallmark of his home.

Her great room was vast, just a few pieces of furniture arranged conversationally. A large print of a red abstract flower hung above the barren fireplace. Several other brick walls were adorned with other abstract designs, all in bright, bold primary colors.

She had an oversize television and a sound system the geek in him admired. All in all, the loft suited a professional, reserved woman.

How much time, he wondered, would it take to shake her up, encourage her to let down her hair, open just one more button on her blouse?

Waiting impatiently, he paced from the kitchen to the great room and back several times.

He was looking out one of the floor-to-ceiling windows at a still-dark Denver night when she returned.

"I can be ready to go in twenty minutes."

"Perfect."

"What? No gloating?"

He sighed. "Inamorata, you don't know anything about me." And she didn't. Her safety was the only thing that mattered. His ego, everything else, came second.

In well under the twenty minutes she'd estimated, she returned to the great room, wheeling a small suitcase and carrying an overnight bag. "All of a sudden, I have a whole new level of respect and compassion for the people we take into protective detail. It's a total pain in the ass."

And emotionally discombobulating, he suspected, although he doubted she'd admit to that.

She hadn't changed while she had the opportunity. Holding on to some semblance of control?

He waited for her to come to him, even though it nearly

killed him. He wanted to fold her protectively into his arms and hold on like there was no tomorrow.

"I can manage," she said when he reached for the overnight bag.

"We'll send someone back for your bags," he said.

"Wes—"

"Leave them."

She was pale. Despite that, her shoulders were back and her spine was straight. She was as well put together as she was at nine a.m., except for the fact she wore a gun in an underarm holster.

"I want you to keep your hands free."

She closed her eyes for a second. "Of course."

He knew Hawkeye had assigned another couple of agents to protect Inamorata. She was one of the organization's most important assets. That one of the punks had sent a personal message to her and the security firm concerned Hawkeye. Inamorata kept a nonpublic profile; Hawkeye liked it that way.

"Let Ricardo know we're on our way," Wes said. "I'll have someone from Hawkeye pick up my vehicle later."

She grabbed her cell phone from its holster attached to her waistband. She used only one button to call her driver. She confirmed he was on standby, and then hung up. "You know I'm accustomed to being the one giving orders," she said.

"I'm in charge now." He grinned to take the sting from the words. "Get used to it."

He checked the hallway outside the entrance to her loft and then held open the door. He saw her acknowledge the Hawkeye, Inc., operative stationed near the elevator; then, when they reached the ground floor, she nodded to a second.

Wes sheltered her body while she entered the vehicle. He slid in beside her. Before the door was fully closed, Ricardo was rolling.

Inamorata was quiet the entire way to his home on Lookout Mountain. She'd scooted to the far side of the car and fastened her safety belt, putting physical distance between them.

He expected her to rest her head, maybe close her eyes, but she didn't.

She pulled out her cell phone. He shamelessly looked across at the screen. He couldn't make out individual words, but he saw enough to know she was sending e-mails and a few text messages.

Even when she was remote, focused, he wanted her. He knew she wouldn't want him having protective feelings for her, so he tamped those down and let the more carnal ones creep in.

Ricardo slowed as he navigated the turn into Wes's driveway.

The sun was coming up, the clear Colorado sky brightening by the minute. Every light inside the house was blazing, and there was a guard stationed at the front door.

"Hawkeye is deploying a lot of resources," Inamorata said.

"You're worth ten times that to the organization." And to him.

Ricardo parked directly in front of the house, with no regard for the landscaping. Smart man.

Hawkeye had assigned an operative, and the man was already on-site. The tall, broad, bald black man cleared his throat and presented his identification. "Marcus Phipps, sir," he said. "I, er, checked out the perimeter several times. I wanted to look in the windows to make sure everything was okay, but the"—he cleared his throat again—"the, uh, security system wouldn't let me. Kept telling me to piss off."

"That would be Aston," Wes explained. "Aston is the whole-house computer. He runs all the systems, including the security. And he seems to have an odd sense of humor."

"I thought I heard creepy music, not loud, but real subtlelike. Not just because there's almost a full moon or anything."

"You did hear creepy music. It's Aston's favorite." Wes had found playing music you might hear in a horror film kept away solicitors. "If that doesn't work, the next sequence usually does." Wes waited.

"I see you," a disembodied voice said quietly. Then, in a higher octave, repeated, "I see you."

It'd been a long time since Wes had heard Aston's malevolent voice. Really was impressive, if he did say so himself.

"Target acquired, Mr. Lowell. Do I have permission to shoot?"

A piece of metal, positioned in the eave, moved.

"Jesus!" The man jumped.

Inamorata only shook her head. That was his girl.

"Aston, disarm the door and stop frightening our guest," Aston said.

"Guest? He's a guest?" Aston's voice had changed. He sounded very polite, refined even. "Why didn't you say so, sir?"

Inamorata rolled her eyes.

"All clear, Aston?"

"No attempted breaches of the perimeter, sir. Except one of those pesky Pica picas about five minutes ago."

"Pica pica?"

"Scientific name for the black-billed magpie that landed on my fence. Zapped his ass. Feathers everywhere. Quite the sight. Quite."

"Aston," Wes warned.

"I didn't really do it."

Wes would have sworn Aston sounded slightly offended.

"I did consider it, though. They're not on the endangered list."

The door latch made a scraping sound.

"We're in," Wes said. "I'll program the system so Aston knows you're a friendly."

"You don't have a key for the door?" the operative asked.

"Wouldn't matter. Even with a key, unless Aston lets you in, you won't get in. The first shock he gave you when you put the key in the lock would convince you not to try a second. If you did, the second would knock enough sense into you that you wouldn't need a third."

"He really would shoot me? I mean *it*. It would shoot me?"

"I most certainly would," Aston said.

The operative nodded. "I need one of those things."

"I'll see to it, if you keep Inamorata safe," Wes said.

"I'd keep Ms. Inamorata safe even if there weren't a super-cool security system on the line."

Definitely a smart man.

Wes shook the man's hand, accepting his personal promise. "I assume you know Ms. Inamorata?"

"By reputation." He shook her hand. "A pleasure, ma'am."

"Sandy," Aston said. "Sandy Inamorata."

"Sandy?" Marcus asked. He rubbed his hands together. "Hot damn. Sandy Inamorata. I'm in the money!"

She sighed. "It's not Sandy. That doesn't even sound good together."

"Oh." Marcus's expression fell.

"Visions of those five figures disappearing?" Wes asked

Marcus shrugged. "It'd be cool to win the office pool. Been

dreaming of Cabo or Maui. A sandy beach and beer." Then he sighed and shook his head. "Hell, as frugal as I am, it'd buy me a car. But I could dream about Cabo while driving around, right?"

"Sorry I can't help," she said.

Along with half of Hawkeye, Wes had all but given up on trying to guess her first name. Aston was much more persistent. He'd been programmed not to take no for an answer.

"Mandy?"

"Not even," she said.

"Candy?"

"That doesn't sound half-bad," Wes said.

"Candy?" she repeated. "I look like a Candy to you?"

He met her gaze. "Oh yeah. Definitely."

She rolled her eyes. "But still wrong."

Despite Aston's assurances the house and property were secure, Marcus drew his weapon and went in ahead of them. He took a startled step back when a growling Bentley slowly moved toward them, ears cocked forward threateningly. The dog's normally enthusiastic tail was frozen in place, sticking straight up in a way that even intimidated Wes.

Wes grinned. His home was more than a sanctuary. It was a fortress. Anyone who got past Aston would have their ankles shredded by Bentley's sharply pointed metal teeth.

"What the hell is that?" Marcus asked.

"It's not a what; it's a who," Wes said. "Meet Bentley."

Marcus took another couple of steps into the house, and Wes applied light pressure to the small of Inamorata's back, urging her inside. The less time she was completely exposed, however slightly, the better.

He closed the door behind them. The always alert Aston slid the bolt home, locking them in without being commanded.

"Down, boy," Wes said.

"Err…"

"Let him smell your hand."

Marcus raised his brows.

"He's serious," Inamorata said.

Marcus, like a man who was afraid of losing his limb, slowly put out his hand. Like a normal dog, Bentley approached and sniffed.

"Amazing," Marcus said. He scratched behind the creature's ears. "Any other surprises?"

"Don't tell him," Inamorata said.

At the sound of her voice, Bentley turned his head and then raced over to Inamorata. He jumped up, and his pink mechanical tongue hung out.

Sometimes Wes wondered if his tongue did the same thing when he thought about her.

She crouched and made ridiculous cooing noises and scratched Bentley's belly. He fell to the ground and rolled onto his back. Then he purred.

Slight programming glitch. Wes sighed.

As she scratched, the purrs got louder.

"Maybe I'll wait until version 2.0 is released," Marcus said. Then he looked at the dog, as if considering what the mutt was good for. "At least he doesn't shed."

"He pees oil, though." Inamorata played with Bentley another few seconds, then smoothed her skirt and stood. "Once he even did it on the carpet."

"Twice," Wes corrected.

"Another programming glitch?"

"I'm working on it."

"I'll take a quick shower," Inamorata said. "Then Ricardo can drive me to the office. I don't suppose Aston can brew coffee while I'm getting ready?"

"You can shower," he said. "Tell Aston what temperature you prefer. But then you're going to sleep."

"I'm—"

"Exhausted. You're exhausted, Inamorata. You'll be more useful to everyone after a few hours of rest."

"Lowell."

She raised her eyebrows in a way that would have left weaker men shaking in their shoes. But Wes wasn't weak. He was strong enough for Inamorata. "My house, my rules."

After clearing his throat, Marcus excused himself, saying he needed to get the lay of the house and find the coffeepot.

Wes figured it was a good thing he'd gotten himself assigned as part of the protective detail. Inamorata would have chewed up a lesser man. They'd be nothing more than puppets in her very capable hands. And she'd push herself past the point of exhaustion.

Probably no one but him would even see it in her.

Her shoulders were pulled back, her spine straight. Every hair was tucked into place. Her skirt looked freshly pressed, despite the fact Bentley had jumped on her. But there was a slight weariness etched beside her green eyes.

When he spoke, he lowered his voice by an octave, despite his determination to tuck her in and fuck her so hard she slept for a week. "Think about the case, about the advice you'd give to anyone else."

She glanced at her watch and sighed. "A few hours." Then she looked at him. "I'm not turning off my phone."

With Inamorata, a compromise was a win. He wasn't a proud man where she was concerned. He'd take the compromise.

She headed for the master bedroom.

He took that as a win too.

There was a guest bathroom down the hall, and she'd opted for the one in his room.

Bentley, a pile of nuts and bolts and wires, ran after her, probably tearing another chunk out of the hardwood floor in his attempts to find his footing.

Another Hawkeye, Inc., employee arrived with her luggage. Wes absently wondered if Inamorata had packed any lingerie, although the idea of her sleeping in one of his shirts appealed to him. The idea of her sleeping in nothing at all appealed even more...

He heard the sound of water running, which meant she'd soon be naked, if she weren't already.

He headed for the kitchen and answered a few questions for Marcus. He showed the man how to interface with Aston both verbally and through a keyboard.

"Before you go..."

Wes stopped at the doorway.

"I haven't figured out the coffeemaker. Everything around here is high-tech. Bet you even have one of those robotic vacuum cleaners."

"Aston is somewhat attached to the vacuum, so you'd better watch what you say about Lexie."

Marcus rolled his eyes. "I won't dis Lexie, if you just show me how to make the coffeepot work."

Wes laughed. After showing Marcus how to brew coffee—this model ground its own beans and filtered its own water—Wes headed for the bedroom, glad the shower was still running. He never wanted to miss a naked Inamorata.

Her clothes were in a neat pile on a chair near the foot of his bed. Her shoes, those high, spiky things that made his thoughts careen in half a dozen illicit directions, lay at an angle, one on top of the other.

True to her promise, her phone was on the nightstand on the side of the bed she'd chosen as her own. She hadn't put away her gun. It lay next to the phone. Generally, when she was at his house, she left it in a holster with her clothes. Sometimes, she had it in an oversize purse.

He thought about all the nights she spent at home, alone. Were her phone and gun always within inches of where she slept? He knew she was a highly trained operative. She'd even done protective service herself. But damn it, who took care of the protector?

He kicked off his shoes and walked into the master bath, a room roughly the size of a studio apartment in New York City.

Steam billowed everywhere and fogged the mirrors. Bentley was sprawled on a mat outside the shower. Humidity plus metal equaled a good recipe for rusting every one of his parts.

Wes pointed to the bedroom. Bentley put a paw over his eyes. Like a kid, Wes supposed. *If I can't see you, you can't see me.*

"Out." He snapped his fingers.

Bentley stood slowly and walked from the room with his head hanging low.

Through the opaque glass door, her slender body seemed to have an ethereal look.

She ran her hands through her hair and then stretched, arching her back.

His cock instantly hardened. He wanted to be inside her. Now.

Wes tossed a couple of towels over the rack that was placed above the unit. Close enough to keep a towel handy so you could dry off in the shower, far enough away not to get wet. Then he opened the shower door.

She turned to face him, but she didn't look surprised. "Joining me?"

He unbuttoned his jeans and shoved them down. He stepped out of them as he pulled his shirt over his head. Unlike Inamorata's tidy pile, he tossed his clothes in a careless heap.

The enclosure, with its dual showerheads, was more than big enough for two. Even though he hadn't known her when he'd had it built, he'd been glad the first time they'd shared.

She moved in deeper. After he closed the door, she rose on her tiptoes to link her arms around his neck.

There was nothing like a warm, willing, wet woman. *This* woman. "If you think you can distract me from your punishment, you're mistaken."

"Punishment?" She shivered.

"For leaving earlier. For not calling when you should have."

"Wes…"

She leaned into him. Gently he turned her away.

"Uhm…"

"Put your hands on the wall."

Slowly she did.

He squirted some liquid soap into his hand and worked it into a lather. "Stay still," he said. "Spread your legs."

It took her several seconds, but she followed his order.

He washed her back and reached around her to lather her stomach. She wiggled back a little. "Stay still," he repeated.

"You're a torment."

His cock jutted forward. He was more than interested in fucking her hard and fast. He cupped her breasts, then squeezed them, simultaneously pinching her nipples.

Her knees sagged forward, but she caught her weight with

her hands and pushed herself back into position.

"That's my girl." He tightened his grip on her nipples.

She moaned.

"Have you ever worn nipple clamps?"

"Yes."

"During your BDSM play?"

"Yes."

"And...?"

"Almost always when I masturbate."

He twisted her nipples just a bit.

"Oh...Wes..."

"Stop?"

"No!"

He lowered his head so his lips were a fraction of an inch from her ear. Warm water sluiced over both of them. "Tell me what you want, Inamorata."

"More."

"Harder? You're always wanting it harder," he said.

And she was. She didn't have a reputation as an extreme player, but she clearly preferred a small amount of pain to a lot of pressure. It shouldn't surprise him. Inamorata was an uptight woman who walked a razor wire of demands and decisions at Hawkeye, Inc. It made sense she craved that edge of pain to make her forget and help her get off.

She was moving, her hips grinding backward. The tip of his cock was rubbing her ass, and even that was enough to make blood pound through his body. She mumbled his name again and leaned her upper body a bit forward, letting him support more of her weight and making it easier for him to squeeze her breasts.

He recognized the signs of her impending orgasm, but until

now he'd had no idea she was responsive enough to climax without him even touching her clit. He increased the pressure on her breasts as well as her nipples. "You're not going to come from just this, are you?"

"I might," she confessed. "Just keep up that pressure a few more seconds."

"I forbid it."

She went still. "You forbid it?"

"You may not come, Inamorata."

For a moment, she didn't say a word. When she did speak, her voice was low, soft. "Even if I ask? If I beg?"

His cock got harder. "You can beg." Jesus, yes. "And it may or may not make a difference." He released one of her breasts and trailed his fingers down her spine to that tiny dip near her rounded butt. He kept a tight squeeze on her captured right nipple while barely touching her back. She'd subconsciously note the differences in pressure, and it was his intention she'd respond to each. "Spread your legs."

She didn't hesitate.

"Farther."

She did. Could this woman be any more delectable?

He stroked her spine, and she began to move again in response to his movements.

Wes cursed himself for three types of fool. He'd been an idiot to let Inamorata set the pace for the last six months. He'd had the idea that if he was patient, things would progress naturally. She'd stay at his house for an entire night, they'd have breakfast, occasionally drive to Denver headquarters together.

Hell, he could get crazy and ask for a whole weekend together, maybe even take a trip to Steamboat Springs, spend a day skiing, then celebrate après ski on a patio overlooking a run. Hell, he'd settle for drinking wine in front of a fireplace and showing her around the town.

And the nights... The nights would be filled with the softness of her sighed submission, the quick intake of her breath as she shouted out his name on a climax.

But the longer he'd waited, the more comfortable she seemed with treating his house like a place to find sexual relief on the way home from work, a rest stop on the way back to her regularly scheduled life.

Well, he sure as shit wasn't comfortable with the way things were. He wanted more. It was time to push. He risked losing her, but anything was better than the status fucking quo.

He trailed his fingers lower, between the crack of her ass and then down to her cleft. "Your pussy is wet." And it wasn't just from the water. "You do like a little pain with your sex, Inamorata."

She didn't respond, didn't need to. Her silence was answer enough.

He gave her clit a quick pinch. She gasped.

He slipped a finger inside her cunt.

"More. More, more, more."

"Don't come," he warned her even as he slipped a second finger inside.

She ground her pussy against his hand.

"Keep still," he told her. "And I mean it."

"Damn it, Wes!"

"Keep still." He kept her on the threshold for a few more seconds, and then he withdrew his fingers and slowly released his hold on her breast and nipple. He turned her to face him.

"Beast," she said, her breathing ragged. She wiped stray strands of blonde hair from her cheeks and cleared water from her face. "You're an absolute beast."

"Part of your punishment, Inamorata. But only part of it." His cock ached for him to take it in hand and give himself some relief. He figured it'd take oh, three, maybe four strokes. "Aston, water off."

The stream of water stopped. He grabbed one of the thick towels. "Stay still." He patted her face, then moved lower, rubbing harder than he would have previously on her nipples.

She moaned slightly.

"Sensitive?"

"Yeah." Her eyes closed while he rubbed again and again.

"Uhm, Wes…if you keep that up—"

"I've already told you not to come. You're not planning to disobey me, are you?"

She swallowed. "No."

He took mercy on her and continued to dry her, easing the towel down her body. He paused when he reached her stomach. He crouched in front of her and gently dried her midsection. He looked up and caught her gaze. "The next time I have you alone, I'm going to shave off the rest of your pussy hair." Her pubic hair was well groomed and trimmed. He liked it. "I like the sight of your cunt, wet and drippy. I don't want it hidden." And he wanted to push her boundaries.

Her eyes were wide, but for once, she was silent.

"The correct response is, 'Anything you say, Sir. And I'd prefer anything you say, Sir.'"

She moistened her upper lip.

He'd never seen her do that before. The sight of her tongue, so pink, so pleasing… His cock throbbed in anticipation, in demand. "Say it, Inamorata. Let me hear your submission."

"Anything…anything you say. Wes."

He dragged his pulse back under control. With deliberate

concentration, he rubbed her thighs, then her knees. He was refusing her orgasm; he couldn't just spill his load all over her in the shower. "Put one of your feet on the bench."

"That's obscene."

"You did it earlier tonight," he reminded her.

"Not with you crouched in front of me."

"You'll have no secrets from me," he said.

Even though the bathroom was still steamy and warm, she shivered.

She lifted her leg, and he dried her calf.

"You're driving me mad."

"Not quite," he said. He ran the nubby cotton up the inside of her leg, then gently patted her pussy.

He parted her feminine folds and took his time.

"Wes!" She shifted, obviously trying to keep her balance, but she kept her foot on the bench.

"Stay in position," he told her again. Keeping her labia spread, he replaced the towel with his mouth.

She moaned when he licked her clit.

He kept up the onslaught, faster, slower, feeling her body jerk and respond. She dug her hands in his hair, but she kept her foot where he'd told her.

He loved the scent of her, soap and woman.

Her body tensed, and she sucked in a breath. He moved away from her. "When you come, it will be with my cock inside you."

"Can we make that sooner rather than later?"

He stood, and she released her hold on his hair. Without being told, she put her hands back on the tile.

"Put your right leg down and your left leg on the bench," he instructed.

She moved slowly but didn't question his order. Yeah, he should have pushed Inamorata months ago.

He dried her other leg. When he neared the apex of her thighs, she rose onto her tiptoes in anticipation. He avoided the area entirely. Instead, he shifted to dry her shoulders and back.

She was trembling, and he knew it was from denied sexual gratification, just the way he liked it.

He turned her to face him. "Walk to the bed," he told her, "lie on your back with your legs and arms spread. If you want me to tie you, disobey me." He wondered if she'd argue or whether desire and worry and exhaustion had clouded her mind.

"If I do what you want, will you finally fuck me?"

She was trying for the upper hand, making this about sex and nothing else. The anger that had been on slow boil heated several degrees.

"Hard?" she asked. "Fast?"

His grip tightened on her shoulders. Having the naked and not-so-submissive Inamorata in his arms made the throbbing in his cock nearly unbearable. "Keep it up and I'll just tie you to the bed and go to sleep."

"You wouldn't." She took hold of his cock and stroked him firmly.

He closed his hand around hers. If she kept it up, he'd come in less than seven seconds. "Try me."

"You want me as bad as I want you." She squeezed his cock.

How had he not noticed how long her eyelashes were and how seductive she was when she looked at him through them? "No doubt."

"But you'd still tie me to the bed without fucking me?"

"Like I said, try me."

"You'd lose out too."

"I'd live." He hoped. He loosened his grip on her hand and her shoulder. "Now move it." As she opened the shower door, he gave her ass a sharp slap.

"Ow!" She turned to face him.

Her lovely green eyes were wide, her pupils dilated. Her breaths were shortened. Yeah, this relationship could become more and more interesting. "I told you to move it," he repeated.

"Yes, Sir."

If only those words had been more respectful instead of sassy. He was mostly dry, but he grabbed a towel and wrapped it around his waist. He tossed her damp towel in the direction of the hamper. He watched her walk toward the bed. Her hips swayed with her graceful movements.

She glanced over her shoulder, and she did that funny little thing with her tongue and upper lip again.

In the months she'd been turning his life and libido upside down, he'd never just stood and appreciated her body's movements. She generally slipped out of his bed and into her clothes, obliterating any chance of intimacy before it started. Now that he had the opportunity, he'd take it.

She mesmerized him.

He was a big man, and his bed was high enough off the ground that she had to crawl onto it. Little vixen took her sweet time. He didn't give much consideration to the fact she might not follow his orders. In the shower, he'd smelled her arousal. She wanted an orgasm as desperately as he wanted to give her one.

"Like this?" she asked, spreading her legs slightly. She'd followed his exact instructions, but not the spirit of the order.

"Living dangerously?"

She spread her legs a little farther.

"Better. But not good enough." He dropped his towel to the floor and wasn't surprised when Bentley raced over and grabbed it. The dog and the soon-to-be-shredded towel disappeared beneath the bed. Wes had forgotten to program manners into the mutt. Another thing to remember for the upgrade. Good thing Bentley was so lovable. And a double-good thing he'd left Inamorata's shoes untouched.

"How's this?"

She did like to live dangerously. "The next time you are deliberately disobedient, I won't be so lenient."

She shuddered, but the action appeared to be more from anticipation than any real fear.

"This time, though, I want your legs over my shoulders."

"Finally," she said. "You're going to fuck me."

As if he could do anything else. Seeing her there, on her back, legs and arms spread wide in invitation, diverted blood from brain to his dick.

He wanted to take her slow and easy, with several lengthening strokes.

"I want you," she said. "Now. I want you to make me forget. I want you to wear me out. Take me. Punish me. But don't make me wait."

As he put his first knee on the bed, she spread her legs even farther apart. The invitation, both verbal and physical, pummeled what remained of his self-control.

He grabbed a condom from a drawer in the nightstand and sheathed himself. When he had more patience, he'd have her do it for him. "Lift your legs," he told her, maneuvering between her thighs.

He moved in, his cockhead poised at her entrance. "You have the most beautiful pussy." He saw she was moist, ripe. "Put your legs on my shoulders."

"You do like this obscene look," she said.

"I like you exposed, hiding nothing," he corrected. "There's nothing obscene about that."

Their gazes met. This side of Inamorata invigorated him. She was holding nothing back. She was as vulnerable as she'd ever been.

He was done waiting.

This time, he didn't bother with the foreplay.

He took her hard, fast, in a single brutal thrust.

She cried out, not with pain but with a shout of pleasure. Bentley scampered from beneath the bed and whimpered.

"Does he have an Off button?"

"He will tomorrow," Wes said. He gave her a few seconds to accommodate him. He shifted the majority of his two hundred pounds onto his elbows so he didn't smash her completely.

She wrapped her arms around his neck. "Yes," she said. "Fuck me."

Her encouragement was all he needed. Her pussy was wrapped tight around him. Her muscles squeezed him, and he'd never known a more perfect feeling.

He fucked her.

There was nothing slow, leisurely, or sweet about this joining. He cared about this woman, deeply. If he didn't, he wouldn't be half this pissed. This wasn't about making love. They'd do that another time. This was about fucking and possessing and proving a point.

Inamorata, independent and proud, had been through a lot, even though she wouldn't likely admit it. The privacy of her home had been violated, her housekeeper had been hurt, and the bad guys wanted her. If he could, he'd take all that away. With his body, he telegraphed the frustration he couldn't express with words.

With her legs over his shoulders, he drove into her deeper than he ever had before. She gasped each time he entered her. "Play with your clit," he told her.

She reached between them to touch herself. He readjusted his weight to support himself on his hands.

"Oh," she said.

He grinned. "Working for you?"

"Don't deny me an orgasm this time. Please?"

Instead of answering, he drove into her.

She called out his name.

"Take it," he said. He fucked her again and again.

Her body tensed. Oh *yeah*.

"Wes?"

"Come, baby."

She did, hard, milking his cock. His teeth gritted to distract him from his impending orgasm, he made sure she rode hers as long as possible.

Only then did he allow himself to spill.

He groaned. Because of her capitulation, her knowing he wanted her and wouldn't tolerate her hiding, the thrill of taking Inamorata this time was better than the first, six months ago.

She brought out the caveman in him. He wanted to protect her, claim her as his. When he had seen her in her loft, taking care of others, he'd wanted to drag her by the hair back to his place and take care of her. Which, he realized, he'd all but done. He had no regrets. He didn't want Inamorata fighting her battles alone, not when he was around.

He excused himself to the bathroom and brought back a washcloth for her. She reached for it, and he shook his head. "Stay still." He soothed her swollen cunt with the cool cloth. "I don't want you sore for round two," he said.

Her mouth opened wide. "Round two?"

"Inamorata." He sighed. "You didn't thank me for your orgasm. We'll keep doing this until you learn some manners."

She shuddered.

He leaned over her and sucked on her already tormented clit. She cried out. "Not nearly done with you yet," he said.

Chapter Four

"Be back in five minutes," Wes said. "Don't you dare think about getting out of bed."

As if she could move.

Despite her overwhelming exhaustion and Wes torturing her with orgasm after orgasm, Inamorata was certain she wouldn't sleep. When she was working a case, rest was the first casualty. She'd puzzle out the few things she knew, maybe make a flowchart of the details. She'd stare at information until her vision blurred and what-ifs collided in her mind.

Tonight, she'd humor Wes and stay in his bed until he fell asleep; then she'd get up and get some work done, call the office, check on Martha's condition, see if there'd been any update on Sam's whereabouts and if there was anything known about the hoodlums he'd been hanging with.

That was her plan. But that plan didn't factor in Wesley Lowell's hypnotic, seductive power.

Before she'd left his home, he'd made sure she'd had half a dozen orgasms. And now... He'd fucked her so hard she had almost no energy left. Her breasts tingled, her nipples ached, and her pussy throbbed.

She couldn't get enough, couldn't stop thinking about what he'd done, couldn't stop thinking about what was still ahead.

Everything he promised, threatened, she wanted.

She looked forward to being across his lap with his hand on

her ass. She more than half hoped he was serious about making her wear nipple clamps. She drew a breath, wondering if he had what it took to truly make her let go, mentally as well as physically.

And if he did, what the hell did that mean to her, for her?

When she played at the club, she kept herself emotionally detached. She was able to enjoy the physical sensations, the pain that brought a flash and sizzle of pleasure. But she'd never done anything other than have sex with men she'd been involved with.

Part of her was scared witless. Mixing emotions and BDSM would lead to vulnerability. So Wes's determination to stay in her life and give her what she wanted sexually was a prescription for disaster. Until now, she'd been smart enough to step around that minefield. She'd avoided long-term relationships and refused to give away even a portion of her heart to anyone other than her sister and Martha.

Her love for Hawkeye had nothing to do with romance and everything to do with gratitude. He was the big brother she'd never had. He was friend and mentor, confidant and world-class ass kicker. He'd given her a chance when no one else would. In exchange, she'd volunteered for duty that put her in the line of fire to protect him.

That she was in Wes's bed instead of insisting on sleeping in the guest room, that she was lying here while he settled Bentley on his battery charger bothered her more than just a little. Until now, until Wesley Lowell, nothing had scared Inamorata.

"Lights off, Aston," Wes said, returning to the bedroom and shucking the jeans he'd pulled on. "Shades closed. Keep out that sun so we can sleep."

"Anything you say, sir."

Clearly Wes liked to be obeyed. Aston hadn't just

controlled the lights and the shades. He'd responded linguistically as programmed.

Wes climbed into bed, and suddenly the king-size mattress seemed too small. He reached for her and pulled her against his body.

She went rigid.

"Stop fighting me," he said. "Not everything between us has to be a battle, Inamorata."

The battle wasn't between them. The battle was internal. She wanted him as desperately as she wanted *not* to want him.

"I'll only make you stay here a few hours," he said.

In less than twenty seconds, his breathing changed, and she realized he was asleep. No one fell asleep that fast.

She tried to scoot away, but even in sleep, he held her fast, exerting more pressure to keep her by his side.

His semierect cock nestled in the crack of her behind. There was something so intimate, so unexpected, so pleasurable about the connection. A few minutes later, she realized she didn't want to move. That thought should have galvanized her into action. Instead, it enticed her to surrender.

Yeah...this man was definitely dangerous.

She hadn't consciously made a decision to sleep, just rest, but the scent of coffee woke her.

She opened her eyes, coming instantly awake.

Wes stood next to the bed, freshly showered, his dark hair still damp. He'd dressed in black jeans and a black long-sleeved T-shirt. She might have salivated even if he hadn't been holding a cup of steaming coffee.

"You've never woken up in my bed before. I like it."

So did she, but she'd be damned if she'd let him know that. "Don't get used to it," she said, scooting into a sitting position. She dragged the sheet with her, keeping her naked body covered, not that a sheet or blankets would stop Wes from touching, from taking.

Her eyes burned, lined with the grit of too little sleep. She'd sell half her soul for that first fortifying sip of caffeine.

"There's no update on Martha's condition. To Hawkeye's knowledge, there have been no demands from the kidnappers. And there's been no activity on Sam's phone. Seems as if the friends might have lied about their names."

Only another operative would know that information was more important than coffee. Only he would know how much that mattered to her.

"Since you've never had coffee at my place," he continued, "I took a guess at how you might want it. Hot."

"Check," she said, propping a pillow behind her.

"Strong enough that a spoon can stand straight up in it."

"Check."

"I've never known you to have a sweet tooth, so I guessed no sugar."

"Check."

"With a dollop of cream, not milk."

"Check again." So maybe she could like this guy. "We're in total agreement. Can I please have the damn cup now?" He finally handed over the goods. The first sip scalded her mouth. She sighed in satisfaction.

"No attempted breaches of the perimeter last night. And all the Pica picas are fine." He looked at her, pointedly, smolderingly.

Her pussy moistened.

Coffee, a status update, and a look that promised more than words could. Yeah, he was good.

Obviously fresh from an overnight charge, Bentley barged into the room, knocking the door open. He launched himself at the bed, hit the box spring, and fell to the ground. He shook his head and tried again.

"Worse than a kid for ruining the mood. I think he's glad you're here," Wes said. "That makes two of us."

"Are dogs allowed in your bed?"

"I've never thought about it. He's never tried to jump on the bed before, so it's never been an issue. He doesn't shed. You want him up there?"

"As long as he doesn't get oil on the bedspread. And as long as I don't spill my drink."

Bentley backed up a few steps, then took a running leap at the bed.

"It's probably better to put him up there than have him bend or break something." Wes scooped up Bentley and put him on the bed.

He was gentle with a nonhuman pet, and thoughtful, but too damn direct with her. In bed was one thing; out of it was another.

She lifted her coffee out of the way, and Bentley scampered into her lap, his feet snagging on the cotton bedding. She scratched behind the mutt's ears. True to form, he purred, if that's what the sound could be called. "Uh. What was that?" It was a deep, almost guttural moan this morning. Not as feline as last night's purr, but definitely not doglike.

"Guess that adjustment didn't work." Wes frowned.

Bentley settled and sprawled out while she drank her coffee

"I put your suitcase in the second closet," he said. "Your overnight bag is in the bathroom. I hope I got that right."

For the first time since she'd known him, he looked a little uncomfortable, as if he was unsure of himself. She found that endearing. "I'll call Ricardo and let him know I'll be ready to go in about twenty minutes."

"Make it thirty. I'll get you some breakfast."

She looked at him over the rim of the cup. "I don't eat breakfast."

"Not usually," he said. "Today you do."

"I grab coffee and a bagel on the way."

"And today you eat fruit and eggs."

"You're damn bossy, Mr. Lowell."

"Be glad I'm letting you go to the office, Ms. Inamorata."

"Letting me?" she demanded. "Letting me?"

He straddled her, bracing his hands on the headboard. She inhaled the scent of fresh, cool mountain air and the spice of determined male.

"There's a good argument for keeping you in protective custody. I, for one, would be much happier with you working remotely until Sam is found."

"This isn't about making you happy," she said. "It's about solving the case."

"Which is easier if you're safe; otherwise Hawkeye will have two problems on his hands."

She put her free hand on his chest and pushed him back a bit. "You're assuming the worst."

"And you're not being objective."

"You're pissing me off."

"Deal with it."

His jaw was set in a firm line, with a pulse thumping there, just like she'd noticed last night. She'd already learned it meant he was inflexible. She blew out a breath. "Thirty minutes," she agreed.

"It's only breakfast, Inamorata."

So he thought. To her, it was about him asserting himself

into her life, as if they were a couple.

Wes left the bedroom, and she sank back against the pillows and tried to shake off the feeling of being discombobulated. Not only had she stayed at Wes's place, but she'd slept while he'd gotten up, showered, and made coffee. She was normally a light sleeper, waking up a handful of times every night, but here, in the protection of his arms, subconsciously knowing she had nothing to worry about, she'd slept deeper than she had in years.

What the hell had she gotten herself into? If she hadn't started sleeping with him, she wouldn't be in this mess now. She'd be running her life her way with no interference, with no one telling her what to do, assuming they knew better than she did what she needed.

Worse, she didn't know how she was going to get herself out of this mess.

She finished her coffee and all but slammed the empty cup on the nightstand.

Bentley cocked his head to one side and brought his ears forward.

She scratched him while pushing a button to activate voice dialing on her phone to notify Ricardo she'd need him in half an hour. He informed her he was already in the area, on standby.

Then she checked her e-mail. There were hourly updates from Hawkeye, Inc., letting her know there'd been no progress so far.

She composed a couple of text messages. Doing something, anything, made her feel more in control.

The first message was to the medic, asking for an update on Martha's condition. The second was to Hawkeye's private number to let him know she'd be at the office after she stopped by Martha's apartment. Then she called Martha and reached

Sara Stein. According to Stein, Martha was asleep.

With nothing else to do immediately, she threw back the covers and climbed out of bed.

Bentley was poised on the edge of the mattress, looking as if he was going to jump after her.

"Hold on, boy," she said, picturing a heap of nuts and bolts and circuitry strewn across the hardwood floor. She lowered him, and he immediately ran in circles around her legs. If this mechanical contraption could be anymore doglike, she didn't know how.

She crossed to the closet and dug a skirt and blouse out of her bag. She hung them both in the bathroom, hoping the wrinkles would fall out while she showered. She hadn't used an iron since college, and she didn't intend to start now.

Inamorata hurried through a shower, and her breath caught when she was finished. Wes had put a fresh cup of coffee next to the sink.

How could she be angry at a man who brought her two cups of coffee? And screwed her hard enough she was still tender in all the right places.

He'd put her overnight bag in exactly the perfect spot. Almost as effortlessly as if she were in her bathroom, she pulled out her toiletries. She tamed her hair with mousse and pins and bands, then put on fresh makeup.

Once she was dressed, stockings in place, her blouse buttoned and tucked into her skirt, her feet stuffed into take-charge heels, Inamorata felt infinitely better.

She strapped on a holster and secured her pistol, then clipped her cell phone to her waistband. When she shrugged into a black blazer, her armor was complete. She'd kick Wesley Lowell's ass if he got in her way, regardless of the fact he'd brought her two cups of coffee, one of them before she'd even crawled out of bed. While she was at it, there was enough caffeine humming in her veins that she could happily kick Hawkeye's ass too. After all, he'd been the one to assign the protective detail.

After squaring her shoulders, she and Bentley went in search of breakfast and Wes.

Marcus and Ricardo were seated at the glass table. She was touched by Wes's thoughtfulness in inviting her driver to join them. Every morning Ricardo was on duty, she bought him coffee and a bagel. If his sloppy grin was anything to judge by, the gourmet feast beat a drive-through meal.

Wes had his back to her, and he was busy cutting up some sort of vegetable. He'd made a total mess on the granite countertops. There were knives and cutting boards and discarded bowls everywhere.

Classical music, something she didn't recognize, spilled from the high-tech stereo. The food smelled sensational. Coffee was fresh and hot. In that moment, she didn't know why she'd made such a big deal of going home to a cold, empty house in the wee hours.

"Morning," Marcus said.

Wes looked over his shoulder.

"Anything I can do to help?" she asked. She didn't really want to help. She wanted more coffee and a big plate of food. Now that she was in the kitchen, her stomach grumbled. Much as she hated to admit Wes might be right, she was suddenly ravenous. Her mouth salivated at the sight of fresh strawberries cut up in a glass bowl and swimming in cream.

"Just have a seat. You need to keep up your strength."

Somehow, she knew he wasn't talking about the case.

Bentley hissed, sounding more like a snake than a cat.

"Programming glitch," Marcus explained to Ricardo.

Ricardo said something in Spanish that Inamorata didn't

quite catch.

Wes had said he was making eggs. By that he meant he'd whipped up light and fluffy omelets, with onions, green peppers, and ham. He was plating one, and she hoped it was for her.

"I'm happy to be assigned to Mr. Lowell's house anytime," Marcus said, shoveling in the last bite and reaching for another piece of toast.

"Worked my way through school as a short-order cook at a twenty-four-hour breakfast place," Wes said.

Six months and she hadn't known that. Until last night, she'd had no idea he wanted to tie her to his bed and spank her ass.

What else didn't she know about him?

He arranged a few strawberries next to the omelet as a garnish and then slid the plate onto the table.

She sat, and he slid a glass of orange juice in front of her. She'd been missing out on this?

While Marcus loaded the dishwasher, Wes ate at the counter. She took a bite of her food and almost closed her eyes in delight. Even though strawberries were out of season, these were deliciously sweet and vibrant red.

Did he do everything well?

Ten minutes later, her energy level peaked. The fact he was right again would have annoyed the hell out of her if she weren't so high on caffeine and satisfied. "Thank you," she said, crossing her knife and fork on the empty plate. "You were right. I was hungry."

"Words stick in your throat?"

"No."

"Not even a little?"

"Maybe a little."

He crossed the room, apparently heedless that they had other operatives in the room. "It was just breakfast," he said, looming over her.

She had to crane her neck to look at him.

He caught her chin between his thumb and forefinger. "But you can thank me for it later." He bent to kiss her hard and fast. He left her speechless, breathless. "Good morning, Inamorata."

Ricardo carried his plate to the sink. Marcus whistled, completely out of tune with the classical music.

And she noticed the bulge in Wes's pants.

Her cell phone signaled an incoming e-mail. She grabbed for the device, grateful for the distraction. She ignored Wes's grin and Marcus's chuckle. Ricardo headed for the door, saying the car was ready and waiting.

Marcus and Wes discussed arrangements for a second agent to arrive, so there'd be twenty-four-hour coverage at the house. "You promise Aston won't shoot the new people?" Marcus asked.

"No promises," Wes said. "You may want to ask him nicely."

She scanned the message from Laurents. There'd been no suspicious activity at Martha's house overnight. He was heading home for some shut-eye and would be back within ten hours. Barstow had crashed in the guest bedroom. He was awake and fresh, so he'd take the next shift.

After draining her juice, she pushed back from the table. Wes was holstering his gun, a massive, powerful piece of weaponry that she probably couldn't wrap her hands around. She didn't even ask if he was going with her. His actions said enough. She decided not to argue. If he wanted to be her flunky, he was more than welcome. Maybe he'd fetch lunch too.

In the car, she gave Martha's address to Ricardo.

Her phone rang before they hit I-70. "It's Stein," she told Wes after checking the caller ID. She answered on the second ring. "Inamorata." The operative succinctly outlined the situation. Within the last few minutes, Martha had gotten a call from her son. One of the bad guys wanted Inamorata's phone number. If they got it within the hour, Sam would be released. "Give it to them," Inamorata instructed. "You have the phone number for the bad guys?"

"Sam called from his phone. We asked for another callback number, just in case. He wouldn't give us anything."

Getting a fix on Sam's phone was good enough. If they could stall long enough, Hawkeye ops would arrive and defuse the situation before it escalated.

"Give it half an hour, then call them back."

"I'm not sure Ms. Montano's going to wait that long. She's feeling much better today. Feisty. Mother-bear kind of stuff." Stein's voice dropped a little. "She's desperate to see Sam."

"Understood. Distract her. Keep her in the loop and let her know what's going on. Give her something to do to make her feel useful and occupy her mind." She thought. "Have her bake those cookies. Tell her as much of the truth as possible and let her know this is bigger than just my phone number, bigger, even, than what happened to Sam. Try to get her to see the bigger picture and draw a map of how her help is necessary. Update headquarters."

Before the sentence was completely out of her mouth, Wes's phone rang. Stein was good. She, or one of the agents with her, had already notified Hawkeye.

Wes started giving instructions to his team, setting up traces and taps, seeing if they had any fix on GPS coordinates. His deep voice sounded powerful, competent, in control. He knew what to do and in what order it needed to be done.

A part of her melted, despite her intention to remain detached. She'd never had a man take charge like this. She'd always been far more competent about security issues than any man she'd slept with. But Wes was her equal in all ways.

He'd pushed his way into this case, doing this for her, because he wanted to protect her. Because he cared about her. Whether she wanted a relationship or not, in this moment, she was glad he'd asked to be part of the team.

Earlier this morning he'd taken her places she'd never dreamed existed. Despite the fear, she had an odd fascination with him. She might have protested, she might have run, but damn, she wanted more. She wanted everything he had to offer.

She'd never wanted to be dominated by a man she was personally involved with. But now she couldn't stop thinking about Wes and his demands.

She informed Stein they were diverting to headquarters. The always brilliant Ricardo met her gaze in the rearview mirror, silently confirming the change of plans. Finally, she sent an update text message to Hawkeye's cell.

In less than twenty minutes, they neared the downtown Denver high-rise that housed Hawkeye, Inc.'s Colorado operation. Wes notified the head of security of their imminent arrival, although it wasn't technically necessary. Hawkeye had GPS tracking enabled on her cell phone. Headquarters knew where she was 24-7.

The company also tracked the driver and the car. Their software package notified management if any driver went more than nine miles per hour over the posted speed limit, in case an operative was in danger and couldn't make a cell phone call. Well, supposedly that was the reason. Some of the constant surveillance tactics were wearing. She tuned them out as much as possible. When surveillance was needed, it was nice to already have it in place.

"We'll get Sam and figure out what the hell's going on," Wes promised after ending his call. "You can let Martha know I personally promise that."

In that moment, Inamorata believed him. She was just beginning to understand how fiercely Wes felt about his cases.

She sent a text message to Martha, relaying Wes's message.

Ricardo pulled into the underground parking lot and stopped the car near the elevator.

"Wait," Wes said. He got out of the vehicle and closed the door.

She fought back her customary impatience. Wes was following procedure, and she knew how important it was to cooperate. She'd bet more problems were caused by clients who'd become impatient with their protective detail than by any bad guy. And now that she was on this end of it, she understood it better. She drummed her fingers on her thigh, annoyed to not be jumping out of the car and immediately heading up the stairs to oversee the situation.

When the elevator dinged its arrival and the doors slid open, Wes verified the credentials of the agent in the compartment. He then opened Inamorata's car door.

He held on to her hand longer than necessary, harder than necessary. Their gazes met and locked. Suddenly she remembered the taste of him and the way his hands felt on her naked body.

His gaze swept over her. When this case was over, she had decisions to make. He might cut her some slack right now, but he wouldn't going forward.

"Your office, ma'am?" the security guard asked.

"Situation room," she said.

The man punched the button for the ninth floor. It seemed like ten minutes before they arrived. In reality, it had probably only been two minutes, tops.

Once she and Wes were in the situation room, stress vanished. She was in her element, and her training kicked in. She knew what to do, and she could block out the pesky issues of a personal life.

A handful of techs were there, some appearing rough and unshaved, as if they'd been dragged from bed, some looking fresh after a good night's sleep, and one woman looked disheveled enough that she might not have seen the inside of a bedroom or a shower in several days. Each person around the conference table had a notebook computer, and there were a few extra computers powered up, ready to work.

Wes cracked his knuckles and took a seat at the head of the table. Inamorata introduced herself and Wes to the techs and thanked them for leaving their regular work on such short notice. She gave a quick synopsis of the situation, along with the cast of characters. All Hawkeye, Inc., techs could operate on a minimum of intelligence, but she knew from experience that the more people knew, the faster they could make connections. "That the bad guys want access to me, to Hawkeye, gives us pause."

The female tech, introduced as Jilly, chomped another chunk of ice and said, "Shit."

Inamorata turned the meeting over to Wes. "Lowell?"

Wes stood, effortlessly taking command of the room, the situation. "Inamorata has given you a list of the players and an overview of the situation. Here's what else we've got." He leaned over the keyboard and tapped a few keys. Several wall-mounted monitors came to life.

"Martha Montano," Inamorata said when a picture of Martha appeared on the screen. Inamorata hadn't even noticed Wes taking the picture last night in her loft, but obviously he had.

A picture of Martha's cell phone and its number appeared, split screen.

"Next," Inamorata instructed.

A picture of Sam appeared on a second monitor. "Samuel—goes by Sam—Montano," Wes said. Another picture appeared, of Sam's phone, along with its assigned number.

"We're still tracking Sam's phone," one of the techs said. "We should have a fix any minute. Surprised it's taking this long, unless they're on the move."

"You know who this is," Wes said.

On another screen, Inamorata's picture appeared, along with a picture of her phone. Having her private information available within seconds no longer surprised her. Information, including a log of missed calls—all from Wes's number—appeared next. "So much for privacy."

"Someone's been stalker calling you," Jilly said. "Unrequited love? Or one of the bad guys?"

"That's not from the bad guys," she said. If the techs were persistent enough, they'd know in under two minutes that she and Wes were involved. She hated that part. No one would care, but she did. She liked her personal life kept private.

"Unrequited love," Jilly said around a mouthful of ice. "Someone's got it for you, bad. 'Morata, you're smokin' hot."

Inamorata shook her head and ignored the comment as the contents of the text messages she'd sent to Hawkeye and Martha were displayed. That much information did surprise her. She'd thought her communication with Hawkeye was confidential.

"Good thing Mr. Stalker Guy didn't send you any naughty text messages," Jilly said.

Good God.

"Don't send nekkid pictures," Jilly said. "At least until this is over and we stop getting all up in your business. Just a suggestion."

"Nekkid pictures are MMS, not SMS," a male tech chimed in.

"So?" Jilly asked, once again reaching for the gigantic cup in front of her. "Multimedia texts are a bit more challenging than simple ones, but all the more fun to crack. And they're a shitpile more fun to look at." She spoke quickly and with more than a hint of an East Coast accent. "You should see some of the nastiness our ops take pictures of with their camera phones. Honey, I could retire on the blackmail money."

Inamorata's phone rang.

Wes's large fingers moved over his computer keyboard, and the incoming number lit up on the wall monitor.

"It's Sara Stein," Inamorata said, saving Wes, oh, maybe half a second.

She answered, and the call was broadcast in the room.

"As soon as we hang up," Stein said, "Ms. Montano will call Sam. The bad guys will have your number at that point."

Game time.

Inamorata ended the call.

Silence momentarily hung over the room. A blast of wind rocked the windows. The heater kicked on, sending warm air through the vents. When they'd left Wes's home, the sky had been vibrant blue. Now it had turned to a threatening gray color. The pissy weather suited Inamorata's mood perfectly. She hadn't had enough sleep. Her friend's son was mixed up in something he had no business being involved with. Martha had been tied and victimized. And Wes had taken a good relationship and potentially ruined it.

"Here's what else we know," Wes said. He displayed pictures of David and Lance. "No last names," he said. "We know one of them, maybe more, work or worked with Sam. It took Ms. Montano some time to find a paycheck stub so we could find out where he worked. We have an operative on the way over to speak with the owners, and we're working on accessing their computers."

Polite code for *hacking*, Inamorata suspected.

"There's supposedly a third man. We don't know who he is. No name, no picture."

The next few minutes dragged.

She paced. Wes stayed hunched over his computer. Jilly pried the lid off her cup and poured ice into her mouth. She crunched and crunched. Inamorata pictured the woman's enamel wearing down, bit by bit.

On the screen, green arrows lit up between Sam's number and Martha's number.

"We're on," Jilly said, rubbing the cup between her palms.

Sugar and caffeine. Probably the only food groups she consumed, Inamorata guessed.

"Audio coming live," Wes said.

The sound of Martha's voice was faint. Wes hit a few keys, amplifying her voice.

"Promise me you're okay," Martha said to her son.

Background noise made Sam's voice all but indistinguishable.

"Got it," one of the techs said.

"Static?" Inamorata asked.

"Wind," Wes guessed. "Could be outside."

They heard Martha give out Inamorata's number.

A moment later, the background noise was filtered.

"I love you, Mom."

"Are you coming home now, Sam?"

The connection ended.

Inamorata swore. "How are we doing on locating Sam's phone?" she asked Wes.

"Different part of town than earlier."

"Can't get a fix," the female tech added, checking her notebook. "They're on the move."

What had she expected? They bad guys would stay still, GPS would locate the phone, and they'd go pick up Sam, apprehend the bad guys, and be home before lunch? She had a rich fantasy life.

Very often Inamorata simultaneously juggled multiple ops. And she was never this involved in one case. She made arrangements and specialized in cleanup and making details go away with local police and federal agencies, sometimes even with the press. Being part of each tedious minute ground on her.

She borrowed a phone to call Martha, leaving her phone free for incoming calls. On the screen, she saw Martha's phone light up. Inamorata squeezed her eyes shut when Martha answered.

"*Sam?*"

"No," she said. "It's Inamorata."

Martha sobbed.

"Got a fix on Sam," Wes said.

She exhaled. "We're on our way to find him," Inamorata told Martha. "We've got his location. Hang tight." She smoothed back her hair as she rang off. This job was a whole lot easier when she wasn't personally involved.

She secured the GPS coordinates from Wes and notified Hawkeye. Within minutes, resources that had been on standby were deployed.

She gave the phone back. Then she stared at hers as if that could make it ring.

On the screen, they saw Martha's phone light up; then, seven seconds later, Sam's did. The call ended shortly after.

Obviously he hadn't answered. Inamorata wasn't a particularly religious person, but she sent up a quick prayer that Sam was okay, as much for his sake as for Martha's.

For the next few minutes, they watched several repeats: Martha's phone lighting up, followed by Sam's, then Martha's shutting down. Inamorata stared, unable to look away from her friend's desperate attempts to reach her only child.

Inamorata rubbed her temples.

"Incoming."

The sound of Wes's voice distracted her from staring fruitlessly, helplessly at the monitors.

Moments later, her phone received the signal and lit up. The shrill ring seemed to bounce off the walls.

"Do you know the number?" Wes asked.

She shook her head.

"We'll broadcast," Wes reminded her. "We're recording."

She nodded. After the next ring, she answered. "Inamorata."

"Do you know who this is?"

She frowned. She talked to lots of people every day. "No. Want to tell me?"

"It wouldn't mean anything to you. But it should. If it wasn't for you, my cousin would be alive."

For her specifically? Or for Hawkeye? She waited. Seconds dragged into a minute.

"I need Hawkeye's help."

"Depends what you need." Hawkeye had his own nonnegotiate policy. Rules could be bent, but rarely broken.

One of the techs typed a message that scrawled across one of the monitors. *Closing in on Sam Montano. GPS from this guy's phone seems to be coming from the same location.*

She nodded. "Are you looking for personal protection?" she asked the caller. "For you or a family member? Someone you care about?"

The caller laughed. "We both know Hawkeye does more than that."

"We're a personal security firm."

"You're a fucking paramilitary operation, Ms. Inamorata. You operate outside the law."

Personal protection covered a lot of ground. "Why don't you give me your name? At least I'll know who I'm talking to."

"Zack Jonah."

The name sounded familiar, but she couldn't immediately place it. "I'm sorry, Mr. Jonah, I'm afraid—"

"My cousin was Nathan Danville."

Her knees went weak. Her breath threatened to strangle her. The past was back to haunt her. And goddamn that it had involved Martha and Sam.

"Yeah, now you remember. Now my name means something to you."

She swallowed the cloying memories. "Not at all." She wished she sounded a bit stronger, more forceful.

His voice lowered, became menacing. "Arizona. Six years ago."

As if she'd ever forget. She remembered the year. The month. The day. The hour. The minute. And most of all, she remembered Chloe. And the blood. Inamorata felt no remorse for her part in it, no matter how wrong she'd been. The only regret she felt was that she hadn't wielded the knife herself. "Six years was a long time ago. I've worked a lot of cases since then."

She signaled Wes to run Jonah's name, but he was a step ahead of her, already on his computer. She knew what he'd find eventually. A sealed file, deep in the archives. He'd keep digging until he found every connection between the cousins.

He looked over at her, a puzzled frown chiseled between his brow.

He'd bumped into the record sooner than she'd expected.

"You were supposed to take care of my cousin, not let him die. Does everyone there know how bad you fucked up? Does everyone there know you killed my cousin?"

"I'm afraid I've been involved in a lot of cases." She locked her knees in place, and she pretended her spine was made of steel and that it could actually support her. "I'm sorry, Mr. Jonah, I don't see—"

"Don't play games with me, bitch," Jonah said. "You'll do as I say, or I'll start by sending you pieces of the sniveling kid we've got here. He wants his mommy, and I want to get my hands on that murdering little slut and my money. I'd say we both want something, wouldn't you?"

"What are you asking for, specifically?"

"I want her. You've got until noon tomorrow."

Chapter Five

The line that linked the phones on the monitor went blank.

"He disconnected," Wes said unnecessarily.

Everyone in the room was watching the same monitors and listening to the same transmission. He looked over at Inamorata. He doubted anyone else saw what he did. The woman was shaken.

Her skin had paled. Her cheekbones were more pronounced, the line of her lips had compressed. Her arms were folded across her chest. She'd known he'd find a file marked Confidential. She'd known his top-clearance security wouldn't be able to get past the Access Denied lock.

Wes watched her rub her temples. More than Jonah could know, she remembered Danville. His Inamorata wouldn't forget a single detail.

Wes's phone rang. He moved away from the conference table to answer the call from the field-team leader.

After the thirty-second brief, he put the man on hold and repeated the update to Inamorata. "Our team's in place outside the house. Phones are still transmitting their location. There's a good possibility they're in the house and this could be over soon." He met Inamorata's gaze. They both knew in this business nothing was a sure deal, and they had to be prepared for any possibility. "We're waiting on your command."

"No-knock entrance," she said. "Front door and back, simultaneously." She straightened her shoulders, once again competent and in control. "Don't alarm the neighbors, but get in there and get him. Get them."

Wes repeated her command to the team leader.

He activated the speaker function on his phone and set it on the table.

"Go, go, go," they heard the team leader call.

The situation room was silent. Wes returned to his seat, but he didn't take stop looking at Inamorata. Beautiful, stubborn, and a force to be reckoned with, the woman needed a keeper. He wanted to take her in his arms, wanted to force her to lean on him. Her shoulders were slim, and yet she seemed capable of taking the weight of the world on them. Did she have any idea how much easier life could be if she shared the load?

The other end of the line remained silent significantly longer than it should have, and tension in the situation room heightened. Jilly had even stopped chomping on ice.

When the team leader spoke, his words were clipped. "We have two phones, a throwaway and one that appears to have belonged to Mr. Montano. The house is otherwise empty. It's vacant, and there are no signs of any struggle." There was a momentary pause. "We missed them by minutes."

Inamorata sighed.

"Roger," Wes said.

They'd need every minute between now and noon tomorrow.

"I'll let Martha know," Inamorata said. She grabbed her phone from the table and left the room.

He admired her guts. She never flinched from difficult actions, except when it involved their personal relationship. No wonder it pissed him off every time she ran.

Wes and the rest of the group watched the monitors for a couple of seconds longer than they should have. Then, driven by disappointment, by being outsmarted, the team resumed work. They had names, had some dots they could start to connect, Sam's place of work and confirmation of where they'd recently been. They'd worked miracles with far less information.

He left the room, looking for Inamorata. She stood in the hallway, her shoulders pressed against the wall. "So close. So *fucking* close," she said.

"Want to tell me about Nathan Danville and Zack Jonah and the woman Jonah is interested in?" Wes wanted her focused.

She rubbed her temples in that same absent way she had earlier. She didn't want to spill the details. But she would. He'd find out anyway; they both knew it. A sealed record was a pain, but in a case this big, Hawkeye would unseal it.

But shortcutting made sense; it gave him and the rest of the team an edge that could potentially save Sam's life. Inamorata, his Inamorata, would realize her personal embarrassment meant nothing in face of that fact.

"In the records, we gave her an assumed name of Chloe. Her real name is redacted."

He nodded, trusting her on that.

She took a breath, closed her eyes wearily for a moment, then opened them again, looking more determined than ever. "Chloe was born in the Middle East. Danville was an important businessman with money and connections and unusual tastes. Chloe's family sold her to him. They thought Danville would marry her, but they were wrong. They got the cash; he got Chloe. She was thirteen at the time, a young, beautiful virgin. She was a freaking child, Wes, taken from her home to be some wealthy man's plaything."

Wes swore.

"You'll ask Hawkeye to unseal the records, as you should," she said. "And he will. You'll find out I had been working in personal protection in Danville's household for about six months, mostly for Chloe, ending with the night he was killed. And before you ask, we were never intimate. I don't sleep with clients."

"I would never have thought you would," he said.

"Chloe was seventeen when I was assigned to her detail."

And that meant Inamorata had not been a whole lot older than Chloe at the time.

"It took me a while to figure things out," she continued. "Hawkeye didn't have any clue what was really going on in the household when he accepted Danville as a client. When we'd done the intake assessment, we'd been told Chloe was his younger sister, but it didn't take me long to see things didn't add up.

"He didn't send her to school. She was enrolled in online classes. She was forever on the computer, even when she wasn't taking classes. She was always in chat rooms, and the Internet really was her only contact with the outside world. When Chloe went out in public, I went with her rather than any of the men assigned to the detail. He didn't want her tempting any of them. He kept her wrapped up in head scarves and jeans, even in summer. I didn't know he was having sex with her.

"I'd been with Chloe for a few months when I learned her horrible secret. One night, when she was around fifteen, Danville had this big party for influential guests. All men. After dinner, while the men were having cocktails, he called for her. He exposed her breasts in front of his guests. The story is a little more lewd than that, but you get the picture."

He did. And he was disgusted by it.

"Danville told her to go to his bedroom and wait there,

naked. She pretended not to hear him."

He didn't want to know this part of the story, but Inamorata was relentless.

"As punishment for pretending she couldn't hear him, he cut off one of her ears. That night, when she told me the story, she took off her scarf and showed me. It was amazing how well she kept it hidden, with her long hair and the scarves. But I'll never forget the first sight of it."

Wes waited.

"She called him all sorts of vile names, words she'd learned from him. He said he thought about cutting off her tongue, but he liked it when she—"

"I get the idea."

"She became personal to me. I should have left when I learned what a vile animal he was, but I couldn't leave Chloe. She begged me to get her out of there. I started thinking of ways to do that. But before I could, Chloe retaliated while he was sleeping."

"She killed him?"

"It's more complicated than that. The report will show a lot of things about me, including the fact I helped Chloe get away." She tipped back her chin. "I did nothing to save the son of a bitch's life. I could have saved him, maybe. Probably. I could have notified someone—the authorities, the staff, another agent, even his doctor. But I left him to bleed out. In fact, I locked the door and told the rest of his detail he'd gone to bed for the night.

"Danville cursed me with his dying breath. I will never forget the sound of him gurgling on his own blood."

Her voice was a little unsteady. She'd done the right thing. She believed she'd done the right thing, but if she thought the event hadn't shaken her, she was wrong.

"Hawkeye should have fired me. I took the law into my

own hands, and I involved other agents in getting Chloe away. Hawkeye never faulted me for helping the girl. I came clean with him, and he didn't turn me in. On my watch, an important client was killed. And Zack Jonah is technically right. I did have a hand in killing Danville."

He waited, saying nothing, not disagreeing, not judging.

"Hawkeye covered for me as best as he could. My name didn't find its way into the press, but the company got a black eye. We lost a lot of other clients as a result. My actions hurt the business, cost us a lot of money."

He said nothing as he watched the pain of the memories turn her dark green eyes a couple of shades lighter, and then the fire of determination made the color darker.

She tipped her head back. "I'd do it all again. Only this time, I'd hurry along his demise rather than just watch him bleed. There wasn't an attempt to reattach Chloe's ear. Her family disowned her. It was her obligation to do what her man said. Even if it meant letting..." She trailed off and then took a shallow breath. "I haven't had any contact with her since then, for her own safety.

"She changed her name when she went to a women's shelter. I understand she had reconstructive surgery—Hawkeye donated the money—and she altered her appearance somewhat. I was hoping no one would ever find out what her real name was or where she is, that she could live as normal a life as possible."

The enormity of this settled in his gut.

She'd do anything to protect Chloe. Even though Chloe was now a young woman, not a child, she remained Inamorata's priority.

Realizations clicked into place. This was a hell of a wormy deal.

Martha meant the world to Inamorata, and Sam was

Martha's only child. And protecting Chloe put Inamorata at odds with taking care of the other people she loved. She wouldn't give up Chloe, even for Sam, even for Martha.

"Since he was there, Jonah obviously knows Chloe's real name. And we can't let him spill it to the world," she said. "If he says it, I need you to do some electronic voodoo to blank it out."

She didn't ask for much. Everyone on the team was as big a nerd as he was. But he didn't say that to her. Wes knew what Inamorata needed from him: emotional stability, objectivity, not to let the enormity of this overwhelm her. She needed him, whether she realized it or not. "Jonah mentioned money."

"I don't know anything about that."

"I doubt Jonah really wants revenge for his cousin's death."

"Sometimes family is tight," she said.

"And more often than not, it's about the dollars," he countered.

"Not big on family love? Sounds a little cynical, Mr. Lowell."

"Would you avenge Aimee? Martha?"

"I'd want to."

"But would you?" he pushed.

"It's different."

"This isn't about Jonah's grief, Inamorata. Think it through."

Appearing resolute, she shoved away from the wall. "I'll notify Hawkeye. If Jonah isn't making idle threats, we can expect him to deliver Sam's right ear to us."

"Agreed." This was bigger, more complicated than he'd originally thought. And with every passing minute, Inamorata seemed more remote and inaccessible, drawing into herself. That was something he wouldn't tolerate.

He understood her better now than ever before. The realization fueled his need to crack her shell and see the vulnerable woman she'd once been. "We'll set up a command room in the guest house."

"The situation room here is fine," she said.

"Here's the deal," he told her. "We're leaving here in less than five minutes. Until Sam is safe and the situation neutralized, you'll be following my orders."

"I—"

"You can shut up now," he said politely. "And go back into the situation room while I make plans." He devoured the distance between them. He curled his fingers into her shoulders and forced himself to back off the pressure he wanted to exert. "You may have had the idea I'm flexible where you're concerned. I'm not. If you object to the way I handle the situation, take it up with Hawkeye. If you want to stay involved, I suggest you keep your pretty little mouth shut except to say, 'Yes, Wes.' Understand?"

A lesser man would have been intimidated by her glare.

"I'll take it up with Hawkeye."

"You know his number." He slowly released his grip on her. He wanted to kiss her, wanted to shake her, wanted to fuck her, wanted to tuck her behind him to keep her safe.

He stepped aside, and she moved past him, back into the situation room. Smart move. He hadn't moved beyond his intention to go caveman on her.

She went to a secure line to call Hawkeye. Wes gave the gathered crew instructions to return to their workstations or home offices, whichever they preferred. But they were now the A team until this job was finished.

He told one of the guys to order the needed specialized equipment and have it delivered to his house. Jilly and another tech volunteered for duty at his place.

"Thanks," he said.

"Wait," Jilly said. "Before I agree to move out of this place, you gotta tell me you have an ice maker. You do have an ice maker, right?"

"It makes cubes or crushed ice."

"Crushed ice?" She looked skyward as if in thanks.

"If it can't keep up, I'll have bags of the stuff trucked in. And all the soda you can drink."

"Soda's gotta have caffeine and sugar," she said. "None of that diet crap. That shit's no good for you."

"Hello, irony," one of the guys said.

"I'll see to it you have whatever you need," Wes promised.

"You're not going to have any teeth left," another of the guys told her.

"Then I'll fit in with the rest of you."

Wes liked Jilly's style.

He ordered Inamorata's car to be brought around and summoned two security guards to accompany them to the vehicle.

Even though she was standoffish with him, she thanked the team for their hard work and dedication. Everyone promised frequent updates and said they'd be on the job until Sam was reunited with his mother. Inamorata was a bit of an enigma around headquarters, and she had a reputation for ruthlessly kicking the asses of agents who were incompetent, but fiercely protecting those who were competent. She was well regarded, and only he knew the toll the job took on her.

Wes didn't relax until Inamorata was safely inside his house. Without being told, Aston locked the doors. Bentley turned excited figure eights around her ankles. She bent to scratch behind the mutt's ears.

"That's some wicked purr," Marcus said, double-checking

that the door was secure.

Bentley fell over in pleasure. But the pup's antics weren't enough to make her smile.

"Welcome home, Mr. Lowell," Aston said. "Glad you could join us, Amethyst."

"Amethyst?" she repeated. "I look like an Amethyst?" This time, she did smile.

"Garnet?"

"Afraid not."

"Ruby?"

"Not a gem," she told him.

"Ah. Well, we'll forget Amber, Topaz, and Sapphire, then, shall we?"

"Everything secure, Aston?" Wes asked.

"A Pica pica pooped on a fence post," Marcus said. "I think Aston electrocuted his feathered ass."

"I did no such thing," Aston protested. "Animal-rights activists would be up in arms. Can't have that."

"Haven't seen another bird around here all day." Marcus shrugged. "That's all I'm saying."

"It's the weather," Aston said. "Dreadful wind. Fifty-seven percent chance of snow flurries. Temperature dropped from forty-seven degrees to thirty-four in the last hour. With the windchill, it's twenty-nine degrees."

"Thank you for the weather bulletin," Marcus said. "I was gonna wear shorts."

"Report?" Wes asked Marcus.

"I'm expecting more backup, and I heard from headquarters that several techs are moving into the guest house. And I understand a couple more protective agents have been assigned to the area."

Wes nodded. "Aston, security red alert."

"Acknowledged."

"We're expecting more agents," he told Aston, repeating what Marcus had already said.

"They'd best be prepared with proper identification."

"Aston—"

"You did say red alert, sir."

Wes shook his head. The advances in Aston's artificial intelligence were astonishing, even to him. Back in the day, Aston could say only a few things and generally only in response to a direct order. Now he seemed to have a mind of his own. In the next upgrade, Wes would make Aston behave more respectfully when told to play nicely with others, Pica picas included.

Inamorata shrugged out of her blazer and hung it in the coat closet. She took his jacket from him and put it on a hanger as well. He raised his brows but said nothing. In six months, that might have been the first domestic act she'd ever performed for him.

Bastard that he was, he liked it.

Seemingly reading his mind, she said, "Don't get used to it. And you can make dinner."

That was his Inamorata.

"I'm going to change," she said.

"Can I get you anything?"

"Coffee," she said. "Please."

She walked off, and Bentley followed her.

Wes stood there until she walked into the master bedroom and closed the door behind her. There was a weariness in the set of her shoulders he hadn't seen before, even when her sister had been in danger.

He wanted peace for her again.

"Since you're here, sir, I'll do another perimeter sweep and check the guest house," Marcus said.

"Affirmative." While he trusted Aston, he also believed in redundancy, especially when Inamorata's safety was on the line.

Wes carried several pieces of electronic equipment from his home office into the kitchen. There was already a large screen mounted to wall. He sometimes used it as a computer monitor when he was working on Aston's upgrades. Other times he set the monitor to display pictures of the ocean or, in winter, a summer scene with a bald eagle soaring into a clear blue sky. Lately, he'd taken to looking at pictures of Inamorata. Some of them were even suitable for others to see.

He poured the existing coffee into a thermal carafe and then set the maker to brew half a pot of decaf. What she didn't know wouldn't hurt her. She was wired enough not to sleep for a week, regardless.

He interfaced with Aston and uploaded the info Hawkeye had on file. He sent a personal request to Hawkeye for the contents of the sealed Danville file and told Hawkeye to keep Chloe's real name and new identity redacted. And he asked Hawkeye to look at the money angle. Finally he set the computer to run his own query on Zack Jonah.

When Marcus returned to the house with assurances other teams were in place along the access roads, Wes poured Inamorata a cup of coffee, added a generous splash of creamer, and headed for the bedroom.

He closed the door behind him. When he saw her, he turned again and locked it.

"Fuck me," she said.

Inamorata stood near the bed, naked. Her clothes, gun, and phone were all in a neat pile on the chair. She'd taken all the pins out of her hair, and the long blonde locks fell across her shoulders. Her green eyes were wide. Her slender shoulders were pulled back.

The sight of her body held him momentarily speechless.

Her legs were spread about shoulder width apart. The nest of curls at the apex of her thighs hid more of her sex than he preferred. He wanted her bare, exposed, nothing hidden. And that went for more than just physically, he knew. He wanted all that from her mentally and emotionally as well.

Her hips flared in a seductive, feminine way that made his cock strain against his slacks.

Her stomach was flat, and her nipples were alluringly beaded at the tips of her small breasts. Her mouth was slightly parted.

As he stood there, trying not to slosh the coffee over the rim of the cup, she put her hands behind her neck. It was a calculated, deliberate action. The movement thrust her breasts more toward him, made her back arch slightly, and screamed submission. "Inamorata."

Her gaze unflinchingly on him, she lowered to her knees.

His cock started to throb in demand. "I need answers, Inamorata. We need to talk. We need to talk about Chloe, about the toll on you—"

"I don't want to talk," she said. "I want to feel."

He'd been there. There was a point where the emotional cost was too high a burden to carry. He knocked around a punching bag when he got to that point. The operative in him understood.

"Give me what I want," she said. "I'm on my knees. I'm waiting for you."

The internal debate raged.

"The case will be there. Give me this."

She looked up at him, and he was lost. "Tell me what you

want, Inamorata. No more hiding."

He watched as indecision chased across her face. She obviously just wanted a scene, wanted to forget, wanted to keep her secrets locked up. But he had no intention of playing this her way any longer. He'd give her what she wanted, but it would come with a price.

"I want to suck your cock."

"Why?"

"Because you'll enjoy it."

"Stop playing games with me."

"Damn it, Wes, you understand submission as much as I do."

"That's what you think you're offering?"

"That is what I'm offering."

"Tell me what submission means to you."

"It means I'll do what pleases you. Pleasing you pleases me. It's not about you taking control; it's about me giving it, offering it freely."

"It's about more than getting spanked?"

"Yes."

Back at headquarters, she'd seemed remote and detached. Now she'd turned to him to help slay the dragon. He was incapable of resisting. "Tell me what scares you."

"Nothing. I'm not scared."

Her answer was fast, too fast. She looked away, the lie hanging thick on the air between them.

He'd know they'd made progress when she could tell him the truth about everything. No secrets, no hiding, no determination to carrying the world on her solitary shoulders. No doubt she was strong enough; she'd had plenty of practice.

"Can't you...?" she trailed off and sighed. She looked at

him through the alluring curtain of her blonde hair. Then she started again. "I'm trying, Wes."

She might be on her knees a few feet away, but she had his balls firmly in her hand. He wasn't man enough to resist her.

"I'm not running. I'm not fighting you. I'm on my knees. I'm naked. I'm here."

Absently he wondered if the cup's handle would snap in his grip.

"Life is precarious and precious. And right now, I don't want to think. I never wanted to remember what happened six years ago, but the truth is, I never forget. I meet Danville more often than not in my nightmares

"Some people go for a run. Some take a hot bath. Some people drink a whole lot more than they should. And we've both seen the chain smokers and habitual drinkers. More than half the people we know are adrenaline junkies. I'm probably one of them. You make gadgets to try and rule the planet when you're stressed. And I've seen your home gym. There are torture places with less stuff. Me? When I need to forget or when I need to feel, I want to have sex. Mindless. Mindless, not meaningless. With you it will never be meaningless. Can we see how far it goes?" she asked. "Just for now? Can you let this be enough?"

Rather than running, she'd stayed. She'd gotten naked, and she was pleading with him to take her.

She'd said "*mindless. Mindless, but not meaningless.*"

It was more than he dared hope, even yesterday. But he was a greedy man. What she was offering was far less than he was ultimately willing to accept. It was a start, though, and he recognized that. "So what you're offering, Inamorata, isn't truly your submission."

They both knew it.

"I'm offering you my body," she said.

"But not your mind, and you're really not surrendering your will. I'm not a nameless dom at the club willing to play with you for an hour and then thank you for your time. I don't want that. If you're honest, you'll admit you don't either."

He turned to put the cooling cup of coffee on the nightstand and to give himself a few seconds to think with his big head. He wanted to be inside her, bad. And if he didn't think it through, that's what would happen. He'd be in her. And she'd run and feel justified doing it.

He removed his gun and holster and put both in the top drawer of the nightstand. Then, more in control, he faced her. "I'll give you what you want, Inamorata, but I want you to be clear on my position. You're not zoning out. If sex is what you want, sex is what you'll get. I'll fuck you senseless, but you'll be fully engaged. You'll participate. I won't just order you around while you act like an automaton."

"Your rules," she said. "I'll do my best. Right now, that's all I can give, Wes. You want it. You want *me*. Accept it."

Then, for the first time ever, she took the initiative.

She lowered herself to all fours. She tipped her chin back; then she began crawling across the hardwood floor toward him.

Bentley obviously thought that was great fun. On his uncertain metal feet, he scampered after her, sliding around and biting at her toes.

Wes pointed at the corner. "Go sit, Bentley."

The dog cocked his head as if suddenly forgetting he knew any commands.

"Go."

With a whimper of protest that sounded almost caninelike, Bentley moved off toward the corner.

"Resume what you were doing," he told her.

She stopped grinning and crawled the remaining few feet

that separated them. Then she knelt up and reached for his belt buckle. Deftly she unfastened it. When the belt separated, she unbuttoned his pants and lowered the zipper.

"You're hard," she said.

There was an understatement.

She drew his pants down, then reached inside his boxers and curled her hand around his cock. Looking up at him, she moved her hand back and forth. If she kept that up, he'd last about thirty seconds.

He clamped his hand around hers.

"Let me finish undressing you."

From her position on her knees, she removed his shoes and socks, then pulled off his jeans and lowered his boxers. He pulled his T-shirt over his head and dropped it on the hardwood floor near the rest of his discarded clothing.

"You've got a great cock," she said.

"You've got a great cock, Sir," he corrected.

She looked up at him.

"I told you what you were offering wasn't enough," Wes said. "If you're offering your submission, Inamorata, then give me your respect."

"I—" She licked her upper lip. "You've got a great cock, Sir."

He liked the way the term of respect sounded on her tongue. He liked the way she looked on her knees.

"May I suck it?"

He might jack off if she didn't. He curved his hand around her neck and guided her head toward his cock.

She opened her mouth and licked the head of his shaft. He closed his eyes. She pulled back slightly, then moved forward to take more of him with her second stroke. "Yeah," he said. Yeah. That was definitely it. She repeated the action, taking a little more of him this time.

Having the lovely and delectable Inamorata on her knees, her mouth wide, her legs spread was enough to make him lose his load. He was determined not to do that.

Her mouth was warm and moist, and her determination was second to none. She opened her mouth to accommodate his girth, and he gently thrust. She gagged, her eyes watering. She pulled back. He released his hold on her while she shook her head.

Inamorata wiped the back of her hand across her mouth and instantly returned to her previous position. "Sorry, Sir," she said. Looking contrite, she opened her mouth and folded her hands behind her back.

Obviously she'd been with some experienced players. Although he was sure she hadn't sucked cock in a while, she knew how. His gut tightened the way it had when she told him ten men, maybe a dozen, had tied her to her bed. It didn't matter how many men had tied her, how many men had fucked her, how many men's cocks she'd sucked. He was going to be the last.

He cradled her head again. She licked the head of cock and ran her tongue around it several times. This time she seemed more relaxed and more confident of what she was doing.

She put a bit of pressure at that sensitive spot just below the tip, and he said her name in a warning tone.

She laughed a little as if relishing her power. If she only realized how much power she had over him.

"I like the way you taste," she said. "Musky. Male. Powerful." She pulled away completely, looked up at him, and then moistened his throbbing cock all the way down.

She kissed and licked his balls with great attention. She worked her way back up, running her tongue firmly up the underside of his throbbing cock.

"That's a girl," he said.

Inamorata was part seductress, part submissive. Her eyes had darkened, and her cheeks were flushed. What the hell had he been thinking the last six months, letting her passively lie beneath him while he rode them both to orgasm?

With her mouth, she captured the head of his dick again. She sucked and licked while determinedly working her way lower, pulling up a little, then sliding down a little farther as she relaxed.

His cock swelled, and he felt a drop of pre-ejaculate leak from the tip. Wouldn't be long before he had to stop her.

Inamorata took a deep breath.

Fuck if he could take much more. He held her head firmly, drawing her closer to him as she sucked his entire length into her mouth and down her throat.

She stayed there for several long seconds. Much longer and he was going to lose it. Because the feeling was so delicious, because he'd fantasized about being lost in her, he gave a couple more good thrusts before pulling out.

Her mouth remained opened slightly; her breath came in uneven little pants. Her eyes were wide and dewy with tears.

"I'm not done with you yet. Get on the bed. Spread your legs. Spread your pussy. Show me how you masturbate."

He saw the struggle cross her face. She frowned, and she looked down; then she looked away. "Yesterday you told me you were too busy to masturbate. We both know that was a lie."

"Yes," she whispered.

"Show me."

She moved slowly, either because she was stalling or because her muscles had stiffened from being on her knees for so long. Still her motions were graceful as she stood and walked to the bed on bare feet.

His cock jutted, throbbing painfully. He ached to bury himself in her, pound her hard, take her, possess her.

She grabbed a pillow and tossed it in the middle of the mattress. Then she crawled onto the bed. She rolled onto her back and positioned the pillow beneath her hips. She spread her legs as he'd instructed; then she used her left hand to part her labia, exposing her clit.

She sucked her right index finger into her mouth and kept it there long enough his cock started to twitch. Vixen.

"Do you have any nipple clamps?" she asked, after removing her finger and rubbing the saliva-slickened tip across her clit.

His gaze was transfixed as her clit became a hardened nub and the moisture glistened there.

"Nipple clamps, Sir?"

"You masturbate with them on?"

"I like the stimulation," she admitted. "I think you found that out last night." She paused as if she wanted to say more. Her cheeks flushed a slight, alluring pink.

From embarrassment? Inamorata could be embarrassed? Who knew? "Go on," he encouraged. "I don't want you hiding from me. I want to know what you want, what turns you on, what satisfies you."

"The constant pressure arouses me. I have a hard time getting off without them, truthfully."

He crossed to the closet and pulled out a box. Obviously Bentley could no longer contain himself. As if he had a real nose, he wandered over and started sniffing the box Wes had placed on the floor. Wes sighed with frustration. "That's it," he told the contraption of nuts and bolts. He picked up the wriggling mutt along with the doggy bed and put them both in the closet and closed the door. "Where were we?"

"You've been holding out on me," she said, stroking her pussy as he'd instructed. "I didn't know you had a grown-up toy box in your closet."

"You haven't been asking for what you want. If you had, this box would have come out a long time ago."

"What else do you have in there?"

"You'll be finding out, Ms. Inamorata." He placed the box on the end of the bed. He took out a bottle of lube and put it on the dresser, then pulled out a bag that contained several different styles of clamps. They varied in intensity from simple, adjustable tweezer-style clamps to biting, teeth-laden alligators and almost everything in between. "Any preference?"

"Do you have clover clamps?"

He raised his brows. "You do like pressure." He pulled out two sets, each linked by a sturdy silver chain. He offered them to her. "One is more intense than the other." He liked clovers better than any other kind, but the women he played with could rarely tolerate the pain. He liked them because they tightened as he pulled on them. The others, especially if they were more decorative, came off too easily. "Give me your hand," he said.

When she did, he put one of each clamp on her pinkie finger.

"Which set?" he asked.

"These." She removed the tightest one and gave him the set.

He put the others away, then stowed the box back in the closet.

"Put them on me?" she asked, a bit breathlessly.

"My pleasure."

He bent over her and sucked her right nipple into his mouth. She arched and squirmed. The harder he sucked, the more she moaned.

He released her, then took her breast and squeezed it, plumping it and squeezing her nipple again.

"Yes," she said, pleaded.

He affixed one of the nasty little clamps to her right nipple.

She cried out. "I'm getting close to coming."

"From the nipple stimulation?"

"Mainly from you," she admitted. Her words were thready, as if she was dazed. "I love having my nipples tortured, but I don't come this fast by myself. It's your touch, Wes, the way *you* pleasure me."

"Don't come," he said. "I won't be easy on you if you do."

"I understand."

"I want to play with you, and I want you to think about the pleasure I'm getting from watching your reactions. Nothing else matters, Inamorata. Got it?"

"Yes," she said around a gasp. "Yes, Sir."

He moved to the far side of the bed and drew her left nipple into his mouth, sucking and biting until it became a hardened nib.

"You're good at that," she said.

He used a whole lot more pressure than he'd generally use with a woman, at least initially. He knew how to measure out pain, ratcheting it up a bit at a time. But with Inamorata... She didn't just have a high pain threshold—she had a high pain demand.

He watched her slide a finger into her slick passage.

The bite of pain had seemingly increased her arousal tenfold. He moved his mouth and pinched the tormented little nipple between his thumb and forefinger. Her head thrashed on his pillow.

"Wes! Sir!"

"Hang on, Inamorata."

"You…" She sucked in a breath and looked at him for only a second before closing her eyes again. "You said you wanted to see me masturbate."

"I did. I didn't say I wanted to watch you come. Change the tempo. Pay attention to your breathing. Be a good little sub." Truthfully he couldn't have been any more pleased with her. Her letting go of her inhibitions thrilled him.

He twisted her nipple.

She cried out.

"Did you come?"

"No!"

"Are you lying?"

"I'm…close… Please?"

"I usually like you to beg. But this time, don't. The answer is no."

"But…Sir!"

He replaced his touch with the second clamp.

Her hips rose and fell as she stroked her cunt faster and faster.

"Stop."

She froze.

"Take your hand away from your pussy and put it beneath your ass."

She opened her eyes and blinked at him. "Are you serious?"

"Do I need to repeat myself?"

She swallowed convulsively and drank half a dozen deep breaths. Slowly, she did what he said.

"I can smell your arousal," he told her. He knew, though, without the sexual distraction, the pain of the clamps would become just that, pain. At this point, or certainly within the next two minutes, it wouldn't drive her to an orgasm; it would just be uncomfortable. The size of his cock hadn't diminished. His whole body urged him to claim her. "Dig your heels into the mattress," he said, "and lift your hips. Keep your legs wide apart."

She nodded and did as he said.

Sex with her had always been good, but he'd had no idea it could be this spectacular. "Your pussy is all red, swollen," he said.

"Yes, Sir," she whispered.

"With your hands, spread your butt cheeks."

She hesitated only a fraction of a second, but long enough.

"How do your breasts feel?"

"A little sore now."

He went over to the dresser and squeezed some lube onto his right middle finger. She blinked, obviously guessing his intent.

He climbed onto the bed and knelt between her thighs. "Tilt your hips more." As she did, her anal whorl was more exposed. "Beautiful," he said. "Spread those cheeks even farther apart." *Yeah.* That was definitely more like it. His woman, displayed for him. "Any idea what you look like, Inamorata? Your nipples are perfectly clamped. You clit is swollen; your pussy is dripping moisture. You look wanton. Keep your hips high!"

She moved back into position.

"Do you have a safe word?"

"I won't need it."

"You might," he countered.

She shuddered, and he noticed her abdominal muscles tighten in response, keeping her in position. "I've never needed one."

"You've never submitted to me."

"Italy," she said on a shaky exhalation.

"Italy?"

"I was born there."

How much more was he going to discover about her? "Use your safe word to stop play entirely. But be aware, if you use your safe word, we won't go back to where we were and continue."

"That's not fair. You make me chose a word and then take away the option to use it."

"You always have the option, Inamorata. But I believe a safe word is for when you've truly gone past your comfort level or you're afraid you'll go there. Either way, things need to be discussed and discontinued. I will watch you constantly. I'll read your pain level; I'll check in. I don't believe in safe words because you don't like what I want you to do or you want to negotiate. Use it wisely."

"I understand."

She hadn't said she agreed, only that she understood. "Tell me to stick my finger in your ass, Inamorata."

"I've, er, never done this," she said.

Christ. Inamorata was *nervous.* And he was harder than he'd ever been. "Let me know when you're ready." He waited. After several seconds, he pressed the tip of his finger lightly against her.

Finally, when he was almost sure she'd chicken out, she said, "Please. Please, Wes, Sir, put your finger up my ass."

"That's what you want?"

Instead of answering, she dug her feet deeper into the mattress for purchase and made her entire pelvic area available to him. She thrust against his finger in silent invitation. With gentle thrusts, he drove his finger inside her by slow measures, deeper and deeper until it was buried to the hilt. She breathed in and out rapidly. "Now move your hands, but keep yourself in position. Put the chain to your nipple clamps in your mouth."

She struggled to comply.

"This is diabolical. You're diabolical," she said. She had to bring her head forward and use her hands to grab the chain and situate it between her teeth.

"Do not release it."

She lay back down and then yelped. She immediately brought her head back up, which would force more pressure onto her abs.

"More effective than being tied," he told her.

She nodded but then winced.

Each time she moved, the pressure on her nipples would intensify. Trying to get away from his touch would cause her pain, but he intended to make it impossible for her to stay still. When she came, he knew she'd scream. "You'll wait for my permission to come."

The chain in her mouth served as a pseudogag as well.

He captured her gaze, and he saw she understood his instructions.

He began to finger fuck her tight hole. She moved slightly in response.

He moved his position and lowered his mouth to her cunt. She started to shake her head, but the pain shooting through her nipples obviously stopped her.

He inserted two fingers from his free hand into her pussy and spread her wide. "So tight, Inamorata," he said. "Hot." He licked her vulva with a long sweep and then pressed his tongue against her clit.

She mumbled something that might have been his name.

He was relentless. He started soft and slow, allowing her

response to grow. Then he increased the pressure on her clit. He watched her oh-so-sexy responses and increased the width that he spread his fingers in her pussy. Her muscles constricted, and he imagined the way she'd feel wrapped around his cock. While she writhed, he continued to thrust his finger inside her ass.

Her head moved from side to side rhythmically. He saw the motion dragging her nipples up and away from her breasts. She winced.

Obviously she wasn't quite *there* yet.

He sucked her clit into his mouth and exerted a tiny amount of pressure with his teeth.

She began to thrash.

Now, now she was there, clearly not feeling the pain any longer. She'd crossed that magic threshold.

Her moans became whimpers, and her muscles tensed.

He released her clit and then laved away the hurt. "Do not come," he said against her pussy.

Even with the chain in her mouth, he heard her muttered pleas. He didn't respond. Instead he inserted a second finger in her rear entrance.

She cried out.

"Hang on," he told her. "You can take more."

She moved her head slightly. The motion wasn't quite a nod since the pressure on her nipples was too much.

"Take it, Inamorata."

She closed her eyes.

He slid his fingers from her pussy and then slapped her cunt once, hard. She screamed and convulsed, and he felt her orgasm crash over her.

He kissed away the sharp pain. Long seconds later, her climax receded, and she released the chain from her mouth. He eased his fingers from her tightest hole. She gulped in oxygen and exhaled shakily as she dropped her hips to the pillow beneath them.

She finally opened her eyes. The green color had turned dark and intense, stormy, and she was focused only on him. A half smile played around the corner of her lips. She looked lovely, sated. Maybe a bit dazed.

But in true fashion, she recovered quickly.

She sat up and simultaneously reached to take off the nipple clamps.

"Leave them," he said.

Her eyes widened, and she opened her mouth as if she was going to argue. He curled his hands around her wrists. "I said leave them."

"Sir, the clamps hurt. Can I—"

He cut her off with a wave of his hand.

"We're not quite finished. You came without permission. Then you released the chain from your mouth. And once you'd already been disobedient, you didn't use that pretty little mouth to thank me or even show the good manners to apologize for your transgression. Then you thought to take off your clamps and get out of bed? Any of those actions might have been forgivable. But all of them? In under fifteen seconds? Impressive, Inamorata. And inexcusable."

Chapter Six

Inamorata's mind swam.

She knew the rules of a BDSM scene. The dom was in charge; the sub followed orders implicitly. Anything, everything was grounds for punishment. In the scenes she'd participated in, she'd been punished for coming, even when the dom pushed so relentlessly she was incapable of preventing it. Just like now.

Wes had repeatedly warned her not to orgasm. She knew about control, sexually and in her personal life. For a while, she'd fought the climax, using tricks she'd learned for dealing with stressful situations.

She'd pictured herself being somewhere else. She'd surrendered and breathed, trying for physical detachment.

But when his mouth had found her pussy, the physical onslaught of his tiny bites had combined with the biting pain in her nipples and trumped her attempts to think logically.

Wes said he would always watch her during a scene, and she believed him. He'd been paying attention. He surely had known just how close she was to an orgasm.

No doubt about it.

He'd known she was on the edge and incapable of stopping the moment he delivered that single vicious slap to her already aroused pussy. He'd known her orgasm would be immediate and powerful. And the clever bastard had continued his sensual torment, ensuring she rode the climax completely. He'd wanted her to come, and he'd made damn sure she had.

But he was right about her immediate response afterward. She hadn't thanked him a single time; in fact, she'd shown him she preferred to run after he satisfied her. "Thank you," she said, quickly, trying to make amends. "Thank you, Sir. That was amazing."

"Too little, Inamorata. Too late."

Her heart pounded.

He climbed off the bed.

What had she gotten herself into? He was a powerful dom, more intense than any man she'd played with. She'd never been with a man this focused, a man she couldn't manipulate. It thrilled her, terrified her.

He crossed the room and moved her items to the dresser top. Then he hooked the chair leg with his foot and dragged it into position near the bed.

He remained standing, powerful legs spread a little farther than shoulder width apart. His arms hung loosely at his sides, but his hands were curled into fists. A lock of dark, dark hair fell across his forehead. The gray of his eyes was steely, harder, more inflexible than she'd ever seen.

His cock jutted forward impressively.

The idea of being fucked by him filled her mind, crowding out any rational thought.

"Get on the floor and crawl to me. Then, when I'm ready, you'll get your ass over my lap."

She shuddered. Had she actually been excited yesterday by the idea of him spanking her? Now that the time was here, nerves and fear collided, nearly paralyzing her.

"I suggest you get that sweetheart of a butt over here, Inamorata."

She moved slowly, feeling unsure. He was upping the stakes. Part of her wondered if she'd actually go through with this.

But even as the internal debate raged, she climbed off the bed and lowered herself to the floor, getting on all fours. She crawled toward him, aware of the pull of the vicious clamps on her nipples.

She loved the way they felt when she was hot, aroused. But she hated them after she'd climaxed. The pressure went from amazing to irritating. After a minute or two, they became painful.

She moved toward him slowly, trying to minimize the sway of her breasts.

When she was about a foot away, he said, "Stop."

She froze.

"Kneel up."

As delicately as she could, she moved into position. She wasn't sure exactly what he expected, so she erred on the side of being overly respectful.

She bowed her head, spread her knees wide, and placed her hands palms up on her thighs.

Her heart thundered.

For a long time, he said nothing. She forced herself to draw in several deep breaths as she patiently waited.

Somewhere in the last half hour, she had forgotten what she wanted to forget. Wes had taken her somewhere else, someplace dizzying, someplace that might be more terrifying than the past.

He took hold of the chain linking her nipple clamps.

She sucked in a sharp breath.

"Easy," he said. Then he tugged on the chain.

She gasped and broke position, leaning forward to grab his

wrists.

"Kneel up," he snapped.

She took a couple of shallow, panting breaths as she eased back into position. Her eyes watered with the pain of having her nipples so distended.

"Nice," he said.

She heard a note of approval in his voice, and her heart soared. There was something about this man that made her weak.

"How does that feel?"

"It...it hurts."

"It hurts?"

"It hurts, Sir," she said. The harder he tugged, the tighter the clamps became.

She kept her head bowed, but she desperately wanted to look at him. Did he like what he saw? Did having her like this, on her knees, supplicant, give him a hard-on?

"Would it hurt as bad if you were distracted?"

She almost, *almost*, looked up. She couldn't read his reaction in the set of his jaw or a smile of approval. In this position she had nothing but the lifeline of his tone of voice to guide her.

"Moisten two of your fingers and play with your clit."

She thought she'd feel self-conscious, but she didn't. She slipped two fingers into her mouth and exaggerated the time it took to moisten the tips. She sucked and licked and moved her fingers in and out.

"I think they're moist enough," he said drily. "Play with your pussy."

Having him there, tugging on her chain, watching her, made the act of teasing her clit that much more incredibly sensual.

"You're distracting yourself from the pain in your nipples," he reminded her, tugging again on the chain. "You're not going for another orgasm you're not permitted to have."

"Yes," she said, surrendering to the sensation of stroking herself. The pain in her nipples seemed to dissipate, no longer quite as sharp.

"Tell me why you're going to be punished."

"Because..." She whimpered as he yanked on the chain. Her pussy was becoming wetter and wetter. She could smell her arousal, and that meant he had to be able to as well. "Because I came without permission."

"And?"

She could barely think with the way the orgasm was building, with how sore and aroused her pussy was, with how tender her anus was. He kept playing with the chain, increasing the pressure and her desire. "And I let go of the chain from my mouth."

"This chain?" He twisted the metal in his hand, dragging her nipples together and sending a sharp pain through them.

"Yes!"

"And?"

"I didn't thank you or apologize." She paused. Then she went for the truth both of them knew. "Because I started to get off the bed—"

"Run away," he corrected.

More than anything, she knew that was what upset him. Six months of sleeping together and she'd never stopped running.

"What do you deserve for that?"

"Spank me, Sir. Spank me."

He abruptly released her chain. She closed her eyes, but she didn't stop playing with her pussy. She didn't look up. She didn't betray—except through her accelerated heartbeat—that fear was colliding with her mounting arousal.

"Good girl."

The unexpected approval was welcome.

He moved to the chair and sat down. "Position yourself over my lap."

The silence surrounding them seemed to reverberate in her head.

"It's up to you," he said softly. "What do you want?"

She knew the question wasn't about what she wanted in this moment. He was asking about long term. She could run now, and he'd let her go. But if she didn't, he might not ever let her.

Inamorata moved slowly, keeping her motions economical. To her, this was about more than surrendering to her punishment; it was about surrendering to Wes's mastery and control. Focusing on each movement kept her sharp and the gnawing panic at bay. Gracefully she rose and draped herself over his muscular thighs.

She felt his strength against her contrasting femininity.

The clamps tugged her nipples down, and she placed her fingertips on the hardwood floor for balance.

"Tell me the rules," he said.

"Rules? I don't know your rules."

"If you were in charge of the rules, what would they be?"

"No getting up."

The words hung between them. *No running away.* "That's a good start," he said.

"No screaming?"

"Scream all you want. In fact, I'll expect you to."

Her heart rate accelerated. "No cussing?"

"Doesn't offend me."

"Count the spanks?"

"Yes. Anything else?"

Her heart was in her throat. She was over his lap, her rear upturned and exposed for his punishment. "Can we just get this over with?"

"Who's in charge here?"'

"You, Sir."

He trailed his fingers down her spine. "Rules?"

She squirmed. "Keep my legs spread?"

"Yes."

He trailed farther, over her lower back, then between her buttocks, teasing her anus, then her pussy. He pinched her clit. "Legs spread," he reminded her. "And turn your toes in."

She did as he instructed.

Despite her nerves and fear, her pussy was wet.

"Those clamps are still tight?"

"Yes, Sir." Since she was across his lap, breathing was more difficult.

"How many spanks do you deserve?"

"However many you decide, Sir."

"Answer the question."

His tone of voice sounded like a whiplash. "Five. One for each infraction."

"That's insulting."

Even as she'd said it, she knew he'd never go for it.

"Ten?"

"Much closer."

She moved slightly.

"Eleven?" she asked. When he didn't answer, she tried

again, "Twelve?"

"Twelve it is. And thank me for each one, since you forgot to thank me for that stolen orgasm."

She nodded. "Yes, Sir."

He placed a hand on the small of her back, and she drew a steadying breath. His first open-handed slap landed unexpectedly hard on her right buttock.

She gasped, arching her back against the pain.

"One?" he prompted.

Shit. That had been harder than she expected. "One," she said. "Thank you."

Before she was quite ready, the second landed directly on top of the first. "Two! Thank you."

"Why are you thanking me?"

She blinked, thrown out of her experience of the pain. "To show my appreciation for your discipline. And for taking the time to discipline me."

Bastard that he was, he landed the third smack directly on top of the other two. He either wasn't very skilled, or he was diabolical. The few square inches burned and itched. "Thank you!" She drew a breath. "Three."

He slipped his hand between her legs and stroked her pussy.

She moved back a bit, pressing greedily against his hand. Just when she got close, he moved. His slap caught her beneath both ass cheeks, across the tops of her thighs. "Four," she said, the word somewhere between a scream and protest. "Thank you." In future, she'd be better behaved, no doubt. She'd had spankings before, but this was unlike anything she'd ever experienced, slower, more deliberate. And that he could do this with just his hand... She wasn't sure she had the guts to try anything else, like a belt or a crop.

His fifth strike caught her left butt cheek, right across from the place he'd spanked her right cheek. "Five." On a whisper, she managed, "Thank you."

She knew his general pattern now, and she relaxed into it. His sixth and seventh spanks were directly on top of the fifth.

Her buttocks felt raw; she felt humbled.

He shifted, forcing her slightly forward. She was more on her tiptoes, and she put her palms flat on the floor. They were barely halfway done. She wasn't sure how much more she could take.

"The next ones are going to be quicker. I warmed you up. The next ones are your true punishment. Understand?"

She nodded.

"Answer, Inamorata."

"I..."

"You can do it."

"Yes," she said.

"You remember your safe word?"

"Italy," she said.

"Do you want to use it?"

There'd been no inflection in his tone. The decision was hers. He waited, not stroking her, not moving at all. She thought about it, considered it. She could end this now. But Inamorata had never backed down from anything. There was something cathartic about this. There was something strangely compelling about a man she'd been involved with for months taking this to the next level.

It was punishment, yes, but so much more. Everything she'd always liked about BDSM, she was getting. Escape. An adrenaline cocktail made from nerves, pain, and the grit of determination.

"Would you like to safeword out?"

"No."

"Good."

The undisguised approval in his rich tenor voice made the decision even more of a rush. She'd missed BDSM, and she was sorry she hadn't explored it with Wes before now.

"In that case, we'll proceed. No need to count the next ones. And you can thank me at the end."

She closed her eyes. In the past she'd been able to surrender to a beating. But those had been at the club, more for fun. She'd never experienced anything like this, like Wes.

"Ready?"

"Yes."

"Ask me."

"Please, Sir. Spank me."

He moved his hand to the middle of her back and splayed his fingers to keep her body still. She'd known her lover was intense. He brought that to all their lovemaking. He reined blows all across her buttocks, catching the insides of her thighs, the delicate flesh between her legs. This focused intensity was shocking.

Pain melded with her protests, and she shouted his name and a handful of curse words. Her world exploded.

Then, as suddenly as he'd started, he stopped.

She was sobbing, cussing, shaking. But she didn't try to get away.

"One more," he told her.

"That wasn't twelve?"

"Eleven," he said.

"But…"

"Let me know when you're ready," he said. "I want you fully aware for the last one."

That he had enough presence to realize she was slipping into her head was astounding.

"You'll feel this one," he told her. "And you won't forget it. Spread your legs farther apart."

She knew what was coming, and she was nervous.

"Take a breath," he told her.

She did, but she still wasn't prepared.

He caught her cunt full on.

She screamed.

She arched her back; her eyes watered.

He remained there, his hand on her back. He didn't try to move her or touch her intimately.

After she'd swallowed a few gulps of oxygen-starved air, her pulse started to return to normal, and the pain slowly receded.

Despite her initial unkind thoughts several minutes ago, there was nothing unskilled about his schooling. He'd known exactly what he was doing. His punishment had been effective and memorable.

She'd be unable to sit comfortably the rest of the day.

"I'm waiting."

Waiting? She shook her head. Then she remembered. "Thank you, Sir."

He helped her stand; then he swept her off her feet and carried her back to the bed. "Roll over onto your stomach."

He left her for a few minutes, and she heard water running in the bathroom. He returned to the bedroom and pressed a cool, damp washcloth against her burning pussy.

"That feels amazing."

"Your ass looks beautiful," he said. "Red. Swollen. You may get a bruise..." He touched her.

She yelped.

"Here."

"Yeah."

"The badass Inamorata will have a red, swollen butt beneath her tight skirt. Oh yeah, and a swollen cunt. I don't want you forgetting who you belong to."

She shuddered. She'd never forget his touch, his mastery.

"I'm going to fuck you," he said.

She turned her head so she could look at him. His jaw was set in a firm, implacable line. His cock was rigid and throbbing. He looked every inch the capable, rough, and tough Hawkeye agent who'd just brought her to the edge of her endurance.

"There's no way to fuck you without it bothering your butt."

"Or my pussy which you slapped."

He shrugged. "That too. Since this will hurt anyway, I'm going to take you from behind so I can pinch your ass, maybe even spank some of the areas again."

"I think I'm going to like it," she said, as excited as she was nervous.

"If you don't, I need much more practice." He grabbed a pillow that had somehow ended up on the floor. With her help, he was able to position it beneath her abdomen.

"Let me suck your cock for lubrication," she said.

"I'm going to use a condom."

"Okay, then let me suck you until I'm sure you're hard."

"Baby, you take off your clothes, and I'm like a rock."

"Well then, let me suck you because I'm a greedy little sub who's hungry for your cock."

"Inamorata—"

"Let me suck you, Wes."

His eyes were dark and smoky. Tomorrow she might be sorry this had gone so far. Tomorrow she might rue being needy and vulnerable. Tomorrow she might run.

But in this moment, she wanted him. She wanted to soak up every possible second of the delicious naughtiness.

He knelt on the bed. She moved slightly so she could take him in her mouth. She started by licking his cockhead, paying extra attention to that sensitive spot beneath the head.

He groaned.

She went lower and lower, taking more of him.

He grabbed her head, digging his fingers into her hair.

There was definitely something heady about making a man as big and strong as Wesley Lowell lose control. He jerked his pelvis, but then he pulled back.

"This is a little more than getting me hard and lubricated."

"Does that mean you're enjoying it?" she asked innocently.

"Enough sass." He took hold of her chin and placed a finger across her lips.

She nodded.

He kissed her forehead before removing his finger. He gently bit the back of her neck before moving away to roll a condom down his impressive cock.

He moved between her legs and positioned himself at her entrance.

"Take me," she told him.

He needed no further urging.

He grasped her hip bones, holding her steady. "You are one sexy woman, Inamorata."

"Fill me, Sir." He did.

Her skin felt raw. Her rear was on fire. As he pulled back, he gave her an occasional gentle slap, reigniting the burn and driving her mad. "I need to come," she said.

"So soon? Didn't you just have an orgasm or two?"

Half a dozen or more. But who was counting? "It's not my fault I'm a poor sub and you're so magnificent." She'd say anything as long as he didn't deny her.

He laughed as he continued to slide in and out, faster and faster.

"Please…?"

"You've earned it." He reached for her clit and gently slid his thumb across it. "Ride it."

The orgasm crashed over her. Her insides seemed to turn upside down. The climax crashed over her. She shuddered as she cried out his name.

After the orgasm receded, he took her again. This time he claimed her harder. Harder, faster, deeper.

Unbelievably, a second orgasm grabbed at her insides, even as his cock pulsed and grew inside her. She panted as he held her steady. "More," she said. She wanted more, wanted as much of him as he could give her.

He pounded her.

"I can take you. Give it to me."

"You'll be the death of me, woman."

"Would it be such a bad way to go?"

He pushed a moist finger deep into her ass. The orgasm that had been threatening swamped her. Her muscles squeezed and contracted, and she felt the orgasm that was dragged out of him.

"Fuck," he said, the single word guttural, an exclamation, not a curse.

He stayed there a long time, keeping a firm grip on her.

He put an arm beneath her, supporting her the way he always tried to.

She could stay like this for the rest of the day. But she knew better. This scene, this surrender hadn't simplified things with Wes; it had made their relationship more complicated. From here, they couldn't go back to where they'd been. She knew him well enough to know he wouldn't let them.

He withdrew from her. She collapsed onto her stomach while he discarded the condom and let the banished Bentley out of the closet.

Wes brought her a cool, damp washcloth and pressed it against her tender flesh. Even with everything going on around them, he took the time to care for her. She steeled her heart against the cracks he was starting to make in it.

He left the cloth against her skin and moved away. He grabbed clothes from a shelf in the closet and got dressed. "I'll meet you in the kitchen when you're ready. I want to make sure the rest of the crew gets set up, and I'll bring them up to speed on the pertinent details."

Wes, Bentley on his heels, left the bedroom. The door closed behind him with an audible *click.*

For the first time, he'd been the one to walk out. While it was nothing like the way she left, she noticed, keenly, the absence of his kiss and his touch. He was all business, as remote as she usually was after they had sex. She wasn't sure she liked a return dose of her behavior.

Inamorata finished with the washcloth, then tossed it toward the hamper as she climbed from the bed.

She took off the heinous clamps one at a time. She winced when the first one came off, moaned when she removed the second. Had she actually asked him to put them on her? She dropped the clamps on the dresser.

She caught sight of her reddened ass in the full-length mirror. He'd spanked her hard. And he was probably right about the little bruise she was going to have on one cheek.

But the scene had been successful. She was no longer overwhelmed by the helpless feeling that had engulfed her earlier. For a while, she'd forgotten, and that helped her refocus.

In so many ways, he was good for her. Having someone to share the load was nice, a novel idea.

But she intuitively knew the cost he would demand would be too high.

She pulled on a thong and stockings and then slipped into her skirt. It was like donning a figurative set of armor. Once she was fully dressed, she would be in charge again rather than a woman who'd recently begged a man to dominate her.

After putting on her bra, she shrugged into her shirt and buttoned it. As she slipped into her high-heeled shoes, she checked e-mail on her phone. The screen was blank, except for the routine mandatory updates. She sighed with disappointment, wishing more information had been sent over. In the half hour or so she'd been alone with Wes, no progress had been made.

Taming her hair after Wes's hands had been in it took some time. Finally, satisfied, she refreshed her makeup and then strapped on her holster and slid her gun into it.

She headed for the kitchen, and when she walked in, conversation died. Jilly stopped chomping on her ice. Wes looked up from the computer he'd been studying. Marcus straightened his shoulders. Another man was in the kitchen. This geek she didn't know. He sported a down-to-his-ass ponytail. Despite the windchill and falling snow, he was wearing a sleeveless T-shirt and a pair of shorts to show off his impressive number of tats. He glanced up at her, smiled warmly, then put his head back down. His fingers had never stopped moving across the keyboard.

Bentley came skidding over. She petted the animal's back and realized his purring was louder than ever. "Any updates?

Demands from the kidnappers?" Even as she asked, she knew the answer. If there'd been a demand, she would have been the first to know. "But you do have news?" she asked, straightening. Outwardly she was cool, calm, competent. Inwardly her nerves weren't so steady. As much as she hated to admit it to anyone, even herself, she was glad Wes was here.

"Yeah," Wes said. "We have a couple of leads on the money angle."

From his flat tone, she knew she wasn't going to like what he had to say.

Chapter Seven

She crossed to the coffeepot and poured a cup. She propped her hip against the counter. After taking a sip of her coffee, skipping the cream she preferred in favor of keeping her hands occupied, she said, "Let me have it."

"We've been looking at Danville's financial records."

How they'd accessed those, she didn't want to know.

"Data never dies," Jilly said, as if that explained everything.

"And it's never buried as deep as you think it is," the male tech added. "Wanna know how much Jilly paid for that piece-of-shit SUV she drives? She can't drive a bargain to save her life."

"Screw you, little dick," Jilly said amiably.

Wes stood straight up and folded his arms across his impressively wide chest.

For a moment, she was a woman, not an operative. She drank in the sight of the man who'd effortlessly dominated her. He'd dressed in a black T-shirt, slim-fitted jeans, and running shoes. He hadn't taken the time to comb his hair, as if he didn't give a damn who knew what he'd been doing to her, with her, in the bedroom.

He didn't seem more relaxed than he had earlier, and she realized that, for him at least, their sex hadn't been an escape.

"I brought the team up to speed," he said. "On a need-to-know basis."

And what he meant, she knew, was he'd kept her personal story as private as he could.

"Before we go any further, this man you don't know is Gary Smith."

Gary Smith? Mr. Tattoo Ponytail Goatee had an innocuous name like Smith?

"Gary, meet Ms. Inamorata."

He slid off his bar stool and extended his hand like a true gentleman.

She put down her coffee. At that moment, that was a sacrifice.

"I've heard a lot about you, ma'am, Ms. Inamorata." He actually bowed over her hand. "Any first name?"

"Yes," she said. "Of course."

"Good try," Jilly said before chomping on a particularly big mouthful of ice.

Smith shrugged. "Can't blame a guy for trying," he said. He took his chair again and bent over his computer, seeming to disengage from the update.

She knew better. Wes had handpicked the techs, bizarre ink and caffeine habits notwithstanding.

She picked up her coffee, took a welcome sip, and waited.

Wes cleared his throat before speaking. "The night Chloe vanished, so did two million dollars."

Even for the Danvilles, that was a lot of money. She took another drink, giving herself time to process the information and what it meant. "I assume we're not talking cash."

"A couple hundred thousand in cash was reported missing," Wes said. "Not pocket change and the person who took it had to know where it was and have the means to access it. But the two million was a wire transfer out of his account, hours before he was killed."

"Clever girl, Chloe," Jilly said.

Inamorata tried to reconcile what she remembered of the girl-woman. Had sweet, resolved Chloe truly been capable of that? "Where did the cash go?"

"We're on it," Smith said. He looked up from his keyboard, then, seemingly needing to do something with his hands, played with the end of his ponytail. "Looking for balances, account numbers. Could be tricky if the money got moved out of the country."

"Clever girl, Chloe," Jilly said again.

Above the rim of her coffee cup, Inamorata met Wes's gaze. He was smart. If he thought this related to Chloe, it probably did. She didn't at all like the direction this was going. What he was suggesting changed her perception of that night, that entire time, and her involvement.

Wes spoke quietly but firmly, "You said Chloe was a computer geek."

"She was a kid."

"I hacked the Pentagon when I was in elementary school," Jilly said. "I think I was ten. I guess I could have been nine, come to think of it. Yeah. Must have been nine."

"So we're essentially keeping you out of prison?" Inamorata asked.

"I put it as the top thing on my résumé. Even Hawkeye was impressed." She tipped an impressive amount of crushed ice into her mouth. "Either Hawkeye or jail, I guess."

"Just another part of Hawkeye's community-service program," Smith said.

"Back to Chloe," Inamorata said. "I'm having a hard time with this one." At the time, the girl had been seventeen and scared, in a foreign country, the possession of a man three times her age, disowned by her family, and she'd been treated brutally. "I don't see how she could have even known how to do any of this."

"But she might have had online friends who could," Wes said.

She had to concede that point. There were predators out there, and Chloe had been vulnerable.

"Think about it," Wes said. "If you believe the act was revenge related rather than premeditated, what provocation did she have that night? Had Danville done anything unusual, made any requests or demands that were out of the ordinary?"

"Anyone can snap," she said. "The wrong word, fear of something happening."

"Chloe?" he asked. "We're not talking about anyone in general, we're talking about Chloe. And we're talking about that night."

She thought back. Chloe had been gaining confidence. In the few weeks before Danville's death, she'd stopped hiding behind scarves, and she'd spent more time than usual in front of her computer keyboard.

"Okay," Inamorata said, putting down the coffee cup. "Let's assume it was premeditated." The words nearly stuck in her throat. "Let's assume someone helped her and that she got away with two million dollars. We'll add in that she knew someone who encouraged her to kill Danville."

If there was a connection, she knew he and his crack crew would find it. Part of her irrationally hoped there wasn't a connection.

She drummed her fingers on her thigh. "Why would Jonah care now? Danville's been dead six years. Jonah could have gone to Hawkeye anytime in the last six years. It's not like our phone number is secret. It's right there on the Contact Us page of our Web site. So why now?" she repeated.

"How do you know he hasn't gone to Hawkeye before now? That he's getting more desperate?"

Shit.

She grabbed her phone from its case and left the kitchen, Bentley nipping at her heels. She wandered to the great room as a pleasant, female voice encouraged her to wait while her call was connected.

She looked out the floor-to-ceiling window, toward Denver, where the lights were starting to brighten. A gentle snow fell. It looked like fairy dust, and at any other time, she'd have appreciated the view.

Bentley sat and wagged his tail. He tipped his head to the side, but he remained silent. She could get used to having this mechanical mutt in her life, could get used to watching evening claim the land from this vantage point.

"Inamorata," Hawkeye said once he was on the line. "The plot thickens."

"Where is Chloe today?"

"So much for pleasantries."

There was noise in the background, as if he was at a party. She heard him take a drink. Probably something refined, maybe a fine wine as he entertained a prospective client. One thing was sure, Hawkeye didn't slug beer from a bottle, or, heaven forbid, a can.

"She's not in the US, if that's what you're asking. And we've still got her under surveillance. It's not as tight as it was initially, but we're watching her. She and her little boy are living as close to a normal life as possible. She married a guy she met online while she was living with Danville. They're currently in the middle of a nasty divorce."

She sank onto the arm of a leather chair. Chloe? A mother? Marriage and divorce? "What about the two million?"

"If she took it, she deserved to keep it."

She sat there, stunned. "It's true." Inamorata exhaled.

"We don't know she took it, but it seems logical."

"You knew."

"We knew two million dollars was transferred out of Danville's account the day he was killed. He could have done it himself. It could have been an automatic withdrawal, maybe a payment on his new boat. We didn't spend a lot of time looking into it."

"We're wasting time looking into those financials."

"Maybe not."

"Tell me about Jonah."

"No love lost between the two. Danville didn't name him in the will, to our knowledge."

"Has Jonah gone looking for Chloe before now?"

"Apparently not."

"I need resources. I need access to his computers. I want someone at his house. He might have Sam there."

"We're working on finding his home address," Hawkeye said. "All intel is being shipped to Wes."

"Damn it, Hawkeye. You never told me any of this."

"You needed to move on."

"I still see him," she said quietly. "In my dreams. Not all the time anymore. Not as often."

"I don't make a habit of playing God," Hawkeye said. "What was done was done. In the grand scheme, the loss of Danville from the planet doesn't seem like a particularly bad one. It wasn't the first attempt on Danville's life. He wouldn't have hired us if he hadn't needed to."

"He was killed on my shift." She tried to ignore the fact her hand trembled a little. "I was paid to protect him."

"You were there for Chloe as well," Hawkeye corrected. "You wondering about Chloe's motivations would have had you second-guessing your actions."

Hawkeye said nothing else, and the silence grew between them. He'd obviously moved away from the party to take her call. It occurred to her that to other people, this was Friday night. Others had plans, went out to dinner, celebrated the upcoming weekend. Life went on.

Eventually, she exhaled.

"Look at the big picture," he told her.

"You know, Hawkeye, I don't even know what that means." She used to know. Now she wasn't sure.

After a few seconds, he hung up.

Her hand shook as she replaced the phone in its holster.

She was aware of Wes moving through the room toward her. "I may have screwed up," she said, watching his reflection in the window.

"Did you do the best you could at the time?" he asked, placing his hands on her shoulders.

In the window, she saw no judgment on his face. "I thought I did."

"It was good enough for Hawkeye," he told her. "You were held blameless."

"I could have saved Danville."

"Maybe."

"Maybe," she agreed.

"And would that have been the right thing?"

She thought about that. After she left his room, she'd collected Chloe. The teen had been in hysterics, covered in blood, unable to speak, unable to say what had pushed her to that last desperate act.

Inamorata had cleaned up the girl, helped her dress, and driven west, getting way the hell away from Arizona. She'd called Hawkeye as soon as they'd left the house.

Danville, had he survived, would have gone after Chloe.

Inamorata wouldn't have been safe either. Maybe he'd have killed them both. *Or maybe not.* Regardless, had it been her decision to make? "It's complicated," she said.

He squeezed her shoulders reassuringly. "Take all the time you need," he said, "but I'm going to have Aston close the blinds. I don't want you exposed like this."

"Hey, Wes!" Jilly called out.

"Duty calls." Louder he shouted back, "Be right there, Jilly!"

Wes bit the side of her neck, not at all gently. He reached around her and cupped her breasts in his palms. He drew her nipples between his thumbs and forefingers and pinched, hard. In the window, she saw her mouth open in surprise and shock. His touch was a reminder, and, she hoped, a promise.

"Aston, close the blinds."

"As you wish, sir."

"Do you like everyone calling you sir?" she asked.

"The way you do?" he asked. "With that inflection? That kind of respect, knowing what it means? Only interested in hearing you say it."

Quietly, all the blinds in the room began to descend.

"And I especially like it when you say it and then open your mouth to take my cock."

Tweaking her sensitive nipples one last time, he released her and walked away, leaving her in the uncomfortable silence, alone with her thoughts.

She drew a few steadying breaths and straightened her clothes. In seconds, the man could turn her world upside down.

When her pulse had returned to near normal, she returned to the kitchen. "Update?" she asked.

"This here freak made himself useful when he showed up. He brought the kid's PC with him," Jilly said, pointing at a small notebook computer.

"Sam's?" Inamorata asked.

"One and the same. I started working on his e-mail accounts."

"Accounts?"

"He has several, or he's letting someone else use his computer."

"Loves me some getting paid to hack and whack. Oh yeah, life is sweet," the ponytailed tech said. "Some people actually have to work for a living."

"Jilly means we're utilizing Sam's personal computer to see if we can get any information about the people he's been hanging out with or maybe get clues as to his whereabouts," Wes said.

As if she didn't know what Hawkeye, Inc. did to keep its clients safe.

"He has a colorful browsing history," Jilly said. "Stuff he wouldn't want his mama seeing."

"I'm working on getting past the network security at his work site," said the ponytailed tech.

Of course. It *was* after hours.

To Inamorata, the rest of the evening was annoyingly uneventful. Things would likely remain that way until noon tomorrow.

She talked to Martha and Sara Stein several times. Not satisfied she was getting the whole story, she called the medic, twice, to check Martha's condition. She had a sense Martha was hiding how much pain she was in, but the medic assured Inamorata Martha really was recovering from the injury. Mentally, she was just as strong, despite the anguish. She was coping as well as could be expected.

Inamorata drank a gallon, maybe a gallon and a half, of

coffee. She refused dinner and burned up the caffeine by relentlessly pacing the kitchen.

Another operative arrived to work with Marcus, and Aston, seemingly aggravated by all the intrusions and demands on his systems, did threaten to shoot.

"If you don't behave, I'll keep Lexie locked up," Wes told Aston. "And you won't be able to play with her." Sometimes dealing with Aston was like dealing with a toddler.

"Indeed? Very good, sir."

"Isn't Lexie the vacuum cleaner?" Marcus asked, his eyes widening. "How do they play?"

"You don't want to know," Wes told the man.

"Dude, I wouldn't miss it for the world."

Wes set up Jilly and the ponytailed tech in the guest house with several large cups of ice. Marcus and the other protective agent would take turns bunking in the bedroom at the back of the house.

"Everyone's been instructed to notify us if there are any updates," Wes told her when he returned to the kitchen.

She was sitting on a stool at the kitchen island, checking her phone, again, for e-mails. There hadn't been a single new message in over an hour. She looked at him and pushed back the strands of hair that had become unruly and fallen across her forehead.

"Nothing's going to happen until tomorrow," he told her.

"I hate this part. The waiting."

"Secure the house, Aston."

She heard bolts slide into place, and then Aston began to perform an audible systems check. She wondered if she'd ever get accustomed to all Wes's gadgetry.

"In the meantime," he said, crossing the room looking dark and dangerous, "I'm planning to fuck your ass."

She blinked. "My...?"

"Your tightest hole, Inamorata. You're going to hold your butt cheeks apart in invitation. Any questions?"

She slowly shook her head. At his husky, demanding words, blood had slowed in her veins. It had nothing to do with the falling temperature and everything to do with the hypnotic effect he had on her.

"When I get in the bedroom, I want you naked, bent over the side of the bed. I want the clover clamps on your nipples. Have your legs spread and your hands holding your buttocks apart so the first thing I see when I walk in the room is your hole. And because I'm kinky, leave on those sexy little heels."

"Kinky?" She blinked. She didn't know what else to say, since her brain suddenly resembled scrambled eggs. She asked, "You have a shoe fetish?"

"I didn't. Turns out the sight of you in those shoes does dangerous things to my man parts. So yeah, I might have a shoe fetish."

She laughed.

"You've got ten minutes." He moved in closer. "Don't keep me waiting."

She slid off the stool and into his waiting arms. He gently pulled her against him. This man undid her. Alternately stern and understanding, capable of giving her what she wanted as well as what she needed, constantly pushing, coming after her when she panicked and ran, infinite patience, knowing when to be tough and when to be gentle...

She was falling for him.

He put his hand in her hair and eased back her head. Pins surrendered and fell to the ceramic floor in a clatter. Without being told, she opened her mouth for him, to him.

He placed one hand on her buttocks and drew her closer, then encouraged her onto her tiptoes.

He claimed her mouth gently at first, then, as she melted into him, with a little more force. His tongue was demanding; *he* was demanding.

She opened her mouth wider, and he intensified the kiss, leaving her breathless.

Slowly, oh so slowly, he ended the kiss.

"Ten minutes, Inamorata."

"I'm not sure I can wait that long."

"Don't even think of trying to sneak in an orgasm."

She opened her eyes wide. "Me?"

"Your butt isn't blistered enough from your last spanking?"

"I want you inside me, Wes. Sir. I won't come unless you're there."

"I'm not sure you said what you were supposed to."

She wriggled out of his arms and started toward the bedroom, moving her hips suggestively.

"Keep it up, woman."

She looked over her shoulder and smiled cheekily. She liked having as much power over him as he had over her.

As she neared the door, Bentley scampered after her.

"Come here, Bentley."

The dog ignored him.

"Bentley!"

The dog ran even faster but obviously wasn't paying attention to where he was going. He ended up skidding into a wall with a loud *crash* before falling over. "I'll deal with him," Wes said when Inamorata started to head his direction. "He needs to be charged."

Bentley jumped up almost instantly. He shook his head. The vigorous motion must have loosened a screw in his ear. His entire right ear fell off, and a screw went spinning across the floor. "Bucket of bolts," Wes muttered, walking over to pick up the nutt and his missing pieces. "Doesn't let you off the hook," he said to her. "Ten minutes."

Inamorata, aware of his gaze fixed on her, pulled her blouse over her head and dropped it on the floor as she walked.

"Nine minutes," he said. "Maybe less. Aston, lights at twenty-five percent."

"Good night, Mr. Lowell. You as well, Lindsey."

"Lindsey doesn't sound half-bad." She waited a beat. "But it's still wrong."

"Hey, Aston," Wes said, "get going on the Italian names."

"Indeed, sir. Good night...Carmela."

"Nope."

"Alissandra?"

"Three strikes, you're out." She closed the bedroom door. She walked toward the bathroom, kicking off her shoes and discarding the rest of her clothes as she went. If she was fast, she could freshen up before he came in search of her. "Aston, I want a shower."

"Certainly, Giuseppe. What temperature?"

"One hundred and one," she said. "And Giuseppe is a boy's name."

"My mistake."

When Aston told her the water had reached the perfect temperature, she pinned her hair on top of her head to keep it out of the water, then got in the shower and rinsed off quickly, aware of the clock ticking.

She dried off, put on some lotion as a concession to the dry Colorado air, and then slipped back into her shoes.

The clamps sat on top of the dresser. They'd looked so much more appealing before her nipples had been abused earlier. What had she been thinking when she'd selected the most intense pair from his collection?

Still, he'd requested she wear them. Requested? More like ordered. That thought was enough to arouse her, make her wish away the minutes until he walked through the doorway.

She pinched each nipple to arousal and then attached a clamp to each. She tugged on the chain to make sure they were tight.

Following his instructions, she moved to the side of the bed. When he walked through the door, the first thing he'd see was her rear. Although he'd teased her with a finger earlier, she was an anal virgin. But earlier, he'd been gentle. He hadn't proceeded until she was comfortable. His penetration hadn't hurt; in fact, the added sensation had made the sex all that much more powerful.

Despite that, the idea of his cock filling her rear passage made her nervous.

She positioned herself, reaching to part her buttocks and expose her anus to his view and possession.

She listened for any sound of Wes's arrival, but it was hard to discern anything subtle over the pounding of her heart.

Her nipples started to throb. The pain felt doubly worse since her breasts were being smashed against the mattress. Her legs felt a little fatigued, but she remained in position because she knew it was what he wanted.

She started to think of all her favorite movies as a way to distract from the focus on her aching muscles and her tortured nipples. Long minutes passed, and she resisted the urge to look over her shoulder or take a momentary break.

"Good girl."

She jumped. She had no idea how long he'd been there, watching her. But his approval made her glad she'd followed his rules.

"You have no idea how hard my cock is as I stand here,

watching you behave exactly as I told you to."

Her entire body responded to the sound of his voice. Her stomach tightened; her heart rate accelerated; her pussy moistened in readiness.

"The shoes are great," he said. "And the rest is even better."

She was hyperaware of his movements as he crossed the room and knelt behind her.

"Keep your cheeks apart."

He placed his hands on top of hers, spreading her even wider. His hands felt cool against her heated flesh.

"Better," he said.

She wanted to protest that this was obscene, but she knew he'd object, and she knew this view of her turned him on.

He licked her, front to back.

She cried out, startled, edgy.

He circled her rear opening with his tongue; then he slid inside her. He was completely carnal.

He slid his tongue in and out, moistening her, and turning her on more passionately than she ever remembered being.

"I'm going to get the lube," he told her, pulling away a little. He slowly stood, keeping his hand on her as long as he could. He kept talking to her, and his voice seemed to mesmerize her. "We'll go easy. But I am going to fuck your rear, Inamorata."

"Yes." Suddenly, she wanted it as much as he did. She turned her head to the side to watch as he put lube on two fingers. She squeezed her eyes shut, wishing she hadn't just watched him do that.

"We'll go slow," he told her again. "Don't panic."

"Easy for you to say. You're the one with the cock. A big one."

He slowly moved behind her. "I'm still fully dressed," he

told her. He pressed his jeans-clad thighs against her naked skin and leaned over her.

She sensed his determination, and his scent was as crisp as the cool Colorado fall night. While she'd showered, he'd obviously been outside.

Instead of immediately sticking one of those slick fingers in her ass, he used his other hand to stroke her pussy.

After several seconds of his slow onslaught, an orgasm began to build. It was impossible with the way fear had been clawing at her only moments ago.

"I want you on the edge," he told her softly against her ear. "This time isn't about punishment; it's about making this better for you."

She nodded.

When she was close, when her insides started to clench, he skillfully eased back. On his next forward stroke, he pressed the tip of one finger against her tightest hole. Somehow he managed to press his thumb against her clitoris, igniting all her nerve endings at once.

She felt the scratch of denim along with his strength as his thighs pinned her against the bed. The weight of his upper body pressed her harder into the bedcovers. He overwhelmed her.

He finger fucked her both places, and the sensations were so overwhelming she barely noticed him stretching her.

"Doing okay?" he asked her.

"Yes."

"Ready for more?"

She tensed.

"Okay," he said with a laugh. "That's the last time I'll ask. I'll trust you to tell me if something's not working. Fair enough?"

He resumed stroking her, touching her, bringing her to the

precipice again. Before she was quite ready, he inserted a second finger. The feeling was amazing, too much and not enough. Both passages felt slick, ready.

He kissed the side of her neck, then her nape; he moved her around so she could no longer think. She was about to come when he pulled away. "Damn it," she said, turning her head to scowl at him. "You were about to make me come."

"The orgasm you get in the next five minutes will make it worthwhile."

"You talk big, Mr. Lowell."

"Ms. Inamorata, you're going to eat your words. Put your hands behind you and keep your butt spread."

She watched him undress.

The man's body never failed to amaze her. His shoulders were broad, his hips narrow. His thighs were unbelievably powerful, especially for a man who spent more time at a computer than he did in the field.

His cock was always impressive, and now, as hard as it was, as thick as it was, she felt suddenly very small and feminine.

He put on a condom and moved across the room toward her.

She expected to feel nervous, but within seconds, he had her right back where she'd been—on the edge. He knelt behind her again and worked that magic with his tongue, against her clit, in her pussy, pressing on her perineum.

As he licked her and tasted her, he inserted a finger in her rear, then added a second finger. "How does that feel?"

"It hurts a little," she confessed. "Not terribly, but it's not pleasant."

"Bear down on my fingers," he told her.

She followed his instructions, and the experience completely changed for her. It no longer seemed like a struggle, and the pain lessened considerably.

"Better?" he asked.

"Amazing," she confessed.

"Relax into it," he said. He stroked her, gently pinched her, teased her.

Unbelievably, she began to relax, not fighting herself, not struggling against him.

The feel of his cockhead against her opening made her freeze. His fingers were one thing, but this intensity *there...* She sucked in a shallow breath. On a sharp exhalation, she said, "I can't."

He pulled out. But instead of saying anything, he continued to soothe and arouse.

The next time he placed his cock there, she relaxed a little more. Each bit of the experience made it easier to go to the next.

He gently forced the head of his cock inside her ass; then he pulled it out and went back to stretching her with his fingers.

He never stopped paying attention to her pussy. Amazingly, the next time he penetrated her ass, he went in all the way.

She gasped and cried out, trying to get away.

He took hold of her shoulders, keeping her still. "You're there, baby."

"It *hurts.*"

She knew she sounded peevish. The size of him, the strength of him, was overwhelming.

"Do you want me to pull out? Admit defeat before you even let me try to bring you to orgasm?"

He clearly knew how to goad her. "No. I don't want to admit defeat." But there was no way she was ever going to reach climax when it hurt this bad to have him balls-deep in her ass.

He began to move slowly, and amazingly, after about thirty seconds, it stopped being painful as her body accommodated him.

"How do your breasts feel?"

"My nipples are burning."

"Good. Focus on it."

He put an arm between her and the mattress in order to lift her pelvis away from the bed. "I want you to play with your pussy," he told her.

She maneuvered so she could finger her swollen clit.

He kept one hand beneath her and held her shoulder with the other. He began to thrust, hard, hard and deep, filling her, stretching her, pounding her. "So tight," he said.

She focused, like he said, on her nipples as she played with herself.

As he possessed her, rational thought slipped away. She was lost in the sensations of pain and pleasure that melded into magic.

"Take it, Inamorata. Take me."

"Yes," she said. "I want it; I want you. Fuck me, Wes! *Fuck me harder.*"

He was always in control, but his shortened breaths told her he was on the edge every bit as much as she was.

He rode her uncompromisingly, thrusting his hips in time with his repeated commands that she take everything he was giving.

On his next thrust, she moved her hips back, meeting him.

"Damn, woman."

"Give it to me," she pleaded. "Sir."

He moved the hand that had been on her shoulder to her hip. He then pulled out his other arm from beneath her.

"You want all of me?" he asked.

"Now," she demanded. "Now, now, now!"

His hands on her hip bones, he dragged her backward as he thrust forward. He totally impaled her. She cried out. The orgasm that crashed over her was unlike anything she'd ever experienced. The wrenching intensity of it seemed to shatter her from the inside out.

She was limp, spent, and he continued to penetrate her for several more strokes. Then he tightened his grip on her hips, and she knew the grip would leave bruises, but she was way beyond caring.

When he came, it was with a massive shudder. He collapsed over her.

"I've never felt anything like that," she said.

"I'm not sure I could survive it very often," he admitted. He slowly straightened and trailed his fingertips down her damp spine.

"But you were right," she said. "You made me come from anal penetration. Don't gloat."

"I'll collect my winnings later."

"Winnings?"

"You can give me one of your world-class blowjobs. Without running away after. And if it's a thought, I'll tie you to the bed."

If he kept doing her like this, she wouldn't be going anywhere for a long time.

He eased his cock from her rectum. "Shower?"

"I can't move."

Effortlessly, he helped her roll over; then he picked her up and carried her to the bathroom. "Aston, shower at one hundred degrees."

"Giovanna prefers it a bit warmer, sir."

"One hundred and one," she confirmed. "But it's not Giovanna."

"One hundred and one it is," Wes said. "And Giovanna it's not."

He carried her into the shower and lowered her to her feet. He left her momentarily to discard the condom.

"I could suck your cock now," she said.

"I'm only human," he said, "but you should be good for at least one more orgasm. Put your hands on the wall."

He couldn't possibly be serious.

"Hands on the wall," he repeated.

His tone brooked no argument.

"Legs spread, Inamorata."

When she didn't move quickly enough, he gave her butt a stinging smack.

She thought she was too sore, or at least too tired. But he proved her wrong. Again and again.

Chapter Eight

Every time he saw her, the differences in her astounded Wes. The woman who'd just walked into the command central set up in his kitchen in no way resembled the greedy, sexy sub he'd so recently dominated.

Last night's scene had been intense, heightened, he knew, by the deadline they faced today.

This morning, her slim shoulders were perfectly straight, her hair was yanked back in a no-nonsense clip. Her green eyes were focused and clear. She seemed at ease and simultaneously in control. No one would ever guess the depth of her vulnerabilities or her capacity for uninhibited release.

Bentley, enthusiastic as ever, dashed over to see her, despite a floppy ear.

"His ear is still broken," she said.

"I was preoccupied last night." He hadn't taken as much care with Bentley's parts as he should have.

It was barely eight o'clock, and her phone rang. "It's Hawkeye," she said unnecessarily.

At this point, even Wes recognized the man's ringtone.

She headed out of kitchen, toward the great room. Not that he couldn't listen in if he really wanted.

On one of the monitors, Wes watched a black-billed magpie land on a wire. Seconds later, it took off again.

"Did Aston zap him?" Marcus asked.

Since the magpie landed on a nearby deer, Wes doubted Aston had sent a surge of energy through the fence.

"I like Pica picas," Aston said. "Keep the carrion down. Much more environmentally friendly that way."

"Uh-huh," Marcus said.

Wes topped off his coffee mug, along with Marcus's. Jilly was working on her second cup of ice, drowned in cola. Smith was drinking soda water with lime. Wes had a cup waiting for Inamorata when she returned.

When she reentered the kitchen, she was slipping the phone back into its case. "A couple of weeks ago, the police in Florida found a woman's body," she said. "She was already in bad shape by then."

"Gators," Smith surmised.

Inamorata slid onto a bar stool, in the middle of the computers, positioning herself mostly in the center of the room. Her message was clear. She was here as a member of the team, not its boss. His respect for her took another notch up.

"Last week, they got a positive ID. Cindy Danville."

"Danville?" Wes asked. He didn't like coincidences, didn't trust them.

"Nathan Danville's sister."

"He had a sister?" Wes asked.

"Fuck me," Jilly said.

"Timelining it," Wes said. He moved to his computer and began to type. Within seconds, the new information started to appear on a screen. Along with Sam's disappearance and the date of his new job and the approximate date he'd met Jonah, they now had information about the sister.

He listened while Inamorata continued. "When Nathan Danville died, his sister inherited. Unfortunately no one could find her to let her know. She evidently left Danville's compound when he brought in Chloe. Since Danville's death, Jonah has been overseeing the estate."

"And he wants to own the whole thing," Wes surmised.

"He's spent the last six years helping search for Ms. Danville. He 'spared no resources,' in the words of the Arizona police."

"I'll bet," Jilly said.

"He called them constantly, hired his own private investigators, sent them leads."

"I don't get it," Smith said. "Ms. Danville is dead. End of story."

"Danville was a bastard, and there was evidently no love for his cousin."

"Hard to imagine," Jilly said.

"Hawkeye paid a little visit to the attorney in the wee hours. Turns out, even with Cindy Danville out of the way, Jonah doesn't have a straight shot at the money."

"Chloe?" Wes asked, looking up.

"If Cindy is unable to inherit, the money goes to Chloe."

"What a stinking shitpile," Jilly said.

"Do you have audio of the call with Jonah?" Inamorata asked him.

Wes called up the file on his computer. On one of the large screens attached to the wall, he brought up a picture of Jonah.

Inamorata's recorded voice spilled from the ceiling-mounted speakers. She sounded sure, in control, exactly what he'd expect from her. But being there, watching her, he'd seen her reaction, the way she'd locked her knees, the furl of worry between her brows. No one else knew her like he did. And he liked that.

"Six years was a long time ago..."

"You were supposed to take care of my cousin, not let him

die. Does everyone there know how bad you fucked up? Does everyone there know you killed my cousin?"

"I'm afraid I've been involved in a lot of cases." She'd paused. *"I'm sorry, Mr. Jonah, I don't see—"*

"Don't play games with me, bitch," Jonah had interrupted. *"You'll do as I say, or I'll start by sending you pieces of the sniveling kid we've got here. He wants his mommy, and I want to get my hands on that murdering little slut and my money. I'd say we both want something, wouldn't you?"*

Wes left Jonah's picture up, even though the audio ended.

"At the time," Inamorata said, breaking the sudden silence, "we didn't know about the money. When we learned about the wire transfer, for two million dollars, I assumed that was the money he was talking about." She sighed. "He's not interested in the two million. He's talking about the entire estate. Stupid. Stupid. Damn it. How could I be so stupid?"

"Everyone thought he meant the two million," Wes said.

She looked at him, and her eyes seemed to snap fire. That'd be the last time he ever tried to placate Inamorata.

"There's no doubt he tried and failed to find Chloe. Hawkeye has her so deep even I couldn't locate her if I wanted to."

"How much money are we talking?" Wes asked.

"Hundreds of millions."

Marcus whistled.

"That'd interest me," Jilly said.

"Enough to come out of hiding?" Smith asked.

"You could afford a lot of protection with that kind of money," Inamorata said. "And she's been through a lot."

"She got away, at least in theory, with two million," Wes pointed out.

"And she could lose part of that, maybe half of it in a

divorce. Who knows how much is even left."

"Yeah," said Jilly, "you always hear how people win the lottery and then they go broke."

"And she has a kid to take care of." Inamorata slid off the stool and paced.

He might have to replace the flooring when this was over. He'd never met a woman with more energy. "There's a good chance she doesn't know how nasty Jonah is," he said.

"I'd assume the entire family was a den of snakes," Jilly said.

Inamorata reached for her phone.

Wes wondered if her mind ever stopped.

She didn't leave the kitchen, didn't look at the keypad as she pushed a couple of buttons. A few seconds later, her call obviously connected, she asked, "How old is Chloe's little boy?"

Wes swore suddenly, following her thought pattern.

Five seconds later, she hung up and scrubbed her hand across her forehead.

She met his gaze, and he saw the hurt and frustration buried there.

"How old?" he asked, already knowing the answer.

"The little boy just turned six. *Son of a bitch*."

"Can someone draw me a picture?" Marcus asked.

Since he was personal protection for Inamorata and not actively working the case, Marcus hadn't been briefed on all the details.

"It's Danville's," she said. "Chloe's little boy is Danville's son."

"Fuck me. Didn't I say this was a shitpile?" Jilly asked.

"No wonder she ran," Inamorata said. "The two million dollars makes total sense now. The timing fits."

"She's not going to sit back now and let Jonah have the money," Wes said. "Her money. Her kid's money."

"With what we now know of Chloe, I'd say that's a good bet," Inamorata said. "We may not have to worry much longer. Chloe may just walk right out into the open."

"If she knows someone's looking for her," Smith said.

"She knows, if she's still a computer geek," Jilly said. "We may not know her real name, but since Jonah was an occasional visitor in the house, he does. And you can bet your sweet ass he's got it out there. He's trolling."

Inamorata's phone rang again. She looked at the wall clock. Not even ten. After checking the caller ID, she said, "It's Sara Stein."

"You okay with us listening in?"

She nodded. They both knew involving the team as much as possible made everything flow smoother.

"Make her call public," he told Smith once they were back in the kitchen.

The man tapped a few letters on his keyboard.

He brought up a picture of Stein on the monitor.

Inamorata answered.

Stein didn't waste time or mince words. "Ms. Montano just received a package."

In the background, they heard wailing. The keening, the palpable desperation all but drowned out Stein's voice.

The bastards hadn't waited for the deadline. Goddamn it.

Wes saw Inamorata take a steadying breath. "Go on," she said.

"It's an ear," Stein said. "Covered in blood."

"Is it real?" Wes asked.

"I'm not convinced it is, but I don't want to touch it and

contaminate it. I need a tech."

"On it," Wes said. "And I'll get a sample of Sam Montano's DNA." He grabbed his phone and speed-dialed headquarters.

"Do you need me there?" Inamorata asked Stein.

"I think that would do more harm than good. She's worried about Sam, and she's upset you might get hurt. Of course she's also confused. She doesn't understand why you can't or won't just give Jonah what he wants. I've explained it, but it doesn't help."

Families of kidnap victims rarely understood, Wes knew. And how could they be expected to? To them, the situation often seemed cut-and-dried. Give the bad guy what they wanted, and their loved one would magically and safely return home.

Consumed by her pain and fear, Martha wouldn't be thinking of Chloe or the potentially motherless little boy. To her, Chloe was a faceless person, whereas Sam was her flesh and blood.

He didn't envy Inamorata's position. It was her responsibility to advocate for everyone. The protector in him wanted to solve this damn situation, take control, shove her behind him while he went in with guns blazing.

Frustration chewed at him from the inside out. He'd never felt like this before, never been involved with a woman who carried such a heavy burden.

Once he was connected with Hawkeye's Denver office, Wes outlined their needs. "And get the medic back over there," he said. "Inamorata will want Martha checked out."

She shot him a grateful smile.

"Send a counselor as well," Wes instructed.

"Do you want me to talk to Martha?" Inamorata asked.

"Let's wait to see what the counselor recommends," Stein

said, obviously having heard Wes's comment.

"Were there any demands?" Inamorata asked.

On the screen, Stein shook her head. "Just the package."

Inamorata was quiet for a few seconds. "Keep me posted." She ended the call.

A few seconds later, he disconnected the call he'd been on.

Silence hung over the room, until the wise Jilly reached for her ice. She chomped madly. "Well, boss, what do we do next?"

"Someone take a look at Jonah's name, on the Internet and anywhere else you can think of. See what pops," she said. "If he's looking for Chloe, what bait is he using?"

It would be easier if they had Chloe's name. But even Wes wasn't stupid enough to suggest that to Inamorata.

"We've got Sam's computer," Wes added.

"On it," Smith said, cracking his knuckles.

"Can I have a moment of your time?" Wes asked Inamorata.

"Two minutes," she said.

He and Bentley followed her into the great room. He stood near the mantel, a foot on the slab of stone protecting the floor, Bentley at his feet.

The gas-burning fireplace flickered to life without him touching the switch. He'd forgotten he'd programmed Aston for that nicety.

Inamorata continued toward the bank of windows. Bentley plopped down in front of the fireplace. He tried to curl up, but his middle didn't fold. Another upgrade needed for the next version. Finally he just stretched out.

Inamorata stood silently at the window, one hand on her waist, the other rubbing her nape.

He wondered if she noticed the snow-dusted landscape or if she was lost in her thoughts. "You've got to let Chloe know about the money," he said.

"Yeah. Yeah I do." She leaned her forehead against a windowpane. "But it doesn't mean I have to like it, any of it."

He crossed the room, stood behind her, his hands on her slim shoulders. He rubbed beneath her shoulder blades, and her hands slowly fell to her sides. "Jonah wants her dead," she said bluntly.

"Hawkeye would have already let her know that."

"The money is an added angle, an incentive she might be willing to take."

"Yeah," he said. "It's possible."

"She's been through so damn much, Wes. Danville fucking raped her, cut off her ear. Even his death hasn't brought her any peace."

She surprised him by leaning back into him, letting him support some of her weight.

"She could be tried for the bastard's death if she returns to Arizona."

He wasn't sure whether to respond or to let her process the information by herself.

"Damn. This is a no-win situation."

"She's an adult," he said. "They're her decisions."

"The night I got her away, we promised we'd keep her safe."

"And you've done a hell of a job. You're still doing a hell of a job." He wrapped his arms more tightly around her middle. "Keeping someone safe isn't always as easy as it seems. Hawkeye will continue to give her protection, but we all know life comes with risk."

"You know, Wes, after Chloe, I thought this job would be easy." She gave a half-disbelieving laugh. "Up until then, everything had been okay. There were stressful situations and interactions with people, but nothing I couldn't handle.

"Then I got tapped for personal protection at Danville's. I thought that was going to be straightforward. Spend a few months in a luxurious situation. Nothing could have been further from the truth.

"After it was over, I told myself nothing could ever be worse than that. I made mistakes, I got written up, but ultimately, I'd helped get Chloe away. It made me stronger, forced me to focus on what was really important. Then I nearly lost my sister."

He'd been there; he remembered. He hadn't been directly involved, but he'd been one of the geeks behind the scenes, and he'd personally known Aimee. He'd been there for Inamorata after she returned to Denver from Winter Park. There was no doubt about her competence, and there was no one Hawkeye trusted more for cleaning up after a scene. But her green eyes had been glazed, haunted, shattered.

She'd blamed herself for the situation, even though it hadn't been her fault. Aimee had become an agent because she wanted to.

That evening, Wes hadn't invited Inamorata back to his place. He'd been more direct than that. He'd texted his address to her phone and told her drinks were at seven.

She hadn't asked how he'd found out her phone number. She hadn't talked about her sister. They'd skipped the drinks.

And two hours later, she'd asked him to show her out.

Until now, until this case, she'd kept her private life hidden from him.

"Aimee wouldn't have been involved if it weren't for me," she said. "Martha, Sam..."

He turned her to face him. He wasn't as gentle as he wanted to be. He caught her chin forcefully between his thumb and forefinger. "Shut up. *Shut...up.* You need to focus. You need to be objective. Sam, Martha, even Chloe and her kid are counting on you."

She turned around. "Didn't your mother teach you if you can't say something nice, you shouldn't say anything at all?"

"Inamorata, that was the nicest thing I could have said to you. Platitudes would piss you off."

"But *shut up*?"

"If we were in the bedroom, I'd find some other way to occupy that mouth. But since we're out in the open, I'll have to find another way." Mindless of her hairstyle, he dug his hand into her hair.

"Make me," she said.

"Make you shut up? My pleasure."

He captured her mouth, demanding her surrender, all but fucking her mouth with his tongue.

She squirmed. She moaned from somewhere deep inside. But she didn't fight. She surrendered.

This Inamorata was different from the one he'd been sleeping with for the last six months. He'd often wondered what she'd be like once the ice thawed. But he hadn't been prepared for her heat. He couldn't get enough of her.

His dick was hard, and he wanted to be deep inside her, impaling her. She didn't bring out the gentleman in him. He didn't want to be nice or polite. He wanted to pound her. He wanted to possess her in a way that never let her forget she belonged to him.

He wanted her to share the load, wanted her to need him.

She responded, pressing her tongue demandingly against his.

This complex woman turned him on. She made him forget dates where he'd taken a woman out for a nice dinner and a glass of red wine. Inamorata was earthy, not only responding to him, but insisting he not hold back. She made him want to dominate and to protect. He fully intended to take her for dinner and wine. And when he did, he'd see to it she wore nipple clamps and a butt plug while she sat across the table.

He had no intention of letting her get away. The sooner she realized that, the better.

As if she sensed that, she put her hands between them, ending the kiss. She was smart enough not to push him away. "I need to call Hawkeye," she said. "I'll have him contact Chloe."

He nodded.

He should have known better than to kiss her. Touching her, holding her, inhaling her scent made him hard. He wanted her beneath him, hard, fast, quick, and dirty. But duty called, and they'd both put their responsibilities first. Once this case was over, they'd be having a serious talk.

He released her, but he cupped her breasts.

She sighed softly. "My nipples are sensitive today," she said.

"So, if I were to do this…" He gently squeezed. "It might hurt?"

Her knees started to buckle before she caught herself.

"It might be enough to make me come," she admitted.

He did it again. She closed her eyes, blocking out the emotion he'd seen there.

"Wes…"

"Sir," he corrected.

"Sir. Squeeze harder."

He did, enjoying the sound of her soft moan and the sight of her mouth parting slightly. Then he placed his hand on her thigh and pulled up the hem of her skirt. He moved aside the fabric of her thong, finding her moist core and circling his thumb over her clit.

Within seconds, she came.

He supported her body weight while her breathing returned to normal and she straightened her clothing. "That'll hold you," he said.

"For a while," she agreed.

"Have I created a monster?" He kissed her and headed back toward the kitchen.

Traitorous Bentley looked up but didn't follow him. Could have been the programming to enjoy a warm fire, or it could have been the dog's reaction to Inamorata. Regardless, he ignored his master.

The kitchen was a flurry of activity. Another protective agent had arrived. Hawkeye did believe in being proactive. When a case escalated, so did the resources.

Smith and Jilly were hunched over computers. Marcus was giving the new agent instructions on how to operate the coffeemaker. Every assignment had its priorities.

He heard a slight *hum* followed by a cacophony of barks.

"What the hell…?" Smith asked.

Saturday, he remembered. Cleaning day. "Aston, override."

"That Lexie?" Marcus asked. "The vacuum cleaner," he explained to the newly arrived agent.

Wes rolled his eyes.

He heard Bentley's metal feet tearing up the hardwood floor.

"Sir, could you keep that mutt locked up?" Aston asked.

"Could you override?" he asked the computer.

"I'm programmed for optimal cleanliness. You do have your standards."

"He has been zapping those Pica picas," Marcus said. "I knew it."

Wes moved to the master computer keyboard. He obviously hadn't perfected this whole artificial-intelligence thing. The damn computer wasn't supposed to *argue*. And it sure as hell wasn't supposed to have a soft spot for something that sucked. Well, maybe. He had modeled the programming on his tastes.

The vacuum swept into the kitchen, its bottom half swaying back and forth.

"*Daaaaaamn*," Marcus said. "I need me one of those."

Bentley ran circles around the vacuum, nipping and yipping.

Lexie was about two and a half feet tall, in two round parts. The vacuum had mechanical feet that glided, and each operated individually. Each foot, with bristles that extended, could snake beneath furniture and into corners. Like Aston said, Wes liked cleanliness.

Wes had installed brushes all around Lexie's bottom half. Until now he hadn't realized how much they resembled a skirt. The vacuum stopped near the back of the room, then lowered and began to vibrate. Rather than moving around, it stayed in one place, shimmying wildly.

"Why is Lexie in the kitchen?" he asked Aston. "Lexie's programming is set for the bedroom carpeting. We generally use a broom and a mop in the kitchen."

"Well, yes, sir."

He waited.

"She works quite well in the kitchen as well. Wouldn't you agree? If you were here by yourself all day, sir, you might enjoy her company as well. She does suck well."

Jilly chomped. Marcus roared. Smith stuck out a foot to keep the machine away. Bentley all but leaped up and down.

Wes entered commands on the master keyboard. The trick would be to turn off Lexie and stop Bentley's hysterics without shutting down Aston's main functions. "I want Lexie back in the closet, Aston."

"But, sir—"

"*Override*, Aston." He hit the Escape key twice.

"Oh very well, sir."

A hissing sound spilled from the overhead speakers. If he didn't know better, Wes would have sworn Aston had sighed. Less than a second later, the vibrating stopped, and Lexie moved from the room silently.

"Spoilsport."

"I beg your pardon?" Wes asked.

"As you say, sir."

Lexie gave a quick shake of her bottom half before sweeping across the threshold and out of the room.

"Very funny, Aston."

Time dragged. They ate frozen pizza baked in the convection oven. Jilly consumed a two-liter bottle of soda. Three more pots of coffee vanished.

Inamorata paced, occasionally stopping at the window. Cases were often like this, Wes knew, especially when a bad guy had given an ultimatum. There were long periods of boredom, punctuated by insanely paced developments, sometimes so rapid-fire it was difficult to process them. Then, often, more boredom. Too much time to wonder, to think, to worry.

"Hey, Wes, will you take a look at this?" Jilly asked.

Wes moved in next to Jilly. Her eyes were bloodshot, and she hadn't chomped a single piece of ice in half an hour. Her movements across the keyboard had slowed. She was either exhausted, or she was on to something and wanted to be deliberate in her actions. He'd bet on deliberate.

Inamorata wandered over, taking a place behind Jilly's left

shoulder.

"What have you got?" he asked.

"Seems our boy Sam has a handful of e-mail accounts. He had one account that used his real name. It appears he used that for a cell phone bill and to e-mail his mother. He sent out job applications and résumés from that e-mail as well. The routine things you'd expect."

He reined in his impatience. Jilly had been meticulous; she'd present the information in the same logical way.

She pointed to the screen. "This one has a code name of sorts, SMMount4U, kind of a stupid play on his initials and last name. He wouldn't want anyone reading what's in there."

He *was* a twentysomething-year-old man. The code name might be tacky, but it was excusable.

Inamorata said nothing. If she was shocked, she didn't reveal it.

"He used this e-mail address apparently for hook-ups and for some chat rooms. Could be something there, but I didn't find anything on a quick search."

Wes nodded.

"But I found something else that might interest you." Jilly moused over an icon and maximized it. "This one has a woman's name. Not very original or creative..." She hesitated. "Unless someone's been using his computer, it appears Sam also sends out e-mails under the name Samantha."

Wes met Inamorata's gaze. She hadn't flinched. Obviously nothing could faze her at this point.

"We'll display this one here." Jilly resized the window and moved it to the left side of the screen. "Then there's this e-mail address—his initials and some numbers, maybe his DOB." She opened it and displayed the two side by side. You may want to read this thread from the beginning. Tell me what you think."

Jilly moved to one side, keeping only part of her rear on the stool. Wes commandeered the mouse and slowly scrolled through the e-mails in reverse order.

After the first couple, he got a pit in his stomach.

Jilly knew exactly what she was looking at. She just didn't want to be the one to say what she'd found.

He met Inamorata's gaze. Her lips were set in a tight line. But she didn't waste a second on denial.

Chapter Nine

"Check his financials," Inamorata said. "Smith...?"

"On it, ma'am."

Jilly looked over her shoulder. "I'm sorry, 'Morata."

"I don't shoot the messenger," Inamorata said. But god*damn*, she wanted to shoot someone. She pursed her lips. Ever since the call from Jonah, everything she'd thought she knew had been turned inside out.

If the words on the screen were accurate, Sam Montano not only knew Zack Jonah, he'd been corresponding with him, and they'd been working out details, including financial compensation. *Goddamn him.* The kidnapping was a fucking hoax. How dare the son of a bitch do this to his mother? How dare he cause such anguish and suffering? How dare he allow his mother to be hurt? Inamorata would cut off his balls herself. "Get someone back into his apartment."

Wes nodded.

"Let me see the e-mails from Samantha."

"Why don't you drive?" Jilly asked, slipping off the stool and heading to the freezer to fill up an oversize plastic cup.

Inamorata slid onto the stool. Wes moved in closer, and she was grateful he did. Inamorata was accustomed to doing things on her own. She always had. Until now, until him, she'd liked it that way.

She moved the mouse over to his Samantha e-mail box and

began scrolling through threads. He'd been trolling chat rooms, pretending to be a woman of Middle Eastern descent who'd been in an abusive relationship. *Looking for Chloe?*

Inamorata seethed. She'd rarely been tempted to kill someone with her bare hands. If she got close enough to Sam, she just might. He might be the son of a friend, but the man was scum. He was going down; she'd see to it.

"Try a filter," Wes said. "Make it go faster."

He gave her a few different suggestions on search parameters.

"I don't think he found her," Wes said. "If he had, Jonah wouldn't have involved you."

"We'll keep looking," Jilly said.

Inamorata held up a hand.

Jilly sucked an ungodly amount of soda and ice into her mouth and waited.

"I want you to become Chloe online. See if you can get to Sam or Jonah."

Jilly put down the cup and rubbed her hands together.

"Worth a shot," Wes said.

"Better than waiting for their freaking demands." Inamorata slid off the chair and headed for the coffeepot that Wes thoughtfully kept filled. "Better than letting Chloe expose herself."

"Woman can't live by caffeine alone," Wes told her.

"Tell Jilly. I've been watching her do it."

"Nah," said Jilly. "I need sugar too."

"See?" He closed the distance between them, grabbed a piece of pizza, and shoved it in Inamorata's direction.

"That's not exactly food," Inamorata said, but she bit into it regardless. No telling how long the day would be.

"How about Finally Free in Arizona for an e-mail handle?" Jilly asked.

"It's a mouthful," Wes said. "But if he's got filters on, it'll hit."

Her phone signaled an incoming text message. She put down the slice of pepperoni pizza and read the message aloud. "The blood type appears to be a match for Samuel Montano. But the ear is not human flesh." *Of course.* She forwarded the message to Stein. "I'm going to call Martha in a few minutes," she said. "Give Stein a head start."

Wes nodded. "How much are you going to let her know?"

"As little as possible." The rest of her food seemed to stick in her throat. She wouldn't have finished it, except for the fact she needed to keep up her energy.

After downing a glass of water, she went into the great room to call Martha. Martha sounded much calmer than she had earlier. Stein had obviously already broken the news. "How are you holding up?" Inamorata asked.

Her voice didn't tremble like it had the last time they'd talked. "Worried. Scared. But I feel better now I know it's not Sam's ear." She choked on a sob. "I want my boy home."

"I know you do." She spoke carefully. "We'll do our best to get this wrapped up quickly." That was the best she could promise.

"I want this whole thing to be over," Martha said. "Please. Please make it go away."

Inamorata got a sudden headache. After a few more polite words, she hung up.

From the kitchen, she heard voices on the speakers.

"Update from headquarters," Wes said when she crossed the threshold. "They've found Jonah's last-known address. They're moving in now."

They waited.

"House appears vacant," a Hawkeye operative said. "Entering in five, four, three, two—Go. Go, go, go."

She and Wes looked at each other.

She knew what they'd find. Nothing. No Jonah, no computer. He'd been a step ahead of them the entire time.

And it was nearing noon.

"Vacant," came the confirmation over the speakers.

Wes took the call off audible.

At ten minutes before twelve, Hawkeye called.

"Chloe wants to play."

Inamorata exhaled. She had expected as much, but the news still sucked air out of her lungs. She didn't know whether to be relieved or disappointed. Knowing what she was up against, a plan formulated. "They're not getting her."

"Let me know what you need," he said.

"Do you still have friends in the bureau?"

"Got a couple of numbers around here somewhere."

"Kidnapping's a federal offense."

"Has been since the Lindbergh case," he agreed.

"I want these guys in prison. And I don't want a lot of questions." Sometimes they had the bureau's back. Now she needed a badge at hers.

"I'll get you a couple of the best within the hour, an hour and a half at the outside."

Hawkeye meant he'd send agents they'd worked with before, Feds who wouldn't have a jurisdictional fit about Hawkeye not bringing them in from the beginning, agents who wouldn't ask too many questions and would come up to speed fast. Inamorata knew Hawkeye would keep their agency out of the press and let the bureau take credit for moving quickly and solving the case.

"Let them know about Sam's associates."

"Consider it done."

Her phone signaled a call waiting. She checked the screen for the number. It had a 720 prefix, but she didn't recognize the number. "Jonah," she guessed. "We'll play it his way," she told Hawkeye. "Let him think he's a step ahead of us."

Her heart rate accelerated, and she ignored the crash of adrenaline, the fight-or-flight reaction. She nodded at Wes to take the call over the speakers. When he gave her a thumbs-up that they were tracing and live, she said, "Showtime." She disconnected from Hawkeye and accepted the new call. "Inamorata speaking."

"You got my message?" Jonah asked.

"You mean the package? Yes. We got your message loud and clear."

"You got the girl?"

"Working on it. Trying to convince her is tricky."

"I want to marry her."

"Marry her?" she repeated. She didn't need to try to sound surprised. She *was* surprised.

"If she marries me, she'll get ten times the amount she stole. My cousin left a will," he said. "He wanted both of us to be happy. If I marry the girl, she'll get twenty million dollars."

"What's in it for you?"

"Money. She'll get a divorce within a year. All neat and tidy. She'll walk away with twenty million for a year of her time."

Inamorata's stomach turned.

"What's it to you?" he asked. "You want the kid back. You'll get him."

"I need to talk to him," she said. He'd expect her next

words, so she said them. "Give me proof of life."

"You'll see him when we do the exchange."

"Mr. Jonah, you cut off Sam Montano's ear. You didn't wait until noon to contact us. I have little reason to trust you. There was a lot of blood in that package. I have no guarantee Sam is alive. Give me proof." She dropped her voice and allowed some emotion to seep in. Hopefully Sam was nearby, listening. "His mother needs it. *I* need it. Nothing is more important to us than Sam's safety."

Muffled sounds filtered through the speakers. Suddenly there was silence. She checked her phone to be sure the line was still connected. Since it was, Jonah had obviously muted the call.

At least fifteen seconds passed.

She turned her back to the room, nervous energy nipping at her pulse. Was she giving the Hawkeye team enough time to get a GPS location?

"Ms. Inamorata?"

Wes typed on his keyboard, and a message scrawled across the bottom of the screen. *They're moving. A car...?*

"Sam! Your mother is worried. Are you okay? Do you need medical care?"

"Please, Ms. Inamorata. I want to go home. Let my mom know I'm okay. Mostly. I hurt."

She gritted her teeth. When she got hold of Sam, she'd kill him herself for what he was putting his mother through. "Sam, listen to me—"

"Seven o'clock," Jonah interrupted, evidently having grabbed the phone away from Sam. "You'll meet me at seven, with the girl."

"Where?"

"We'll let you know."

"I need time to get the girl from Arizona."

"Seven o'clock," he repeated.

"Mr. Jonah, surely you see you're asking the impossible. Give us until tomorrow. She might not be willing to come."

"She'll want the money," he said.

There was a loud sound like wind rushing. Then...nothing.

"He probably threw the phone out the car window," Jilly guessed.

After holding on a few more futile seconds, she hung up and slid her phone on the countertop. That had gone better than she could have hoped, but it wasn't good enough.

She exhaled. "I'll need a head scarf," she said to Jilly while making sure she didn't look at Wes. She mentally ran through the things she'd need. She had packed a pair of jeans and running shoes. She had a jacket that would work. "And you'll need to be me."

"I don't own a skirt." Jilly chomped. She looked at Inamorata with a slight frown. "And my ass ain't ever going to fit in one of your skirts."

"Jilly in a skirt," Smith said. He whistled. "I want to see that. Heels too? You going to be able to walk?"

"Fuck you, asshole," she said easily.

"Get someone to go shopping," Inamorata said. "Have the stuff delivered here by three."

"Thank God I don't have to go," Jilly said with a shudder.

"Did we get anything on the cell phone?" Inamorata asked Wes. "Another throwaway?"

"Looks like it," he said.

His lips were tight, and there was a pulse throbbing in his forehead. And this was one of the reasons she didn't get involved in personal relationships. Having to consider another person's feelings could be detrimental to the team.

She was honest enough to admit if the roles were reversed and he were walking into danger, she wouldn't like it.

But as the person who often ran the incident response, she'd see it as the logical thing to do. Even if she didn't like it, she'd keep her mouth shut and take the actions that would lead to the best possible outcome for the team and for Hawkeye's client. "We've got five hours," she told him.

"Great room," he said. "Now."

Jilly and Smith leaned over their keyboards. Marcus shoved his cup on the counter and said he needed to do another perimeter check.

She thought about ignoring him but was slightly concerned he'd toss her over his shoulder or drag her from the kitchen. God only knew what gossip would go through headquarters after that.

She followed him into the great room. Bentley bounded after them.

Wes stood with his back to the fireplace, legs spread, arms folded across his chest. He was breathtakingly gorgeous, dressed all in black. He'd raked back his hair from his forehead, making his eyes seem even more steely. His jaw was set in an uncompromising line.

She might be in charge of his mission, but his posture left no doubt he considered her his woman, which in his male mind, likely meant he was the boss.

"Pick someone else," he said flatly.

She continued across the room and propped her hip against a decorative table. "I'm the most logical candidate," she said.

"Not even close," he said. "Can you take care of yourself in the field? No doubt. Are you the most qualified person at Hawkeye to walk in as Chloe?" He didn't give her time to answer. His voice gravelly, he continued, "But you are one of the most skilled we have at running an op. You're better to

Sam, to Hawkeye, to Chloe if you're not the one in the line of fire."

"Would you be saying that if you weren't fucking me?"

The words hung between them, anger provoking and challenging.

The tic in his temple became more pronounced. "You're lucky I don't turn you over my knee right here, right now." He took a step toward her. "In fact, I may just do that." He took a second step toward her.

Inamorata pushed away from the table and stood her ground.

Bentley ran circles around Wes's feet.

"Be very careful, Wes," she said. "Don't bring our personal lives into this."

When he spoke, his tone of voice was unlike anything she'd ever heard. It was chilly and remote. It matched the darkness in his eyes. "You know, Ms. Inamorata, I'm tired of being careful around you. And if you'd admit the truth, you're tired of it too. You don't want a man you can push around, who will let you do anything you want with no regard for your safety."

"I was put in charge of this case because I'm the right person," she said.

"Agreed. Hawkeye knows what he's doing. But he didn't tell you to pretend to be Chloe."

She refused to back up, even when he closed the remaining distance between them. The air all but sizzled with the force of his determination. "There's a reason I have never had a serious relationship—"

"Until now," he corrected.

He hadn't touched her. Maybe he didn't trust himself. She was grateful regardless. In his arms, she came undone. "I don't consider this a serious—"

"Don't piss me off, Inamorata."

He smelled of the outdoors, of frosted pine and fresh mountain air. Part of her wanted to surrender to his unspoken demands, to ask him to hold her. But she couldn't. He saw this case differently than she did; she recognized that. She folded her arms across her chest and wished he'd back off, even six inches. "I can't help it if you get pissed off. I love my job. I love what I do. And I need the freedom to do my job without worrying what someone else will think. I'm not giving up Hawkeye for anyone, not ever. I don't *do* serious relationships. I don't want one. You knew that from the beginning." When he started to interrupt, she raised a hand. "Hear me out. You're fantastic in the bedroom. If you still want me in your bed after-hours, the way it's been, I can do that. I want to do that. I want to keep things the way they've been. Please don't ask for anything more."

"Your answer is not acceptable, Inamorata."

She dropped one hand to her side, while the other remained protectively around her waist. "Are you giving me an ultimatum?" Her heart thundered. *Not this. Not now.* "Don't you understand? What I do is part of who I am. I can't give that up and still be the woman you desire."

"I'm not asking you to give up Hawkeye," he said. "I'm asking you not to take unnecessary chances where you're not the only person qualified, and especially if you're not the best person to do it."

Now she was getting pissed. "As determined by you?"

"You're twisting my words."

"I *am* the best person to do this, and if you'll quit playing the domineering-man card, you'll realize I know what a snake Jonah is. I know Chloe. I'm the only woman in the organization who has met her. I know how she moves; I know her mannerisms. Assigning someone else to walk in there is irresponsible and stupid."

"Sam knows you. He'll blow your cover."

"People see what they expect to see; you know it as well as I do. Jilly will be there dressed as me. Everyone will assume the blonde in the skirt is me."

He dragged a hand through his hair.

"I never met Jonah. Depending when the estrangement between Danville and Jonah occurred, he may have met Chloe. I was in the house for six months." Her anger dissipated as she looked at him. Yes, he was acting like a rough-and-tough male, but it came from concern, not just a need to dictate her actions. Even though she knew that, it changed nothing. Still, trying to get her point across, she lowered her voice. "I want your support," she admitted. "Even if you don't approve, I'd like to have your support." More than any man, ever, he mattered to her. Right now, she felt emotionally wobbly and unsure. But she was committed to her course of action. "I'm uniquely qualified to take down Jonah."

"You're going to do it, even if I forbid you?"

"Don't," she said, begged. "Just don't."

He reached for her then, dragging her onto her toes and against his unyielding body. He kissed her hard, long, deep, thrusting with his tongue. Despite the tension that seemed to snap between them, she instantly responded to his touch. In his arms, she was a woman who hungered for her man's dominance. Her nipples hardened, and her pussy moistened as response flooded her. Her mind and her instinct for self-preservation told her one thing. But her body told her another.

He placed a big hand on her rear, and she felt the scratch of her woolen skirt against her bruised, swollen skin.

His cock was hard, pressing into her stomach. She curved her hand around him and stroked.

He groaned against her mouth.

Damn, she never wanted to give this—him—up.

And she knew they were both aware of the clock ticking off the minutes. Jonah had said five, but last time he'd acted two hours early.

Wes placed a hand over hers, stopping her motions. She tasted the bitterness of his good-bye before he ended the kiss.

He released her and took a step back.

She swallowed deeply. She told herself there wasn't a lump of emotion lodged in her throat. "I'll understand if you need to resign from the case."

"I don't quit," he said, jaw set.

She hated that it was this way. She remembered leaning against him earlier, how he'd effortlessly supported her and how much his strength sustained her. For a second, she reached up and placed her palm on the side of his cheek. "I'm sorry."

"Yeah."

"We have an op to run," she said, retreating to what was familiar. Work was something she knew how to do. It grabbed her focus, honed her senses. She was good at it. "The Feds will be showing up soon."

* * *

Ultimatum or not, he didn't like this. Watching a federal agent wrap Inamorata in a hijab and show her how to adjust it made his gut clench. Between the skills of a makeup artist Jilly had requested from Hawkeye, a pair of colored contact lenses, and a bottle of dark dye applied to her blonde hair, Inamorata's appearance had been altered significantly. But as far as he was concerned, the scarf didn't cover enough of her face to ensure her safety.

The agent had said women wore scarves in several different

ways, and Inamorata could cover more of her face if she wished.

"She can't have her peripheral vision obstructed," he said.

"It's a balance," the federal agent agreed.

Inamorata adjusted the material in a mirror the agent was holding up. "I only need the element of surprise," Inamorata said.

"We've got her back," the federal agent said.

Was he the only one who thought this was a supremely bad idea?

Even though they had almost two hours before the deadline, Wes brought over a surveillance earphone. "Let's get this attached and do a sound check."

She removed the scarf and draped it across the paper-towel holder.

He'd seen her in plenty of sexy skirts and completely naked, but he'd never seen her dressed in crisp blue jeans, a softly knit mock-neck sweater, and running shoes. The jeans showed the curve of her rear and length of her legs. The sweater was fairly loose so the radio could be attached without any obvious bumps. Regardless of what she wore or didn't wear, the woman was sexy.

She pulled up the bottom of her sweater, and he attached the small radio to her spine. He'd done this dozens of times with other agents. He'd always been detached, but with Inamorata, things were different. Feelings for a woman changed everything, sharpened his senses and thought processes.

He handed her the plastic earbud, and she placed it in her ear canal.

"Comfortable enough?"

"I hardly know it's there."

"That's what I was hoping to hear." He connected the hard

wire and low-profile microphone to the radio.

At least the scarf would hide the earpiece and acoustic cord.

She went into the bedroom to put on a bulletproof vest.

Inamorata and the federal agent, preceded by a Hawkeye operative and followed closely by Marcus, went to the guest house to check reception of the earpiece at a distance. The model she was wearing was new, super-small, and not yet commercially available. Before sending her into the field, he wanted to be sure it worked as specified.

The federal agent whispered to Inamorata.

At command central, they heard the words perfectly.

Wes was grateful the storm front had passed. If the exchange happened outside, they'd need the calmer weather. Wind would screw up the reception.

Jilly entered the kitchen in a skirt and blouse, along with a blonde wig.

Smith looked up from his keyboard and gave a wolf whistle.

She flipped him the bird.

"We'll need a little work on your reactions if you're going to be Inamorata," Wes told her.

"Yeah. Sorry about that."

"For shit's sake, no chomping on ice or slurping soda when you're hooked up to the microphone," Smith said. "Unless you're trying to kill us all."

"Don't tempt me," Jilly said.

Inamorata and her detail returned to the kitchen. Ricardo also arrived.

While Wes wired Jilly and Ricardo, most members of the team took the opportunity to eat. Operatives tended to be pragmatic. Sleep and eat when you could.

Jilly left to put on her bulletproof vest. Then the FBI agent worked with Jilly and Inamorata, helping Jilly learn some of Inamorata's most common gestures and movements. They also practiced people calling out Inamorata's name without her reacting and with Jilly responding.

No one, no one, walked like Inamorata, though. She had a sensual sway of her hips, one that was difficult to copy because it was combined with her internal confidence. She was a woman who knew where she was going and, uncompromisingly, knew what she wanted.

As time dragged on, Wes noticed that conversation became more sporadic. Jokes were cracked but not laughed at, and tension mounted. People needlessly checked their smartphones and the wall clock.

Twenty minutes before seven, Inamorata's phone rang.

"It's a 720 prefix," she said to Wes.

He nodded he was set up. The Feds confirmed their surveillance was also in place, and she answered. They were all tracing the call, the Feds ignoring the fact Hawkeye was skirting the edge of the law. But since there was no real expectation of a positive result, there was no real foul.

After another ring, she pushed the Answer button on her phone. "Inamorata."

"You got the bitch?"

Pleasant man. He needed to learn a few manners. What Wes wouldn't give for five minutes alone with him in a dark alley. That he'd involved Inamorata made Wes doubly furious. He wouldn't need a weapon other than his bare hands.

Wes keyed the sequence to display the man's picture on the screen.

"If you're asking about Bahirah, we've got her," she said.

By prior arrangement with the Feds, they'd agreed not to omit Chloe's real name from the recordings. They wanted as much evidence against Jonah as they could get.

"I want you and the bitch in the terminal at Union Station. One hour. You're late, the kid gets killed."

"I'd prefer somewhere more private."

"Didn't ask what you wanted."

One of the federal agents grabbed his phone and left the room. There wasn't much time to get people in place, especially at such a public, exposed place. There were no metal detectors, no way to control who came in and who left. It was mainly just security guards down there, if he remembered correctly, people who protected the mass transportation. He assumed there were cameras in place, but depending on the number of people there, they might not be a lot of use. For their purposes, Jonah couldn't have chosen a worse venue.

"Stay near the Wynkoop Street entrance," Jonah instructed. "Sam will walk toward you. Bahirah will walk toward me."

Which meant, Wes assumed, Jonah was planning on going out the rear entrance, near the light-rail platform or heading toward the trains. At that time on a Saturday night, people would be coming and going.

Inamorata tried to stall. "Let me be sure I understand—"

Jonah disconnected.

Inamorata swore.

For a couple of heartbeats, there was silence.

"We need to leave within ten minutes," Ricardo said.

Inamorata adjusted the scarf and made sure the earpiece was covered.

The Feds confirmed they'd moved special agents into place at Union Station, on the platform and along Wynkoop. Police were notified and so were transportation officials.

"Play it cool. Keep him talking if you get close enough," the female federal agent said. "We intend to bring in agents behind him to apprehend him before you get close. All goes well, no one will ever know what went down."

She nodded.

Every time he worked with her, her levelheadedness impressed him. She asked enough questions to clarify the situation, but no more.

He helped buckle her into her shoulder holster.

Although there was no need to check her gun and its ammo, she did, just like they all did.

He held her trench coat while she shrugged into it. He then adjusted the collar as an excuse to brush his fingers against her nape.

She turned to face him. "Thanks."

"Be safe." He wanted to hold her one last time, kiss her, make her promise to be safe. Instead, he folded his arms across his chest.

Their gazes met, locked before she headed for the front door. She opened her mouth as if to say something but then closed it again.

Goddamn it, it shouldn't be this way.

"Ma'am?" Ricardo prompted.

"Ready," she said.

Marcus held the door.

"Good evening, Amadora," Aston said.

"Amadora Inamorata," said Jilly. "Sounds good, but it's a hell of a mouthful."

"And wrong," Inamorata said.

"How in the known universe do you walk in these shoes on ice?" Jilly asked.

"Don't think about it," Inamorata advised. Then she did

look over her shoulder. There was apology and regret in her eyes, something that tinted contacts couldn't disguise.

He nodded. He understood her stance. He didn't like it, didn't agree with it, thought she was being reckless. But he understood she was doing what she thought she needed to.

Marcus escorted them outside and into the waiting vehicle.

It occurred to Wes then that after the op was over, she wouldn't be returning to his place. He set his jaw in anger, in frustration.

His stubbornness, her stubbornness had forced the end of something that could have been great.

"Hey, Wes!" Smith shouted from the kitchen. "Feds have a feed from the Union Station terminal."

Chapter Ten

Inamorata wished she were as calm as the others thought she was.

The situation with Wes had crawled under her skin more than she'd realized. Somewhere along the line, despite her internal denial, she'd fallen in love with the irresistible, dominating man. No one had ever made her respond the way he did.

But even for him, even for love, she couldn't turn her back on Martha and Bahirah. That night, as she'd booked them a hotel room that hadn't asked for ID as long as she had cash, she'd sworn she'd keep Bahirah safe. And to her mind, this was the best way to do it.

Still, walking away from Wes was one of the most difficult things she'd ever done.

"Teams are in place," Wes said in her ear, his voice rich, calm.

She held on to the lifeline of his voice, drinking in his reassurance the way she had during their recent BDSM scenes. Even when things seemed to be out of control emotionally, he was an anchor.

"Anyone have a line on Jonah?"

"Negative."

A few minutes later, Ricardo pulled to an illegal stop in a fire lane near Union Station. Her heart was beating double-time. She checked her watch. "One minute."

"No visual," Wes said.

"Ready?" she asked Jilly. "We need to move."

"I'm not sure I like being you," Jilly said. "I'd rather hide behind a computer screen and chew on ice."

"None of us like listening to you chomping on that ice," Smith said.

Ricardo assisted Jilly from the car first.

Inamorata admired the way Jilly handled herself. She smoothed the front of her skirt the way Inamorata would have. And she was completely steady on the heels.

Jilly came around to Inamorata's side of the car, as if she were protecting her.

"Scared shitless," Jilly said. "Yep. Scared shitless."

"Stay sharp. You've been trained for this."

"Just because I'm scared doesn't mean I'm not going to shoot someone's ass."

She knew how Jilly felt. The pain and anguish in Martha's voice had infuriated Inamorata. That a child could do that to his mother was staggering.

And Jonah—murdering son of a bitch.

Inamorata knew revenge shouldn't fuel her, and she kept that dangerous emotion at bay. But that didn't mean she couldn't even the scales of justice tonight.

She adjusted her head scarf.

"My heart is thundering," Jilly said.

"Deep breaths."

"I don't know how you do it, 'Morata."

"Block out everything except the moment. Confidence. Focus. Doing the right thing." Jilly nodded.

"Shoulders back. Stay sharp."

There were surprisingly few people around, and Inamorata was grateful for that. She wanted no innocents harmed.

Jilly moved toward the entrance. Inamorata followed, her head down.

Jilly pushed through the front door with her nondominant hand.

They stopped inside the terminal, staying close to the exit, in case they needed a quick escape.

In a glance, Inamorata surveyed the area. There were rows of polished, glossy, high-backed benches between them and the rear exit. A café was closed up. A janitor pushed a broom across the floor. She saw a young couple who appeared to be in an embrace, but their gazes were too active to be lovers. Feds.

But where the hell were Jonah and Sam? Nearby, one man dozed, his head propped on a backpack. A kid ran around, his parents seemingly oblivious. "Shit. We have a child."

"See what you can do," Wes said.

"Let's move to the left," Inamorata said quietly to Jilly.

Wes's voice filled her ear. "Two men coming in the back entrance. Could be your targets. Wearing baseball caps and jackets."

"Got 'em," said Jilly.

"They're moving toward the men's room," Inamorata said. "Not looking this way. May not be our guys."

"Can you get a visual confirmation?" Wes asked.

She shook her head, even though he couldn't see it. "No. They moved too quickly. The first one to walk through could have been Sam, but the other guy was looking down. No way to confirm him as Jonah." She thought. "Can you get a visual from one of the cameras? Maybe it's not Jonah with him? Maybe one of the others? David? Lance?"

"Another man coming in behind you," Wes said quietly.

"Could be nothing. Baseball cap also."

Fuck. "I'm not liking this." She glanced at the large clock on the wall. Two minutes after. She eased her hand toward her gun. With a slight inclination of her head, she signaled Jilly to turn. Hand on her gun, Jilly spun.

"Sending a couple of federal agents into the restroom," Wes said.

"Gun!" the female federal agent shouted.

People screamed.

A gunshot exploded behind her. The sound was deafening. Time seemed to slow.

The two men came out of the restroom, guns blazing.

Inamorata drew her pistol and took aim at the two men. "Sam and Jonah," she shouted, not knowing if Wes would even hear her.

The child ran into the aisle.

His mother yelled at him.

The boy stood there, as if paralyzed.

Jonah aimed at Inamorata.

The child was between them.

"Inamorata?" Wes demanded.

"Freeze!" a federal agent shouted, drawing his weapon.

Jonah opened fire. His first shot shattered the bench near her.

Inamorata acted, going for the child.

His next shot barely missed the boy.

"A little help here," she shouted. She was still moving forward when she was hit. The force of the bullet knocked her down, stole her breath, maybe cracked a rib. "*Shit,*" she whispered.

"Inamorata?"

She heard Wes's frantic voice but couldn't respond. "Damn it, Inamorata! Talk to me."

She blocked out everything except getting to the child. Jonah fired again and again, obviously intent on emptying his clip. Intent on killing her.

Jonah hit her a second time, grazing her arm.

She crawled toward the boy, grabbed him, and covered his body with hers as bullets exploded around them.

She managed to return fire, once, before pain didn't let her aim her gun. Fortunately she saw the federal agents move on the bastard.

She fought off nausea and kept the boy protected.

Seconds later, there was sudden and overwhelming silence.

Her ears rang, and adrenaline thundered through her.

She looked up to see Sam facedown, a gun aimed at his head. Jonah had been wounded, either from her bullet or from someone else's. She didn't care which.

"Inamorata? Talk to me, woman," Wes demanded.

"I'm okay," she said. And she was, mostly.

"You hit?"

"Grazed. Not bad," she said. Still protecting the boy, she angled toward Jilly. Blood seeped from beneath the woman. "Jilly's hit," she said. "Goddamn, Jilly's hurt."

"Help's coming," Wes promised, his voice a lifeline of reassurance.

The welcome sound of sirens split the air.

"All clear," one of the agents shouted.

Slowly, grimacing with pain, she moved, letting the child up, and used the benches to pull herself upright.

"I think he's okay," she told the hysterical mother. "Help's on the way."

"You scared the shit out of me, Inamorata." Wes's voice seemed unnaturally loud in her ear.

"I scared the shit out of myself," she admitted. Now that the situation had ended, she started to shake. "Thanks for sticking with me, Wes." She needed to see to Jilly, needed to think. She couldn't do that with thoughts of Wes crowding her mind and her heart. "Ending transmission." She took out the earpiece and blinked away the unexpected sting of tears.

She took a couple of steadying breaths to focus. Her steps were slow and uncertain as she moved toward brave Jilly. "How you doing?" she asked the operative.

"Fucking hurts like a fucking son of a bitch. *Fuck it.*"

"You got him." Inamorata lowered to sit next to Jilly.

"He was going to kill us." She sounded offended.

Inamorata took the woman's hand.

"I'm getting blood on this nice skirt," Jilly said. "And I think I might have broken off one of the heels."

Hawkeye himself strode through the door. Inamorata had never been more relieved to see someone. And never more disappointed it wasn't Wes.

* * *

She'd been questioned, poked, prodded, bandaged, and hours later, finally, released. They'd told her she had bruised ribs. She'd been luckier than Jilly, who had two cracked ribs.

Ricardo helped her into the backseat of the car, and she moved slower than normal.

For the first time ever, after an op, she hated the idea of arriving home to a cold, empty house.

She generally liked the quiet and peace to think, to write her notes, maybe take a bath and drink a glass of wine.

But tonight she couldn't stop thinking about Wes.

Over the past six months, she'd come to count on him, on his strength. Sex had been more than a way to relax. It had been a way to forget. She hadn't realized how important he'd become to her.

Until now.

Ricardo escorted her to the entrance of the building where she lived. She told him to take a week's worth of vacation. He'd earned it.

She took the elevator to the third floor and slowly walked to her loft.

When she arrived, she saw light spilling from beneath her front door. A nasty feeling of déjà vu flashed through her. She reached for her gun as the front door opened.

"Don't shoot," Wes said.

Emotion swamped her. Relief, followed by joy. Then she frowned in puzzlement.

"I figured it wouldn't occur to you to come back to my place."

It hadn't. How well he knew her.

"I'm pissed," he told her, taking her uninjured arm and drawing her inside. He locked the door. "But I've been pissed at you plenty of times in the last six months. I figure I'll be pissed at you plenty more times as well."

She blinked, feeling unsure as he led her to the bedroom. "I'm not sure what you're saying." Part of her couldn't believe she was letting him take control like this. Part of her was grateful and wanted the other part to shut the hell up.

"I want you in my life, Inamorata. If it has to be on your terms, I'll live with it, but I won't stop pushing. I intend to wear you down. Like that old saying goes, with enough time and determination, you can piss a hole in a rock."

She laughed, a shaky little sound. "I've learned a few things. I am who I am. I can't change that. But at the end of the day, Wes, I want you there. I have no idea what that means. But I will try to give you more of what you need."

"We'll start by getting you naked."

"I'm banged up," she said, warning him. "But I want sex. I want you."

Several feet from the bed, he released her. She saw he'd turned down the covers, and there was a glass of wine on the nightstand.

"I want you to fuck me, hard."

"After you relax in a bath."

"I want—"

"*I* want your ass in that bathtub," he said. "I think you owe me a few simple 'yes, Sirs.'"

She nodded, never more grateful for his bossiness.

"Say it, Inamorata. I've earned it."

"Yes," she said. Wanting him to kiss her, to touch her, to make her forget. "Yes, Sir."

He helped her undress and then swept her into his arms and carried her to the bathtub which was already filled with hot, steamy water.

"Hawkeye told you I was on my way," she guessed.

"I threatened to quit if he didn't give me information."

"You know, Wes, Sir, you may be the perfect man." He wrapped plastic around her arm to protect the bandage.

She soaked for long minutes, and he gently washed her back and her hair. She finally allowed the enormity of the situation to settle in. "He fully intended to murder Chloe."

"And you too," he said, his voice raw.

There was silence. She knew he was furious. From his

point of view, he had good reason to be angry. But she would do it all over again. They'd never see it the same way, but if they could agree to disagree, they might stand a chance. "If the Feds hadn't been there, he probably would have gotten away with it."

"Now the money belongs to Chloe," he said.

"She deserves it."

"And Sam?"

"He'll be going to prison for a long time, no doubt. It's his first offense, and he could say he was misguided." She sighed. "But I was happy to learn he didn't have a gun. I thought he did, but it turns out he was reaching for his phone. I think he really never considered Jonah would try to kill Chloe."

Wes helped her from the tub and wrapped her in a big, fluffy towel.

"Fuck me?" she asked, leaning against him.

"Inamorata..."

"Kiss me." She reached to put her arms around his neck, but pain lanced up her arm. Being grazed by a bullet and having the wound stitched *hurt.* "Uhm, maybe I should let you be in control."

"You know I love you, Inamorata."

"Good thing," she said. "I don't like being in these things alone."

He looked at her with those dark, intense eyes. She wondered how she'd gotten lucky enough to have him in her life.

"Tonight," he said, "I'm going to make love to you. And soon, I'm going to fuck you so hard you won't be able to stand up."

Epilogue

"First things first," Wes said, looking at Inamorata, spread out on his bed. He enjoyed having her in his bed, in his life. Over the last month, she'd caved a handful of times and spent the night. Once, she'd even brewed coffee and brought it to him in bed, naked. She hadn't invited him to her home since the night of the shooting. But he'd take what he could get while pushing for more. Like he'd told her, "*with enough time and determination, you can piss a hole in a rock.*" He had both time *and* determination.

He'd been looking forward to tonight, to her body being healed enough for her to fully engage in a scene the way they both wanted. She'd been asking him for this for two weeks. He'd made her wait until tonight. "I told you I was going to shave your cunt."

He'd placed a towel beneath her hips and tied her hands behind her back and then fastened her ankles to a spreader bar.

She looked lovely.

He grabbed the can of shaving cream and a damp washcloth from the dresser. Bentley took notice from his doggy bed in the corner. "Stay," he told the mutt. "Unless you want me to lock you outside the room?"

As if he understood, Bentley dropped his head onto his paws.

Wes moistened and then lathered her pubic area. He dipped a razor in a bowl of warm water and then leaned over her. He removed the majority of hair in the first few strokes. And then he became slower and more deliberate, pulling back each pussy lip to remove each hair.

She remained perfectly still.

Within a minute, her pubic area was bare, even more beautiful than it had been before.

He wiped her with a damp cloth. He removed the towel from beneath her hips; then he kissed her cunt. "Gorgeous."

She wriggled and squirmed. He licked her and inserted a finger inside her, searching for, and finding, her G-spot. He stimulated that sensitive spot as he sucked on her clit. She cried out as she climaxed.

"Did you just come?"

She softly swore.

"I beg your pardon?"

"Yes, Sir. I came."

"Ah." He picked her up from the mattress and turned her over. He spanked her hard several times.

She quietly cursed, but instead of trying to get away, she surrendered as he reddened her rounded ass.

He changed the tempo, making the beating more sensual. When he was several strokes in, her breathing changed. "Naughty girl," he told her, seeing her grinding her bare pussy against his bedsheets.

"But—"

"I want you on your knees. And the only correct response is 'yes, Sir.'"

"Yes, Sir," she said obediently.

Since she was so alluringly trussed, he took pity on her and helped her into position. Her head was on the mattress; her butt was slightly in the air.

He tapped her back until she arched it more and more.

He went to his closet and pulled out his toy box. Along with a pair of nipple clamps, he removed a medium-sized butt plug and a bottle of lube. "Keep your gaze averted," he told her.

She squeezed her eyes shut, trying to behave a little, maybe?

After washing the plug, he returned to her.

He reached beneath her to pinch her right nipple, arousing it. Before she was fully prepared, he caught it with the clamp.

She gasped.

He teased her left nipple while tugging on the clamp attached to the right one. She began to rock back and forth. He affixed the vicious clamp to her left nipple.

Inamorata exhaled with a shaky breath. "I think—"

"No," he told her. "You stole one orgasm. You can fight the next one."

He gave the chain a sharp tug. While she was still reeling, he parted her ass, exposing her anus. "It's been a while," he told her, "But you can and will take it." He lubed his index finger and went straight in. She didn't struggle. "Why, Ms. Inamorata, one might think you're enjoying this." He stretched her wider and then grabbed the lube and liberally squirted the plug.

He placed it against her tightest hole. "Bear down." She did, and he pushed. She cried out and fought just a little, until her body accommodated the thickness of the toy. "Okay?" he asked.

Her breathing was ragged, but she managed a breathless "yes."

He wiped off his hand on the washcloth and moved in behind her. "Ask me to fuck you," he said.

"With the plug in?"

"Ask me to fuck you, Inamorata."

She moved back a little. "Please, please, Sir, fuck me as

hard as you can. Make me yours. *Own me.*"

His jaw clenched. Nothing he'd like better.

After donning a condom, he knelt behind her, taking care with the spreader bar. He grabbed her hips and dragged her back. He held her tight as he positioned his cockhead at her vaginal opening.

"Make me yours," she said.

He drove into her.

She cried out at the force of the possession.

With the plug inserted to the hilt in her ass, she was even tighter than usual, and the fit alone was enough to make him ready to ejaculate.

"Damn, Sir. This is… It's…amazing. Sir…!"

He forced himself to hold back long enough to make her come. He tugged on her clamps, played with her clit, changed his angle slightly to ensure he rubbed against her sensitive internal spot.

"Please," she whispered. "Please, Sir, may I come?"

As if he could deny her. He yanked on her clamps. She screamed and climaxed hard, her vaginal muscles milking his cock.

Throwing back his head, he grunted as he came in a hot, steady spurt.

She called out his name, and he dug his hand possessively into her once-again-blonde hair.

Slowly, gently, he untied her and detached her ankles from the spreader bar. He helped her onto her back and removed the plug. "Stay there," he told her, climbing out of bed.

Despite her assurances she was fine, he was taking no chances with her. He'd used her hard, and he knew harder times were still ahead. There was a box full of toys he hadn't gotten to yet.

He returned to clean her up.

He got into bed and pulled her against him.

"Sir?"

"Hmm?"

"Thank you."

He kissed the top of her head. "Aston, lights out."

Bentley yawned, a metallic, grating sound. Another upgrade needed.

The lights dimmed by slow measures.

"Good night, sir," Aston said. "Good night…Esmeralda."

"Good night, Aston," she said.

Wes waited. When she didn't say anything else, Wes asked, "Esmeralda? Your green eyes. Of course. Esmeralda?"

"I thought you said it wasn't in the gem family," Aston said.

"Maybe I'm just tired of everyone guessing."

"And maybe your name is Esmeralda. Shall I beat the truth out of you?"

"Please do. Sir."

THE END

Sierra Cartwright

Born in Northern England and raised in the Wild West, Sierra Cartwright pens book that are as wild and untamed as the Rockies she calls home.

She's an award-winning, multi-published writer who wrote her first book at age nine and hasn't stopped since. Sierra invites you to share the complex journey of love and desire, of surrender, submission, and commitment.

Her own journey has taught her that trusting takes guts and courage, and her work is a celebration for everyone who is willing to take that risk.

If you'd like to encourage Sierra Cartwright to tell us more, she would love to hear from you. Check out her website at http://www.sierracartwright.com.

Loose Id® Titles by Sierra Cartwright

I Heart That City: Double Trouble

The HAWKEYE Series
Danger Zone
Bend Me Over
Make Me

"Met Her Match (A Hawkeye Story)"
Part of the anthology *Doms of Dark Haven*
With Cherise Sinclair and Belinda McBride

The above titles are available in ebook format at Loose Id

Hawkeye One: Danger Zone
Hawkeye: Bend Me Over

"Double Trouble"
Part of the anthology *Body Shots: I Heart That City 1*
With Mechele Armstrong

*The above titles are available in print format
from your favorite bookseller*

CPSIA information can be obtained at www.ICGtesting.com
Printed in the USA
LVOW06s1157010614

388016LV00001B/49/P